SUZANNAH ROWNTREE

A Vampire in Bavaria

Miss Sharp's Monsters, Volume III.

Chapter I.

It was now three weeks since my employer had been kidnapped by anarchists and replaced with an automaton—yet so far, nobody seemed to have noticed.

Indeed, gentle reader, had you been present at the train station in Coburg on that sunny afternoon of an idyllic German spring, you would scarcely have seen anything amiss. The previous train had passed through a quarter of an hour before, allowing a party of two heavily-veiled ladies, one tall bowler-hatted gentleman, and an aggressively villainous-looking navvy to disembark. These four, immediately recognisable to the loyal reader as myself, my employer, and two gentlemen friends—no, not like *that*—now gathered behind the corner of the station, engaged in a hushed debate. Upon the platform itself, a small, fashionable, and expensive-looking crowd had begun to gather. About them stood a girdle of bowler-hatted plain-clothes-men and decomposing revenant policemen, watching the gathered townspeople with eyes of suspicion and distrust. A brass band had appeared and was murdering *Loch Lomond* in a discouraged sort of way, their sound thin and uncertain in the open air.

A scene, you might be pardoned for thinking, with nothing whatever to hint that murder and revolution were in the air.

Our meeting behind the station corner became suddenly animated, as one closely-veiled lady peered at the platform and let out an indignant hiss. "There it is, the infernal contraption! Oh! and it has its arm in George's, the designing thing! Come along, Sharp!"

She made to step out of concealment as though to confront the young couple that had strolled along the platform towards her, but three pairs of hands instantly restrained her with piercing, whispered protests.

"May, stop!"—"Your Highness, please!"—"Ah, *ce puii mei,* a typical aristo!"

She threw back her veil to reveal a face that might have belonged to a china doll—golden curls, snapping blue eyes, and faintly flushed cheeks. She might have been the twin of the lady on the platform, save that her *doppelgänger* was pale and bloodless by comparison. This was, of course, my friend and employer, Princess May of Teck. She was unusually angry just at that moment. No princess likes to narrowly escape imprisonment and experimentation at the hands of a revolutionary cell, only to find that not only has a clever contraption been impersonating her in her absence, but that it has also pledged her to marry the prince she has been determinedly avoiding for months.

"Patience, ma'am," said the man in the bowler hat. "Don't forget that the automaton is rigged to explode. We can't risk unmasking it in a public place like this—why, anyone in the crowd might be holding the detonator!"

This was Inspector Alexander Short of Scotland Yard, a tall and inconveniently attractive man with a long, careworn face. At present he was on high alert, and the point of his nose had gone white with the tension.

"Got it," said the navvy briefly. A short, stocky man, Anton Lupei of the People's Vengeance wore a flat cap, a checked neckerchief and a permanent three-day stubble, more by choice than necessity. He jabbed a stubby finger towards the townspeople peering over the station fence at a respectful distance from the policemen and their royal charges. "There's Hannah. She'll be the one with the detonator."

The fourth member of our party started at the sound of a distant whistle and pulled back her veil, the better to see the approaching train. "Oh, the dickens! That's the royal train—that's Queen Victoria. *They mean to explode the bomb today—now—as soon as the train arrives.*"

I invite the reader to observe the person thus presented to their scrutiny—a young woman in her early twenties, dressed in bloomers and a high-necked blouse, with a silver brooch pinning a gauzy scarf at her throat and a dilapidated umbrella clasped under one arm; in addition to which you may observe dark hair, large eyes, and three livid scars running across the left side of her face. This striking and intelligent young person is (of course) none other than myself: Liz Sharp, of Saint Botolph's Hospital for the Reception of Penitent Working Girls.

(Or so it calls itself. In fact, Saint Botolph's is an institution founded for the purpose of taking in the monster-bitten, stealing their memories, and training them to become a lady's maid-cum-bodyguard to the rich and monstrous of the world. This prevents them, or so it is thought, from becoming embittered anarchist agitators.—With what success, my readers may judge for themselves.)

"They're going to kill Aunt Queen?" May gasped. Her knuckles whitened on the black lacquered walking-stick she carried under one arm—a dashing accessory, adopted less for the sake of fashion than convenience.

"And Prince George," I added with a glance towards the young man walking arm-in-arm with the false May.

"And twenty or thirty other royalties," Short finished grimly. "Quickly, we must make a plan."

"Or we could just take cover and let Hannah make a clean sweep of the whole bloodsucking gang," Anton growled, sticking his hands in his pockets. Neither the sentiment nor the posture was quite correct for a person in the presence of royalty, but Anton was an anarchist himself, and evidently felt obliged to remind us of this fact at every opportunity. He was with us only because—as told in the previous volume of my memoirs—he felt some sort of obligation towards myself; besides which, nearly every other anarchist in Europe was at present violently displeased with him for helping me to stop the revolution plotted by my mad parents. It had been their intention to turn the workers of Europe into monsters every bit as bad as those that ruled us, and Anton, having experienced the transformation, had been unable to stomach the thought of anyone else following suit. As he said himself, what was the point of toppling one set of monster dynasties, only to erect another in their place?

All the same, upon the subject of bombs he was still rather permissive, and it is needless to say that the three of us ignored his present suggestion.

"May, wait here and take cover." I was obliged to raise my voice over the shriek of the arriving train. "Anton, you retrieve the detonator. Short, go with him. I'll take care of the automaton. No arguments! Go!"

Short had opened his mouth to protest, but as Anton

broke away towards the mysterious Hannah and vaulted the station fence, he had no choice but to follow. The truth was that neither of us felt *quite* comfortable with the anarchist's inclusion among our party, but at least, if Short accompanied him to retrieve the detonator, Anton's more combustible tendencies might be restrained.

As for the automaton, it made better sense for me to tackle the contraption myself. Having been both wolf- and vampire-bitten, I was a good deal quicker and stronger than either of the men.—Although not quite so fast, nor so strong, as to successfully confront a real monster. And the platform was full of them.

May caught my hand as I turned. "Be careful," she said, although I only saw her lips move, for the train was almost upon us.

With a nod, I tore my hand from her grasp and leaped upon the platform. Instantly two of the plain-clothes-men converged upon me with lifted cudgels. But Saint Botolph's had prepared me for this, and thankfully neither of them were revenants, who go into a murderous rage when attacked. I had a stout umbrella and two years' study in what our instructor, Miss Nakamura, had referred to (rather misleadingly) as the Gentle Art. Both the policemen went flying, and two steps later I was at Prince George's side.

"Sharp!" he cried, "hang it!—what the blazes?"

The then Duke of York was a slight young man with a short fashionable beard, attired in a custom-tailored morning-suit that might, on a calmer occasion, have brought tears of quiet joy to my eyes. His shirt-front was the exact colour of a snowy Alpine slope on a spring morning, and his trousers that rare and delicate shade of grey found only on the inside of an angel's wing. His tone, however, was startled and displeased. As highly as he thought of me, it cannot be pleasant to be accosted on a train station platform by an umbrella-wielding Amazon.

Still, when a fellow has nearly slaughtered you in the shape of a wolf beneath the full moon, you cease to be awed by his bipedal form. Also, the joke was irresistible. "Oh, I agree, darling; it's no use. We really must stop meeting like this."

George choked. In the same moment there was an unpleasant-sounding *click* from the wasp-waisted form of Princess May's *doppelgänger*, followed by an even more alarming *whirr*. My heart leaped into my mouth. I remembered what had happened the last time I heard that sound coming from one of my inventive father's contraptions.

To think was to act. Tearing the false May from George's side—the dickens, she really *was* a good likeness, with her wide blue eyes and china-doll stiffness—I gathered all my strength and hurled her off the platform, directly into the path of the oncoming train.

There was a sickening *crunch* as the slowing locomotive struck her, carrying her out of sight. Shouts, gasps, screams rent the air. It all sounded terribly real, and for one fraction of a heartbeat I doubted myself—oh, heavens! surely that had not been the *true* May!

Then a withering blast shook the air. With a flash of light, the sweet pungent stink of dynamite burst over us in a cloud of smoke. The locomotive rocked to the side and jumped the tracks, but screeched to a halt before it could drag the carriages after it. The explosion assaulted my sensitive hearing, muffling the ensuing sounds of terror—but I saw the engineer and fireman burst from the listing locomotive, running towards us with wide-open mouths and wildly-waving arms.

Confusion and panic seized the whole gathering. The crowd of dignitaries and the brass band frayed and began to run. Then came a *boom* compared to which the first had been nothing—a terrible, shattering, thunderous sound. The ground shook and a blast of hot, damp air passed through the crowd. A confused moment later I came to myself sprawling across the platform in a tangle of someone else's limbs, my ears ringing and sore. Pushing myself up, I found that I had landed square on top of George, whose top hat had been knocked from his head, and whose alpine shirtfront was smirched with smoke.

The dickens—a *second* explosion?

George's lips moved as he shoved me away. Jumping to my feet, I glanced around me, taking stock of the situation. All was disorder and chaos—smoke and steam was everywhere, people sprawled across the platform, and wails of surprise and terror filled the air.

As the cloud slowly dissipated, I beheld my handiwork with awe and not a little terror. The train itself had shielded the platform from any serious harm, but my mouth went quite dry as I realised just how much damage my impulsive act had caused. Disrupted by the first blast and its derailing, the royal boiler must have exploded. The front of the locomotive had all but disappeared, and the pipes of the interior splayed out like the tentacles of some mad beast. Beside the crippled engine, the wooden fence that bordered the station was all torn and splintered.

Yet, miraculously, no one was hurt. As the princes, princesses and policemen on the platform climbed shakily to their feet, felt themselves all over, and came with astonishment to the conclusion that they were all still in one piece, my horror faded. If I had hesitated, George and goodness knows how many others would even now lie dead beside me. But I had acted promptly enough to avert a real catastrophe.

My spirits lifted. A good afternoon's work, after all! Lives saved, May's *doppelgänger* dealt with, and May herself about to return in safety to the bosom of her family. Tonight, at last, after weeks of anxiety I would sleep in peace.

My hearing slowly returned—in time to hear a voice call out from behind me.

"There's the anarchist!" someone shouted. "*She* did it! Arrest her!"

I turned, and realised that the fingers were pointing at me. I backed a step, and fetched up against the two policemen I had knocked flying. They seized me at once.

More pointing fingers. More shouts.

"Murderer!"

"She threw Princess May under the train!"

"Anarchist!"

"Shoot her out of hand!"

"Yes! Shoot her at once!"

Some of this was to be expected, but that last suggestion went a good deal too far. "What the dickens? George, tell them—"

George had been sitting on the platform, staring at the defunct locomotive in astonishment. Now his dazed expression cleared to incoherent wrath. "Sharp! You—of all people—her *bodyguard—you!*"

"What? No!" I searched the crowd wildly, feeling sure I was

about to be dragged away and summarily executed. Where was Short? Where was May? It was not as though this was England, where a fair trial—or at least *some* sort of trial—was guaranteed me. Just as I was giving myself up for lost, my attention was arrested by a familiar face. Ah, how well I knew that pale complexion, that black velvet coat, the faint mocking smile! My heart beat against my ribs like a bird against the bars of its cage, but I managed to speak aloud.

"Vasily! You owe me this, at least!"

Beneath the concealment of his dark glasses, Grand Duke Vasily Nikolaevitch Romanov gave a sharklike grin. "On the contrary, my dear. Whatever debt I might have owed you was paid the night you threw me out of the dining-room window at Castle Sarkozy. You had better take the anarchist away, gentlemen," he added to the policemen.

Before I could think of anything else to say, an imperious voice cut through the commotion.

"You will do nothing of the sort. Unhand my bodyguard at once, if you please!" A gasp of astonishment ran through the crowd as May stepped onto the platform. Placing a protective hand on my arm, she turned to the Duke of York. "Good day, George. Not injured, I trust?"

He gaped. *"May?* But—"

"Oh, George." Her voice shook with repressed emotion. "That was an automaton packed with dynamite, and Sharp has just saved your life—and who knows how many more?" She turned to me. "How can we ever thank you for all you've done?"

"But—!" George waved a hand towards the locomotive. "That wasn't *you?*"

"Of course not. I am supposed to be in mourning, George!

And even if I were not, I would *never* wear green, not even in a hat!"

For a moment, I had been sure the sentence was about to end differently. May had been in mourning only four months since the tragic death of her fiancé, George's brother Eddy. Since then, both George and his family—to say nothing of the Empire at large—seemed to presume that George would be acceptable to May as a substitute. On her part—well, I suspected she was not indifferent to her royal cousin, yet he really should have known that the *true* May would never have agreed to marry him. Not in such unseemly haste, and certainly not after having killed Eddy herself, that night of the full moon, with an arrow dipped in wolfsbane.

But that's a long story, and one I have told in a previous volume of these memoirs.

George looked shaken. "An automaton? Good Lord! I *thought* you were a little quieter than usual, these past few weeks!"

"Well, I'm glad we have that cleared up." Any other woman might have injected some measure of irony into the words, but May simply made the statement in a flat sort of way. "Now, will you ask these gentlemen to release my bodyguard?—No, mamma! Not now!"

A crowd of shaken but inquisitive royalties had gathered about us as May and George spoke, and now a fashionable woman of majestic girth burst through this ring of people, crying, "May! my child! what is the meaning of this?"

George stepped back as May was folded into the Duchess of Teck's embrace. With the object of his affections thus eclipsed from view, he motioned to the policemen, who released me but did not cease to breathe down my neck.

"May! what is this that I hear?" the Duchess cried at length, releasing her child for an anxious maternal inspection.

"It's true, mamma. I was kidnapped by anarchists and replaced with an automaton."

"But why didn't you *telegraph?*"

I *had* telegraphed—repeatedly. The Tecks had thought I was hoaxing them.

"Really, mamma, I would prefer to discuss it in private." May glanced at the crowd with a faint flush that, as one who knew her well, I identified as embarrassment. In fact, the last three weeks since the Castle Sarkozy affair had been rather trying to May's delicate sensibilities. She had had no money with which to purchase a train ticket from Hungary to Germany for herself, let alone me. After having fled first Paris and then Eger, Anton was next door to destitute; and Short, who had spent money freely in tracking me to Eger and purchasing the equipment we needed to storm the castle and put a stop to the revolution, had cleaned himself out in doing so. The upshot of it was that the four of us had been compelled to limp across Europe in the cheapest possible lodgings and conveyances, earning money along the way in whatever way we could find. I was not quite sure what mortified May more: her penniless circumstances, or the fact that she could do nothing to relieve them—her upbringing not having prepared her to take in washing, to sew baby clothes, nor even to sing popular songs in the street.

As Mary Adelaide continued to demand explanations from her errant daughter, I looked about me for some quiet means of escape. Alas: the policemen continued to breathe down my neck in a discouraging sort of way, and that was hardly the worst of it. Despite the cross-talk act going on with the

Duchess, the eyes of the assembled royalties were fixed on me, and an unfriendly glitter was in all of them.

At least one of the people in this crowd had actually tasted my blood, I thought with a shiver, catching another glimpse of Grand Duke Vasily's dark glasses. Perhaps two, for I was still ignorant as to the identity of the werewolf who had given me the scars on my face. Moving a little closer to George, I dared to hope that I might survive the day. But in the next instant my hopes were dashed, for the crowd fell silent as an imperious voice spoke.

"*Where* is the young person responsible for this outrage?"

Mary Adelaide's voice cut off as though a knife had sliced through it. Everyone turned. The men bowed, the women curtseyed, and I found myself looking down at a little old lady bundled into a wheeled chair, flanked by an entourage that had evidently just alighted from the stricken train.

She fixed me with a gimlet eye and my heart sank like a stone. Queen Victoria, I gathered, was distinctly unamused.

Chapter II.

In the silence that followed the Queen's words, May collected herself into a profound curtsey. "It was only Sharp, ma'am. My bodyguard—"

"What," the Queen interrupted, "is your bodyguard doing throwing bombs at *my train?*"

"I presume she has been taken into custody?" added a gentleman who was standing half a step behind her. He was approximately the shape of a Continental coffeepot, and my heart plunged a little further as I recognised the Prince of Wales.

At his words, the policemen behind me latched onto my shoulders again. May clasped her hands. "George—she saved your life! Tell them!"

I understood the reason for her appeal. Surely Queen Victoria would listen to her grandson, the second in line to her throne—but perhaps May overestimated George's resolve. Caught between May's appeal and his grandmother's imperious stare, George swallowed hard and wilted a little. He was a brave man, and devoted to May, but the sinking feeling at the pit of my stomach whispered that he was not quite *this* brave.

"I'll—we'll discuss this later," he said jerkily. "Too public."

May sent me a worried look. She said nothing, but her hand slipped within mine, and squeezed it in a fierce promise.

"Short about, by any chance?" George added.

"Here, sir!" Inspector Short raised a hand from the back of the crowd.

"My bodyguard, ma'am," George said to his grandmother. "Scotland Yard man.   Very reliable.—Short, will you take—er—this young person into custody? Bring her to the palace for questioning."

"I was trying to *stop* an explosion. Tell them, Short!" I appealed, as he made his way through the crowd towards me.

"All in good time, Miss Sharp." His voice lowered. "Forgive me. Orders are orders."

"This is ridiculous," I said. "Five minutes ago, you were taking orders from *me*."

"We'll explain everything at the palace. Until then…" With an apologetic look, he drew a pair of handcuffs from his pocket.

I glanced at May. Her lips were compressed a little, and I could see the angry helplessness in her eyes. I might try to protest, but I knew my behaviour must reflect badly on her. Princess though she might be, May was of morganatic birth. Her grandmother had been a mere countess, cutting off May's father from the crown he otherwise would have inherited in the small German kingdom of Wurttemberg. As a result, May's impure blood left her suspended somewhere between commonalty and royalty, with little inheritance and no influence at all. It was only her dutiful good sense that had brought her into favour with Queen Victoria, but that favour only went so far.

She could not help me, and I did not expect her to. All the

same, I saw her suppressed indignation, and treasured it up like a hot brick on a cold night.

Reluctantly, I put out my hands and let Short snap the cold steel around my wrists. He sent me a tight, worried smile, and then nodded to the policemen behind me. I found myself marched away, through the station and out to the street beyond. A queue of carriages waited beyond, and beyond them a thin cordon of undead policemen held back the inquisitive townspeople. Their curiosity must have been whipped to a fever-pitch by the double explosion, for upon my appearance they flocked forward with murmurs of excitement. Someone shouted, and an ill-aimed clod burst against the wall of the station behind me.

The werewolf scars on my face burned like a brand as Short helped me to ascend a brougham, which he did with the most gentlemanlike air in the world. As the small carriage began to make its way through the paddocks and copses that divided the new train station from the quaint medieval town of Coburg, I found I had little attention to spare either for the idyllic green countryside, the whitewashed walls and clustered gables of the town, nor the marvellous old castle that crowned the hill above. What fate awaited me in this fairy-tale town? Short and George might reassure themselves that everything would be quickly straightened out, but *they* did not live with a mark of infamy branded across their faces, nor were they suspicious merely by virtue of their low station in society.

All the same, it meant something to know they were on my side.—Figuratively, I mean, for Short was at present seated opposite me, leaning forward to look into my face. Under his scrutiny, my scars became a little warmer. "What is it, Short?"

"Are you quite well?"

"Perfectly." I glanced down at myself, noting a little dust, but no blood nor any other visible injury.

He still seemed worried. "That crowd—you mustn't mind them. It must have looked very bad.—I beg your pardon. I should have allowed you to veil before we left the station."

"Oh, *that*." I smiled at him despite myself. It was kind of him to think of it, even belatedly. "Don't bother yourself. I'm used to it, you know. No one thinks well of a scarred dainty."

"*I* think well of you, Miss Sharp," he said mournfully.

Of course he meant—as a friend. I had long ago made my peace with the fact that Short—a starched collar in human shape—would never return my feelings. There was no future in it. He was a respectable man, and I was—a branded outcast. Who was I, to involve a good man in social ruin? Thus I had laboured to conceal my feelings; with, I flatter myself, a fair measure of success.

But, hang it all! How was I to do the right thing by him when he *would* say such things?

To distract myself, I held out my wrists. "Then surely you can unlock me now?"

His long mouth twisted doubtfully. "It isn't procedure."

"No, but nothing about this is procedure," I wheedled. "Or does her majesty the Queen personally question *every* petty criminal arrested by Scotland Yard?"

"N-o, but I need them to hear me when I speak up on your behalf," he said earnestly. "It is always better to work within the system than against it; and if they suspect me of being on your side—"

"I thought you *were* on my side."

I hadn't meant to let him see my hurt, but Short was always

indecently perceptive, and he surrendered at once. "Of course I am. Give me your hands."

There was an intriguing difference in size between my small, capable paw and his long, clever fingers. "Do you play the piano?" I asked before I could stop myself.

"I used to play at home. My sister Emily said it made her feel better, when she was melancholy, as she could be sometimes." He paused, and the silence added what he did not. He had told me not long ago how his family had perished in a disaster on the Thames. "I haven't played since," he added, keeping his eyes on his work.

I told myself I should say nothing to indicate that I saw him as anything more than a professional acquaintance. Then I promptly disregarded my own advice, because his eyes were drooping sadly and it was better, at any rate, than throwing my arms around his neck and covering his face with kisses. "One day, when all this is over, you must play something for me."

He looked wistful. "Would you like that?"

"Better than anything." I was letting myself get carried away. I could not allow him to know just how far I had gone. He was still clasping my hands, and I quickly drew them back. That broke the spell, and cleared my head a little. "Please tell me you and Anton caught the real bomber, or we might *really* be in trouble.—Where *is* Anton, anyway?"

"I don't know where Anton has gone. The anarchist—Hannah, he called her—set off the detonator before we could subdue her. Your friend said *Oh well*, tripped me up neatly, and disappeared with the woman." Short looked aggrieved. "It's true that Lupei was of some assistance during the Castle Sarkozy affair, Miss Sharp. But we can't trust him."

"I agree, and I *don't* trust him—not quite. But remember that once the detonator was tripped there was no halting the explosion, and of course he did not like to hand over the culprit for execution and revivification as one of those horrible revenant policemen. I only wish I had been able to do as he did, and show a clean pair of heels. Don't worry, Short. Something tells me we haven't seen the last of him."

Short frowned. "That isn't precisely reassuring. Why *is* Lupei following you about like this, Miss Sharp? Does he have designs on you?"

"Designs?"

"He *was* your fiancé, after all."

"Oh, I do wish you wouldn't talk to me like a Dutch uncle," I protested. A thought struck me. "Or—wait. Don't tell me you're *really* my uncle. I've had enough of *that* sort of surprise to last me a lifetime."

"Your uncle!" He let out an exasperated laugh. "I'm not half old enough to be your uncle, Miss Sharp!"

I considered this. I suspected he was younger than he seemed—no older than thirty, despite the dour face, the drooping eyes and careworn expression. "I suppose you're about to tell me you're my older brother, then."

"Nothing of the sort."

"Why so decided? I think I would like to have you as a brother. Wouldn't you like it?"

"No!"

"Well, I like that! It isn't as though I get you into mortal danger above once a month. Less, sometimes."

"Because—" He caught himself, and took a deep breath. "You're trying to distract me, Miss Sharp."

I smiled. "You used to be better at avoiding my arguments,

Inspector."

"I asked about Lupei," he said repressively.

Did Anton have designs on me?

In a former life, before I gained my scars and lost my memories, my name had been Vera Livius, daughter and assistant of the most brilliant inventor in Europe—and the promised bride of a young anarchist named Anton Lupei. Owing to some recent family troubles resulting in the tragic deaths of both my parents—deaths, I hasten to remind my readers, with which I had had *almost* nothing to do—I had foresworn the name of Livius; yet Anton remained loyal to me, likely because his actions had resulted in my being half-drained by a vampire.

Or *had* been loyal, until now. As impertinent as Short's question seemed, I could not help sighing.

"Truly? I'm not sure I understand why Anton should have chosen to follow me. But if I was to guess, I would say this: Anton may be an anarchist, but he has his own sense of honour, and he feels he owes me a debt."

"Then—there is no understanding between you?"

I had to laugh. "Heavens, no! I am no longer Vera Livius. I am Elizabeth Sharp now, and she is quite a different sort of person."

"I suppose she must be." He hesitated, and his hand strayed up, as though feeling that something was safe in his breast-pocket. "We haven't had much chance to speak in private, Miss Sharp," he began, rather diffidently. There was something in his face, in his voice, that filled me with premonitions. But just then, the carriage slowed. Outside was a delightfully narrow street bordered by charming old plaster-and-lath houses; then we turned and entered the rear courtyard of a large, cream-coloured building which must be the palace.

Short sighed, letting his hand fall onto the latch of the door. "Perhaps, when all this is over," he murmured, more to himself than to me. The carriage creaked to a halt, and he helped me alight.

Beneath my calm exterior, I was all in an uproar.—Short wished to speak to me in private? What did *that* mean? Ordinarily, when a gentleman wishes to speak to a lady in private, it means—but then, I was neither ordinary, nor a lady. Dear me, what a goose I was! Building castles in the sky, until I half believed them! Better not to think of it at all. I had *many* more pressing matters to attend to.

We now stood in the courtyard of Ehrenberg Palace—not to be confused with the much older castle that crowned the nearby hill, Veste Coburg. As it turned out, we were but the first in a cavalcade. Another carriage drew up behind us, from which a pale and determined May emerged. A third entered shortly after, from which Prince George descended precipitately.

I let out a wistful sigh. It was just like old times, although the Ehrenberg courtyard provided a little more room than did a second-class compartment on the Orient Express.

May didn't seem to have noticed Prince George, for she sailed towards Short and ordered, "Unchain my bodyguard at once, Inspector!"

"Ma'am," Short said with a bow, "I think you'll find—"

"Oh, do as she tells you, damn your eyes!" George bellowed, catching up with May.

"It's all right," I protested, lifting both hands to wave at them. *"My chains fell off, my heart was free, and all that."*

"She should never have been arrested at all," May declared, taking my hand, and turning on George as though it was all his fault.

With that, a more intriguing drama began to unfold. George reddened. "Beg your pardon for this, May. Demmed ungrateful way to treat you, after what you did."

May blushed. "What *Sharp* did."

"Oh, don't mind me," I put in. "I only tackled the creature, narrowly avoided exploding everyone, and got arrested for my pains." It was not that I must have all the credit, but the starry look in May's eyes alarmed me. I could not deny that had it not been for his habit of turning into a slavering wolf every month at the full moon, George would have suited May admirably; but it was still a terrible idea for May to marry George, for all sorts of excellent reasons.

Neither of them paid attention to me when I spoke. On the contrary, they were too busy exchanging charged looks. Their last meeting had been disastrous, to say the least: it had ended in May declaring she never wanted to lay eyes either on George or me ever again. Harsh words—but we *had* been concealing from her the rather vital knowledge that George and the rest of his family were in fact, contrary to popular opinion, werewolves. Since then, May had forgiven me, but what about George? I was not entirely sure he deserved the same.

May took a deep breath, and began to trace the cobblestones with her black lacquered walking-stick. "Oh, George. I ought to be begging *your* pardon."

He reddened. "Not at all."

"I was cruel."

"No, no."

"I would do anything to take back those words."

"Do not tempt me, May! I shall hold you to that."

May stilled for a moment—a trick of hers, when she was shocked or frightened of something. She had no opportunity to say more, however, for at that moment the Duchess of Teck descended upon us. She had arrived in the same carriage with May, and had alighted from that vehicle with a good deal more ceremony than her daughter. Now she gathered up May in one comforting arm and said, "Don't let's stand about! You must come upstairs and have some tea, George!"

George, so confident a moment before, wilted visibly beneath the force of her personality. "Ah," he stammered. "Don't want to impose. Ought to be pushing off. Give May a chance to rest…"

"Nonsense!" Mary Adelaide trumpeted. "How can anyone think of resting when I am in such agonies of suspense waiting to know what has been going on all this time? Upstairs with you—yes, Sharp too. Come along!"

In this way we found ourselves herded with our luggage upstairs into a suite of luxurious rooms in the palace's first storey.—In truth I was quite impressed that the Tecks had managed to finagle themselves into the palace at all. Coburg was in a few days to host the most glittering event of the royal social year, the marriage of Princess Victoria Melita of Saxe-Coburg and Gotha, to Prince Ernst of Hesse and by Rhine. Bride and groom were, like George himself, grandchildren of Queen Victoria's; and the small town was already filled to bursting with royalties and other distinguished guests. The Tecks had originally not been invited at all, for when one's ancestor has introduced a countess into the family tree, one cannot expect to be treated like *proper* royalty.

If the Tecks were now ensconced at the centre of Coburg's royal palace, it must only be because in the true May's absence, George had gone and betrothed himself to the counterfeit. This luxury was simply the reflected glory of England's heir.

In the lavish sitting-room of these apartments, the Duchess perched on the edge of an armchair, clasped her hands, and looked at the four of us arrayed on two sofas before her.

"The first thing to clear up," she said briskly, "is the engagement. I'm sure it would be terribly inconvenient to break it off at this point, dear. Do say you'll let it stand."

Anyone else might have choked on her tea—George, in fact, turned bright red, inhaled a crumb of shortbread, and went into a coughing fit. Short squirmed in sympathetic agony. I tried very hard not to let my glee show. I might not approve of a match between George and May, but I would never tire of watching their dance.

May, however, replaced cup on saucer with an air of perfect calm. Only a slight heightening of the colour in her cheeks betrayed her emotion. "I don't know that I can, mamma." She turned to George, whose eyes were now streaming, and who appeared to wish himself in Timbuctoo. "I am so terribly sorry for what I said in Strasbourg, George. But the truth is… " she swallowed. "I do not think I will ever bring myself to become the wife of—of—of one in your condition."

"My condition?" he gasped, finally getting the better of his coughing-fit.

"She means a werewolf," I put in helpfully.

George was so far gone in agonies of embarrassment, he did not even send a furious glance my way. "Oh—display on the train—know what you mean—shocking!"

"You were only trying to protect me," May said quickly. She

was certainly blushing now. "I don't wish to be ungrateful! But…I do not think…I can *marry…*"

"Oh, nonsense!" the Duchess said. "Your cousin Ducky is marrying a werewolf on Thursday! If she can do it, I don't see why you can't!"

"I don't see why we have to be this way at all," May said, and this time there was a faintly mutinous tone in her voice.

"Can't rule without it, you know," George said mournfully. "If we weren't monsters—pardon my French—we'd lose the Empire, and then what? Half the globe would be plunged into chaos. Or worse, the Russians and the Germans would gobble it all up between them. Hate it myself, but don't see what I can do about it!"

May sighed, and seemed to shrink in on herself in defeat. "Of course not," she whispered. "I'm sorry, George."

If she had anything more to say, she was forestalled by a rap on the door. Mary Adelaide gave an impatient snort, but called, "Come in!"

One of the plain-clothes policemen from the station entered. "Forgive me, ma'am, but I was only looking for Inspector Short—" He broke off in surprise when he saw me drinking tea with my littlest finger demurely extended. "Beg pardon! But her majesty wished to question the young person herself."

"Her majesty!" I said. "I didn't know this was within her majesty's jurisdiction, Jim!"

The plain-clothes man sent me a hostile look. "Matter of fact, I believe it's within the Kabale's jurisdiction, if her majesty chooses to press charges."

"Which is *not* going to happen," said Mary Adelaide majestically. "I suppose you'd better run along, Sharp."

George leaped to his feet, evidently glad to be released from the intolerable interview. "I'll come and speak up for you! Saved my life, by Jove!"

The Kabale! I had heard of them once before—from Vasily in London, during the Whitechapel werewolf business. From what Vasily had told me, royalties had their own customary laws, and the Kabale was the body that enforced them. As Short, George, and May accompanied me from the room, I wondered whether I felt more curious to meet the Kabale in person, or anxious to dispel the cloud of suspicion hanging over my head. Doubtless the aforesaid cloud was shortly to be dispelled by the warm bright light of truth, and I would not learn more of the Kabale. Just my luck!

One is idealistic, when young. Little did I know in that moment that I was shortly to know far more about the Kabale than I could ever wish!

A door in the broad hallway opened as we passed, and a very young lady stepped out, barely more than a girl. "Georgie!" she burbled, catching the object of her attention by the shoulders, and kissing him fondly on the cheek. "Just who I wanted to see! I say, what's all this I hear about an explosion? Are you hurt?"

George reddened and threw an anxious sidelong glance at May. "Hurt, Missy?—Not in the least.—By Jove! I didn't know *you* had arrived yet."

"Just this morning. Oh, Georgie, I have *so* much to tell you. And to think I haven't seen you since I got married, and had to go away to Roumania! Awful place!"

This exchange helped me to identify the lady, who was very pretty and expensively dressed, with blue eyes and a profusion of golden hair. This must be Princess Marie of Edinburgh, another of the Queen's many grandchildren and the lady with whom George's name had been linked before each of them had gone their separate ways, she to marry Ferdinand, the Crown Prince of Roumania, and he to pay his attentions to May.

"Ah," George said awkwardly in response to this effusion. "You know May of Teck, of course."

"*Everyone* knows the Tecks," said Missy, barely throwing May a glance. "Will you be at the ball tonight, George? I am keeping my card free for you, you know."

"Well—hang it—jolly good of you and all, but won't Ferdinand—"

"Oh! what Ferdinand don't know, won't hurt him! He had to stay home in Roumania, anyway, and in the meantime I mean to enjoy my freedom to my heart's content. But oh, I was supposed to go and loan Ducky a pair of diamond earrings for tonight's ceremony. Don't forget! I shall want at *least* two dances, and a nice long chat."

With that, she tripped away down the hall. George cleared his throat with another sidelong glance at May, who watched Missy's departure with a rather wistful expression. Upon my word, here was a new development—an old flame of George's with no intention of giving up her territory, and May looking like a lost soul over it! Still, perhaps it was for the best in the long run.

George cleared his throat. "Spare me a couple of dances too, May."

"If you like," she said lifelessly. "What did Missy mean by *tonight's ceremony?* Isn't the wedding on Thursday?"

"Oh. No, this is—er—a German custom. Better push on, before Grandmamma sends someone to find us."

In a large and elegant suite at the front of the palace, the windows of which overlooked the flowering gardens and shady park stretching uphill towards the old castle, we found Queen Victoria herself seated in state upon a brocaded armchair. She was flanked by her two elder sons: the coffee-pot Prince of Wales, George's father, and the soldierly Alfred, Duke of Saxe-Coburg and Gotha, the present owner of this palace and father of the bride.

I had an explanation of my actions this afternoon ready to hand, but the Queen began her questions on quite a different line.

"You are scarred, Miss Sharp."

So, my face was to tell against me once more. "Yes, ma'am, just like the Princess Beatrice."

Her frown deepened. Perhaps it was a low blow: she herself had scarred her beloved youngest child by accident.

"You don't sound quite English," she observed. "Are you an anarchist?"

"On the contrary, ma'am. I was trained as a bodyguard and anarchist-hunter at Saint Botolph's."

"That," she said, rather shrewdly, "does not answer the question of what you *are*."

I had met this formidable old lady once before, at the beginning of my employment with Princess May. Then—when not transforming into a wolf and howling at the moon—I had seen the Queen at her most winning: full of affectionate italics. The woman who confronted me now, by contrast, was every inch the Empress, and I warned myself not to underestimate her.

"No, ma'am, I am not an anarchist."

"Why did you bomb my train, then?"

"I was unable to defuse the bomb, so I threw it where I believed it would do the least damage. I'm afraid I didn't stop to consider the locomotive—but even if I had, it was that or let the thing go off in the middle of the crowd."

"Saved my life, what!" George put in. The Queen opened her eyes at him, and he rushed on: "I came to vouch for Sharp's character, ma'am! Er..."

He wilted visibly beneath her stare.

"Thank you, George," she said icily.

Well! I had thought May's *ohs* bad enough, but this was a hundred times worse.

"I might have been killed," the Queen went on after a moment, "along with the Prince of Wales and several more of my children, grandchildren, and servants. I should *very much* like to know how there came to be a bomb at all."

"Ah," I said, happy to be of assistance in clearing *that* up. "It was planted by anarchists, and detonated just as I reached it."

"And the real culprits?"

I looked at Short, who cleared his throat. "I was unable to apprehend them, ma'am." He shot me a meaning look. "Although I did my best."

I smiled at him in thanks. Had he revealed Anton's role in the day's events, the fat would *really* have been in the fire. As it was—

"All this is most unsatisfactory," said the Queen. "A bomb was thrown at my conveyance, and I am asked to believe, first, that it was done with the best of intentions; second, that it was impossible simply to defuse the infernal device; and third, that phantasmagorical anarchists were responsible for the explosion! Really, this stretches belief! Is the crime of *lèse-majesté* to be overlooked so easily?"

A crime?—saving lives, a *crime?* For once, I was dumbstruck.

Then May made a small sound of distress, and George leaped into the breach. "But it *is* true, ma'am! I'll vouch for Sharp any day of the week!"

The Prince of Wales grunted. "Even if it is true, it sets a dangerous precedent. We can't have people throwing bombs at the person of majesty, not even a bodyguard!"

"Why, Bertie!" the Queen said in pleased surprise. "I don't care what anyone says; you *are* very sensible on occasion. Yes, indeed. I *will* be submitting this case to the Kabale. Is there some sort of prison, or gaol, or lockup, Alfred, where she can be held?"

"George, can't you *do* something?" May whispered.

The Queen must have heard. "Was there something else, George?" she asked, softly ominous.

George looked from May to me and then to his grandmother, and I scented his nervous perspiration. His throat worked, and although I had begun to despair of his being able to help me at all, it would have been a great comfort had he tried.

"No, ma'am," he mumbled, looking more than ever like a guilty schoolboy.

"Then it's decided. The Kabale had better deal with this young person tonight. You may go."

Short ushered me from the room with a murmur of, "Courage!"

"I'll take as much as I can get!" I muttered. "What the dickens, Short! I saved all those lives, and they take it as an insult because a bit of smoke blew in their eyes!"

"Hush, Miss Sharp! You ought not to say such things," he warned, glancing behind. But we were well into the corridor by now, and apart from the other two policemen, only George and May had followed us.

Chapter III.

May having bade me a hurried farewell, with a promise to see what she might do, I was taken down to the Coburg police station and locked into one of the cells there. To my surprise, the small gaol was filled to the brim. Short went away, promising to return as soon as he had more news, and I settled in resignedly to wait.

"Crime wave?" I asked one of my cell-mates. I had been locked in with five or six other women, the majority of whom seemed quite respectable to the outward eye.

The middle-aged lady I had addressed was a lean, capable-looking woman who smelled of fish. She shook her head. "No, m'dear. Wave of monsters. Just you sit tight and don't cheek anyone, and they'll let all us suspicious characters out again in a few days."

"Do you mean to say they haven't charged you with any crime?"

"Dear me, no! Only on suspicion. They have to clean up the streets somehow." She directed a knowing smile at one of my other cell-mates, who had brought knitting and was placidly at work on a sock. "English!"

"Ah," the knitter said, as though that explained everything.

My cellmates might be willing to bear their wrongful

imprisonment with equanimity, but I could not help chafing at the forced inactivity. I *had* been charged with a serious crime, and I was beginning to be seriously worried. Surely it was not rational to see in my actions anything but a genuine desire to save lives! Yet what passed for reason with me, did not so pass with the exalted people I had frightened.

For I must have frightened them—I, with my scars, and my knowledge of bombs—I would always be feared and distrusted, not for anything I had done, but because of what had been done to me! But perhaps this would yet prove to be a blessing in disguise. I remembered why, when this Continental trip began, I had been so eager to attend the Coburg wedding. Nearly every royalty in Europe would be here—including the werewolf that had attacked me two years ago, scarring me forever.

My actions today had gained me the privilege of meeting the Kabale face to face. Perhaps I might find my way into their good graces, as I had with May and to a lesser extent, George and the Duchess. Perhaps I might ask them to help me find justice for what had been done to me.

And if not?—Well, at worst I would go to my grave with *some* of my endless curiosity satisfied, for I had been agog to know all about the mysterious Kabale since Vasily first mentioned them.

An hour passed before May arrived, alone this time save for Short. "What a horrible place," she greeted me, looking at the crowded cells with distaste.

"Believe me, I've seen worse," I said, repressing a shudder at the memory of the tower of Castle Sarkozy.

"Oh, Sharp! I feel this is all my fault." May turned to the policeman who escorted them. "I would like to speak to my friend in private, if I may."

In this way, a minute or two later, we found ourselves crowded into a small office room. May dropped into the chair behind the desk looking rather weary and drained—an impression rather magnified than relieved by the black mourning she wore.

"Oh, May, you ought to have been resting," I said apologetically. "I am afraid the last month has been rather hard on you."

"Hard on *me!* Oh, Sharp, how can I rest, knowing you to be in danger? I've been writing letters to Aunt Queen, and to the Kabale. So has mamma, and so has—so has George. This is all very new, Sharp. I had never heard of the Kabale until today."

"I had—a little," said I. "All I know is that it's supposed to be some sort of monster tribunal. What have *you* learned?"

Short cleared his throat. "As I understand it, the Kabale attends to security at events like this, among other things. Their jurisdiction…" He paused. "Their penal jurisdiction extends as far as the death penalty."

"Death! Surely they don't mean to kill me?"

"I don't know," Short said glumly. "It may even depend upon what her majesty requests."

"But it will be a fair trial, won't it, Short?" May put in.

"I don't know," Short repeated. The brave front he'd put on two hours ago as we left the Queen's presence seemed to have melted away, and he was looking at me with his mouth all stretched out and turned down at the corners. "It's never a good sign when a court is a secret known only to the powerful."

"Don't worry, Short," I told him, attempting to look on the

bright side. "To be honest, the fact that the Kabale is such a dreadful secret makes me all the more eager to see it at work."

"From time to time, Miss Sharp, I ask myself why it is that my life has become so eventful since I met you. But that comment makes the answer quite clear."

"Oh, don't pretend you don't like it!" I transferred my attention to May. There was something I needed to tell her—something I had lain awake thinking over through many sleepless nights, these last few weeks. "May, if for any reason I don't see you again—"

"Don't say it, Sharp! We *will* see each other again; I promise you!"

"I only mean to say that I think you're quite right in not marrying George. I know my opinion doesn't weigh much with you—as it shouldn't, for it's your own happiness at stake—but for some of us, the monsters aren't family, or protectors, or friends. They're killers. They have to be, in order to be monsters at all. It means something that you see it that way, too."

"And on this question I will never compromise, you may be sure of it," May said—but she *looked* terribly distressed. If she had learned to think of George as a killer, she had not yet learned to cease thinking of him as a cousin and a friend.

"Not that it isn't a shame," I added. "If it wasn't for the—the teeth, and the claws, and the killing someone to make himself a werewolf, he'd be *perfect* for you. Begging your pardon." I added that last sentence more out of habit than conviction, for May had told me to speak freely, as her friend.

"Oh, Sharp…" May glanced over her shoulder to Short, who tactfully nodded and let himself out of the small room. When we were alone, May reached into her pocket and withdrew a letter written on beautiful thick paper.

"I received this from George," she said, blushing very faintly. "This afternoon—just before I came here. Please read it! I don't know *what* to think!"

I hardly needed the invitation, for wild horses could not have torn the letter from my hands. I unfolded the page and read.

Ehrenberg Palace, 189-

Dear May—May more than dear—I can only imagine what you must think of me. The scene you witnessed on the Orient Express lives in my nightmares, and when I think of it I tell myself I had better despair. You beheld me then as the monster I am, a sight I would have given my right arm to spare you. Dare I plead with you not to judge me too harshly? You saw a savage beast, but one driven out of his small measure of restraint by the danger which threatened you. You saw a wolf, but I am more than a wolf. I am also a man, and that man is entirely yours, heart and soul.

I can have no secrets from you, who know and have seen all. My feelings are the same as they ever were. Of course, there is no definite understanding between us, and certainly there can be no public engagement until our mourning is completed. Nonetheless, I could ask nothing better than to be permitted to recommend myself to you, in hope that the existence of the monster may not be too high a price to pay for the faithful adoration of the man.

Yours,
George of York

"Dear me!" I said, captivated in spite of myself. "Did he write this himself?"

May blushed still more vividly. "Short—Short said his pen was scratching all afternoon. I mean—I'm sure he was writing to the Kabale too."

I handed the letter back to her, where it was smoothed carefully back into her pocket: proof of May's fundamentally prosaic outlook on life. *I* would have kept a letter like that next to my heart. "And how do you mean to reply?"

"I don't know," she confessed. "I can't say yes unless I think I *could* marry him. And it isn't only that he's a werewolf, although that certainly matters."

She seemed reluctant to say more. "Go on," I prompted.

She heaved a sigh. "It stings, a little, that he couldn't tell the difference between me and an *automaton.* How well can he know me, if he could make a mistake like that?"

"I don't suppose he imagined such an impersonation was even possible," I felt compelled to point out.

"And then, there is his family," she said, making a *moue* of disapproval. "You saw how quickly he yielded this afternoon! I don't believe George has ever in his life done a single thing his grandmother might disapprove of. Or if he has, he's been *very* quiet about it."

George had once told me that he spent his life acting as his brother's whipping-boy, constantly tasked with keeping Prince Eddy on the straight and narrow, and standing up to accept the punishment when he failed.—Which must have been often, from what I had come to know of Eddy. I had to agree with May: it didn't seem as though George would be ready to defy his upbringing anytime soon.

Yet—what better spur to change, than the prospect of

happiness in love?

I drummed my fingers against the table-top, trying to think. I did not wonder at May's confusion. I was not in love with George, but I had come to respect and even like him—before Vasily's revelation that it took more than a simple taste of human blood to turn a prince into a monster. It took lifeblood—murder! George was a killer, and had never told us. That felt like a betrayal, even to me, who had never really been close enough to call him my friend.

And yet—George was now a future king. The fate of millions might be tied to his character and choices. With so much power, he could not be ignored; but he might be influenced, and what influence could be so powerful as that of the woman he loved?

I had wagered my life on the hope that Anton might change for the better. Might I not wager a little lost time on the hope of George doing the same?

"If that's the way you feel," I said very clearly and deliberately, "why not tell him?"

"Tell him to go against the *Family?* Oh, I couldn't!"

"Why not? George may be a monster, but I take it he has a conscience, and you evidently mean a great deal to him. Who else will encourage him to speak?"

"Do you think that would be proper?"

"Dear May, are you really asking *me* what would be proper?"

"Touché!" she said with the ghost of a smile. "Still, I don't know, Sharp! George is going to be King one day, and surely I ought to treat him like it. I ought to be showing him respect for his office, if for no other reason. And it doesn't seem respectful to criticise a future king like that. I *hate* women who scold."

I sighed. Sometimes it was easy to forget just how far May's ideas diverged from mine. "Well, if you can't speak to him without scolding, or if he can't be reasoned with without feeling disrespected, then perhaps you are less suited than I thought, and it would be best to give him the flick."

"Perhaps you're right." She nibbled thoughtfully on her lip. "That reminds me of something I was going to ask you, Sharp. Please don't take this the wrong way, but I want you to promise me something."

"I will if I can in good conscience."

"Will you promise to be very careful, and very respectful to the Kabale? I wouldn't ordinarily say this, for *I* don't mind, but there are times when I think you might come across to people as somewhat…"

"Fresh?" I suggested, grinning.

"Forward," May said delicately. "The truth is, people of their station are accustomed to deference, and I would hate you to be in any more trouble than you already are. Do be careful. For your own sake; or for the sake of your friends, if for no other reason."

I was about to point out how polite I had been to the Queen that very afternoon, but then I remembered my comment about Princess Beatrice, and turned my words into a cough. "Certainly I mean to be respectful to the Kabale. I want to know who gave me these scars, and I've a suspicion the Kabale might be able to tell me."

Our voices had lifted somewhat since we stopped discussing George; and now Short re-entered just in time to catch my final words.

"Don't get your hopes up, Miss Sharp. From what I've heard, the Kabale is mostly concerned with preserving stability and continuity, and most of all peace among the crowned heads of Europe. What with the trouble in the Balkans, and the Kaiser's constant sabre-rattling, we might have had any number of wars this last ten years if not for them. Keeping records of bitings and drainings may be beyond their purview."

"How so? During the Whitechapel business, Vasily told me that the Kabale might help me bring Sal's killer to justice. And anyway, *I* should have thought that stability and continuity would be best preserved by penalising the bitings."

"Well, if you must ask, do take care to choose a propitious moment. Ma'am," he added, with a glance at the watch in his waistcoat pocket, "I see that it is nearly five o'clock."

May squeezed my hands, a faint anxious line between her eyes. "I must go, Sharp. I wish I could go with you tonight, but the Kabale doesn't open its meetings to just anyone, and there's that masked ball at the palace. I'll come back the moment I can. *Do* be careful."

"I promise," I told her.

After a moment's hesitation, Short took my hand in turn. "Take care, Miss Sharp." His gaze was oddly intent. "No matter what happens, we won't let anything happen to you."

He ushered May away, leaving me to be returned to my cell by a pair of revenants. Back in the lockup, I put my cool fingers against my hot cheeks and told myself to simmer down, but then I smelled the faint lingering scent of him—pipe-smoke and gunpowder—and had a bad couple of moments. Short and I were friends, nothing more. I really must be careful not to read anything into his behaviour. Loving me was the sort of risk Anton might take, but never Short; and I never meant to risk our friendship by letting him see that a part of me, however small, wished for more.

I settled down on one of the small, narrow benches that furnished the cell, and whiled away the time arguing with my cellmates about female suffrage—an idea which scandalised them thoroughly. To my surprise, I was roused after a couple of hours of this when the door to the lockup opened, and the fresh-faced young policeman who had manned the desk upon my entrance staggered in looking somewhat apprehensive. His arm was twisted behind his back, and my old friend Anton Lupei was propelling him forward with a knife held to his jaw. There was no sign of the two revenants, his underlings.

"Anton!" I cried in great delight. "I wondered when you'd turn up again!"

"You can rely on me, Liz Sharp." He manoeuvred the policeman in front of my cell, and spat instructions at him in villainous-sounding German. The young man unlocked the gate with shaking hands, and Anton beckoned me. "Out you come. The rest of you too—you're free now."

I exchanged glances with the fish-wife and the knitter. All of us looked dubious. I shared their reluctance. What use was escape, when the long arm of the law might recapture us with ease?

"Thank you, Anton, but I was quite capable of picking that lock myself! I *did* bring my hairpins, after all."

"Then why didn't you *use* them?"

"Because if I leave like this, I'll have to go into exile. If I stay—"

"If you stay, you leave yourself at the mercy of monsters," Anton growled. "Don't be a pheasant, Liz! I'm the best chance you'll ever have. Besides, there's someone waiting to see you." Pocketing his knife, he snatched the keys from the young guard and bowled him into my cell. That was alarming, and I slipped out the door just in time for Anton to swing it closed and lock it again.

"Wait a minute," I objected. *"Who* is waiting to see me?"

"An old friend of yours." Before heading back towards the door, Anton tossed the keys into another cell. "Use those to free yourselves, *mes compagnons.* Or stay there, if you're all cowards. Coming, Liz?"

An old friend! Well, I could hardly stay in prison after an invitation like that. Reaching through the bars of my erstwhile cell, I snatched my hat from the bench, settled it on my hair, wrapped my veil around my face to hide my scars, and hurried after Anton. In the police-station itself, the two revenants were collapsed onto the floor like the dead men they were, though there was not a mark on them.

"How did you do *that?"* I inquired, startled. I knew from bitter experience that revenants were well-nigh impossible to fight. Once they were attacked, they went into a murderous frenzy, killing everyone in their path. And since they were already dead, nothing short of instant vaporisation would stop them—neither shooting, nor stabbing, nor lighting on fire.

"They've no free will," Anton said with off-handed pride as he pushed open the door and led me into the streets of Coburg. "They're bound to obey their superiors. I simply had that bootheel order them to sleep."

I think I have mentioned that although small, Coburg was an impossibly quaint and pretty town, full of whitewashed houses boasting cheerful red-tiled roofs and Renaissance-style red strapwork across the plaster. The streets, however, were very quiet and although the sun had not yet set, I saw few citizens out on the streets. Those who were moved furtively, glancing often at their watches or the slanting sunlight.

Anton led me north to a part of town which was slightly shabbier than the rest, although by any English standards it would still have been considered painfully neat and clean. I kept my head down, for although the streets were practically empty of citizens there seemed to be a great many policemen about—from the uniformed German policemen directing the non-existent traffic at every intersection, to the revenants on patrol, or the English or Russian plain-clothes men lurking behind newspapers on the corners and being shooed out of early-closing cafes.

"This place is half strangled," Anton observed, pulling me a little nearer his side as we circled a bowler-hatted loiterer leaning against a public-house door. "I won't rest easy till we're out of it."

I recalled Short's question in the carriage. Why *was* Anton still following me? What did he hope to achieve? Vera Livius was dead, and it made no sense to repay a debt to someone who no longer existed. "I don't know that I'm ready to leave yet, Anton. But you're right, it's dangerous in Coburg. Don't let me keep you here."

"No, Liz—I'm staying for as long as you still need me." His jaw bulged pugnaciously. "Also *Vasily* is here and I still need to kill him."

He spat the name as though it soiled his lips.

"The Grand Duke?" I exclaimed, startled. "Why must you kill him?"

"What a stupid question!" Anton's eyes smouldered with past wrongs. "He killed my cousin Ioanna to make himself a vampire, and then he drained you at Castle Sarkozy. No arguments! He dies."

I considered this. Vasily was treacherous and dangerous. I didn't trust him as far as I could throw him, and he was a tall, stocky man, not built for long-distance flight. All the same, Anton was exactly the wrong person to deal with him, precisely because he was motivated by vengeance.

I could not restrain myself from touching the place at my neck—concealed by my high-necked blouse and gauzy scarf—where Vasily had bitten me and drained my blood. The pain was gone now, the punctures healed to faint, silvery scars; but I thought I would never feel comfortable baring my neck again.

"If anyone has the right to make Vasily pay for what he did at Castle Sarkozy, Anton, that person is me. As for Ioanna, you ought to know he considers what he did to her to be his greatest shame."

Anton spat. "Of course he would say that to *you.*"

"What is that supposed to mean?"

"He knows your weakness." Anton jabbed a finger at me. "Women, you are all the same. This is why the monsters rule the world! *Oh, he's so dashing.* He's a vampire! *Yes, but underneath, he's tormented by the things he's done.* He drank your blood against your will! *He can change.*"

His voice see-sawed comically between his own gruff tones and a high-pitched mockery of my own, and I couldn't help laughing, even as I smacked his arm. "Oh, that's rich, coming from you! I remember not so long ago, Short making similar arguments about a monster I faced in a church in Eger."

During the affair at Castle Sarkozy, the Livius Serum—my father's final, most devastating invention—had briefly trans-formed Anton into a mindless, blood-soaked monster, and I had gambled my life to reach him and save him, rather than kill him as Short had insisted. A shiver ran through Anton at the memory, and all the laughter disappeared from his voice. "That was different," he growled. "I am not a monster anymore. I never will be again."

"That's right," I said gently. "You have had the luxury of choice. But it didn't work that way for Vasily. Once he made his first kill, even though it was an accident, he became a monster forever."

Anton growled. "Yes, they are all of them monsters forever. They must consume the blood of the innocent if they are to survive. And that is why *all* of them must die."

"I don't know, Anton. I have always believed there is hope for wicked people. That is what it means to be a Christian, after all."

Anton snorted. "There's another thing. You're Protestant now, yes?"

"What do you mean by *now?*"

Seeing my puzzled look, he shook his head. "Don't you realise your father had you raised Roman Catholic, in deference to Veronika's wishes when she had you? They stole that along with everything else, at Saint Botolph's. You should question more of what you think you believe."

With that, he pushed open a door on the narrow, shabby street, and led me into a tenement. I followed in a daze, feeling curiously unmoored. Nothing else Anton could have said could have affected me like this. If there was one thing I had always been sure of, it was my faith, and now…even much of *this* was their creation.

Perhaps Anton had a point. As far as any of us knew, once a royalty had made their first kill, they would forever carry a monster within them. There was no going back for them. Perhaps monstrosity ought to be beyond temporal forgiveness. Perhaps the only reason I had ever believed differently was because that was how I had been taught at Saint Botolph's.

But no: if my religion commanded me to love my enemies, it had also inspired me to follow my conscience. Here in my confusion I found one fact to cling to: Saint Botolph's had never wanted me to trust myself. I had stubbornly followed my own heart and conscience in defiance of everything they taught me, and so far, I had not gone too badly astray. I could not put aside what I felt to be right, merely for this—certainly not with lives at stake, even if they *were* monsters. If that was what Anton wanted, I would defy him as stoutly as I had defied Miss Scrimpson.

It felt like shaky ground from which to begin rebuilding everything I believed, but for that moment it was enough.

The tenement into which Anton led me was built around a central stairwell that wound through several storeys towards the roof. As I followed Anton upstairs, I noticed one door ajar, with a pair of bright eyes watching from behind it. When I met the eyes, the door snicked shut. A little way upstairs, another followed suit.

"Are you sure this place is safe?" I asked under my breath. Perhaps my mental upheaval had left me feeling physically vulnerable as well. The hair was standing up on the back of my neck, and although I saw no more open doors, I still felt as though I was being watched.

"It isn't us they're afraid of. How do you think these people feel, knowing their town has become a playground for—"

"Hush!" I murmured. "Not out in the open, Anton."

After that he was silent until the staircase delivered us onto the fourth storey, where the poorest, coldest rooms were. Anton unlocked a door and stood back, motioning me to enter.

I stepped into a large, bare garret room furnished with a low bed, a stove, a table and chair, and not much else. It was the chair which was of greatest interest to me, for a young woman was bound to it. For a moment she glared at me over the top of her gag. I caught a whiff of her scent: carbolic soap, cheap hair oil, and a distinctive human musk. For a moment I thought I was back in Saint Botolph's itself! Then her eyes widened in recognition, and she said something muffled in the back of her throat.

"What the dickens, Anton?" I sprang to the poor girl and pulled off the gag, revealing the features of—Hannah Bunker.

The more attentive of my readers may remember Miss Bunker: she had been an inmate of Saint Botolph's when I left it four months previously.

"Hannah!" The name woke a more recent memory: when Anton caught sight of the anarchist with the detonator just now, that was the name he used. These lodgings evidently belonged to her, if the stockings and petticoats drying before the stove were any indication. "Hannah!" I repeated, blankly. "Don't tell me *you're* an anarchist!"

"Don't tell me you *aren't*, Elizabeth Sharp." Hannah spat on the floor as though to rid her mouth of the taste of her gag. "All along, you and Sal Tanner were teaching your own little clique how to kill monsters! Why didn't you tell *me*?"

"Those meetings were limited to the girls we could trust," I said severely, "and considering your irresponsible actions today, I don't believe we were wrong to exclude you. Exactly what were you trying to achieve with this senseless violence?"

"I was trying to destroy the Kabale."

"The Kabale?"

"Bet you didn't know about *them*," she said triumphantly.

I threw a glance to where Anton leaned against the door with folded arms. He nodded to me, the corner of his mouth twitching in a brief, encouraging smile. Well, how interesting. Short feared that Anton had betrayed us in order to rescue the automaton bomber; but in fact Anton had captured her and brought me to question her. In the view of the world taught us at Saint Botolph's, one was either a bomb-flinging anarchist or a lawful citizen, but perhaps Anton was progressing in a direction that was neither.

"Anyway, what do you mean by senseless violence?" Hannah added. "Who made you the judge of what violence is and isn't appropriate?"

"I don't know," I said honestly. "No one taught me to think about this in any depth. I'm having to make it up as I go along. But the one thing I *do* know is that I draw the line at indiscriminate slaughter of innocents, whether it's committed by monsters *or* by anarchists. Will you tell me about the Kabale?"

She sent me a triumphant grin. "Well, first of all, they're the ones who run Saint Botolph's."

"I beg your pardon?" I said faintly.

"After what happened to Sal, some of us did some snooping," Hannah said. "It turns out the Board is a front. The real instructions come from a secret society of European royalties. How else did you think they stole our memories? That's siren power."

While the royalties of Germany were werewolves, and the royalties of Russia and Roumania were vampires having the power to twist what the mind perceived in the present, the royalties of Denmark and Greece were sirens, having the power to steal or alter memories. It struck me that I had been attacked by each of them in turn. A werewolf had given me my scars. A siren had stolen my past. And at Castle Sarkozy not a month previously, Grand Duke Vasily Nikolaevitch Romanov had drained my blood.

Behind all these sinister events lurked the Kabale. Of course, I already suspected something of the sort. I had been snatched by a werewolf in Stuttgart. I had woken in a hospital in London. Somewhere between those two points, my memories had been removed by a siren. The logical answer was that somehow, a conspiracy of European royalties were working together to cover up their crimes. But—dash it, the Kabale was *official.* Queen Victoria herself deferred to it. I had imagined a gang of libertines and ne'er-do-wells attempting to cover up their reckless crimes.

"I thought the Kabale was only supposed to keep the peace," I said. "Stability. Continuity. Order."

Hannah seized the bait. "Of course! That's what *they'd* think. Any time one of them attacks someone, they have one of their sirens remove our memories, and then we wake up in Saint Botolph's, or on the *Akbar,* without the first idea who we are. And then they indoctrinate us as their dedicated bodyguards. The Kabale is dedicated to stability all right. It's a systematic cover-up designed to keep *them* on their thrones."

"Good Lord," I said blankly. I believed her—dash it, I shouldn't have needed her to tell me. And this was the tribunal before which I was supposed to appear tonight!

Anton pushed away from the door. "It's a good thing someone broke you out of that gaol, hm?"

If what Hannah said was true, there was no possibility of my getting the Kabale to willingly hand over the name of the werewolf who had given me my scars. Meanwhile, the chances of my being forgiven today's events seemed more remote than ever.

Yet if I went away with Anton now, how would I ever know who had given me my scars? How would I ever learn more about the Kabale?—that shadowy organisation, which controlled Europe behind closed doors!

Poor Short, with his affinity for stability and order! I was about to take twenty years off his life, no doubt.

"I'm grateful to you, Anton, but I must go back; and quickly, before there's a disturbance."

"Go back? To gaol?" Anton thrust his arm against the door before I could pull it open. "Are you quite mad?"

"They have to be stopped, Anton. I need to know who is running Saint Botolph's."

"They'll kill you."

"Then at least I'll die doing something worthwhile." I hesitated. "It's my only way of finding out who gave me these scars."

He watched my face intently, and his shoulders slumped in resignation. "I know better than to argue with *that* look."

I forced a smile. "How nice to meet someone who finally understands me!"

"What about *me?*" Hannah interrupted querulously. She struggled against her bonds. "My foot has gone to sleep."

Anton cocked an eyebrow at me.

We could hardly keep her a prisoner, and it was out of the question to hand her to the revenants. "Tell her what happened at Castle Sarkozy, and let her go if you think it would be safe."

"I'll see you back to gaol first," he said, glancing towards the window. "It's getting dark."

Anton was right: twilight had begun to thicken upon Coburg, and full night could not be far away. Night, in a town full of monsters!—I gave a word of assent, and we stole down the stairs again. Once again, I felt the prickly consciousness of eyes watching from the shadows, and pulled my veil close around my face. Just as we reached the final flight of stairs, a door creaked open behind us. I turned very quickly, reaching for my revolver—but I had divested myself of weapons before going to gaol, and my hands came away empty.

In the crack of the door, a pair of rheumy old eyes stared at us. *"Fräulein!"* an old woman croaked. It was one of the tenants who had watched us on our way upstairs a moment ago. *"Fräulein, Herr,* don't you know what night it is?"

I looked uncertainly at Anton. "April the…"

"It's the first night of full moon," she hissed, "and there is a wedding at the palace!"

"Not until Thursday," I said easily. Her eyes lifted to heaven.

"Oh! you foolish English! Do you not know what goes on at these affairs? Do you think you can walk these streets in safety? Go upstairs again! Go upstairs and bolt your door and stay there until morning!"

"It's alright, mother," I said. "We are not as helpless as we seem, and we shan't be out long."

I sensed that Anton wished to move on, and yet those staring eyes held me transfixed. "Wait," the old woman muttered, and her door closed. I heard the chain rattle, and then she shuffled into the hall, holding out a small object that glinted in the faint light filtering through the skylight at the top of the stairwell.

"Take this," she whispered throatily. "Hide it. You may need it."

I lifted the item with a wordless sound of surprise. It was a little tin hip-flask such as gentlemen carry to store their brandy, and I could feel a liquid sloshing inside. A cross was embossed upon the side.

"Saltwater." She motioned for me to hide the flask. "If the werewolves catch your scent, pour it over your shoes to hide your scent."

"Thank you," I said, concealing the flask in the capacious pocket of my bloomers. I already knew the salutary effects of salt in repelling vampires, and having the flask on hand *did* make me feel better equipped for—whatever would happen tonight.

"What about me? Don't I get a weapon?" Anton grumbled as we stepped out into the gaslit streets.

"I suppose she thought I looked particularly helpless."

"You only look helpless because you've muffled up those scars."

"Well, you're not getting my saltwater; I might need it later. Go and make up some of your own if you're nervous. What do you suppose *does* go on at these monster balls?"

"I'm not sure I want to know," he said grimly, casting a glance up at the fading sky.

We stole through the streets like ghosts. No citizens were abroad at all now, and even the policemen were scarcer than they had been. Two of them came pacing towards us along the street. I felt Anton stiffen by my side as both of us caught a whiff of corruption, and a glimpse of the pale fire burning in their shrivelled eye sockets. We crossed to the other side of the street, and edged past them with our hearts in our mouths.

"Revenants!" I whispered when they had gone by. "I heard the Kaiser was planning to manufacture the abominable things for his army, but it seems he's making them for the police force too!"

"He is here in Coburg, you realise," Anton murmured, as we hastened towards the police station. "Everyone is here, and they're making a show of force for people like you and me."

"I'm not an anarchist, Anton. Not really."

"I know. I didn't mean only anarchists."

Shall I ever forget the emptiness of that town—the bars falling across doors and shutters as we passed—the scent of garlic and salt crushed across doorposts and windowsills! With the evening, a dark cloud of fear had fallen upon Coburg. Once again, I wondered what that old lady could have meant by asking if I knew what went on at these affairs. A formless premonition took hold of me, and as we came in view of the police-station, I put my hand on Anton's arm.

"This is far enough. I can go the rest of the way alone."

"I still don't like it, Liz. There are better ways to lose your life than walking into the wolf's jaws."

"You're wonderfully encouraging, do you know that?"

"I have *sense*. Unlike you."

"Then I need hardly tell you not to stay here. Take Hannah and leave Coburg—at once—before things get worse."

"And leave you behind? Not likely."

"Hypocrite," I said, with feeling. "What's the good of sense if it only applies to other people? Chew on *that,* Anton Lupei."

Patting his shoulder in farewell, I darted across the street and sauntered into the police station. The young lieutenant sat at the table again, yawning over a report. When I threw back my veil, he recoiled as though he'd seen a ghost. An instant later, I was staring down the barrel of his revolver.

"Hullo, Jim," I greeted him. "Didn't I mention I was only stepping out for a breath of fresh air? Won't you show me to my room?"

Chapter IV.

Since the gaol was still more or less full, I presumed few if any of the inmates had taken advantage of the keys to escape. As for myself, I worked the young lieutenant like a pump, and learned that the palace, though alarmed by my escape, had counselled the local police not to pursue me. They had methods of their own, which they intended to pursue at the earliest opportunity.

Within my cell, I watched night fall with a cool prickling up and down my neck. I could guess what methods the Kabale might use to hunt me down. Half of them were no doubt wolves, and better capable of following a scent than myself.

That they would have the boldness to do so through the very streets of Coburg—that was a sobering thought. In Germany, unlike England, the condition of the ruling class was an institution rather than a guilty secret. I felt that I had come to the place of power of Royalty itself. Here they were not afraid of me, and if they wished might crush me, and none would dare complain.

I did not regret my decision to return to gaol, but I was grateful for the saltwater flask nestled in my pocket.

This time I did not have long to wait. It was quite dark and beginning to be chilly, when the door to the lockup opened and a pair of plain-clothes policemen entered and spoke to me in English. "Elizabeth Sharp?"

"Yes, that's me. Where's Inspector Short?" I inquired, as they entered my cell and cuffed my wrists. I realised I had been hoping—desperately and against hope itself—that he would have somehow accompanied me tonight.

"Busy," one of them said laconically, covering my head with a black bag that completely obscured my vision.

In this condition they marched me out of the lockup and helped me into a carriage. As the vehicle set off, I asked myself if I might have been better off flitting into the wild with Anton after all, for not even the additional strength I had gained as a werewolf and vampire victim could break chains. With my hands in cuffs I was helpless. Oh well—it was too late now, and I suspected that Anton, at least, was not far away, even if Short's duties kept him occupied.

I distracted myself by paying close attention to what I could hear and smell. In this way I learned that the carriage, after a short trip through cobbled streets, turned onto a gravel road and began to climb a low incline through what sounded—from the rustling of the leaves and lack of an echo—like some kind of open countryside. After a few minutes' drive the cobblestones resumed, as did the echo. The carriage stopped, and I was helped from the box and hurried into a warm stuffy space where I was made to wait. No one showed me to a chair, and for a long time I had little to do but listen to the heartbeats of the policemen to either side of me, and the murmur of voices from a room ahead—the Kabale, no doubt!

The wait went on and on. To pass the time, I attempted to engage my guards in an argument, but they were unresponsive until I asked them to remove the bag covering my head. Then they *did* respond, with a decided negative.

Nothing attempted, nothing gained!

At length the voices fell silent and the door ahead of me opened. My guards marched me within and positioned me to face—what? All I could hear was the faint rustle of clothing and breath: the living silence of a large room full of people.

Footsteps strolled across the floor towards me and I braced for the removal of my hood. Instead, an unfamiliar scent and the warmth of a body circled behind me. I heard the beat of a heart and the sound of sniffing at the back of my hood before the steps strolled away again.

Meanwhile, in front of me, I heard whispers, not loud enough to distinguish any words. They went on and on, and I could not help reflecting what an excellent thing it was that I was not by nature a fearful woman. Otherwise I might really have found the whole affair rather disquieting.—I was tempted to speak, perhaps to suggest a patent cold remedy, since they all seemed to have lost their voices; but the thought of my promise to May restrained me.

At length, someone cleared a throat and addressed me in German-accented English.

"Elizabeth Sharp, following the consideration of all the evidence, a verdict has been reached."

"I beg your pardon?" I said, startled. The bag was still over my head. Would I not have the opportunity to face my accusers, nor to speak in my own defence? Was I not even to *see* my judge?

"The crime," he said sternly, "is *lèse-majesté,* in the form of throwing an incendiary device at a conveyance occupied by royal personages. The verdict is death."

None of it seemed real. Here I was, being condemned to death by an anonymous voice that might have been anyone at all. Nervous laughter broke from my lips. *"What?"*

"However," the voice went on—and now it had adopted a tone of great magnanimity—"in consideration of the great services rendered by you in foiling the revolutionary anarchist Veronika Sarkozy, and in your protection and aid of Princess May of Teck, the Kabale has consented to pardon you of your crime." A pause. "You are permitted to address the court."

Within the stuffy confines of the bag, my mouth had dropped open. A *pardon?* I had committed no crime, and they were *pardoning* me? A moment ago I had been holding back my fear, but now that was overwhelmed by a wave of anger. I was relieved to learn that this sham trial before a secret court was not to result in my execution, but I was dashed if I was going to thank them.

"Gladly," I said. "Now that this afternoon's events have been cleared up, I have a request of my own to make. Approximately two years and three months ago, a young woman named Vera Livius was snatched by werewolves from the streets of Stuttgart while she waited to be admitted to her lodgings. I should very much like to know who was responsible for that attack."

Startled whispers ensued. The spokesman said, "Miss Sharp, the Kabale does not deal with such matters. You would be best advised to consult the Stuttgart police."

It was only the answer I had expected, but if they thought I was fool enough to be fobbed off on their minions in Stuttgart, they were quite mistaken. "Yet you were concerned enough with the attack upon Miss Livius to have her memories removed, and to send her to Saint Botolph's in London to be trained as a bodyguard."

If anyone had raised his voice, the whole room would have been in an uproar. As it was, after some frantic whispers, a different voice spoke. This, I recognised as the Prince of Wales—George's father.

"Miss Sharp, it is a very serious thing to accuse royalties without evidence! You cannot possibly know that any of us were responsible for what happened in—"

"There are werewolf scars on my face," I said coldly. By now, I had completely forgotten May's strictures upon respect. "I also have a siren-erased memory."

"*And* the scars of a vampire bite on your neck," put in a third voice; this one carried a Russian accent. "I wonder how *that* happened."

My blouse and scarf were firmly in place, so Vasily must have told them how he had bitten me against my will to escape the dungeon at Castle Sarkozy. Realising that, I lost my head entirely. "I don't feed monsters for money, if that's what you mean."

At the slur, the room went as silent as the grave. Belatedly, I remembered May's advice, and hurriedly added. "With all due respect—" not that it sounded respectful, now that I'd called them monsters—"why *not* prosecute such crimes, rather than hide them? Among the anarchists there are a great many people who bear scars like mine, or have lost people they love to attacks like the one that destroyed Vera Livius. Covering up such crimes will only exasperate the people and drive more unfortunates into the anarchists' arms. Punish them, and you will truly win the people's love and loyalty."

The first voice spoke again. "The Kabale, Miss Sharp, does not deal with such matters. You have been issued a pardon.

Take care in your future actions, for we may not be inclined to show such leniency a second time. You are dismissed."

The policemen hurried me from the room, and I went unresistingly. No doubt I was a fool to expect anything better from these men. They sat in that room at their ease, cloaked and shielded by power and wealth and all the terror of their monstrous nature. Why should they expose themselves to justice, only because they were confronted by a helpless woman who could not even force them to look her in the eye?

At least I still had my pardon, as insulting as it was.

I was marched directly out and replaced in my carriage. This time I was left to sit alone for perhaps another half-hour, as the carriage remained stationary, only moving when one of the horses shifted its weight. At length the door opened and I heard the tail-end of a man's whisper—

"—make it look convincing—"

—before the policemen took their seats across from me in the carriage, and rapped on the roof to signal their readiness for the journey.

As the carriage jolted into motion, I took a deep swallow and held out my shackled hands. "Can you take these off for me, please? And the hood? I want to get at my hanky."

There was no answer.

Oh, the dickens. I didn't like any of this. That fragmentary whisper had upended all my hopes. *What* was to be made to look convincing? For endless minutes the carriage rolled on through the whispering trees, and my alarm only mounted. Where the dickens was Short? Where was Anton?

I clenched impotent hands within my shackles. I tried to pray, but doubt assailed me there, too. I had been taught to pray at Saint Botolph's, by people who expected it to make me meek and biddable. Before that I had learned religion only because my father was honouring the wishes of a mother who eventually rejected her faith altogether. Was there any substance in what I believed, or had it only ever been a tool of control, an empty gesture to tradition?

The sound of our wheels changed as they rolled upon the echoing cobbles of the town. We must be nearly to the police station now. Abandoning my doubts to their own devices, I told myself I must have been mistaken. After all, my escort need not be planning anything to do with *me*.

But of course, my first hunch proved correct. A shout sounded from outside the carriage, and it pulled to a stop.

"Bail up!" a man shouted, letting off a gunshot.

My hopes fell like a house of cards, but I reacted at once. Lunging forward, I swung my clasped and chained hands in the direction of the nearest heartbeat. A hard body-blow doubled him over. The next instant I reached blindly for the throat of the other.

His hands closed about my wrists, halting me dead.

Good Lord—he must have been monster-bitten too.

The thought had barely time to fleet through my mind before he kicked open the carriage door beside us and hurled me through it face-first. I tucked in my elbows and broke my fall with both hands, but before I could push my way to my feet, a heavy weight of bodies flattened me to the damp pavement.

Even if I could have wielded my saltwater, I had no chance to reach it. My hands and ankles were pinned, and from the sickening stench of rot and death, at least two of my assailants were revenants. I stopped fighting at once, terrified of sparking their murderous rage. Then a whiff of sweet scent reached me. I turned my head away, but it was no use. For one moment my hood lifted, and I took a single breath of fresh air before a handkerchief soaked in chloroform clamped against my mouth and nose. I slipped into a fuzzy dreamland.

Chapter V.

One of the ancillary effects of being monster-bitten is an ability to heal more quickly than normally possible. As I discovered that night, this meant that the sedative with which I had been dosed was only partly effective, and only for a short time. I had the vague impression of a hurried march through echoing hallways, an attempt to fight that resulted in a second dose of the drug, and finally of coming to my wits in a rather uncomfortable predicament.

I sat in a sturdy chair to which wrists, ankles, and body were tightly strapped with leather bands. That terrible black bag still remained over my head, now somewhat damp around the nose and mouth. I strained against my bonds and attempted to overturn my chair, but the whole assemblage was more than a match for me.

I fell back breathing hard. I was sure I had seen a chair like this before; it was the sort of thing Queen Victoria used at the time of the full moon to prevent her from breaking loose. The infernal thing was every bit as uncomfortable as it looked—half restraint, half torture device.

Nearby a door opened and to my amazement the last sounds I had expected flowed through—the scrape of stringed instruments, the tramp of dancing feet, and a babel of polite conversation and laughter. The scent of the place—they must use attar of roses to scent their cleaning supplies—confirmed my suspicions.

Why was I at Ehrenberg Palace?

A muffled gasp reached me from the direction of the party. "Is that her? Do you suppose she'll scream much?" someone whispered.

A murmured answer, indistinguishable amidst the noise of the crowd.

"Oh! I could *never*—" the piercing whisper rejoined, but then the door closed again. I found that my forehead was cold with nervous perspiration.

Do you not know what goes on at these affairs?

Officially, the Kabale had pardoned me. In fact, they had returned me to the town and staged a rather transparent kidnapping.—The details were immaterial. The great fact was clear: I was about to die. I *must* die, for I had challenged the Kabale to their faces, and they had me marked as a dangerous woman. They would tell May and George quite earnestly that my death had been a terrible mistake, the result of a prank gone wrong, a bureaucratic error, or something of the sort.

I writhed in my bonds. I could feel the cool weight of the saltwater in the pocket of my bloomers, but I couldn't *get* at it.

The door opened a second time. I commended my soul to my Maker—if he was there.

But it was only another pair of whisperers: "So it's true! The poor girl!"

"I didn't realise—when they said a *blood feast*—oh, May!"

I nearly choked on my own tongue. "May?" I cried hoarsely.

In the blink of an eye, the black bag whisked off my head

and I found myself blinking into eyes that blazed like blue fire. "Sharp!" she said after a moment, pulling herself together after her shock, "what the blazes are *you* doing here?"

"Oh, ma'am," I babbled. May wore a black evening gown, her neck and *décolletage* winking with faceted jet beads and a mask of black lace concealing the upper half of her face—but what there was of her to see flooded me with an almost childlike relief. "I am afraid I must have forgotten your instructions this afternoon."

She drew herself to her full height. "I don't care *whom* you might have cheeked, Sharp, *or* how badly! They have no right to serve you or *anyone* up as a glorified *hors d'oeuvre!*"

Was her anger for the Kabale, then, and not for me? "You have no idea how much that means to me."

"Shut the door, Alicky," May added, over her shoulder.

The nervous-looking girl by the door nodded and pushed the door closed. With her astonishingly delicate features and the masses of soft, wavy brown hair beneath her tiara, she must have been one of the prettiest girls I'd ever seen.

But I had little attention to spare from May. "What do you mean by an *hors d'oeuvre?*"

Tucking her lacquered walking-stick beneath her arm, May attacked my straps with shaking fingers. "Apparently it's a part of the wedding festivities—a part no one thought to tell me till tonight." Releasing the final strap, she seized my hands and pulled me to my feet. "They're going to kill someone. They're going to kill *you.*"

The princess by the door—Alicky?—covered her mouth with her hand and stifled a sob. I gathered that she, like May, was now learning of the monstrosities that surrounded her for the first time. It was customary with the royalties to keep their daughters ignorant of such things for as long as possible—a practice which had now saved my life.

I put a hand to my pocket, checking that my saltwater was still accessible. "No, they won't, May. Not now that you've freed me."

"We must get you out of here." May hesitated, shooting a glance towards the door by which I must have entered, opposite the ballroom.

I had heard low voices, and an occasional cough, from that direction. "That way is locked and guarded. By the time I got it open, they'd be ready for me," and I shivered, remembering the unusual strength of the man in the carriage.

May watched my face. "Then it must be through the ballroom, since there are no windows."

"What, right in front of everyone?" the pretty girl objected.

May seemed to take that as a challenge. "Yes, right in front of all of them! *This* ought to help." She was still carrying her lacquered walking-stick, and now she gave it a quick twist and pulled it apart into twin halves, each armed with a sharp blade that had been sheathed within the handle of the other. They were made of steel inlaid with silver down the tang, doubtless with werewolves in mind.

Readers of the previous volume of my memoirs will recall that this double sword-stick had once belonged to my mother, Veronika Sarkozy. My memories of Veronika were particularly unpleasant, and when it came to *mêlée* weapons I preferred my battered umbrella, since it seemed less likely to cause serious injury. Still—waste not, want not; so I had given it to May with instructions to carry it with her at all times, where it would be available if I needed it, or might be useful at a pinch to herself.

Alicky clapped her hands over a horrified gasp at May's martial words, but I stifled a snort of laughter.

"May, dear, you can't really expect me to battle my way through an entire ballroom of monsters at full moon."

"Only as a last resort, of course," she said imperturbably, sheathing the blades and setting the walking-stick on a side table, quickly followed by her mask and her jet earrings. "Principally we shall rely upon stealth and imposture. Help Sharp off with her clothes, Alicky. She's a little shorter than me, but that can't be helped."

"Imposture—*Really*, May!" I protested. I felt a little dizzy, as often happened when May got the bit between her teeth. Perhaps she found my impertinence horrifying, but she had charged off on enough of her own private war-paths to give me grey hairs of my own. "We are *not* changing places so that I can slip away and leave you to the mercy of this pack of beasts! You must run and get Short—or Anton—or anyone. Please!"

"There isn't time." May unpinned her necklace and attacked the buttons at the band of her wasp-waisted black gown. "Hang it, Sharp, how do you propose the men will help? Are they going to charge through the ranks of policemen in the hallway, or through the monsters in the ballroom? You must see that stealth is our only hope."

"Oh, May! You are so brave," Alicky whispered admiringly.

"I have seen a *great* many worse things than this, my dear coz," May told her.

—And strangely enough, there was something about the awe in that young girl's eyes that convinced me. It was my job—and my instinct—to protect May, but I could neither force her to go against her conscience, nor coddle her like a child. If I tried to do it, how was I any better than her mother, who had so diligently kept her in ignorance of the world around her? Let me not deceive myself. May was a woman grown, and she bore her own scars, less visible though they might be than mine. She had experience, wit, and willpower; and she had weighed the risks and resolved to take them.

I let out a sigh and began to peel off my own rumpled, travel-worn clothes. "I hope you know, May, how gravely this goes against the grain."

The three of us worked quickly, our fingers shaking in nervousness. Although I was shorter than May, my figure was thicker, so my bloomers and jacket buttoned around her waist well enough. Meanwhile, having laced my corset a little tighter, I slipped into her black evening gown, padded the bosom with a couple of extra hankies, and blessed her mask and jet necklace for covering up the scars on my face and neck. I thought the hair would be the most difficult task, for I was the only lady's maid among us and I have never excelled at dressing my own hair; but Alicky, it turned out, had grown up with enough sisters to learn some of the basics.

In a very short time I was presentable and May was strapped into the chair. "Now, Sharp," May said very seriously, "I shall be all right the moment they take off that dreadful bag, but you are in danger every moment you remain in this palace. For heaven's sake get yourself out of Coburg at once."

"I'll take care of myself; trust me," I replied cheerfully, pulling the black bag over her head. I didn't think it needful to mention that during my Kabale hearing the black bag had never come off at all. She would only worry, and I didn't mean to leave her here any longer than I could help it, anyway.

Alicky and I slipped through the door into the ballroom,

I hiding behind May's black-bordered fan and gripping the sword-stick for dear life. The immense room was supported by twenty-eight immense pillars, each of which was carved to look like a giant holding a blazing candelabra in an outstretched hand. A high gallery ran around the ballroom, and beyond was an intricately-moulded ceiling featuring inlaid paintings, from the centre of which hung a massive crystal chandelier. Below—ah, below was the crowd, a mass of dim shadowy splendour in the old-fashioned candlelight. Everywhere were tail-coats, uniforms, and medals on the men; everywhere was silk, taffeta, velvet, feathers, and the blaze of a thousand jewels on the women. I wondered if there was a single European royalty who was not present.

The moon must not yet have risen, for none of them had actually turned into werewolves. But I caught a glimpse of fang here and a flash of red eyes there, for the vampires had no need for the full moon to reveal their monstrosity.

I put a hand on Alicky's arm. "Quickly," I whispered. "We must find Prince George and tell him that May is in danger."

Alicky had her mask on again, a golden oval that concealed her whole face and made her look serene and confident—an illusion belied by the quick thump of her heart. "But May said you must leave at once."

"May worries about me too much," I said—a statement which, even at the time, I felt might be somewhat hypocritical. Somewhere, Inspector Short must be feeling an unaccountable urge to bury his face in his hands and groan. Still, what else could I do? May had taken my place, and every fibre of my soul revolted at the thought of turning my back on her in such a predicament. I checked that my saltwater was tucked securely into my waistband at the hollow of my back, before towing Alicky through the crowd in search of George's slight figure and pointed beard.

"Ah!—there he is!"

Having glimpsed George in the shadows as I passed one of the gargantuan pillars, I turned Alicky and myself about to face him. "Your grace! Thank goodness, I've been looking for you everywhere.—Why, what a dashing outfit, if I may say so!"

He was all swaddled up in silks and furs, looking more like an Asiatic prince than a supremely unimaginative English gentleman. When I accosted him he looked taken aback for a moment; but then his attention fell upon my companion. "Oh—Sunny!" he gasped, snatching the mask from his face.

Alicky uttered a sound of terror and shrank behind me.

My own scalp prickled as I looked into that unmasked face, both familiar and strange. His voice had not the piercing boom I was accustomed to hearing from those lips. Elongated canine teeth had turned his words to a lisp, and his eyes—ah! his eyes were red!

I recoiled a step. Then a well-known figure emerged from the shadows beside George's double.

"Ah! I thought I recognised that voice! Your servant, ma'am." Grand Duke Vasily Nikolaevitch Romanov lifted my unresisting hand to his lips. I do not like to admit to such feminine weakness, but in truth it was all I could do not to faint away on the spot.

Vasily turned to George's vampire double with, to my relieved surprise, a fluent lie. "Sir, I don't believe you've met my very good friend, Countess Vera Domonkos. Countess, of course you know of my cousin Nicholas."

"Er—of course," I murmured, dipping into the profoundest

curtsey I could manage. My mistake was now clear. George had not mysteriously become a vampire. Rather, this must be his cousin on their mothers' side: Nicholas, son and heir of the Russian emperor.

The Russian prince merely stared at Alicky with burning eyes. "Thunny," he lisped again, reaching out impulsively before stopping himself. "It hath been tho long. Are—are you well?"

Behind me, Alicky seemed to have recovered a little of her voice. "Y-yes, Nicky. What a surprise to see you again."

"How could I mith your brother'th wedding?" A yearning silence elapsed. I only wanted to flee, but the princess behind me was latched onto my neckline, and I did not like to tear May's dress. As for Nicky, I don't suppose he'd seen me at all from the moment he realised Alicky stood beside me. He looked at her like a lost puppy and said, "Wath I wrong to come? Forgive me. I *had* to thee you again. I've mithed you terribly."

If the neckline on my dress had been any higher, Alicky would have strangled me by now. "Oh, no, please don't apologise," she whispered. "It's only that I...I see you made the change, after all." Nicky looked guilty, and she added in the voice of one trying to make the best of something that grieved her, "It thuits you—I mean, suits you."

"You angel," he said meekly, "will you honour me with thith danthe?"

"Oh," she said faintingly, "really, I don't think—"

"Oh, Thunny, *pleathe,* don't be afraid of me! I don't think I could bear it!"

"Afraid of you, Nicky!—never!" she lied bravely. Releasing my dress, she put her trembling hand in his. "Forgive me. It's only that—I've never *seen* you like this before, and it is rather a shock!"

The two of them swept into the stream of passing dancers, leaving me alone with the vampire who had drunk my blood against my will. Vasily, when I turned to face him again, was watching Nicky and Alicky with a cynical smile. "Ah, young love! They worship each other, but she will not consent to marry him because she does not wish to make the necessary sacrifice."

"Can you blame her?" I asked, fixing upon my face a smile I did not feel. With Vasily beside me, I felt like an electrical wire, stripped raw and sparking. It was difficult to search for George with my nerves burned to shreds, but then by chance I caught a glimpse of him among the dancers—the *real* George, attired in impeccable evening dress and dancing with Missy of Roumania.

"I must go, if you'll excuse me," I said, but Vasily's hand fastened upon my arm, turning me inexorably to face him. This close, his scent washed over me—the faint scent of carrion on his breath, overlaid with sterile cedar. My heart quickened as I recalled the moment his sharp teeth punctured my skin. There was something exhilarating in his closeness, something that made me feel intensely alive.

"Leaving so soon, my dear *Countess?*" His voice was low and mocking. "You know, it isn't mannerly for the guest of honour to depart before the ceremonies begin."

So, he knew why I was here—and what the Kabale planned for me. I took a quick, shallow breath. If I had one enemy in this world, it was Vasily Nikolaevitch. He had drained me and attempted to betray all of Europe to the anarchists. In return, I had thrown him from a third-story window and nearly killed him.

I might have been safe, even surrounded by monsters as I was, if I had only done as May told me and escaped at once. Of all the people in this crowd who might have recognised me, Vasily was the one who bore me the greatest grudge—a grudge he meant not to relinquish, if his actions at the train station this afternoon were any indication.

This, reader, was the man who held me fast, reminding me that I was supposed to be tethered blind and helpless in the anteroom yonder, waiting to be eaten.

I ran the tip of my tongue over my lips. "What do you want from me?"

"Perhaps there's nothing you can give me any more."

His words stabbed like a knife, but I would not be cowed. "You did not betray me to your tsarevitch."

He gave a sharp-edged smile, but all he said was, "Come. Dance with me."

He didn't wait for me to agree, instead sliding a hand to my back and leading me into the flow of dancers. Thankfully it was a waltz, one of the few dances I knew, and I was able to follow his lead without instantly betraying myself.

His left hand enfolded the fist in which I gripped May's sword-stick. He had seen the weapon before, in Veronika's keeping. If he wished to tear it from my grasp, there was little I could do to stop him.

"Speak your piece," I whispered as the flow of bodies engulfed us. "I have no time for this."

"Here? Don't be foolish." His elongated teeth gleamed in the candlelight. "Enjoy the dance, *ma tigresse.*"

"A tigress I may be, but not yours." All the same, despite the danger, the monsters, and the scent of blood curling tendrils of fear through every chink in my armour, I must confess I enjoyed that dance. All around us was dim candlelight and flashing colours. Vasily held me close, directing me with assurance through the steps of the dance, and my whole body thrummed with elation at his touch. What witchcraft was this? Vasily had always held a terrible, seductive magnetism for me—the beguiling call of a precipice, the tactile sleekness of a viper, the febrile ring of sharpened steel. Surely, after what this creature had done to me in Castle Sarkozy, I ought not to feel it still—but I did. He had drained my blood, violated my will, and betrayed my cause. I knew him now for the danger he was, and never in my life had I felt so feverishly *alive.*

I didn't know if the silver blades sheathed within the walking-stick would hurt him. Perhaps, before this night was over, I would plant them between his ribs, and see what they did. Perhaps, before this night was over, he would break my neck with those corded hands that even now guided me through the shadows and light of this dark, glittering world. If all this was written in the stars, why not surrender to this brief intoxication? I had rejected every other advance he had made.

At length the flow of the dance carried us to the far end of the great ballroom. There beneath the gallery a stair led to the upper level. As Vasily drew me from the stream of dancers and tugged me into the shadows, I came back to my full wits. I had lost sight of George while we danced. How long would it take me to find him again?—and then how would we recover May?

"Where are you taking me?" I demanded.

"Somewhere we can speak in private." Still I resisted, and

he let out a sigh. "You need my protection, Sharp. But I need yours no less."

I had seen Vasily with every shred of civility and manners stripped away by starvation and cruelty, and there was something of that same desperation in his voice now. This time when he tugged me towards the staircase, I did not resist.

"What do you mean, protection?" I panted as we emerged upon the upper gallery. "Speak quickly."

We were alone here, for the musicians were seated at the other end of the gallery, above the great double doors. Apart from them, only a couple of plain-clothes men strolled to and fro keeping watch over the revellers. There was no chance of our being overheard, yet Vasily pulled me close and lover-like against one of the great pillars supporting the room. His carrion breath brushed my cheek as he spoke. "The two of us have something in common, my dear. And that is that the Kabale wants both of us dead."

It was the last thing I expected him to say. "The dickens they do!"

He covered my mouth with his hand. I stiffened with fear. He must have heard my heart racing, but he only leaned closer.

"Hush! It was because of the affair at Castle Sarkozy. The Kabale knows everything; they interrogated some of the anarchists who escaped the castle that night. They know I made an agreement to help Veronika create the Livius Serum. They know I promised Russian neutrality once she used the serum to start her revolutions. There's no forgiving a thing like that: they've already condemned me to death. Nicky agreed to shelter me for three days, but after tonight…"

I pushed his hand away from my mouth and tried to put some distance between us—difficult, considering my back was up against a pillar. "Wait a bit! Why is it *you* they're punishing? You were acting on your emperor's orders, surely."

The words were hardly out of my mouth before I realised what a ridiculous thing it was to say. Of *course* the Kabale couldn't condemn an emperor to death, and none of them wanted to start a war. So Vasily became the scapegoat—a whipping-boy for the tsar, just as George had been for Eddy.

Vasily's red eyes glowed with anger. "My tsar disowned me. After everything I have done for Holy Russia—after everything I endured in Castle Sarkozy—I am to be cast aside like a raddled dainty. I, Vasily Nikolaevitch, a prince of the Romanovs!"

"Infamous," I said dryly. I, too, had endured a great deal in Castle Sarkozy, most of it at his hands—yet he had never made anything like an apology, nor even a gesture of thanks. "What can *I* do about it?"

"Hide me from them."

"You can't be serious. I have no money, no power…" My sideways slither around the pillar came to a halt in the angle it made with the rail of the balcony, and Vasily leaned a hand on both, trapping me.

"Of course I'm serious. I must hide among the commoners, and you are the only commoner I know."

"Go and boil your head," I said shakily, putting a hand to where the saltwater bottle nestled against the small of my back. With his heightened senses, he must know what effect his proximity had on me, and meant to use it against me like a weapon. "You drained my blood and tried to set all of Europe alight. Why ever should I help *you?*"

Those terrible teeth glinted in the candlelight as he smiled and held up a long index finger, tipped with a long sharp nail.

"First, because I'm rich."

"You're offering to *buy* me? Again?"

"Why not? Everything has its price, and mine is one I think you might find it pleasurable to pay, which is my second reason."

He was too close, and once again I felt like a stripped wire, ready to go up in sparks. I had to swallow hard before I could get the words out. "Are you unaware that you smell like a deadhouse?"

"Do I?" He smiled with all his teeth. "Does that stop your heart beating like a bird in a cage? Does it make you unsheathe those swords and fight me? Does it make you run when I do—this?"

His elongated teeth brushed my lips a moment before his lips did. I had nowhere to run, even if I had wanted to; so instead I did unsheath the swords, so that both points settled against his shirt-front.

He backed away, but only by an inch. "You still manage to surprise me, Miss Sharp."

"As I think I always will surprise you." I was myself again now: the anger had cleared my head. How well I recalled our very first meeting in Piccadilly on that memorable night during the Whitechapel werewolf affair! "Here's where you mistake me, Vasily. You knew from the first I was no dainty, but you've never stopped trying to make me one. You saw my naiveté and inexperience, and you took it as an invitation to conquest. What did you think of me?—that I was some sort of untempted Aphrodite? I am Athene, the mailed virgin, and I will never submit to you."

I had the satisfaction, then, of seeing him look for a moment completely taken aback.

"Then don't submit to me," he said with a shrug. "But you *will* help me, for my third reason."

How much he liked the sound of his own voice! I had no time for this: I must get away from him and rescue May, before it was too late. "And that is?"

"That I know the identity of every member of the Kabale, and I can help you destroy them."

My racing heart stuttered to a halt. "I…You would do that?"

"Well, naturally," he purred. "I don't mean to remain a fugitive forever. If we tear the Kabale apart, both of us can return to our rightful places. As for my fourth and last reason"—his mirthless smile widened—"know that if you refuse, you will never leave this ballroom alive."

The room was so hot and airless that for a moment I thought I might be about to faint. Once again it was my anger that saved me. Forcing myself to breathe, I considered his reasons with increasing fury.

My pride forbade me to take his money, and was now flaying me alive for having succumbed to his charms long enough to enjoy that brief dance. Destruction of the Kabale, though? *That* was a prize worth daring a great deal for. It was not only my own wrongs I had to avenge. So long as the Kabale ruled, the monster-bitten could never hold their attackers accountable. More families like mine, driven mad by grief, would turn to anarchy and revolution in one last grim hope for justice. Unbind the Kabale, and we unbound the knot that tied the royalties of Europe into one solid, impregnable phalanx. Divided, they could be weakened. We might force them to listen, to bend.

It was a shame that he should have ended by threatening to kill me if I refused to help. That made everything quite clear:

he wished to use me as his tool, not to work with me as my friend.

Thickly, I said, "You drank my blood."

"You are too generous to hold that against me."

"Good Lord! Have you *ever* been made to face the consequences of your own actions?"

He laughed as though I had made an excellent joke. "Not that I can recall, and at this stage of life I hardly mean to begin. Your answer?"

I did not want to answer—at least not until I had managed to put some more space between us. Thankfully, the sound of footsteps interrupted us and Vasily turned away from me. At the far end of the gallery, the musicians had risen quietly and were now leaving through a door that opened behind them. In the lower part of the room, silence had fallen.

A premonition struck me—*May!*—even as a voice announced, "Ladies and gentlemen, distinguished guests! The moon will rise in a moment. Your attention, please."

"Oh, no," I gasped, leaning over the railing. Vasily had delayed me too long, and now the worst was about to happen.

The dancing having ceased, the assembled royalties stood watching as a black-clad, hooded figure was escorted from the small room where I had left May. Beneath us, under the gallery at this end of the room, stood two young people—the bride and groom, no doubt, Victoria Melita of Saxe-Coburg and Gotha and Grand Duke Ernest of Hesse and by Rhine. The bride seemed nervous, her slim white fingers locked around the stem of an ancient, jewel-encrusted goblet.

May was dragged to the open space before the happy pair and forced to kneel. She did not resist as two uniformed princes, with formal solemnity, stretched out each of her arms and pushed back the sleeve.

George! where the dickens was George? There beside the bride I could see the red-gold hair and rich ivory silk of his dancing partner, Missy of Roumania. There in the shadows beneath the gallery on the other side of the room I saw his *doppelgänger* cousin half supporting a pale and terrified Alicky. But of George himself, there was no sign.

Below, the bride's father announced with a very embarrassed English throat-clearing, "Er—the bride will now drink the lifeblood of this condemned criminal from a silver cup. Ladies and gentlemen, our Ducky's first moon."

It was then that May seemed to have realised that she was not to be unmasked. In clear, autocratic tones she cried, "A criminal? I *beg* your pardon!"

At that, the groom stepped forward and boxed her ears so forcefully that May fell to the parqueted floor with a cry of pain. A strangled sound escaped my lips. I sprang away from the pillar, but Vasily pinned me back against the white marble.

"Imbecile!" he hissed, "do you *want* to die?"

"It's May—it's May of Teck!" I whispered, and his grip loosened in surprise. I darted past him towards the gallery directly above the spot where the ceremony was taking place. Someone was already there, a tall dark shape leaning over the rail in bristling, horrified stillness. He turned and saw me. "Ma'am—" he began, and then stopped. *"Miss Sharp?"*

As I live and breathe, Inspector Short! He must have been stationed up here, like the other plainclothes-men, to keep guard of the proceedings. His face was ghastly with horror, but he moved to intercept me. "It's no use. I beg of you, don't—"

"I must," I said grimly. Even ten minutes ago I would have

been overjoyed to see him. Now it was too late: all my being was concentrated upon the small, lonely figure of my dearest friend, surrounded by monsters. "It's May."

"God help us," he said softly.

I leaned over the gallery-rail. Below was the flash of a blade and little moan of pain from May as the groom slashed her wrist open. Together, Ernest and Ducky held her wrist over the silver cup as drops of blood pattered into it.

My stomach heaved at the sight of blood.—I had seen blood before, of course, but never May's.

Below, Alicky of Hesse fainted into Nicky's arms and was borne from the room.

Before I could act, a change forestalled me—the very thing I had been dreading. The moon must have risen, for its white light silvered the eastern windows. With it, a change came over the room—a chorus of snarls and growls as many of the guests fell subject to the terrible change. The room was suddenly full of writhing, mangled bodies and the sharp scent of wolf.

Releasing May's arm, the groom fell to all fours as his shirt and coat burst along the terrible, ridged spine of his back. Ducky shrieked and recoiled, nearly spilling the half-full cup of May's blood.

No longer supported by her cousins, May fell to the floor. Her blood trickled across the parquetry, but Missy dashed forward, steadied Ducky's hand, and pulled May's slack arm over the cup once again. I caught a glimpse of elongated teeth bared in a triumphant smile—why, Missy was a vampire!

My mind darted back to that afternoon in the palace hallway, when the Crown Princess of Roumania had waylaid George and demanded to dance. Did Missy know? Did she scent, in that black-hooded, bloomered form, her rival May of Teck?

My throat was dry, my fingers white on the baluster. May was bleeding to death, surrounded by monsters—but what could I do, alone, against so many? I had fought the monsters often enough by now to be suitably afraid of them.

"We must do *something*," Short whispered beside me, but he didn't move, either.

"Drink!" the bridegroom cried in a terrible, half-beastly voice as he rose to his hind feet, now fully wolf. "Drink!"

The chant rose: "Drink! Drink!"

"Drink!" Missy cried, pressing the silver cup into the bride's hands.

With a sob, Ducky put the cup to her lips and promptly choked on it. Blood flecked her lips, nearly black in the dim candlelight. The chant dissolved into cheering—a terrible, bestial shouting and stamping. In a wink the veneer of civilisation in this room had broken, leaving only savagery. It was awful—it was unholy.

I had known these people were monsters—I had known they must kill in order to rule. I had never imagined *this*—this solemnisation of the bloodshed with fine clothes, with music and dancing and ceremony. They did not deplore this: they celebrated it—not as a painful necessity, but as a rite of passage.

Beside me, Vasily stood watching in an attitude almost of boredom, as though this was a sight he had seen a hundred times before; but Short was bent over the baluster, his fist pressed to his horrified mouth.

Beneath me, with a yelping laugh, the werewolf bridegroom snatched the silver cup from his bride's hands and tossed the whole terrible draught down his throat. He threw back his head in a triumphant howl—which suddenly, unaccountably dwindled to a man's thin yell.

Utter silence fell, and every monstrous face turned towards him.

Above May's crumpled form, the bridegroom flailed, clutching at his throat. He fell to his knees. His body moulted—shrank—grew larger and smaller in a moment of grotesque struggle—then at last dwindled to its natural man-shape.

"Poison!" Ernest cried then, in a voice that was nearly a scream. *"Poison!"*

Murmurs of surprise and horror filled the air. The monstrous crowd backed away as though fearful of sharing the groom's disgrace. The bride put bloodied fingers to her horrified mouth. Missy seized her sister and shrieked, "You haven't changed, Ducky—why aren't you *changing?*"

That quickly, a clear space opened up around my fainting friend; and with it my opportunity.

"Miss Sharp!" Short flung out a hand to restrain me, but he was too late.

Unsheathing my mother's swords, I vaulted over the baluster and hurtled downwards to land, with a bone-jarring jolt, upon the floor below. I swept a circle with my left blade, sending May's tormentors scrambling backward to avoid me. With my right, I sliced free the gauzy cotton scarf she wore about her neck and then wound it about her wrist in an attempt to stanch the flow of blood.

To do it, I had to drop my swords, but still no one moved—only stared at me, silent and horrified. I finished my task within moments, then turned to reach for my swords and came face to face with the groom. Ernest sat on the floor where he had dropped—half naked, terrified, and very much an ordinary man. A man!—and the moon shone bright through the ballroom windows!

For an instant I could only gaze at him in amazement. Then he reached out and tore away my mask, revealing my face to the crowd of silent monsters before me.

"You!" he hissed, "the anarchist from the train station!"

His words fell into the silence with perfect clarity. A mutter, a gasp, drifted through the watching crowd. Some of them backed away. Some called for the police. Some of the males put themselves bravely between me and the ladies.—I felt a wild desire to laugh.

These creatures were accustomed to prey—meek, frightened, trembling prey. As long as I had known the monsters they were terrified of the anarchists, surrounding themselves with bodyguards and henchmen living and undead. Tonight, they were also afraid of whatever had defanged the unfortunate bridegroom.

They were afraid, most of all, of *me.*

That fear was now my only hope of saving May. So long as they remained paralysed, we had a chance. Snatching up my swords, I leaped to my feet, pointing both blades at the monsters.

"I am Nemesis the implacable, the daughter of Justice!" I declared. "I am come to tear the masks from your faces!"

The crowd dissolved in panic as they scrambled to get away from me. Someone shrieked in terror. Their movement saved me, blocking up the stairs and doors by which the plainclothes-men in the gallery above and the revenants in the antechambers beyond were trying to enter the room.

I turned, searching for Short—I could not both carry May and defend her at the same time. There was no sign of him. Instead, a dark shape dropped from the gallery above and landed in a crouch on the floor beside us—Vasily.

"This way," he said, lifting May from the floor. Turning, he darted towards a door set in the shadows beneath the gallery. I backed a few steps, still ready for battle; but none of the monsters had it in their minds to give chase—not yet. At the door, I turned on my heel and followed Vasily.

"Athene *and* Nemesis! How busy you must be!" he remarked dryly as I caught up with him.

"They were similes, or *figures of speech involving the comparison of one thing with another thing of a different kind, used to make a description more emphatic or vivid,*" I rattled off, feeling in my pocket for the saltwater. "Hold still a moment; I'm going to pour this over our feet to confuse our scent."

"Can't they follow wet footprints?" Vasily asked, but he did as I asked. "I take it this means you'll accept my offer, at any rate."

It took me a moment to recall our conversation in the gallery; but then I gave a hard-edged laugh. I had the Kabale to thank for this night's work—for the awful ceremony in the ballroom, for my own close brush with death, and for my friend's injury. Vasily was correct: this alliance of monsters must be destroyed. And now that I had extricated myself from the ballroom without taking any harm, so that he had no threats to hold over my head, I did not particularly object to availing myself of his help.

"I do accept," I said. "Help me end the Kabale, Vasily Nikolaevitch Romanov, and you shall have all the protection I can give."

Chapter VI.

Except for the monsters in the ballroom and the revenants flocking to their aid, the palace was wellnigh deserted. We could move without being seen, and within five minutes we had made it back to the Tecks' suite at the rear of the building. The sitting-room was lighted only by a single lamp, turned down low. Vasily deposited May on the couch while I darted into May's dressing-room and snatched the first-aid case from my valise, as well as the basin and ewer from the dressing-table.

"You'd better not have tasted her while my back was turned," I growled at him when I returned.

He looked affronted. "A lady of her station? Never."

I cast a silent glance to the heavens, then whisked the black bag from May's head. She looked waxen-pale, slumped against the cushions in my ill-fitting clothing. But her eyelids fluttered, and after a moment a gleam of blue escaped them.

"Oh, Sharp," she whispered faintly, "you came back for me! How foolish!"

Something was wrong with my voice, and I had to clear my throat before I could reply. "It isn't the first time, my dear, but let us hope it will be the last." I handed her bleeding arm to Vasily. "Hold that above her heart."

May lay still, very calm—calmer than I should have been under the circumstances. "Did you tell them it was me, then?"

I nearly dropped the soap with which I was washing my hands in the ewer. "Heavens, no! Look at me, May." I waited until her dizzy blue eyes focused on me again. *"No one can know it was you beneath that hood!"*

"But Alicky knows…"

"Then you must persuade her not to tell!" I sat back on my heels, staring at May without quite seeing her. My mind was busily at work, stitching together scraps of evidence. While the bride had failed to transform, the groom's transformation had been undone.

Veronika Sarkozy had brought May as a gift to Dr Livius, meaning to draw her blood for more experiments.

"You're of morganatic blood." My voice seemed to come from far away. "Royal blood—tainted blood—blood that won't let you transform into a monster. And now that Ernest and Ducky have drunk it, it won't let them transform either."

May attempted to sit up. Her voice rose by an octave in fear. "What do you mean?"

"Your blood," I said, lifting catgut and needle out of the vial of alcohol in which I stored them, "your blood is able to defang the monsters.—Did *you* know this, Vasily?"

He looked as dazed as I felt. "It's as I said. One doesn't drink the blood of a lady of her station."

"No one else knew what to think either," I surmised, remembering the utter terror that had marked all those faces at the sight of what May's blood had done to the Grand Duke of Hesse. "They condemned me to death this evening only for daring to lob a bomb in the direction of a royal train. If they find out you helped me escape, took my place, and then defanged two of their own—why, your life wouldn't be worth a brass razoo. Your part in all this must remain a deadly secret." I fixed my eyes on Vasily, who had listened to all this with a look of quiet calculation. "Your grace?"

He transferred that calculating gaze to me. "Naturally, Miss Sharp. So long as the agreement between us continues—"

"Hang the agreement," I cut in, pointing at him with the sterilised needle. "If ever you betray this secret—no, if *anyone* betrays it—I will personally hunt you down and stake you through the heart. And I'll do it *before* I see to May's safety. Am I understood?"

A tooth glinted appreciatively. "Perfectly, Miss Sharp."

"Excellent." I addressed myself to May's injury. The cut was deep, but had no more than nicked the artery; and a clot was already forming, stopping the flow of blood. "This will pinch."

Although we had nothing with which to numb the pain of the stitches, May was able to remain tolerably silent, and Vasily held her wrist tolerably immobile as I stitched the gash closed and wrapped it in a clean bandage. This done, I applied arnica to her reddening cheekbone where Ernest had struck her and helped her to her bedroom, where I coaxed her gently out of her borrowed bloomers and into her nightgown.

For much of the operation she was silent. Then, as I began taking the hairpins from the Newport knot in which her hair had been dressed, she passed her arms around her knees and shivered a little. "Sharp?"

"Yes?"

"I think I understand Alicky a little better now," she whispered. "You know that she is in love with George's cousin Nicky?"

"Yes, I saw them together."

"This evening when Alicky told me how everyone was trying to make her marry him, and how horrible the thought was to her, all I could think of was George's letter this afternoon. I wondered if it was really so wise to turn aside from one's own happiness like that. I was nearly ready to find George and tell him my answer was yes." She swallowed hard. "I think I have been very foolish."

"Or very sheltered, which is quite a different thing." I sighed. "You see now what these people are capable of."

"They meant to kill someone," she whispered, shivering a little. "As a *celebration*."

"If you marry George, you will be part of this world forever. You can still escape, you know. In fact, it may be wise to leave Coburg at once."

"Oh! of course I cannot marry him now," she said with a shudder. "I was ignorant before, but after what I have seen tonight…!"

I felt a little dizzy with relief. As long as I had known May I had been quite sure she would always side with her family above me. Yet now that the monstrosity of her class was laid bare before her, she recoiled from it in distaste. Would she have responded the same way, if not for our friendship? But the great thing was that she *did* recoil.

She turned, taking my hand. "As for leaving, I don't know if I can—not without betraying myself. But you must go at once, since the Kabale has condemned you to death. I'll give you whatever money you need—only you must get safely away from here."

I certainly could not stay in the palace, and yet—"I don't want to leave you alone in a town full of monsters. Since

Ernest unmasked me in front of everyone, they know I was there—and I very much fear someone may put two and two together, and realise who was beneath the black bag, even if they don't recognise the walking-stick, or the dress, or the scent."

"But if I flee, they will *know* it was me. To seem innocent, I must stay—at least long enough for everything to die down."

"The dickens," I murmured. She had a sound point there. "Perhaps…at any rate, I don't mean to leave Coburg myself."

"You *don't?* But, my dear Sharp—"

"I told you the Kabale has been covering up monster attacks," I reminded her. "I'm sorry, May—but I *must* do something about it. I must leave the palace, but I won't go far; and if I can, I'll find someone else to watch over you in my place." I smoothed my hands over my face, battling to clearly see the path ahead of my feet. It was late, and I was tired—but if what we had learned tonight was true—

"I won't need money; not at once. But I must ask a favour."

"Of course—anything."

I took a deep breath. "Your blood."

She went into one of her startled stillnesses. I knew I had overstepped her bounds at last, but I could not stop now. "Europe is ruled by monsters. But your blood—your blood is the key to that."

Still she did not reply. I thought she shrank away from me, a little.

"I know these monstrosities horrify you as much as they do me," I whispered. "Now it lies in your power to *do* something about them. I know you have always believed yourself destined for greatness—"

"Defang them!" she murmured. "What—royalties?

anointed kings?"

I leaped to my feet, too passionate to remain still any longer. "It isn't only a few bad ones who kill people. Surely you must see that by now. Simply *drinking* blood doesn't accomplish the transformation into a monster. It must be lifeblood—it must be a killing. A person was drained to create every last monster in that ballroom." I turned on her with the ruthless truth, unspoken until this moment. "It isn't only Eddy who has killed someone. It's George, too—it's the whole pack of them."

She did not try to argue; she only looked up at me with piteous large eyes. "Please, Liz. Give me at least a little time to consider it. I feel very tired—I have lost a great deal of blood tonight."

"Oh, May, of course you have. I didn't mean to be a brute."

At that moment we heard a voice clamouring faintly from the hallway—none other than George himself.

May clapped a hand over her mouth, and I confess I felt my own prickle of fear. On that night it was easy to imagine that speaking a certain name aloud might conjure up the one meant, despite George being about as far as humanly possible from resembling the Prince of Darkness usually evoked by such superstitions. Overcoming my nerves, I hurried through the door into the sitting-room just in time to behold the Duchess sallying forth from her own bedroom, her front hair waving about in curling-papers.

"Who on earth is hammering at the door? It sounds like a train station in here.—Oh, Sharp! So glad to see you. Is May back too?"

"Yes, ma'am." I threw a glance into the room behind me, satisfying myself that the sleeve of May's nightgown covered her wound.

"And why is there a Grand Duke on the sofa?" Mary Adelaide added.

Vasily, stretched out in a posture of languid indifference, blew the Duchess a kiss. I observed that the bloody paraphernalia of May's injury had disappeared.

"Vasily—er—escorted me home after the hearing," I invented.

"Ah, I see!" The Duchess stifled a yawn and went to the door, which was still rattling violently.

I could think of no way to stop her. The door burst open when she turned the knob, and a large grey wolf sprang into the room. I unsheathed the sword-stick, but then Short followed, looking rather wild.

"It's all right, Miss Sharp!" he cried, lunging for me, and seizing my arm. "He's in his right mind!"

"May! May!" the George-wolf barked. He dove beneath the couch, nearly tipping it over with the startled Vasily upon it. I was about to comment that if George was in his right mind he had a funny way of showing it—but then, with a yank of his snout, the blood-stained cloth I had used to clean May's wound, and the half-closed first-aid case, spilled out from beneath the furniture. With a horrified whine, the George-wolf recoiled.

The door creaked away from the wall and Mary Adelaide appeared in blank astonishment from behind it. "Good heavens!" she yelped, catching a glimpse of the evidence. "Sharp—what on earth—! May, my child!"

"I'm here," May said faintly from her room. "And I'm all right."

The George-wolf leaped up and raced towards her with

another whine, this time of welcome. When he reached her threshold, however, he seemed to recollect himself, and swerved into the wall rather than hurl himself into a lady's bedroom. There was a thump, and the pictures on the wall jumped. Then, shyly, he poked his snout around the corner.

"It's all right, George," she said wearily, getting up and coming to the doorway. The werewolf, with his sulphurous yellow eyes, crouched at her feet with a whine in his throat. I noticed that although May avoided looking at him, she did not flinch from the creature.

"There was a mix-up about the blood feast tonight, mamma," she said, pushing back her sleeve to show the bandage on her arm. "They meant to kill Sharp, but I was taken for her by mistake."

Short turned to look at me in silent horror.

"Oh," Mary Adelaide said shakily.

"You did not tell me I would be witnessing a murder tonight, mamma."

Her voice was ominous, and the Duchess wrung her hands. "Oh, May! I…I could not bring myself to tell you. I thought perhaps you would be better served to see it with your own eyes."

"And to feel their knives in my own skin?" May asked. George let out another, more agonised whine. There was a moment's silence. "Inspector Short?"

"Yes, ma'am?"

"What is George doing here?"

Short seemed lost in confusion, but the George-wolf let out a series of abbreviated yelps:

"Came to warn you! Gelded Ernest, what! Kill you if they find out!"

My mouth was dry. "George, how did you know it was May?"

"Knew Sharp's bloomers! Had to have swapped. Only explanation."

"Oh," May said blankly, and I could think of nothing to say either.

Beside me, Short cleared his throat. "There's no need to panic. If anyone else had come to the same conclusion as his grace, it's safe to say we'd already know about it."

"The room was crowded and warm," Vasily put in. "In such a place it is difficult to be certain of scents, at least."

"But people are sure to guess," I said soberly, "even if they don't *know*. Everyone saw me, and everyone knows who my mistress is." There was a suffocating silence. "She'll have to be guarded, but not by me. I'm no longer any use to you, ma'am."

I would have taken the opportunity to propose my replacement, but the Duchess breezed forward, beaming. "Such long faces! You forget that May is engaged to marry George. That is protection enough, surely? No one will dare to touch a future Queen!"

George pushed to his feet, apparently unable to prevent his tail from wagging. "Yes! Yes! Take care of you, what!"

May's cheeks flushed very slightly pink. "That would be dishonest," she began, sounding—to my finely attuned ear, at least—rather alarmed.

"Only pretend," George put in eagerly. "Not real. Break it off later. When safe."

"I don't think I could do that to you," she whispered.

But I had heard enough. "No, it's a brilliant idea—at least for the duration of the wedding. In fact, it might be the reason no one has bothered you already, ma'am."

"Nothing can be announced while the two of you are in mourning—but there are ways to make it look *quite* convincing," Mary Adelaide put in wisely, crossing the room to take May's hand. "You must spend *all* your time together." And then, in a piercing whisper, over May's protests, "Don't be like that, dear girl! What will become of us if you *don't* marry well, I should like to know!"

"That's settled, then," I said, to cover up the awkwardness.

The George-wolf looked rather thoughtful and not entirely happy. I felt for him. He had his wish, and would be permitted to court May in the guise of her betrothed—but conscious at every turn that it was all a pretence, at least so far as she herself was concerned.

"Thank you, your grace," I told him, collecting my first-aid case, and stuffing it back into my valise. "I'll send a bodyguard before dawn, I hope. In the meantime, don't allow anyone else to enter this suite, unless they use the password *Sal Tanner.*" I looked down at the sword-stick in my hand, then offered it to May. "This will need to be hidden, for it's too distinctive for either of us to be seen with it. And there's one other thing…"

"Your old journals?" she said softly, catching on at once. In my past life as Vera Livius, I had been an inventor, keeping records of my discoveries in a series of notebooks. One day, I hoped, I would have the chance to familiarise myself with their contents once again.

"Take good care of them," I told her. "I'll return to collect them one day."

May nodded, squeezing my hands. "I'll put them away safely, depend upon it."

"Thank you, ma'am." I turned to Vasily. "Shall we flit?"

Thus far Short had remained more a silent observer than

an active participant of the conversation, but now he settled his hat upon his head and picked up my valise. "I'll come with you, in case there's any trouble with the police."

"Why, thank you, Short—that's very thoughtful of you."

"Also I want a word," he added, sounding nearly as ominous as May had a moment ago.

"It's a free country," I said amicably, leading the way into the corridor. "—Or if it isn't, it ought to be. Come along!"

Chapter VII.

None of us spoke more than absolutely necessary until we had safely navigated the long quiet hallways of Ehrenberg Palace, and Short and Vasily had charmed their way past the revenant policemen guarding the rear courtyard entrance. When we were out in the narrow, cobbled streets, Short took my arm, pulling me a few steps away from our carnivorous companion.

He pulled a long face—well, longer than usual. "I still don't quite understand what happened tonight, Miss Sharp."

His tall form and thick woollen greatcoat shielded me from the cold night air, and I stifled a happy sigh. Vasily had known me to be innocent upon our first meeting, but had seen my inexperience as an invitation to conquest. Short, by contrast, had assumed me to be a reprobate, but he had come to see—and on some level, to respect—the truth. Smiling at him fondly, I filled him in.

"You were right about the Kabale, Short. It was the most dreadful farce, and they sent me straight to Ehrenberg for the blood feast. If May hadn't found me and taken my place, I'd be dead and Princess Ducky would be howling at the moon alongside her werewolf intended."

The corners of his mouth drew down in distress. "One

hardly knows what to think. Of course I knew the monsters must kill—but to make such an occasion of it—"

"I know," I said in a low voice. "Somehow I had always thought the bloodshed was an unpleasant detail—a side effect. But it wasn't. All along it was at the centre of who these people are, and what they do. The whole system is built on it."

"Yes," Short said, after a moment, as though reluctant to admit it. "Miss Sharp, what did you mean by that crack about Nemesis?—if I might ask."

"Oh, it wasn't a crack. I was quite in earnest."

"I learned a little classical myth in school, you know. As I recall it, Nemesis was the goddess of divine retribution, hounding criminals and evil-doers to their own destruction. Is that what you mean to do to the assembled royalties of Europe?"

"Why not?" I said brightly. "*Something* must be done. If not May, then me, and if not me, then another poor creature would have been ritually slaughtered tonight, to make one of them a monster. Of course, I should very much like *not* to do anything about it, but what then? What will happen at the *next* royal wedding? Good heavens, what do you suppose they do at their christenings and funerals? I shudder to think how long this has gone on already."

I couldn't quite see his face in the dark as we passed from one lonely globe of gaslight to the next. "Of course something must be done, but what do *you* mean to do about it? Change doesn't come in a day, nor at the hands of a single person. There are proper channels, and in my experience, those who ignore them generally end up throwing bombs."

"Oh, of course I don't mean to do *that*," I assured him. The corners of my mouth wanted to curl up in anticipation, and

I realised—now that I had had a moment to reflect—that I was feeling more or less on top of the world. For so long I had wanted to do *something* about the monsters that ruled our lives and had stolen everything I once held dear. Now, at last, I knew what it was. "Nor will I be alone. Vasily and I have a plan."

"You and *Vasily?*" he cried in horror.

"Don't sound so surprised!" From several steps behind, Vasily was laughing at him. "Didn't you know, Inspector? Danger is irresistible to Miss Sharp, and so am I."

"I still have saltwater in my pocket," I warned him.

We were now beyond the immediate environs of the palace, venturing into the poorer streets north of the town's centre. Each door, each window was locked and barred, and the streets were almost dead—but only almost.

Before Vasily could respond to my challenge, a woman's scream thrilled in the night air quite close to us. My heart quickened, and I stopped, listening.

"It came from that direction," I said, pointing, "and I'll bet it's because someone was disappointed to miss their blood feast tonight."

My two escorts glanced at each other. "What did I say just now?" Vasily observed.

Short turned to me. "Miss Sharp, we must get you to safety."

"I'm not in Coburg for safety," I rejoined, but before the argument could develop further, a voice shouted from the same direction as the woman's scream. The words were indistinct, but the accent and timbre was familiar to all of us.

"That's Anton!" I cried.

Short muttered under his breath. The next moment all

three of us set off at a run.

We came upon the battle in a by-way flooded with moonlight. A woman shrank back against a wooden fence, clutching at her torn blouse. Anton stood before her wielding a long, sharpened stake that looked as though it had been recently uprooted from a garden—supporting tomatoes, if my nose could be trusted. He faced a red-eyed vampire in impeccable evening dress, who sprang upon him as we ventured upon the scene.

With a loud *crack* Anton's stake spun away, striking the nearby wall of a house and rebounding as Anton went down beneath the monster's overwhelming strength.

The vampire threw back his head to grin mockingly at us—the moonlight glinting on white, pointed teeth. I dove aside and caught up Anton's weapon, but Vasily caught my arm to hold me back.

"Not the stake!"

Doubtless the creature, being a vampire, must be a member of Vasily's own family. All the same, mature consideration convinced me of the sense of his words. There was only one thing you could do with a stake, and that was to kill. We were already in enough trouble for defanging a pair of werewolves.

Instead, I reached for the flask of saltwater at my back.

Uncorking the flask, I sent the remainder of the precious liquid arcing out in a thin stream that struck the beast across its face. Saltwater is like acid on a vampire's flesh, and the creature recoiled with a thin shriek, clapping its hands to its face. Sensing his chance, Anton flung the creature off him and retreated to my side, snatching the stake from my hand.

By the time he had it and turned, poised to strike, the narrow street was empty save for the girl and the four of us. Her gaze fell upon Vasily, and with a squeak of fright she took to her heels. She must not have been far from home, for she vanished into a house not far away.

"Where did it go?" Anton panted, looking about as though he expected to see the vampire peering from one of the windows above us.

Vasily gave an eloquent shrug, but I pointed upwards. "It went away across the roofs, as you did in Eger."

Anton swore creatively in Roumanian. "And you let it escape to kill *again?* I had it! I was *this* close to ending the bloodsucking insect, and you distracted me!"

"It seemed to me as though you were in dire need of Miss Sharp's assistance," Vasily said.

Anton startled and turned. "You!" An instant later he had the Grand Duke pinned against the nearest wall by the throat, stake poised. "Give me," he said through clenched teeth, *"one reason* not to ram this through your black heart."

"Oh, you anarchists are so excitable," Vasily said in a bored voice. Anton snarled.

I threw Short a glance, half expecting him to step in with calming words. Instead, he lifted an eyebrow at me. "I'm having trouble thinking of any particular reason, myself. What about you, Miss Sharp?"

After Vasily had half-drained me to escape from Castle Sarkozy, Short had said something about wanting to kill the vampire. It had only been a muttered aside, in the heat of the moment—or so I had thought. Was it possible Short had been *serious?* For a moment I could only stare at him. Then I sighed, and pulled Anton away from the vampire by the ear.

"He has promised to help us destroy the Kabale," I explained. "And since they condemned me to death tonight without uncovering my face, I've decided to accept."

Short let out a horrified yelp. "Destroy *what?*"

"You heard, bootheel," Anton said gleefully. "Bloodsucker, I apologise. That is a very good reason to keep you alive a little longer."

"Wait, wait, wait," Short protested. "Destroy the Kabale?—the very organisation responsible for keeping the peace in Europe? And you mean to enlist *these* renegades to help you?"

"I'm enlisting you as well," I pointed out ingratiatingly. "You're *tremendously* respectable, Mr Short." I let go of Anton and patted him on the back by way of apology for yanking him about by the ear. "Do you have lodgings, my friend?—and is there room for me and the vampire?"

Anton shot Vasily a suspicious look. "Yes, but he stays within a barrier of salt."

"Done," I agreed, overriding Vasily's protests. He had asked for my help, and if he did not like the help we were willing to give, he was quite welcome to face the Kabale alone. "Shall we, gentlemen?"

Short did not speak again as Anton led us north, although every time I glanced at him I saw that his lips were pressed thinly shut and downturned at the corners. Poor Short! the night had caught him by surprise, and he did not yet know what to make of it. In that moment I made up my mind to be very patient with him, for he had stayed by my side through a great deal of trouble, and had offered to kill a vampire for me—Now, of course, I blush to think how badly I underestimated the strength of his objection to what I meant to do.

Anton led us directly to the tenement I had visited with him this afternoon. We climbed the stairwell—this time no eyes dared to watch from cracked doors. Anton fished keys from his pockets and let us into the garret.

"Why, this is Hannah's place," I said as the whole party entered. The stockings were gone from before the stove, and the carpet-bag from beside the bed.

"I sent her away and took on the lease." Anton bent to light a cracked oil lamp on the table.

"Hannah?" Short put in. "The *bomber?* You just let her *go?*"

Anton shrugged and went to investigate the cupboard next to the stove. "I told her what became of Veronika's plans, that the revolution was called off. She will be harmless, for a while at least." He straightened with a sound of satisfaction, holding up a brown-paper bag full of salt—evidently Hannah had stocked her cupboards with the needful. "Over here, bloodsucker." He began pouring a careful circle around Vasily, who watched with a scornful smile.

"How long is a *while?*" Short wheeled abruptly to face me, and his voice sank to a murmur. "Miss Sharp! It was all very well when Anton was willing to stay with us and help us, but today he has abetted a dangerous anarchist, to say nothing of assaulting a foreign dignitary in the street—"

"If you mean the vampire," Anton cut in, "when I committed my *assault,* he was trying to bite a girl in the neck."

"How did you know she was unwilling?" Vasily drawled, a gleam of tooth showing in his smile.

"Shut up," Anton snarled, "or I'll stuff the rest of this salt down your black throat. He was a prince. It doesn't matter if she pretended to be willing or not."

Short pulled off his hat and ran a hand through his hair, disarranging the fair locks in a way I couldn't help finding rather distracting. "Miss Sharp, not only is one of these men an anarchist, but the other has already betrayed you twice! How can you trust either of them?"

"I *don't* trust Vasily." I made no attempt to lower my voice, for the vampire would be sure to hear me regardless. He swept me an extravagant bow from his narrow circle. "As for Anton, I know exactly where our aims coincide."

"If it's destroying the Kabale, she can trust me in that," Anton pointed out, replacing the salt in the cupboard, and throwing a lump of coal into the stove. He straightened, wiping sooty fingerprints on his trousers. "Although I still say we should burn down the whole town on top of the monsters."

The tip of Short's nose whitened, and he jabbed a finger in Anton's direction. "That man belongs in gaol. And the vampire belongs in Russia where he can't do any harm—"

"I thought you were going to kill Vasily yourself," I reminded him wickedly.

"Tell the bootheel to get in line," Anton growled. "I was there first."

Short remained focused on me. "Miss Sharp. I'm only trying to keep you safe."

"You're a little late for that, Mr Short." I might have tried to be more conciliating, but I confess the night had left me keyed up to an extraordinary pitch. "It was Vera Livius who needed protecting in Stuttgart two years ago. Give me credit for a little more strength tonight."

His lips paled as he pressed them more tightly together, but he had no response to that. I turned to Anton. "The main person we need to protect right now is Princess May, now that I can no longer act as her bodyguard. Vasily is wanted by the Kabale, and Short is already acting as Prince George's bodyguard. There's no one else we can trust, so it will have to be you, Anton."

There was a brief silence. Then Anton bellowed, "Never! Death before dishonour!"

Short threw up his hands with an inarticulate sound of despair, and Vasily remarked drily, "I was of the impression that you wished to *preserve* Princess May's life, Miss Sharp."

"I do believe we're making progress," I cried, "here at last is something the three of you agree on!"

"I will *not* spend my days nurse-maiding a useless aristo," Anton groaned. "Ask me anything but that!"

"May isn't useless," I began.

"She is!" he bellowed. "She had to be well-nigh carried across half of Europe, and you and Short waited on her hand and foot the whole way!"

I sighed, for despite the fact that he had stayed out of her way as much as possible, I had dared to hope that Anton might have warmed to May during the course of our journey. I did not like to tell him the whole truth, but he needed to know exactly why May required his protection.

"What if I told you she recently transformed the Grand Duke of Hesse and his intended bride into common mortals like you and me?"

Anton's eyes narrowed. "It cannot be done. You are pulling my leg!"

"Honour bright! Short saw it too. One moment Duke Ernest was a wolf; the next he was just a very startled man in the moonlight. That's why May needs protecting. If the others find out it was she who did it, May will be dead, and with her all hope of bringing down the Kabale."

"What is this fairy-tale you're telling me? How can someone

like May—wait." Anton's eyes narrowed. "Her blood. That's why Veronika and Kurt wanted her blood?"

Short pulled a hand down his face, muttering something under his breath. I felt the same alarm myself. If Anton knew the secret of May's blood, what was to stop him draining her dry?

There was no help for it now. "Morganatic blood defangs monsters," I explained, having outlined the events of the evening in a few words. "We know it, May knows it, and if the secret gets out, every monster in Europe will know it. She's in terrible danger as long as she's in Coburg, and I can't deal with the Kabale if I'm trying to keep her safe. *Please,* Anton."

He looked from my face, to Short's, to Vasily's. If he'd had any doubt of my story, their expressions must have convinced him that I told the truth. Pulling off his cloth cap, he let out a low whistle. "So that's your plan for dealing with the Kabale? Use May's blood to defang the monsters?"

He watched me closely. There was no helping it: he would learn the truth from May, if not from me. "I don't know," I told him. "She may not consent to being used in that way, and I will not force her. But no one will be able to use her blood at all once she is dead."

Anton scowled. "You are foolish not to secure her blood now."

"As Vasily secured my blood in the dungeon of Castle Sarkozy, you mean?" Anton opened his mouth, but I raised a hand for silence. I would not play games with May's life. "No, listen. May is mine to protect, and I have already involved her in too much danger in return—so please, believe me when I say I will shoot you out of hand sooner than let you lay a finger on her against her will."

Anton swallowed. "You should know I do not bow to threats. I will obey you without question, but first I will speak my mind. I think this is folly."

"Don't stop there," Short said in a deceptively mild voice. "What would *you* do, Lupei?"

"I would forget about drawing fangs," Anton said. "Maybe I was making a little joke before, with the burning the whole town. But I could make some bombs, just some *little* bombs, and set them off under the palace, yes? And the house where the prince of Russia is staying, and the other house where the Kaiser is. You could even get your friends out first."

There was a resounding silence in the aftermath of his words. I felt that Short was trying to catch my eye, but at least he had the sense not to speak.—Yes, I wanted to shout at him. Yes, I *did* know that Anton was still dangerous; that was why I kept him so close to me. After his disillusionment at Castle Sarkozy, I might be the only person in the world he still trusted. He might be a mad dog, but if I abandoned him now that was all he would ever be.

Yes, he was dangerous—but he was less dangerous now than he had been a month ago on the Orient Express, and as long as he was willing to follow me I could try to lead him into something better. He was not, like Vasily, a creature of deception. I knew that if he meant to harm May he would say so.

So I said flatly, "I don't mean to kill anyone if I can help it, Anton."

He made a face.

"I don't mean to start a revolution either," I added, as much to Short as to Anton. "But the Kabale has been covering up the crimes of royalties all over Europe, subverting justice. All I need to do is tear the masks from their faces—bring their crimes to light. Truth will bring justice to all of them in the end." I put out my hand. "I hold you to nothing, Anton. I only ask for your honesty. If you cannot in good conscience guard May as faithfully as I would, you are free to leave me."

He looked at my hand, and his eyebrow quirked. "I am not leaving, for two reasons. One, because I have done terrible things to you and others, and I have given up the right to make my own judgements for a little while, until I trust myself better. Two, because it is *my* garret. If anyone should leave, it will be you."

I couldn't help a laugh, even though I felt like a small child riding a large and very wayward horse. "You wouldn't do that to me, Anton."

His face sobered. "Never."

"Then you'll nurse-maid the princess?"

"As tenderly as a mother, since you ask it. But I ask one boon." Anton glared at Vasily, who stood leaning against the invisible barrier made by the salt he could not cross. "I will guard the princess, but afterwards I get to stake the bloodsucker who murdered my cousin."

Vasily gave a sharp-edged grin. "Not if you want my help destroying the Kabale, you won't."

Anton snarled in return, but I laid a hand on his shoulder. "Don't be unreasonable. We need his help. But," I added thoughtfully, "if he does *anything* to betray us, all agreements are off and you have my leave to incinerate him."

Anton took my hand. "Done," he said. His eyes narrowed at Vasily. "I'll be watching."

"How fortunate! I do my best work before an audience."

"Miss Sharp," Short said in a low voice. He stood beside me, twisting his bowler-hat in his long, sinewy hands; and I realised that he was almost miserable. "I, too, think you are being foolish. Didn't I tell you how often the Kabale has prevented all of Europe igniting in war? Break them, and you complete the work Veronika started, and set all the monsters at each other's throats. Only a month ago, you were ready to die rather than let that happen. What has changed now? You're no anarchist—are you?"

I swallowed hard. My exhilaration was slowly ebbing, giving way to exhaustion, and I was beginning to realise he was in earnest. "Of course not. Veronika meant to kill the monsters, to upend the whole system. I only mean to unmask and expose them."

"To destabilise them," he said.

"Yes."

"And I tell you now, if you destabilise the monsters, you will destabilise *Europe.*"

There was a difference—couldn't he see there was a differ-ence?—between me and Veronika. If the monsters went to war with each other after I had exposed and neutralised the Kabale, that would be because of their own rapacity, their own contumacy, and not because I had spilled first blood. Moreover, if I weakened them, perhaps a war would not be so dreadful. Only let the monsters begin to be held accountable by their subjects, and we might see fewer wars fought over the greed, or the perceived slights, of a few.

I was too tired to put all of this into words. "Europe is already unstable, Short. Just look at *those* two." Anton was circling Vasily, growling threats, while the vampire spat occasional veiled barbs. "The monsters eat the commoners;

the anarchists throw bombs at the monsters; and the Kabale tries to smooth it all over and paint it to look pretty, and beneath is only festering sores."

Short looked at the two of them and scowled. "And you'd entrust your friend's safety to *that?*"

"Sooner than I'd trust it to anyone else in that palace." I put a hand on his arm and he stiffened, looking down at it with his eyebrows stitched hard together. "At least you and George will be watching her too. But I think Anton will be quite safe. He promised to follow me, and he's always been honest with me. You know I'd never entrust May's safety to someone I can't trust."

Short drew back, out of my reach. "Lupei might be able to follow you, Miss Sharp." He pronounced my name with a stumble, as though he'd been about to call me something else. "But I cannot. What the Kabale did tonight was deplorable, but we *need* them. I cannot help you destroy them."

"*Need* them?" I asked blankly.

He didn't answer.

I don't believe it had ever occurred to me that he might back away from me like this. After everything we had done together! After helping me hide Eddy's body—after giving me comfort when Vasily had drained my blood—after telling me how disillusioned he'd become with the way the world was ruled.

We had stormed Castle Sarkozy together, but then we were facing anarchists. Now that I turned to face the monsters, he meant to abandon me.

He must have seen the shock in my face, for he clasped my hands between his own. "Leave Coburg, Miss Sharp. Leave, before the Kabale recaptures you—or those two kill you" (a nod towards Vasily and Anton). "What we saw tonight was dreadful, but this is no way to repair things. I'll find you a place to hide until the hue and cry dies down. *Please.*"

I hesitated, shaken in my resolution by the sheer desperation in his voice. Lately I had come to a profound respect for Short's judgement. Could he be right? Was I about to do something dreadful?

Or had I been correct all along? He was a policeman, after all. His whole life, no less than May's, had been spent in propping up the monsters' rule. Wistfully, I recalled our conversation in the carriage this afternoon, only a few hours ago. He had said, then, that he was on my side. But he had also said that it was always better to work with the system than against it.

How could he still believe this after what he had seen tonight?—when the system itself—monsters, revenants, and live policemen together—was rotten to the core?

Perhaps he sensed the thoughts that crossed my mind, for his hands tightened on mine in a grasp that was nearly painful. I smiled up at him and clung to what I knew. "I am not my mother, Short. I will not harm a hair of anyone's head if I can help it; but I *must* reveal the truth. If you can't join me, you must respect my conscience."

He released my hands and stood back, bowing his head. "I am sorry to see you take this path." A deep sigh. "I had best return to the palace. I've stayed away too long."

"Take Anton with you," I said quickly. The verbal sparring-match between the anarchist and the vampire had stuttered out, and for some time now the two of them had been watching Short and myself with feline amusement (Vasily) and a grim smile (Anton). Now Anton picked up his cloth cap and moved forward. Short nodded in resignation.

"As you wish."

"I am greatly obliged," I told him softly. Having given Anton a few quick instructions, promising to have a more solid plan in place by tomorrow night, I bade him and Short farewell, and latched the door behind them with a sinking feeling in the pit of my stomach.

In the wake of their departure, Vasily snorted. "The bootheel is quite mistaken, you know."

"I see that you're using anarchist argot now," I jibed, but he ignored me.

"The reason we have not yet had a war owes less to the Kabale than it does to sheer blind luck. We might not actually drink each other's blood, but we are all waiting the next opportunity to tear out each other's throats."

I felt empty, like a corpse drained of blood. "Why?"

"For the same reason Alexander sat down and wept: that there was only one world to conquer." He ran a tongue over his sharp teeth. "The problem with Europe is that there are too many Empires, and all of them want the world."

Chapter VIII.

Having covered the windows with a board to block the light, I slept until late the following day and was still deeply asleep when a voice spoke from across the room.

"Miss Sharp?"

My heart jolted me upright as I grasped for a weapon. My battered umbrella was in my hand before I remembered where I was: alone in Anton's garret with the monster that had once drained me.

Even after a night spent on the floorboards of a dusty garret, Vasily Nikolaevitch Romanov exuded sheer predatory power and lazy self-assurance as he sat neatly within his circle of salt, observing me with inscrutable eyes. For a moment I was no longer in the dim Coburg garret, but trapped in the black dungeon of Castle Sarkozy—trapped in the nightmares that had haunted me since—helplessly waiting for the creature to pounce.

Then he said: "Don't you have an appointment in an hour?"

His spell broke. I put down my umbrella and rubbed the heels of my hands across my aching eyes before peering at my pocket-watch. Indeed, it was noon; and I had asked Anton to bring May to meet me at one.

"The dickens," I murmured. "Face the wall, your grace. I am

going to get dressed."

"You ought to call me Vasya," he offered, turning in his circle of salt to obey, "since I am pretending to be a commoner."

I restrained an unladylike snort as I slid out of bed and seized my washcloth.

At least the panic of waking had banished my sleepiness and awoken my busy mind. "The first thing I need is to see the entire Kabale with my own eyes, since I was hooded at my hearing. When is their next meeting?"

"Tomorrow night," he answered. "But why is that necessary? I know all of them. I can give you a list."

"I want to see them myself," I insisted, finishing my morning ablutions and drawing on corset and padding over the chemise and drawers in which I had slept. "I'm very much afraid I don't trust you as far as May can spit."

"Dear me!" he said thoughtfully, no doubt envisaging such an experiment. "Well, at least I am not alone. You don't trust the horse-faced policeman, either."

Over my corset, I wore a sturdy belt from which hung my capacious pockets and a coil of thin, sturdy rope. At Vasily's words, I halted in the midst of settling these around my waist. "I beg your pardon?"

"I couldn't help but notice that you didn't favour Short with the knowledge of your plans."

"Humph!" I said. "He isn't part of this operation, so there's no use including him."

All the same, I could not help but feel a pang. I felt awfully queer without Short by my side—tender and vulnerable, like a hermit crab that has lost its shell. At some point—perhaps in the hospital in Eger on that awful morning after Vasily's bite—I had come to depend on him as a shield. Now he was gone and Vasily was watching me from the circle of salt, his mouth twisted in a knowing smile.

After a quick breakfast of stale bread and cheese, I pinned my hat to my head and shrouded my head in my thickest black veil. Emerging into the streets, I found that Coburg had ventured out-of-doors during the daylight hours and, apart from the presence of a great many policemen, seemed to be in high spirits—no doubt glad to have survived the night. Stopping at a small news-stand, I noted there were no reports of last night's occurrences. Of course the press was not free in Germany the way it was in England, but when I made discreet inquiries of the vendor, I satisfied myself that there were not even any current rumours.

At least that would make *my* work easier, for otherwise every passer-by in the street might be watching for me. Turning down the street leading to the Marktplatz, I found a carriage waiting at the corner with its blinds drawn. Anton sat beside the coachman, his hat pulled down over his eyes. I nodded to him and knocked on the door to the rhythm of *Rule Britannia;* it opened to me, and I slid into the warm dark interior opposite May.

"May!" I cried, throwing back my veil as the carriage jolted into motion.

She seized my hands with a look of relief. "Oh, Sharp, you are in terrible danger. Everyone is so very angry with you—they are calling you an anarchist."

"And you?" I scanned her face anxiously, finding to my relief that the blow dealt her last night had not left an obvious mark. The bandage on her wrist was hidden by long sleeves and gloves. "Anton has been taking care of you?"

"Yes, although he frets mamma and papa terribly by refusing

to stand up straight, and by chewing toothpicks in their presence."

"Oh! he *only does it to annoy, because he knows it teases*," said I, quoting *Alice.* "The important thing is that he's there. Tell me what has been going on at the palace."

May swallowed hard. "Aunt Queen and the rest of the family are all very indignant. All of them are blaming you for what happened to Ernest and Ducky. I am to have nothing more to do with you, of course. The police have been told to keep watch for you, but there is to be no hunt—not yet. George says the German cousins mean to handle that themselves, as soon as the moon rises."

I hummed thoughtfully and made a mental note to stock up on saltwater. If it could really prevent werewolves picking up my scent, I must avail myself of it at once. "And no one suspects it was you under the bag?"

"I don't know," May said thoughtfully. "Do you remember the Crown Princess of Roumania?"

"Missy?—The one who waylaid George in the passageway yesterday, and then held you down last night so Ducky could collect your blood?"

May shuddered. "Yes—she's Ducky's sister. She came to visit me this morning. She didn't stay long, but she asked a great many questions about you, since someone told her you were my maid. I think—I think she was trying to threaten me. She said very decidedly that she meant to find out who it was under the hood as well." May swallowed hard. "I don't know whether she knows, or only *suspects.*"

"All the more reason you should keep up this pretended engagement with George."

May blushed faintly. "George came to see me this morning

when I was having tea with Missy. When he put his arm around my waist, Missy choked on her cake."

I raised a mocking eyebrow. "Careful, now. I thought we agreed that you oughtn't to fall in love with George."

"Of course not! But it is only…" She interlaced her fingers. "All my German cousins have always looked down their noses at me for being morganatic. But George…George doesn't care. He likes *me,* and he doesn't mind who knows it."

"Eddy liked you too," I reminded her.

She shook her head. "N-o, I don't think he did. Not like George does. I think Eddy was much more in love with himself than he was with me." She put gloved fingers to her lips, as though surprised to hear such sentiments crossing them. "I mean—I ought not to speak ill of the dead, but—"

"Oh! I understand what you mean," I said, laughing at her.

"And I *don't* think I am in any danger of falling in love with George," she said, becoming serious again. "Oh, Sharp. He has told me the story of how he became—what he is. He said he owed me that, at least."

"Was it very bad?"

She nodded, serious. "The thing was arranged for him when he was very young—scarcely more than a boy, although he did not try to excuse himself for that! He was sent down to the Old Bailey, and they presented him with a condemned woman who had been convicted of killing her husband. Oh, dear! A happy wife does not do such things—he said it himself. Perhaps she was only trying to defend herself. He still wonders whether he was right to do it, but what else could he have done? He was a boy, and he has always been in awe of the family."

"He could have refused to play their game," I said. In my

heart I could not judge him too harshly, however, and I added: "Perhaps he was a boy then, but he is a man now. It is not too late to stand up to them. What happened after the tea party?"

She became very solemn. "After Missy left, George and Short and mamma and I had a conversation. Sharp…is it true what they told me; that you mean to destroy the Kabale?"

"I don't mean to throw bombs at them," I said defensively.

"Oh, Sharp, of course not, but…"

Her words hung in the air. I twisted my fingers, plucking up the courage to say more. How I wished there was another way! How I wished I need not ask this of her!

"If I could dose the Kabale with morganatic blood," I said at length, "it would not hurt them, but they would no longer be monsters—no longer trusted or respected by their fellow royalties. Their power would be broken, for a time at least."

"Oh," May whispered, shrinking in on herself a little. "You still want my blood."

"It's the only way I can see to end the Kabale without hurting anyone."

"And if I refuse—what then?" Even in the gloom I could see how pale she was. "Will you start hurting people, then? Will you take my blood by force?"

Her words were soft, but they were like a stab to the heart. "May!"

"I am sorry," she whispered, "but I must know! Inspector Short said you've gone too far—and George and mamma agreed with him."

Bitterness overwhelmed me. Short no doubt thought I was becoming a full-blown anarchist, and I could not imagine May disagreeing with her mother and suitor for very long. "If you believed that, why did you consent to meet me?"

"But I *don't* believe it, Sharp! Or, I don't want to believe it—but what else am I to think? Am I to take you at your word the way I took my family at their word, when they said they were not monsters?"

It was a fair question—and she had hit me in my weakest point. May's blood was my only plan. What else could I do? Would I descend to blackmail, or assassination?—Perish the thought!

I cleared my throat. "Perhaps I will find someone of morganatic birth who *will* help me. And in any case I will find out who the members of the Kabale are, and publish their identities and deeds..."

My voice trailed away. Publish them how? Perhaps the English, or even the American press would be able to print what I knew; but the newspapers of the Continent were controlled by the monsters, and the illegal underground papers were nearly all anarchist organs, many of them dedicated to the business of revolution and correspondingly unhappy with me for my interference in the Castle Sarkozy affair. How would I get the truth into the hands of those who needed it most?

I sighed. "If that's all I can do, then I will do that. But even if the truth about the Kabale was known, it wouldn't break their power; and if the uproars of the last century have taught us anything, it's that almost no one gives up power of their own free will. If all I can do is get the word out, I fear it will only mean harsher suppression, greater conflict between the monsters and the anarchists—and ultimately, perhaps, a more violent revolution when the whole festering sore comes to a head."

May's lips parted. "Do you really believe a revolution is

coming?"

"A better question might be whether you really believe this can go on forever."

She looked down at her clasped hands and spoke in a half-suffocated voice. "I don't want to cause a war. I don't want to destroy my family and betray my empire; and I don't want to give up my blood. Surely you, of all people, understand *that.*"

My blood had been taken twice now, without my consent. I had determined never to give my consent in the future—and I could hardly blame May for feeling the same way. "Of course I do, May, and I hate asking this of you."

She smiled faintly. "Perhaps you will find someone else."

"That's a long shot, but I am obliged to you for the wish." I peered out at the window, noticing that we had wound our way through the Coburg streets nearly as far as the train station. It would only be a short walk back to the garret from here, and I rapped with my umbrella on the carriage roof to be let off. "Thank you for the information. Might I borrow Anton this evening? Would it be possible to enlist George or Short as your protector for a few hours?"

"Of course."

"Then send him to me at sunset." As the carriage drew to a stop, I looked at her with wistful fondness. "I hope we can remain friends, May, even if we cannot bring down the Kabale together."

"Always," she said fervently, wellnigh crushing my fingers in her grasp.

I alighted from the carriage deep in thought and watched it draw away. Only after a moment did I recall the scars on my face, and put up my hand to lower my veil. Before I could do so, a second carriage pulled into the space recently vacated by May's, and the door opened.

"Elizabeth Sharp, I presume," said Princess Missy, sweetly dangerous.

I found it suddenly rather difficult to breathe. Slipping a hand into my pocket where I carried my replenished flask of saltwater, I said, "I have not the pleasure of your acquaintance, ma'am."

This morning her eyes were of a pretty blue, and her teeth were of an ordinary length; but she leaned forward, smiling thinly as she scattered the musky scent of roses. "I am Marie of Roumania, and you have destroyed my beloved sister," she said. "You had better start running, Sharp. For the Kabale means to hunt you down; and whatever is left of you when they are finished, I will burn—along with whomever it was beneath the black hood."

Chapter IX.

At the last part of Missy's announcement, the witty rejoinder faded from my lips. She gave me a thin smile, slammed the door of her carriage and signalled her coachman to proceed. There was nothing else I could do. I must only hope that Anton, atop May's carriage, would see that he was being followed and shake Missy off the trail.

I returned to our lodgings with a heart full of foreboding. It fretted me a great deal to think that I had got May into so much trouble. At this point, I thought gloomily, she might have to marry George just to escape the monsters' vengeance.—*Why* could not I have left well enough alone, and thanked the Kabale with becoming humility for sparing my life?

Well, it was too late for that now. I must be patient. I did not despair of convincing May to give me her blood, and in the meantime my time in Coburg would not be wasted if I could only learn the Kabale's identity. Once I had seen their faces, I would have all the time in the world to plot my next move.

I stopped on my way home to purchase a live chicken, then returned to the garret to a deeply bored Vasily.

"Feeling hungry? I brought you some food." I placed the

wicker cage within the circle of salt.

At the sound of clucking, he made an affronted face. "This is a *chicken.*"

"So?"

"I do not drink the blood of chickens!"

"Then glamour it to look like something else."

He turned away from the cage with a sniff. "If you won't let me leave, the least you could do is bring me something worth reading."

"I gave you *The Small House at Allington.*"

He made a face. "Anthony Trollope. Fox-hunts and beefsteak. I should infinitely prefer Nietzsche."

"You look like the sort of person who would prefer Nietzsche." I put my hands on my hips. "I met Marie of Roumania on my outing. She wants revenge for what May did to her sister, and I fear she may already suspect who it was. We have to stop her."

"We?" He arched an elegant eyebrow. "Princess May is more than adequately equipped to thwart any vampire attack, surely."

"You don't imagine that Missy will fall for *that,* do you? And in the meantime, I haven't managed to convince May to let me have her blood. So, if you have any other ideas—"

"Kidnap her and siphon some off, as the serf suggested."

"As I told Anton, that's *your* sort of trick, not mine."

"Then I cannot conceive why you should ask me."

"Because Missy is a vampire like you," I protested. "Surely you must know how dissuade her."

He shrugged. "Tell your friend that she must give up her blood, or Princess Marie will strangle her. It's true enough."

Only last night I had compared Anton to a wild dog, but

Vasily was no better, and the ease with which his thoughts resorted to kidnapping or blackmail sent a chill down my spine. Had Short been right? In accepting Vasily's aid, had I made a deal with the devil?

"A penny for your thoughts," he said unexpectedly. "Your face is a study."

"Oh, nothing," I said. "I was only wondering how one develops such an appalling character as yours. Not only are you content to prey upon ordinary people like me and your endless dainties, but you are all too willing to betray those of your own class as well. Is *nothing* sacred to you?"

He hissed lazily. "My class, bah! My loyalty is to my Empire—Holy Russia."

"That is strange, seeing that you have more and angrier anarchists in Russia than anywhere else. Are you sure Holy Russia returns your affections?"

"It doesn't matter what a rabble of peasants and provocateurs think of us."

"You truly don't fear consequences for your actions?"

"Why should I? When I killed Ioanna, did a thunderbolt fall from the heavens to strike me?—No. We have too much power to be unseated from below. And what use is it to change now? Those who want change will never accept less than total revolution. They would choose the worst of anarchists any day over the best of monsters."

"And whose fault would that be?" I sighed. "You might give it up."

"And assuage my conscience that way? Oh, no. It is far more agreeable to regret the past in luxury than in penury, my dear." He gave a sharp-edged chuckle.

"Well, *I* don't mean to have regrets, whether in luxury or

out of it. And certainly not because I stole May's blood."

"There is also blameless luxury," he said with a grin. "My offer of employment still stands. Why not, Athene? I take it your employment with Princess May is at an end."

I narrowed my eyes at him. "If it's a bodyguard you want, I'd sooner guard Missy of Roumania than you. At least *she* has never drained my blood."

"Ah, but would it not be worth accepting merely for the sake of the look on Inspector Short's face when he hears of it?"

"I *beg* your pardon?"

Vasily smiled. There was a knock at the door, and a familiar voice called, "Miss Sharp?"

"Ha! I knew I could hear those flat feet ascending the stair," Vasily said.

Giving up trying to get any sense out of the vampire, I marched to the door and threw it open. "Short? Just the man I wanted—"

My voice trailed away as I glimpsed his face—pale and set, the thin lips almost colourless as he shoved through the door into the room. His left hand dipped into the pocket of his greatcoat, while his right landed heavily on my shoulder.

"Elizabeth Sharp," he said, "you are under arrest."

I was surprised half into laughter. "Et tu, Short! and on what grounds?"

"You're wanted in London for questioning in the murder of Sarah Tanner," he announced, in the same vein of concentrated fortitude.

Was he serious? I stopped laughing. "That's nonsense: Scotland Yard had *months* to question me about that."

"Don't argue, Miss Sharp," he added in a pleading voice.

"I'm only trying to get you safely out of Coburg before you get yourself killed."

I backed one slow step, and then another, for I could guess what he held in his left-hand pocket. "What an awful lot of trouble you are going to, with all these trumped-up charges! Vasily, here, favours outright kidnapping."

"That's against the law," Short said defensively.

"Oh! I beg your pardon. Of course, this is a *lawful* kidnapping."

"Don't argue," he began again.

"I don't mean to argue," I said, backing another step. "I simply won't go with you, and that's that."

"You can't stay here," he said in desperation. "They know where you live."

My heart seemed to stop beating. "I beg your pardon? They know where I *live?* How do they know *that?*"

His lips thinned. "Because I told them."

I could scarcely believe my own ears. If he had struck me with his fist, I might have felt it less. "Oh, you *Judas,*" I heard Vasily say, as if from a great way off. His voice was full of relish.

Short loomed over me, pale and bloodless. "I promised them that if they held off, I'd see that you did no harm. That's why I'm here. Give it up, Miss Sharp! Come back to London with me—you'll be safe there, and the Kabale will let it all go."

"You betrayed me to the Kabale," I whispered. "And what about May—did you betray May, too?"

A horrified look. "No, of course not."

He seemed exhausted, all the lines on his face etched deep and tight, adding ten years to his age. I did not think he was lying to me, but I was suddenly unsure. "I mean it, Short. I saw Princess Missy in the street this morning—she means to know who it was. She means to have her revenge—on May—and if I don't do something to stop her—"

"George will protect May," Short cut in. *"You* are coming with me. Pack your valise."

Leave Coburg—miss the meeting of the Kabale tomorrow night—leave May to George's doubtful care? "Not on your life. You can arrest me in two days. Today and tomorrow; that's all I ask."

"Today, Miss Sharp." Short withdrew the handcuffs from his left-hand pocket and advanced upon me. I took one last backwards step and with a sweep of my foot, opened the barrier of salt that contained Vasily.

The vampire stepped out and caught Short by the throat, half lifting the taller man from the floor. Short barely had time to gasp; dropping the handcuffs on the floor, he clawed at the vampire's unbreakable grip. "Miss—Sharp!"

"What's that you say?—Oh." Vasily turned to me in mock seriousness. "He wishes to know if you mean to let me drain him."

"It's daytime," I pointed out, stooping to retrieve the handcuffs, and digging into Short's waistcoat pocket for the key, which was attached to his watch-chain. "You can't bite anyone during the day."

"That is not a *no.*"

"Then how about this: if you so much as scratch him, I'll light you on fire," said I. "Here, bring him over to the stove."

The heavy steel box, mounted upon four tapered feet, was the most likely place to tether a prisoner. Vasily held the indignant policeman down while I cuffed him to the stove. "On the bright side," I told him as I straightened and fastened the key to the watch-chain I wore about my own neck, "at least you'll be warm."

Released from Vasily's crushing grip, Short glared daggers at both of us. "Give it up, Miss Sharp. The Kabale know where to find you, and your best hope is to come with me now."

I recalled May's warning—that the monsters meant to deal with me tonight. "They won't bother us while the sun's up. They'll wait for moonrise, and I'm not afraid of them at moonrise. I have all the salt and silver I need, and friends who will help me."

Friends other than himself, I meant—and that one struck home.

"Vasily Nikolaevitch and Anton Lupei," Short said scornfully, "friends? You know very well neither of them are helping you out of friendship. Lupei means to win back your hand. He'll turn you anarchist if he can—if he hasn't already. And the Grand Duke?" For a long, charged moment both men looked at each other with murderous eyes. "He'll ruin you the moment he gets the chance."

"Oh, yes," Vasily said with a malicious grin, passing an arm around my waist, *"that* is the jealousy talking."

Short actually bared his teeth, for all that I had already shrugged Vasily away. "Unhand the lady, you leech."

"Order me about at your peril, bootheel!"

"With pleasure." Taking a small perfume-bottle from some hidden pocket, Short reached up and sprayed it straight into the vampire's face. There was a strong, flowery scent that I recognised at once. Vasily straightened with a sound of protest, but then collapsed elegantly at my feet as the spray took effect.

Short pocketed the flask with a grim smile. "Laudanum! Marvellous stuff."

Made from concentrated poppy-juice, laudanum could put a vampire to sleep in moments. No doubt the slight dose administered to Vasily would be of short duration. He would be awake soon enough, and in the meantime Short was restrained by his handcuffs; small damage had been done. Confining my remarks to a reproving click of the tongue, therefore, I dragged Vasily's slack body into the ring of salt.

"You had a werewolf sedative, too," I observed, closing the ring with the assistance of a broom. "Do you have any left? Now that you've put the Kabale on my trail, you might at least give me the means to fend them off without killing anyone."

"I should have thought they would teach you that sort of thing at Saint Botolph's," he rejoined.

"Dear me, no! We were given to understand that our own employers would give us all the specialised training we required. The monsters are careful not to let just *anyone* know their Achilles-heel, you know. Imagine the diplomatic uproar in Saint Petersburg, should the English begin teaching vampire weaknesses to people who might very well go to work for the Germans." Putting the broom aside, I turned back to him. "Please," I coaxed. "The silver and wolfsbane are all very well, but you and I both know what damage they might do in careless hands."

Short's mouth lengthened dolefully. "I won't give you the means to dig yourself deeper."

"They *did* give you training, didn't they, when George hired you? But not me, because May is not a monster! I like that!"

Short didn't answer that at once. Instead, he returned to what I had said before his altercation with Vasily. "I thought *we* were friends, Miss Sharp."

Something in his desolate tone pulled at my heart. Ah, there was a part of me that wanted to please him, to leave all this danger behind and go away with him. Once, perhaps, the same impulse to please that had made me conceal the truth from May, might have inclined me to yield to Short. But I was stronger than that, now. I had stood up to Anton and my own parents at Castle Sarkozy. I knew that without honesty, there could be no love of any kind.

I said: "I thought we were friends, too, but then you barged in here and tried to arrest me."

"If I did anything less, would you have heard me?"

"You make a great many assumptions about me," I said coldly. But after a moment I relented, and kneeled down on the floor to face him. "All right; I am listening now. Speak your mind."

"It's as I told you last night," he said in something close to despair. "How can I put it any more clearly than that? Tear down the Kabale, and you'll tear down all the governments of Europe."

"Would that be so terrible? I only want to hold them accountable for their evil deeds. Only darkness is destroyed when you shine a light on it; is that any argument against lighting the lamps? Or did you see *nothing* wrong with the blood feast we witnessed last night?"

"Of *course* I did!" He yanked at his handcuffs, making the stove-pipe rattle. The chain held, however; and he only leaned forward, his eyes blazing in his pale face. "Of *course* I abominate what they do! Can you think me so lost to all right feeling?"

"I don't know," I said with the sense that I was watching

this argument from a very long distance. "I would not have thought so, but neither would I have thought to be arrested by you."

Short fell back against the wall, silent for a moment. "The royalties are monsters," he said flatly, after some time, "and the world is suffering because of them. I thought once that it was only a few bad apples that caused the trouble—but no, these people have turned murder into an institution. Still, what can we do? If we tear them down the world will be consumed in the kind of violence your parents nearly unleashed at Castle Sarkozy. If one must choose between monstrous order and monstrous chaos, it's better to have the order."

"What can you mean, Short? Is order a human life, made in the image of God, and infinitely precious? Is it right to trade lives for such an intangible thing as *order?*"

"When order dies, people die! Ask them in the slums of London. Ask them in the rice paddies of Kashmir. I have been in both places; I know what they would say."

"Perhaps they would. Yet everything you say still amounts to this: it is expedient for us that a few undesirables should die for the people, and not that the whole nation should perish. Does it make the blood feast right, that the privileged are willing to tolerate it for the sake of a little peace and stability?"

"Of course not, but what else can we do?"

"*This,*" I cried, "this: the very thing I am doing now! ...Do you know, Short, you sound exactly like Vasily?"

He scowled. "In what way?"

"None of you believe that a monster will ever be anything but a monster. Anton believes it, so he wants to destroy them all. Vasily believes it, so he considers himself free to do as he likes without fear of consequences. You believe it, so you think it fruitless to challenge them."

"It is better, at any rate, than trying to keep them as pets, and allowing them to take liberties with your person." His lips folded shut for a moment, but then he said in a voice that shook with some repressed emotion: "There is something wrong with you, Miss Sharp. You are drawn to danger. You desire monsters, and it fills me with terror for your safety."

They were hard words to hear, for could I honestly say the monsters held no appeal for me? I remembered how Vasily's proximity affected me last night. "Perhaps I do," I said, trying to keep an answering quiver out of my voice. "But I also truly desire their redemption. And I will not be shamed for that by you or anyone."

"You believe they might change?"

"I know it," I said simply, "because of May."

For an instant he watched me with wide and startled eyes, as though trying to interpret the meaning behind my words. More than that I did not dare to say. Short was my enemy now—he could and would use whatever I said against me.

Then his eyes flickered and narrowed, and he moved. He was only tethered to the stove by his right hand; his left was free, and his lanky frame gave him a formidable reach. It was this hand that shot out and seized the long chain of my watch where it hung around my neck, and dragged me close to him.

His scent of perspiration and pipe-tobacco enfolded me; his face was close to mine, pale and determined, and his brown eyes, ordinarily drooping and sad, had narrowed into something blazing and passionate.

I could not move; indeed I could scarcely breathe. Here was a new side to Short, and it bereft me of motion, breath, and thought. Strangely, although my limbs had turned to water, I do not recall feeling particularly afraid of him. Only—close.

He pulled again at the chain; there was a click as he unlocked the handcuffs. Only then did any kind of coherent thought return to me. Recoiling, I tore the chain from his grasp, plunged my hand into my valise and came up with the small revolver I kept for emergencies. True, it was loaded with silver, but it would still do damage to a policeman. I levelled it at Short's breast even as he advanced upon me with his handcuffs.

Short stopped with the barrel tickling his buttons. For a moment we stood facing each other, quite at an impasse. If he had a firearm of his own, he could not reach it while I held him at gunpoint, and as for me, what could I do? We were friends—once, if not at present. I could never bring myself to shoot him, and if I kept him around much longer he was sure to realise it.

So instead I touched my tongue to my lips and whispered, "I think you had better leave, Short."

At first I thought he meant to be stubborn, but then he backed towards the door, not taking his eyes from my face. "You can't make them change, Miss Sharp," he said as he went. "You are a great many wonderful things, but you are not a miracle-worker.—Good-day."

The door closed behind him; and I waited to listen for his footsteps going away down the stairs before I rushed after him and shot the bolt.

Chapter X.

Anton struck a match, illuminating the interior of the hospital cupboard in which both of us were presently attempting not to smash anything. I sighed as an array of cleaning supplies became visible.

"Explain to me why we're doing this again, Anton."

"Damned if I know," he muttered. *"You* said we must be ready in case the aristo agrees to share her magic blood. *I* wanted to seal our new lodgings with salt before the monsters tracked us there, too."

I sighed, holding my candle to his guttering flame. "And what do you think?—Of May, I mean?"

Anton snorted. "You should find an alternative now and save yourself the trouble. She will never willingly defang the monsters. She spent all afternoon batting her eyes at that stuttering mastiff."

"It's only a pretence," I said, running the candlelight along the shelves in front of me.

Anton gave a derisive snort.

"It's true," I added. "Nothing would suit May better than marriage to George—even she realises that. But she won't do it, because he's a monster."

Anton shrugged. "Every woman likes to be chased a little.

You will see."

I would have disagreed with him, but so many of my judgements had gone wrong in the last twenty-four-odd hours, that a moment of doubt struck me. I had used May to justify myself to Short, arguing that if she could change, anyone could. What if I was wrong? What if May succumbed to George's appeals and her family's insistence?—Or, if I believed her too constant for such weakness, how could I be sure she would give me her blood?

No, no: if I could not depend on May, then I could depend on nothing, and everything I hoped to achieve was meaningless. Still, it was galling to remember how many things had gone wrong today—how, for example, I had congealed into a jelly when Short had made his escape this afternoon. Really! It wasn't as though he was a monster, like Vasily. It wasn't as though I was afraid of him. It wasn't as though I shouldn't have been able to get the better of him, despite his superior height and weight, in any physical confrontation. What was *wrong* with me?

I found I had been staring at the shelves in front of my nose without really seeing them. They were mostly populated with linens, and I turned too quickly to inspect the shelves behind. My skirts flared out as I turned, catching upon a cluster of mops and brooms standing in a corner. Anton reached out with a sound of warning, but I moved quickly, opening my arms to catch the wooden sticks. They fell into my welcoming embrace with a soft clatter, and one of them hit me on the cheekbone. Anton hissed, stiffening into motionless silence. Although we had waited until midnight to begin our raid on the hospital, there was still at least one nurse on duty; possibly a doctor as well.

As we waited on tenterhooks, I realised I had failed to catch the last of the brooms.

It fell last of all, a solid wooden bar that just evaded my outstretched arms. I made a desperate lunge, but only succeeded in knocking a wooden box from its place on the shelf. The next moment the broom fell with a thunderous clatter, and the box followed it with an even louder crash.

Only then did I see what was stencilled in large German lettering upon the side of the box: *Syringes.* Anton swore, but when I picked up one of the cases that had spilled out—about the same size and shape as a case for spectacles—I found the hypodermic intact within, complete with glass tube and two needles.

"I have them," I whispered, pocketing three just in case.—We knew that May's blood would defang a monster that drank it, but from now on the monsters would be more wary of what they imbibed. I hoped that injecting her blood would be simpler and just as effective.

At that moment—much too soon—the door swept open upon us, and we looked up into the face of a formidably starched and bleached matron. For a moment she stood speechless in horror—then she turned away from us, raising her voice to a shout.

"They are here! Quickly!"

I heard from the echoing passage-way the slow tramp of feet—I smelled the rotten stench of long-dead corpses!

"Revenants!" said I, jumping to my feet and seizing my umbrella. "We've outstayed our welcome, I think."

Anton pushed the matron aside and stepped into the passage, drawing his revolver from his pocket. Half a dozen revenant policemen shambled towards us, shrivelled and sticky with decay, a cold spark of blue fire burning in the sockets of their shrunken and missing eyes.

I caught Anton's arm. "Don't shoot; they'll go berserk if we offer the least resistance."

"Elizabeth Sharp. Anton Lupei," droned the foremost of the revenants. "You are under arrest. Come quietly or you will be macerated."

"Macerated? What does that mean?" Anton breathed.

I glanced behind us, where, at the far end of the hallway, was the open window by which we had entered. "Believe me, you don't wish to know."

I tugged Anton by the back of the waistcoat—first one step, then another, nearer the window. He backed away slowly, keeping his revolver trained upon the corpses, reluctant to turn his back upon them.

We were nearly to safety when, without warning, the creatures burst into swift motion.

"*Now!*" I shrieked.

I made two steps of it to the window, dove through the open casement and scrambled to my feet in the cobbled street beyond. Anton tumbled through a moment later, almost landing on my head. I helped him to his feet.

"Run," I gasped, as a revenant followed through the window. "*Run!*"

There was no time to make any sort of plan. We dashed down the street together in the direction of our lodgings and whatever safety they might provide. I had saltwater in my pocket, the flask knocking against my thighs with each step as I ran—but even if I could have stopped to dig it out, would the revenants be troubled by it the way other monsters were?

Anton, less hampered by his clothing, was some steps ahead

of me. I had little warning for what followed. Suddenly there was a scent of perspiration immediately behind me—a panting breath on the back of my neck. I shrieked a warning to Anton just as the creature behind fastened its hand in my hair and hurled me to the ground.

I fell to the cobble-stones, unable to roll away because of the grip in my hair. Its weight descended, pinning me to the ground. Through tears of pain I looked up into glassy eyes carrying the blue revenant spark. We were immediately beneath a street-lamp, and I saw my attacker's face for an instant quite clearly. My stomach did something quite unpleasant as I recognised it as the young lieutenant from the police station yesterday afternoon.

His face was perfectly blank, just like the dead, but I heard his labouring heart beating faster than any human heart should as he reached into his pockets for his handcuffs.

Terror held me immobile. Was this revenant, or mortal? If I attempted to resist, what then?—All revenants were dangerous when crossed, but this one was quicker and stronger than most, since it had outstripped the others in a matter of moments. What destruction might this creature cause, should I trigger its berserk rage?

A shot rang out—then another, and another. My assailant reeled beneath that onslaught. Hot, living blood soaked the revenant's breast, but had I had any doubts of its monstrous nature, they must have disappeared as the creature kept its grip on me. As Anton swooped out of the night to my defence, it merely raised a defensive arm.

"Anton, no!" I shrieked, as the anarchist collided bodily with the revenant.

It grabbed for his throat, but the impetus of his charge

rolled the thing off me and I scrambled to my feet, clutching my umbrella. There came the sound of a heavy blow. Anton grunted and rolled across the street, his revolver clattering across the stones to my feet. The living revenant advanced upon him, handcuffs forgotten. Instead it unhooked the truncheon from its belt and rained down blow after vicious blow.

Anton threw up his hands in a posture of defence, but the maddened revenant took no notice. It only beat him in a murderous rage, each blow eliciting a grunt or cry of agony.

"Anton," I shrieked again. By now the other revenants had closed in about us, a tight, silent ring of uniforms and glittering eyes, rotten flesh and ready truncheons. My hair had come down, getting in my eyes and offering a ready handhold to any of the other policemen who cared to assail me, but they seemed content only to watch while Anton was beaten to death before them.

I had no weapon that could do anything to any of them—nothing but trigger their violence in return.

"Stop it," I screamed, since it was all I could do. "You're going to kill him! For pity's sake!"

"The law knows no pity," said a cold, grey voice.

My heart nearly choked me as I turned and saw—the yellow, sulphurous glow of a werewolf's eyes. The great beast approached on silent, slinking feet, its teeth and eyes reflecting the light of the lamp beneath which Anton was being murdered. More eyes and teeth caught the light behind it. I drew in a quick breath, counting perhaps five distinct wolf-scents.

May's German cousins, determined to have their revenge for last night's defanging! I swallowed hard; and beneath my skirts, I moved my foot until my toe brushed the revolver Anton had dropped.

"Please," I begged. "Call it off. It'll obey *you*."

"Enough, Huber," the great wolf barked. "Stand down. This is *our* business"

Abruptly the beating halted. The revenant stood to attention, stiff as stone. For a moment the only sounds were Anton's ragged, sobbing breaths, and his tentative movements as he pulled himself from the ground.

I dared not take my eyes from the great wolf, which fixed its blazing eyes on me from beyond the silent circle of policemen. "Should have finished *you* in Stuttgart," it growled.

My heart stood still.

Could it be true?—could this be the monster that had given me my scars?

"End it now!" another yelped, crouching to spring.

With a sob, I dropped to the ground and swept Anton's revolver up to point at the great wolf. How many bullets had been used already? I had forgotten to count. Perhaps the gun was empty. Perhaps there was one bullet left.

"Stay where you are," I said sharply to the great wolf. "Otherwise—this is loaded with silver. And it's *you* I'll shoot first."

"Then shoot," the wolf answered, but its hackles were up, and its ears flattened.

"I won't kill anyone if I don't have to. I'm not what they say I am."

With a grunt of pain, Anton rose to his feet. From his voice, I could hear his own teeth were bared. "I *am* everything they say I am."

"Send your corpses away," I told the wolf. "Or, I repeat, it's *you* I'll shoot."

There was a great deal of snarling—the other wolves, little more than shadows in the darkness, had spread out to surround us. But for the present—just for a moment—I had the upper hand of their leader, and royal precedence meant none of them would dare to move without his permission.

Who *was* this wolf?

"Back to the station, Huber," the wolf commanded.

At that the revenants turned and marched away, leaving Anton and myself to face the wolves on our own.

"Now tell your friends to leave," I directed. "But *you* stay. If it's true that we met before in Stuttgart, then you and I have unfinished business to discuss."

Reluctantly, the wolf spoke to its companions—not in human speech, but in growls. In the shadows beyond the lantern-light, black shadows began to slink away; and I felt myself once more mistress of the situation.

"All right: I am going to let you go; but on one condition."

"You presume a great deal, to impose such conditions," said the great wolf, beginning to pace to and fro before me.

"Tell me your name." I think I must have forgotten everything else—Anton, the revenants, the other wolves, the danger that hemmed me in on every side so long as I remained in Coburg. For more than two years I had dreamed of little but this moment. "Tell me if you are the one who attacked me and gave me these scars."

The silence bristled with unsaid things.

"What if it was me?" the wolf demanded. "You ought to thank me. You are a very important person now, Vera Livius—entitled to all sorts of special consideration, to special training, to elevation to the highest circles of society. No,

I think it suits you well to be a victim. Now nothing that happens to you will ever be your fault."

"How *dare* you," I choked. Anton's revolver was slippery in my hands. I tightened my grip, so angry for a moment that I might almost have pulled the trigger. But then a whiff of scent behind us, and the scrabble of claws on stone, warned me a moment too late.

Anton cried out. He must have tried to shield me, for a heavy blow threw him against me. We fell to the cobblestones in a confused tangle of arms and legs. There was a wolf atop us—a wolf that must have been waiting in the shadows for my attention to be distracted. Pain burned down my leg as its hind claws raked me. Its great elongated jaw opened as it fought to get its teeth in Anton's throat.

I couldn't breathe. I couldn't move. Only my right arm was free.

The other wolf yelped, "Take him! Leave her to me!"

They meant to kill Anton, and then me. I had no more contingencies up my sleeve. Only a revolver in my hand, and I didn't even know if it was loaded.

I do not mean to excuse myself. The plain truth is that it was his life or ours. There was no time to think or reason, even if there had been anything but terror in my mind. I reached around Anton and thrust my revolver between those glistening jowls. Hot wet breath enveloped my hand. Then I pulled the trigger and shot the creature through the brain.

The gun's report echoed like a thunderclap through the wet streets, leaving an awful silence in its wake. The great beast collapsed atop Anton; then, slowly, it shrank and shed its fur and became a bleeding, shattered, naked man.

Anton rolled the corpse off us. I got up on my elbow,

sweeping the revolver to cover the great wolf, which cringed as my smoking barrel steadied upon it.

"Did I not warn you?" My voice was faint and muffled in my own ringing ears. "I am no longer the poor defenceless girl you savaged in Stuttgart. Now run, you dog. Run, if you value your miserable life."

It backed away, its eyes glowing with reflected light and impotent rage. I could still smell its fellows further off in the street, slinking through the darkness.

"Run!" I shrieked, my voice thin and hysterical. I got my own revolver out of my pocket, shifted my aim, and pulled the trigger a second time. My bullet struck chips from the cobblestones beneath the great wolf's paws. That broke its resolve. I doubt anyone had dared to shoot at the creature before. Now it turned tail and fled into the night. With a scrabble of paws the others followed.

I climbed to my feet panting and vigilant as a single terrified thought danced its way through my mind.

I had killed a man—a royalty. I had done the very thing I'd promised May and Short and myself never to do.—I had become like my mother.

None of them would ever trust me again.

Anton pried both revolvers from my shaking hands and drew me after him into the shadows. I followed, unresisting. After a moment I remembered an important detail, and soaked our feet in salt water to confound the scent. My hands shook as I tried to replace the stopper on the hip flask. Anton did it for me.

"Ah, Liz!" he whispered, his rough voice softer and more caressing than I'd heard it since he was speaking to Vera Livius at Castle Sarkozy. "Why did you do it, my love?"

I took a deep, shaking breath. "H-he was going to tear out your throat."

His hands tightened on mine as we limped towards our lodgings. "You ought to have let him."

"You don't mean that."

"Tch! Do you think I like being a wanted felon enough to let you become one, too? It's no more than I deserve."

"Don't you dare," I said with a catch in my voice. "I don't give you leave to speak about yourself like that. Besides, it was my life at stake as much as yours. Are you much hurt?"

"A few bruises. I'll feel it tomorrow, but I'll mend."

He pulled me protectively to his side as we reached our new lodgings near the Marktplatz, a narrow tumbledown house for which Vasily had magnanimously allowed me to pawn his pocket-watch. It was larger than our former lodgings, and more private, with room to give Vasily a larger circle of salt in a whole room of his own. Anton stooped to ensure that the barrier of salt we'd found time to scatter across the threshold remained undisturbed. What he saw must have reassured him, for he pushed the door open and helped me over the threshold with a sigh of relief.

In the scantily-furnished front room, Vasily was sitting on a wooden armchair staring hungrily at *The Small House at Allington,* which lay near the wall by the door.

"At last! I thought you would never return. Will you pass me the book, please?"

I stooped to retrieve it, noticing a red scuff upon the wallpaper where a little of the book's dye had come off. It must have been thrown with great force.

"So, you decided to read it, after all. I see you have met John Eames."

"That young man is an *imbecile,* and yet I cannot stop reading."

I could not suppress a shudder as I reached across the salt circle to hand the book back to him, but Vasily accepted it meekly enough. He nodded towards Anton, who in the flaring gaslight was a terrifying sight, bleeding from a burst eyebrow and a scratched breast, tenderly cradling his bruised forearms. "The peasant looks dreadful. Will you desire him to remove himself? He is spoiling the view."

Anton turned to me. "Liz, we should go at once. It is no longer safe here—"

"Something the matter?" Vasily raised an eyebrow.

With a growl, Anton advanced upon the vampire. "We were ambushed by werewolves. I don't suppose you happen to know anything about that, hmm?"

"And what if I did?" Vasily said provokingly.

With a growl, Anton jabbed towards Vasily's midsection, crossing the salt into his prison. Unholy glee lit in the vampire's eyes. Moving quicker than thought, he seized Anton's wrist and twisted it so that the anarchist landed on his knees with a whine of pain.

Vasily bent over him murmuring, "Shall I twist this just a *little* harder? Shall I take it off altogether?"

"Stop it, both of you," I snapped, although my heart was in my throat again as I recalled the inexorable strength of those hands. "The last thing I need right now is either of you being put out of commission. *Vasily!*"

The vampire hissed and shoved Anton out of the circle again, scattering the salt.

"Liz—I swear to you…" Anton began, breathing hard, and levelling a finger at Vasily.

"I don't want to hear it," I said. "Those werewolves must have scented us somewhere in the town; do you imagine they came in here to have tea with Vasily? I would have smelled them all over the house."

Anton got up with a snarl and swept the salt back into its ring surrounding Vasily. "Very well," he growled, "but I tell you it is not safe. I stay here tonight, and we will leave at sunrise."

"Again?" I said wearily. "I had terrible trouble finding this house, and it cost a pretty penny. And now you want me to find another?"

"No, no, no!" Anton threw his hands in the air; the broom fell with a clatter, making me jump. "Not in Coburg! You must *go*, Liz! Whatever you are trying to do here—"

"Not you too, Anton."

I think that got through to him, for his shoulders slumped and for a moment he stood with head bowed, running his hands through his hair.

"They will kill you," he said at length.

"They have been trying to kill me all day. It is only another twenty-four hours until Vasily takes me in to see the Kabale myself, and after that we can go where we please."

Anton let out a gusty sigh, but then his eyes narrowed at the vampire in the salt circle. "You, bloodsucker."

"Peasant?"

"You will take her where she can spy on the Kabale?"

"Of course. I have a stake in this too, you know."

"Well, you had best guard her well," Anton growled, "because otherwise, *I* will have a stake in you."

Chapter XI.

The remainder of the night was undisturbed by monsters, although I wished I could tell whether this was because they had lost our trail or were simply too frightened to expose themselves to further danger. It was wretched to think that perhaps I had justified them in their fear of me—that I had become a monster myself!—I was no pacifist; I believed I had a right to defend myself and others against murderers however princely—but I could not help feeling that I had put myself beyond the pale of society, by choosing to exercise that right.

More than that: I wanted a better and more lasting victory, than one of mere brute force. I wanted, not to destroy my enemies, but to persuade them—and I could not help grieving for the creature I had slain.

I slept fitfully and woke early, whereupon I swathed my face in a thick veil and ventured out to keep watch upon the tenement which had been our first base of operations.

I concealed myself in a nook of someone's front garden, where I had not long to wait. In the grey half-light between dawn and sunrise, there came a sound of tramping feet as a band of revenant policemen converged upon the tenement. At their head, looking rather grim and worried, was Short himself.

It made me feel a little ill to see him in the company of revenants. I dared not move as they passed my hiding-place—I hardly dared to breathe until they vanished within the tenement.

Surely they had been sent to arrest me for the killing of the werewolf last night. As far as the Kabale was concerned, I had sealed my own fate. But what about Short? How could I bear it if Short thought ill of me?—But I *must* bear it. I remembered Castle Sarkozy, and all I had learned there. I could not yield what I felt to be right, merely because it meant opposing someone I liked.

Every minute the light was getting stronger—a lovely clear sunrise, heralding a warm and bright day. I had already put myself in enough danger by coming here and lurking in a garden. Having climbed the wall again, I stood in the street shaking my skirts to remove a few wisps of straw that clung to them.

I should go away, but I found I could not. I wanted to see Short's face when he emerged from the house having found his birds flown.

I walked slowly up the street and then down again. On my second lap, I passed Short and his revenants as they emerged from the tenement and turned back in the direction of the police station. From the opposite side of the street, I risked raising my veil as Short passed. He did not look my way, but I could no longer see the lines so deeply etched at the corners of his mouth.

Then I knew that there was a part of Short, no matter how much he might deny it, that felt pleased at my escape.

I started back to our lodgings feeling a very little better, and able to think on other things. I had been correct in my guess after all, and the monster that scarred me was in Coburg. I knew at once what I meant to do to him: he must be defanged if I could manage it, and exposed at the least. But in order to do so, I must either catch him in his wolf form, or convince someone else to discover his name.

I returned to the house to find Vasily still reading in the front room, cursing John Eames under his breath. Anton had returned to the palace to take up his duties as May's body-guard, leaving me to lay my plans for tonight. This required a conference with Vasily, followed by the construction of a shopping-list, which I wrote sitting in the window of an upper room that looked down upon the narrow street leading to the marketplace.

Happily I was still in the possession of my valise, which included a red evening frock which May had given me, since it was a colour she never wore.—The discrepancy between May's taste and that of her mother had endowed me with a varied and colourful wardrobe. The dress was as usual somewhat snug around the waist and loose at the bust, but I was a skilled needlewoman, and a few tucks here, and the letting-out of a seam or two there, quickly rendered the gown wearable.

I was lost in my work when a flash of rich colour drew my attention to the street below, and I looked down to see a lady in a plum-red coat among the passers-by. A strand of hair escaping from beneath her hat and veil was the colour of red gold, and at the sight of it my heart stood quite still.

What was *Missy* doing here?

It was now about ten o'clock in the morning. The sun was well up, and the town was astir. Hastily pinning on my hat and veil, I went downstairs and opened the front door just wide enough to admit my nose. Missy turned a corner and disappeared from view, whereupon I hastened out on her trail, following the distinctive scent of musky roses towards the palace. Here, instead of entering the building, the scent led towards the great Schlossplatz before it, where a green park led uphill towards the castle. The square and park were both sunny and warm, and between the palace and the Neoclassical façade of the great Landestheatre there marched a neat row of shops that included a café. Brightly-coloured sun-shades had bloomed on the pavement outside, and what appeared to be the upper-crust of Continental society was seated beneath them having breakfast or taking tea.

Missy sat alone at a table for two, and I almost laughed aloud when I saw that her attention was fixed upon the very elegant-looking couple at a neighbouring table—George and May.

May's black mourning-dress drew the eye all the more surely by contrast with the pale, sun-washed stone and vivid grass of the Schlossplatz. She and George seemed deep in conversation, as oblivious to Missy's scrutiny as they were to Short and a somewhat battered Anton, who watched from another table at a discreet distance.

Seating myself immediately behind Missy's back but facing the feigned lovers, I unfurled a newspaper to conceal myself from Short. I never could resist eavesdropping upon May and George.

"Say you like it?" George urged, gruffly shy.

He was speaking of a jeweller's box he had slid across the table to May, and she had turned faintly pink. I bit an anxious lip. Some girls merely like jewels, while others would strangle a beloved grandmother for them. After four months' acquaintance, I had concluded that May was very nearly the latter.

"Oh," she said, and I could hear the wistful longing in her voice. "I couldn't possibly—"

"Nonsense! Who am I to shower with jewels, if not my promised wife?"

To my left, Missy's teacup clattered as though she had nearly dropped it upon the saucer.

"But it's so *conspicuous,*" May murmured. All the same, she did not resist as George slid a sparkling ring onto her hand. Catching a glimpse of the gem, I suffered a moment's shortness of breath. May was in danger!

Then again, perhaps George was only behaving as he should. A jewel so extravagant made sense only if a serious understanding was in place between the two of them. Its very size made it the sort of protection May desperately needed.

"I couldn't possibly," she said. Evidently, despite her lust for diamonds, she could not quite bring herself to accept such a gift when the engagement was purely illusory.

"Bah," George said earnestly. "You ought to see some of Grandmamma's collection. It will all be yours one day."

"George! As though I would marry you for the jewels!"

"Can't be for my brains, what?"

"*George!*"

To both our surprise, he burst out in guffaws of laugher. "Ha! ha! Had you there, by Jove! Ought to have seen the look on your face!"

"Oh," May said, fluttering between laughter and wrath. "You *beast!*"

She said the word in fun, but it wiped the laughter from his lips—and that must have recalled May to the reality of their position as well, for she fell silent and glanced self-consciously around the café. I dove behind my paper, but it wasn't me May's gaze fell upon: it was the rigidly attentive Missy.

May turned back to George and leaned forward with both her elbows on the table. Her voice changed, becoming low and—dare I say it—alluring. "For such a thoughtful gift, surely I ought to give you *something* in exchange. Go on, name your reward."

It was George's turn to blush. For a moment it seemed as though he could not get any words out. Then he cleared his throat and said, "A lock of your hair?"

A lock of her hair!—to remember her by, no doubt, when the present masquerade was done!—I sighed. I could not quite help liking George.

"Please," he added in a whisper.

May twined a loose curl around her finger. There was a light gleaming in the depths of her eyes, and an odd tug at the corner of her mouth.

"Why not a kiss?"

Missy bent her teaspoon in half as easily as though it had been a daisy's stem.

"By Jove," George stammered.

Sweetly malicious, May leaned a little nearer to him and murmured:

"Who am I to shower with kisses, if not my promised husband?—After all, they will all be yours someday."

Oh, the saucy thing! what a wild morning she *was* having, to be sure!

George turned scarlet and seemed to have lost all capacity for thought or speech. The reader knows with what ambivalence I regarded George; but hang it! it would have been sheer cruelty to let her go on tormenting him like that. I was extraordinarily tempted to get up and stage an intervention, but before I could do so, Anton stepped in.

He got up from the table where he and Short had to all appearances been studiously ignoring each other, and limped straight up to Missy.

"What are *you* looking at?" he asked truculently.

The princess startled, affronted. "I *beg* your pardon!"

If Missy thought she was going to intimidate Anton, she was quite mistaken. He spoke impassively, but I could tell he was enjoying himself. "I'm *her* bodyguard, and I don't like the way you've been staring."

"Well, I never! Do you have any idea who I am?"

"No, and I don't care to know. I'm an honest working man. I'm only here to make sure no one gives *her* the stink-eye, so you might want to move yourself along before I do it for you."

George swivelled around in his chair and seemed to catch sight of his former love for the very first time. His jaw dropped open. "Hang it, Lupei! That's the Crown Princess of Roumania! I say, Missy, I can't *think* what might have…"

His voice trailed away as he noticed the teaspoon tied into knots, and the china broken up into tiny pieces on Missy's table.

Seeing the direction of his gaze, Missy blushed brightly, but then rose to her feet with an assumption of dignity. "Don't bother, George. I was just leaving, anyway. It is very dull to dine alone, but that's marriage for you—as I'm sure you'll learn yourself, in time."

It was a feeble blow, but it discomfited George. Poor Missy! For a moment, as we all watched her retreat towards the palace, I even felt sorry for her.

As he went back to join Short at their table—the inspector had covered his mouth with his hand, and seemed quite mortified—Anton caught my eye and sent me a conspiratorial wink.

Ah, he *was* enjoying himself. Besides which, he'd sent Missy packing and left the coast clear for me to speak to May.

Getting to my feet, I brushed past May in the direction of the café's interior. As I passed, I slipped a small item upon her table—the silver brooch, in the shape of a crescent moon, that Sal Tanner had left me before she died. I was in the café's ladies' room, dabbing at an illusory stain on my black dress, when May followed me.

"Oh, Sharp!"

To my surprise she seized me by the arm, pushing back my veil to peer into my face. "Sharp! Is something the matter?—are you hurt?"

"I'm perfectly well, thank-you," said I with a laugh. "Only I wanted to speak to you and satisfy myself all was well. And here I find you tormenting poor George like the very dickens!"

May glanced at the great sparkling diamond on her finger. "It serves him right for tempting me with such pretty things, when he knows very well I can't refuse them!"

"Monster or not, you must not find him so very repellant if you were willing to kiss him."

"Speak one more word, I dare you," May said, drawing herself up to her full height; "and I'll—I'll—Oh, Sharp! I heard such dreadful things of you this morning. They say you killed Prince Chlodwig of Lippe!"

I couldn't meet her eyes.

"Please, Sharp. Tell me it isn't true," she cried, seizing my hand. "Lupei would say nothing without your leave, and I feared—"

"I'm afraid it's quite true," I confessed before she could go any further. "Five of them ambushed us last night. It was a matter of life and death, and I—I had no other way to stop them."

"Oh," May whispered, letting go of me. "Oh, *dear.*"

"I'm so sorry, May! Anton was right; I ought to have sacrificed him." I took a deep breath, swallowing the lump in my throat. "Are you going to turn me in?"

"Oh, Sharp, *no,*" she said very gently. "I know what it's like to kill someone when you never meant to. If you say it was a matter of life and death, I believe you."

"If it had been a vampire, I might have done something with saltwater or laudanum; but for a werewolf there is only silver or—"

"Wolfsbane," she finished, with a sad smile, "I know."

She held out Sal's silver pin, and I replaced it at the throat of my dress.

"There is one thing I have learned, at any rate. The beast who gave me my scars was there last night." In a few words, I summed up the night's events and revelations. "May, have you any idea who it might have been? I thought, since the attack occurred in Stuttgart…"

"—That it may have been one of my Württemberg cousins?" May added with great composure. "Honestly, I haven't the faintest notion. I will make inquiries if you like, but I am afraid that apart from George, almost everyone seems to have sent me to Coventry."

If May was being ostracised by the other monsters, then surely they must suspect! "Hang it, May, I wish you were safely out of this. Was Anton recognised from last night, do you think?"

"Not that I've heard; but…" Her voice trailed away. At length she sighed. "George and Short are in league with the Kabale, you know."

I nodded. "Short told me in person."

She darted a shrewd glance at me, but did not otherwise respond. "Both of them have urged me to dismiss Lupei and find another bodyguard. I don't think the Kabale knows my new bodyguard is in league with you—if he keeps throwing his weight around like he did just now they will soon guess—but in any case George and Short know, and…"

And if they became any more desperate to stop me, they might arrest Anton, or betray him to the Kabale. Moreover, they might easily put two and two together and realise he must have been my companion of the previous night. I told myself I was playing a dangerous game, that I ought not to risk Anton's life by trusting in men I now knew would ally themselves with monsters and revenants; yet somehow I still could not bring myself to think of either Short or George as enemies.

"Forgive me, May. I've put you in an untenable position, I know."

"If I asked George, I'm sure he'd manage to have a plainclothes-man reassigned to guard me."

"It won't go on much longer."

"But why must it be Anton?"

"Because he is the only one I can trust. We cannot turn to the police—not even the human sort." Not even Short, I thought with a pang. "They're all tools of the monsters, and it's the monsters you need protection from. George is all very well, but you said yourself he won't stand up to his family for you, and neither will a policeman. You *must* have at least one guard who will defend you for your own sake; and if not Anton, then someone else."

She sighed. "I understand; but it seems very dangerous for both of us."

I hesitated—then took the plunge. "There is another reason. I wanted Anton to know you the way I do. You know how savage and bitter he can be. If he is ever to be a happy and productive member of society, I think he must be shown that even in palaces there are men and women of principle who refuse to become monsters."

"Oh," she said meditatively. "I did not think of that. I beg your pardon, Sharp. In that case I will do my best."

"Well, you'll need to be quick about it," said I, attempting a smile, "for tonight Vasily and I have a meeting to attend; and tomorrow I shall be leaving Coburg, and likely taking Anton with me."

I paused. The problem of how to protect May should Anton be forced to leave Coburg tomorrow had occupied me with little hope of resolution for much of the past couple of days. If only I could trust George or Short! In desperation, I considered the possibility of asking Vasily to do the job—but no, I trusted him even less than I did Anton or Short.

It was at this juncture that the door opened like a pop-gun and we found ourselves face-to-face once more with—Missy of Roumania.

Dash it! She must have doubled back to the café, evading Anton's notice along the way.

May was the first to speak, in a nasal drawl that betrayed how excessively she disliked the other princess. "Dear me, Missy! you again?"

Missy let out a soft, slow sigh of triumph, but her eyes were murderous.

"So I was right," she breathed. "The two of you *are* working together...and *you* are the one who ruined my sister."

Her gaze fixed on May. I reached into my pocket, fumbling for saltwater; but May spoke before I could intervene.

"I told you myself I was no criminal. If anyone had believed me, Ducky would be none the worse off today. Now if you'll excuse me, I believe you are in my way."

Missy seized May by the arm as she passed. "You think George will protect you? You are wrong. No matter what he sees in you, he'll never defy his family for you. In another few years, he'll be on the Kabale himself, and you..."

She gave a hard, sharp little laugh.

"*You,* poor little May of Teck, will be a headstone in a Coburg cemetery."

Chapter XII.

With such breathings-out of threats and murder, Missy departed. I bade May a hasty farewell, warned her to remain safe, and exited the café by the rear before retreating to the safety of our new lodgings to complete my preparations for the evening.

I worked feverishly, wrapped in desperate cogitation. With Prince Chlodwig's death, my position in Coburg had become completely untenable—perhaps in Europe. Yet the thought of leaving the principality had only become more unbearable with this morning's events.—May was in terrible danger. Now that Missy had guessed at her role in the events of two nights ago, only George's protection now lay between her and death, or whatever other penalty the Kabale might have in store for her. As for Missy's other threats, I knew I would lie awake worrying about them. George loved May sincerely, I knew; but was that love enough to counterbalance his family's influence? His attempt to intercede on my behalf two days ago after the explosion at the train station had ended with me in gaol awaiting trial. Before the formidable combined authority of his grandmother and father, he had folded like a damp newspaper.

I bore him no ill-will. Prince George was one of whom

I expected no heroics; but the truth was that May needed someone to shield her against the most powerful people in the world, and not even I had the ability to do so.

I laid down my needle and arched my back in a stretch, meditating bitterly upon the irony. All this time I had been afraid that May would abandon me, and she had stuck by me, as true as steel. Now she herself was in danger, and I realised I ought to have been worrying about George instead.

Not a comforting thought; and oh, the dickens! how could I leave her alone in Coburg? or what could I do to help her if I stayed?

I still had no solution to the question when some hours later, Vasily and I set out on our mission. The Kabale was to meet, as I had already deduced they did on that memorable evening two nights previous, in the great hilltop castle that loomed above Coburg in frowning medieval splendour. As our hired carriage rolled through the Schlossplatz and into the large park separating the castle from the town, we joined a procession of carriages bearing coats-of-arms famous across the world.

I had purchased us new masks, and now fitted mine over my plainly coiffured hair, which I had adorned with a few paste jewels and a nodding black feather. Sal's crescent-moon brooch adorned the black ribbon about my neck, but May's unwanted red gown, with its black lace and jet beads, provided the necessary glitter of luxury. I flattered myself I looked sufficiently extravagant not to be immediately recognisable as the interloper at the blood feast. As for my scent, I had bathed in saltwater and applied a strong perfume, and must pray that I did not run across anyone who knew me well enough to recognise it anyway.

As I smoothed the black lace mask over my face, I caught a glow of red eyes and felt Vasily watching me attentively from his seat opposite.

Trying not to feel like a small rabbit pinned by the gaze of a hawk, I touched the tip of my tongue to my lips. "How do I look?"

He smiled, a hint of sharp fang showing between his lips. "Good enough to eat."

"I can push you out a window again," I threatened. My heart was fluttering again, keying me up to a great nervous pitch. I knew he could hear it, but I kept up the pretence of calm all the same. "I take it this means I pass muster."

"You make a better princess than dainty." There was a strange ring in his voice; like sincerity, if I had not known better.

Was I only imagining it, or had something in Vasily's manner towards me really changed, these past two days? He no longer seemed to be playing a game of seduction: could it be that he had taken my words to heart, or had he simply gained what he wanted—my help—and decided he had no further use for me?

Our masks prevented our being recognised, and Vasily's red eyes and fangs, together with the borrowed name of one of his innumerable cousins, gained us admittance to the castle when we were stopped on the bridge that crossed the moat to the gatehouse.—Oh yes, it was a *real* castle, built for effect, not for show, and a formidable stronghold, even in the modern age. We passed through the imposing gatehouse in the first ring of walls, then through the tunnel-like gate in the second, emerging at last in the lower courtyard. Flaming torches lit the space much as they must have done in the days when

Martin Luther flung his inkwell into the Devil's face, in one of the rooms in the tall plaster-and-lath buildings that loomed over us. I wondered if the prince in those days had been a wolf. Perhaps there might be a grain of truth in the legend of the inkwell, after all.

Vasily stepped down from the coach with a sweep of his long black cloak and reached up to help me down. He led me into the building on our left, and as our footsteps echoed across the parqueted floor in the richly-furnished vestibule, I thought I recognised the acoustics from two nights ago. Not that conditions were quite the same, for we were now surrounded by royalties—some like ourselves masked in an attempt at incognito—who helped themselves of glasses of champagne from passing trays and murmured among themselves in a funereal manner. My mouth went dry as I noticed that some of them now wore mourning, no doubt for the unfortunate Prince Chlodwig.

I felt half suffocated among so many monsters. Much to my surprise, I found myself pressing closer to Vasily's side, my heart beating erratically at the thought of what might happen if my mask was for any reason removed.

Vasily pressed my arm in a way that was no doubt intended to be comforting, but it only wound my nerves tighter. For an instant memory assailed me: I felt his mouth against my skin, his arms crushing me against him in the dungeon of Castle Sarkozy. I found myself putting up a hand to cover up the bite-marks in my neck. Vasily had convinced me to leave the scars visible tonight—if anyone asked, I was a high-born dainty, and my enemies were looking for a werewolf victim, not vampire bait. All the same I felt exposed—vulnerable—naked.

Massive double doors barred us from going any further.

I caught a glimpse of the Prince of Wales' coffee-pot figure ahead of us being ushered through them—and was that *George* beside him?—or was it the tsarevitch, Nicky?—but Vasily steered me after the majority of the crowd, climbing one of the double stairs to either side of the room. These led us to a gallery overlooking a hall, where a crowd of spectators were taking their seats. Vasily drew me aside into the shadows by the door at the back of the gallery, where we might hopefully make our escape if necessary; but still we had an excellent view of the long table dominating the room's centre, where a selection of princes were taking their seats, somewhat varied as to things like height, mustaches, and medals; but otherwise they were rather a homogenous group.

The Kabale! My heart quickened again, this time with excitement. The Prince of Wales I knew was a member—but I had never imagined that Missy of Roumania would be the sole woman there, nor for that matter had I expected Nicky of Russia. I did not recognise the others, but I counted them and studied their faces, wishing I had dared to bring May with me. Not only would she remember each face, but she would be able to draw each of them in detail later on.

As the gathering fell silent, a voice announced, "The quota is full. Seal the room."

"Seal the room!" a voice cried at the threshold; and the doors slammed. The Kabale took its seats and began to conduct its business—which it did in barely-audible undertones. As someone was asked to read minutes, I tugged at Vasily's sleeve.

"Will you tell me who these people are?"

He lifted a long-suffering eyebrow. "I was happy enough to do that two days ago, Miss Sharp."

"Perhaps; but this way it's harder for you to lie to me."

Behind his mask, it was impossible to see his expression. "I don't suppose it ever occurred to you that I might wish to tell you the truth."

"It did, naturally." I fished a piece of notepaper and a pencil stub from their hiding-place in my corset. "Hope for the best and prepare for the worst; that's my motto. Now, I recognise Uncle Bertie; who's the bloke to his left?"

Vasily emitted a gentle sigh. "They are mostly the heirs of Europe," he explained. As he listed their names, I jotted them down, together with a brief description, thus—*Crown Prince of Germany—tall, beaky,* or *Crown Prince of Greece—high forehead, may put out an eye with that moustache someday.*

I wondered if one of them could be the great wolf I had confronted last night—the one who had attacked me in Stuttgart two years ago. The chances were good he was somewhere in this very room; but how could I tell which?

"Now," said the German Crown Prince—who was acting as the meeting's chairman—"in the matter of the anarchist, Elizabeth Sharp."

Thus neatly did the Kabale label and package me for disposal.

There was a throat-clearing, and the Prince of Wales stood ponderously. "Recent events have proven that Miss Sharp will not hesitate to use violence against her betters. Since it is too dangerous to deal with her ourselves, and since she has so far evaded the police, I move that a price of one thousand pounds sterling be placed on her head."

"With respect, Uncle Bertie, I don't think we need give up quite yet." Missy now flashed the red eyes and elongated fangs of a vampire as she spoke. "It may interest you to know, gentlemen, that I am in possession of information which I think will shortly lead to Miss Sharp's arrest."

My apprehension turned to suffocating dread as I recalled the most injurious piece of information Missy held.—*May!* Was Missy about to expose my mistress before the Kabale?

"What information might this be?" someone asked in a haughty drawl.

"It's true that Miss Sharp fled her lodgings last night or early this morning," Missy said with a sharp-edged smile. "But she is in Coburg still. I spoke to her myself this morning."

There was a mild sensation; hands fluttered and voices murmured in ears, not just downstairs around the table, but also throughout the assembled onlookers in the gallery. As for me, my relief made me feel a little light-headed. Why was Missy not implicating May?—or had I simply not listened long enough?

Vasily's hand was on my arm, his voice in my ear. "Time we were gone, I think."

"No," I whispered, "I must hear more."

"You *spoke* to Miss Sharp this morning?" the German prince demanded, "and you failed to tell us? Your Highness, need I remind you that as a female, you appear at this board only by sufferance?"

"Perhaps one day I may be permitted to forget it." Swallowing her flash of temper, Missy smiled and went on. "Miss Sharp has committed a terrible wrong against my beloved sister. Ducky ought to be spending this week like any bride: basking in the love of her family and betrothed, accepting the good wishes of her subjects, and making her first kills. Instead she and Ernest both mourn the loss of their heritage and of the unfortunate Prince Chlodwig. Gentlemen of the Kabale, I claim the right to bring Elizabeth Sharp to justice myself. Give me two days, and I will present you with her bloodless corpse."

The cool confidence with which she spoke ran over my body like ice-water. So, Missy intended to keep May's involvement a secret, but only because she wanted to drain me herself. A cheerful proposition, I must say!

"Permission to address the table!" It was a familiar voice—booming, strident—and it came from a masked gentleman in the gallery opposite. I had to wonder why he bothered with the mask; no one who knew George could have mistaken his voice.

The chairman waved in assent, and George snatched off his mask. "Strongly object to my cousin's request, by Jove!" he said in a voice jerky with embarrassment. "Not cricket, what! Not a personal vendetta. Ought to be a matter of justice. Trial by jury, and—and all that."

His suggestion was met with all the enthusiasm of a mouldy tea-cake in my lady's drawing-room.

"Miss Sharp forfeited her right to a trial when she murdered a royalty."

"Doesn't seem right, that's all," George pled, which was very sweet of him. "Bound to argue self-defence if you gave her the chance—and who's to say she wasn't right? Not saying I think she *was,* mind you! But demmit, shouldn't she have the chance to prove it?"

"We have no such custom," the chairman said, with frozen disdain. "If commoners *will* kill and maim royalties, they must be prepared to suffer the ancient penalty."

George's jaw bulged. "Whose ancient penalty do *you* mean, Willie? The English Crown rules in partnership with a House of Lords that once forced the Crown to sign the Magna Carta, and with a House of Commons that once cut off the very head that wore the Crown, demme! Don't see what is so very dreadful in Miss Sharp's merely defanging those heads, and it's quite in the ancient English custom, if not yours!"

Really, if George had tossed one of Anton's bombs into the centre of the room at the close of this remarkable speech, he could not possibly have caused a greater sensation. I clapped a hand to my mouth, but my muffled shriek of delight went unheard amidst the uproar that suddenly swallowed the room. Chairman Willie leaped to his feet. "Your effeminate English customs are next door to *democracy!* Imperial Prussia will never stoop so low!"

Beside me, even Vasily chuckled. His breath was cold on my cheek. "I told you they were ready to tear each other's throats."

"Hang it, George," the Prince of Wales bellowed before his offspring could say anything else. "To think I should live to hear my own son excuse the murderers of the sainted Charles!"

George paled, evidently appalled by his own temerity. "Not at all, sir, but the British Constitution—"

"Hang the British Constitution," Uncle Bertie burst out, "and sit down and shut up before you embarrass yourself any further!"

"Do as he says, George," said Missy with a thin smile. "You'll get the rest of us English in trouble, which might be very embarrassing for *one* of us, at least."

Evidently this was a veiled allusion to May herself; but the threat was wasted on George. At his father's command he had already collapsed into his seat; and now he slunk behind his mask and relapsed into silence. Poor George! I could never have imagined him defying the Kabale like that, but the attempt had evidently wrung him out, and I wondered how long it might be before he would pluck up the courage to try again. Alas—it seemed that Missy was to be proven correct.

The golden-haired crown princess now leaned forward in her chair. "Well, gentlemen? Have I your permission to track down and drain the anarchist myself?"

Despite some dissent—it seemed that the German princes felt peculiarly averse to entrusting a female with such a delicate task—the motion was carried. After that it seemed that the question of Miss Sharp was shelved, and the Kabale moved to other business. Thinking it was time to make our departure, I went to pull on Vasily's sleeve, but my attention was arrested when Chairman Willie announced:

"Now, in the matter of the living revenants…"

"We should leave," Vasily breathed, but I held up a hand.

Another of the Kabale climbed to his feet, clearing his throat—the heir to Coburg, Ducky's brother, Prince Alfred. "Gentlemen—and lady—the proposed experiment has now been carried out upon Lieutenant Huber, a brave young man in our police force. I can confirm that the thing went off without a hitch. The result was an unliving revenant of far greater intelligence, speed, and effectiveness than the dead sort. I can confirm that the subject's existing psyche and personality did not constitute a barrier to his effectiveness. Orders were obeyed promptly and without question." He cleared his throat. "Of course, in the commission of his duties, Huber was shot multiple times in the torso and is now subject to the same rate of decay as undead revenants. A wreath and a posthumous medal has accordingly been forwarded to his next of kin."

"Ah, I knew it!" I hissed, causing Vasily to seize my arm in a warning grasp. Huber *was* a revenant—converted without the preliminary step of death. But now—the true horror of this discovery struck me for the first time. If the Kabale could convert even living men and women into mindless berserkers, revenants had now become far more easily accessible, to say nothing of longer-lived.

"If Huber is now subject to the same limitations as other revenants—is, in fact, dead," someone put in, "then how much have we really gained?"

"Time, your grace," the prince replied. "An unliving revenant, so long as he is not mortally injured, may remain effective for not less than the duration of a natural human lifespan. Imagine a totally compliant army or police force, ready at any moment to be deployed to battle, with no risk of premature decomposition. Or consider our recent troubles with Saint Botolph's and *Akbar* inmates. Clearly our training regimen has not been as effective as might be desired. Convert the present inmates to unliving revenants, and we shall have no more troubles of the sort we have had with Elizabeth Sharp."

Most of the Kabale seemed in favour of the idea. The only debate was between those who were ready to adopt a motion at once, and those who asked to witness the conversion of a living person to a revenant first, to satisfy themselves that the process was safe and could be reliably duplicated.

As for me, I could scarcely breathe. Reluctant as I am to admit unwomanly weakness, I felt that I was about to suffocate, or faint. The Kabale had already deprived us of home, family, and social standing; and now they planned, with all the composure in the world, to deprive us of our free will.

Below, a resolution must have been taken, for the Kabale had now begun to discuss whether it was appropriate for Grand Duke Ernest of Hesse to retain his dukedom now that he had been defanged, and the Prince of Wales was making a long and prosy speech about the importance of setting the correct precedent.

I gasped for air. I had thought that the monsters had taken everything from us. How foolish I had been! They meant to go further, and take away our minds.—"Oh, God," I murmured. In that moment, I felt that there must be a higher power to hear me, for otherwise I lived in a world gone mad! It was a comfort to hope that whether I succeeded or failed, these people would face justice in another world, if not our own.

"*Now* shall we leave?"

At Vasily's voice in my ear, I started. His hands hovered at my elbows as though he meant to support me, but was not sure of his welcome. His proximity was too much.

"Give me a moment," I murmured. "I need air."

Pushing the door open, I staggered out of the gallery into the passage that ran the length of the building from the stairs up which we had come. It was cooler here, and I drew in a grateful breath. With it came a familiar scent: fresh soap, tobacco-smoke, and a hint of masculine perspiration.

Behind it: rotting flesh.

"Good evening, Miss Sharp," said the grave, pleasant voice of Inspector Short.

I turned with a gasp. Short had been leaning against the wall beside the door through which I had just now come. Three revenants blocked the stairs to my left; three more were ranged across the passageway to my right.

"Short," I breathed. I was trapped, and I did not even have Vasily to rescue me. If I called for help it would only attract the attention of the monsters in the gallery.

Short threaded a proprietary arm through my elbow. "Best you come quietly."

"It's a fair cop," I said, resigning myself. I was fairly caught. Escape would have to come later. At least I had my lock-picks with me.

"This isn't an arrest, Miss Sharp," he said, signalling his revenants to follow, and hurrying me down the passage leading deeper into the castle.

"Where are we going, then?"

"Away from here, as quickly as we can."

I could have laughed. "You needn't have gone to all this trouble, Short! Vasily and I were about to leave, ourselves. And speaking of Vasily—" I dug in my heels, employing my considerable strength to force Short to a halt. "If this is no arrest, then I think I will go back and ask him to accompany us."

Short turned to face me, his lips pale and thin. "No, don't. I don't think he would care to join us."

"What, do you mean to say he's on *their* side?" I injected a little acid into my tones.

"No, I mean he would not wish to go where we are going."

I looked him up and down. Short was coiled like a spring, pale to the tip of his nose and looking as determined as I had ever seen him: ready for some battle I only dimly sensed was coming. With a sigh, I twisted my elbow from his grasp. He let me go, but his eyes remained fixed on me with watchful resolve.

"All right. Just *where* were you planning to take me, Short?"

"You killed someone last night."

"Not by malice aforethought, I assure you."

"I know." He took a deep breath. "But you must leave Coburg now, before anyone else dies."

"By which, I presume, you mean another blood feast?"

His throat worked as he swallowed. "That's *their* business," he said, pointing in the direction of the Kabale. "You are mine. I'm taking you to Australia, and if you have an ounce of sense you'll come quietly, before you get yourself killed—or start a war."

I felt scarcely able to believe—even now, even surrounded by his revenants—how serious he was. This man had been my friend; but now he meant to stop me, and he would not take *no* for an answer.

And then his face softened. "Please, Miss Sharp. Don't look at me like that."

He reached out, the tips of his fingers skimming gently across my hair. My breath was suddenly uneven. All else disappeared: there was no one in the world but Short and myself and that soft, gentle point of connection.

I realised what he was doing a moment too late, when he took the first of my lockpicks from my hair.

"Short," I protested, but it was only in a whisper. Some enchantment was upon me. I could not have moved if I tried.

His fingers brushed through the black waves of my hair, finding and claiming the last of my hairpins. My dark hair slipped down my neck, uncoiling from its knot. How shall I describe the sensations his touch awoke? In Vasily's hands I had been a nerve stripped raw. In Short's hands I was a stream of sweet and flowing water.

It struck me that it had never been desire I felt for Vasily, after all. *That* was only ever fear, but this—ah, this was something far more potent.

He released me, breaking that strange enchantment.

"Let us talk this over." The words rang tinny and false in my own ears. We had spoken yesterday, and what good had it done? "But not here. Let me go back for Vasily, and when we are all safely in the town again—"

"Absolutely not," Short said, putting my lock-picks in his pocket. "If you turn back you are lost."

"I am the mistress of my own actions, I think." Now that he was no longer searching my hair, I was beginning to recover myself. I backed away, keeping a wary eye on him and his revenants; but he spoke in a voice dark with warning.

"I can't allow you to do that." His hand had dipped into the pocket of his greatcoat.

At this moment we stood in a large apartment on the second floor of one of the castle's bowers: it was parqueted, and long painted panels lined the floor and ceiling. The six revenants stood between us and the passage that led back towards the gallery, towards Vasily.

"You can't stop me," I said, more boldly than I felt. "You won't risk your corpses going into a berserker rage."

"No," Short said grimly, "in that you are right. But still I cannot permit you to leave."

A match struck. A fuse hissed, dispensing a sharp whiff of gunpowder. I turned in horror, just in time to see him toss a small canister through the air. It struck the ground at my feet and rolled some way beyond, into the passage. For an instant I thought it was a real bomb. Then it went off in a blaze of light, with a deafening bang that rattled the chandelier.

It was not a serious explosion—little more than a flash

and a bang, but those were quite enough. My vision was dazzled; a high-pitched whine swallowed my hearing; my nostrils and throat were clogged with the smell and taste of gunpowder. For a moment I could not have told you which way was up or down, for Short had judged my condition to a nicety, and my senses—rendered delicate by wolf-bite and vampire-bite—were wholly overwhelmed.

I must have fallen to the ground, for the first thing I felt was the parquet-flooring beneath my hands. As a little vision returned to me, I saw Short's dim shape looming over me and heard his voice from far away: "I *am* sorry, Miss Sharp."

His hand supported my head again. I smelled the heavy perfume of laudanum a moment before he up-ended a whole vial of it into my mouth. I coughed and spluttered and tried to tell him that I was not a vampire and would not be rendered unconscious in this way, but the majority of it went down my throat.

A sleepless night some months ago had sufficed to prove that laudanum was far less effective upon me than upon the un-bitten, the result bearing much more resemblance to intoxication than anything else. Doubtless I had the werewolf bite to thank for that, but all the same I felt a moment of panic as Short forced the drug past my lips.—If I was not in my right mind, how would I escape?

A moment before I would scarcely have thought that *Short* might pose a serious obstacle to my movements, but now—I must act quickly, or never have the chance to finish my task.

I was nearly blind and deaf, but desperation and long training told me what to do, and the movement required was simple enough. I swung my right hand up and over, breaking Short's grasp on the back of my neck, trapping his arm and forcing him to his knees beside me. With my left I lashed out, by sheer luck jabbing him in his unprotected throat. Then I was up on my feet, staggering towards the door and the six revenants guarding it. Despite the fireburst of light that still obscured my vision, I thought that if the revenants remained obediently where they were, I might find my way out—

The room slid sideways and I found myself on the floor again. The flashbang must have upset my sense of balance—that, or the laudanum was beginning to work. When Short tackled me from behind, I could only summon a drunken flailing as he pinned my wrists to the floor. The next moment I felt the cold bite of his handcuffs, before he got up and pulled me to my feet.

"So it *is* an arrest," I said in a voice that seemed muffled and far away. The words tasted bitter on my tongue. He'd taken my lock-picks, and I'd let him do it without raising a hand to stop him, because his touch had stolen my wits. Did he know I felt this way about him? Did he set out on purpose to use my own heart against me?

If Short replied, I didn't hear it. Instead, another sound came from the passageway and I felt him stiffen in surprise as he turned to face it.

I blinked once, then twice at the shape of a man approaching in a predatory lope from the doorway. Vasily? Hope ran through my veins—and fear. I was glad to see Vasily. I feared for Short.

"You," Short growled, putting me behind him. "Don't interfere, you monster."

"Language!" I murmured. I felt terribly dizzy, but at least Short had released me. I glanced around the room, trying to think.

Vasily closed the door behind him and shot the bolt, sealing us off from the passage leading back to the Kabale. My hearing was still very muffled but I heard his words well enough: "This is the hardly the way to get a lady's attention, Inspector. Even *I* know that."

"You have no right to tell me or anyone about the proper way to address a lady," Short growled, pulling the perfume-bottle of laudanum from his coat pocket. "You drained her blood."

"And very delicious it was too."

If Vasily was trying to make Short lose his head, he succeeded spectacularly. Short stiffened. "On second thoughts, laudanum is too good for you," he murmured. Then, to the revenants: "Take him!"

"This is between you and me. Tell your corpses to keep back," Vasily snarled.

"I don't answer to you," Short said, with serene fury.

Quicker than thought Vasily leaped, his hands outstretched to fasten around Short's neck. Short didn't flinch. His hand swept out of his other coat pocket, loaded with a glass bulb of saltwater. He lunged forward as gracefully as a fencer and smashed the bulb against Vasily's forehead even as the revenants latched onto the vampire's outstretched hands.

Glass and saltwater exploded. I smelled burning flesh. Vasily shrieked and bucked, managing to throw one of his revenant attackers the length of the room. I threw myself aside to miss it and collapsed to my knees again, my head swimming.

The revenants went wild, wrestling Vasily to the floor, beating and kicking him. Their unnatural combined strength was too much even for a vampire: every time Vasily attempted to drag himself to his feet, they crushed him down again.

Short stood over the scrum, breathing hard. Blood dripped from his clenched fists. He must have cut them breaking the saltwater bulb against Vasily's head, but he didn't appear to notice.

He only stood there and watched with a terrible satisfaction in every line of his grim, brooding figure.

The reader must not believe I was watching idly. By now my vision had cleared sufficiently to show me the door leading into the next apartment, away from the Kabale and the savage beating occurring on that side of the room—yet, shaking and addled as I was, I was in no shape to take it. Instead, I pulled myself to hands and knees and crawled through the stench of salt-corroded vampire towards the great windows at the side of the room, which looked down upon the castle courtyard. The journey seemed interminable; and when once I reached my goal, it was as much as I could do to pull myself to my feet and throw open the casement.

My senses were still overwhelmed. The laudanum weighted down every limb, and Vasily was sobbing in great, terrible gasps.

"Short," I cried. "Stop it. Stop it. They'll tear him apart."

"He won't die of it." Short turned towards me, all white with blazing eyes. "What are you doing?"

"This is barbaric." My legs chose that moment to let me down, and I collapsed onto the windowsill with the void at my back, catching at the jamb to keep myself from tumbling out.

A little red kindled in his sheet-white face. "Barbaric? Draining your blood against your will—*that* was barbaric."

Really?—He would pause in the middle of kidnapping me

to get his revenge on Vasily for drinking my blood? I might have been flattered, if I was not so afraid for him.

"This isn't like you."

"Don't pretend that you know me," he said hoarsely. "No one else will make him pay for what he did."

At that, I could not help laughing, although even in my own ears the sound was a little wild. "Oh," I cried, "the irony!"

He flushed. "You're tipsy, Miss Sharp. Come down from there. It's time we went."

"Call off your attack dogs first."

"They won't kill him, and I can't risk him following us."

"We can't leave him here—the Kabale means to kill him!"

"*Serve him right if they do,*" Short hissed.

He stepped towards me, reaching out. I tipped backwards, feeling the night air whisper at my neck.

"Not another step."

He halted, paling. "Miss Sharp—"

"Free Vasily," I told him, praying that my shackled hands wouldn't suddenly lose their grip on the jamb, "or on my word of honour I will throw myself out this window."

I tried to remember how high up I was, and whether there was anything beneath to break my fall. Even with all my wits about me, I was hardly capable of surviving such a plunge, and at that moment I was liable to plunge face-first like a rag doll.

But I was hanged if I meant to let Short intimidate me like this.

"Miss Sharp, I implore you." He took another step.

"Don't go calling my bluff," I slurred. "We already know my sense of self-preservation is highly deficient, and besides, if Rebecca from *Ivanhoe* could do this I don't see why I shouldn't."

"Miss Sharp," he repeated with a despairing gesture, "you are impossible! Dying for what you believe in—that I can understand; but dying for *him?*"

Not for Vasily, but to spite Short, I thought, because he had won my trust and now used it to betray me.

He flinched. "Is that truly what you think of me?"

"The dickens. Did I say that aloud? Never mind." I shifted my grip on the window-jamb. "Go away. I'm not coming with you."

Short turned to the revenants. "Stop that," he commanded.

Silence fell, but for Vasily's groans. I didn't look at him; I was quite sure there was blood, and at that moment I could not bear to see more of it.

Short turned to me, pale to the lips. "Answer me, I implore you. Is that what you think?—that I am only doing this to betray you?"

"I thought you were my friend."

"Your friend," he said in a very flat, emotionless voice. "It would have been nice to know this. *I* thought I was your spaniel, to be bought and sold, to follow at your heels until dismissed."

My heart struck me.—It was true. I had been so frightened of letting Short see my true feelings that I had scarcely thought even to show him friendship.

"Don't listen to him, Miss Sharp." That awful, rasping voice was Vasily. He pulled himself with an effort to his knees. He looked dreadful—his face deformed with red bubbling flesh from the saltwater bulb, his clothes and flesh alike torn from his beating. "It's a trap."

"It's no trap," Short kept his attention on me. "Please, Miss

Sharp. Come off that window-sill. Don't destroy yourself for my sake."

A thump made all three of us jump. The commotion we had caused must have finally summoned attention. Now fists pounded on the bolted door, and voices demanded entrance.

"Quickly!" Short cried, reaching out to me.

"We bring Vasily."

"No. I won't risk it."

The revenants had fallen back. All Short's attention was on me. Now Vasily leaped from the ground—bared his teeth—threw himself at Short.

"Short!" I shrieked.

Short turned, whipping his hand from his pocket. The vampire grabbed for the lapels of his coat. Short fell back a step, bringing up the perfume-bottle. Vasily's clawed hand flashed, ripping open Short's coat.

The blow sent the perfume-bottle flying across the room, along with a small, glinting object that rolled across the parquetry and settled shining at my feet. I blinked at the thing in confusion. It was so incongruous that for a moment I had trouble figuring out what I saw.

A golden ring, sized for a woman's hand.

A wedding-ring.

At the centre of the room, Vasily had lifted Short from his feet, and was crooning something in soft and angry Russian. Short clawed at his hands making unintelligible choking sounds, gesturing futilely for his revenants to attack.

My hands slipped on the windowsill, and my heart leaped into my throat. Steadying myself, I looked again at the shining thing on the floor at my feet.

Short had a wedding-ring in his pocket.

I remembered his question in the carriage on the way to Ehrenberg Palace, the morning the bomb went off at the Coburg train station. I remembered him asking to speak to me alone when all this was over. I remembered his hand straying to his breast pocket, now torn open by Vasily's attack.

More memories assailed me: Short asking for a kiss in Eger—Short cradling my hands between his own on the Orient Express—Short threatening to kill Vasily at the hospital of the Vincés sisters.

Short's voice breaking as he spoke of being my spaniel.

"Oh," I whispered as the thing struck me. *"Oh."*

Short loved me—Short, whom I had believed could never love a woman like me—Short, whose closeness had always raised in me a wistful longing, sharp and painful like a memory of a long-dead friend.

Amidst the thumps and blows shaking the door, I heard a queer gasping sound from Short. I looked up and saw that he was on his feet again, gasping for breath. Vasily still gripped his lapels, but now it was for support. The vampire's head had fallen forward, as though he was struggling to keep his eyes open.

He had breathed a little laudanum, after all, before the bottle flew.

Breaking Vasily's grasp, Short turned towards me. "Make your choice, Miss Sharp. Leave Vasily and come with me, or stay with him to face the Kabale. Which shall it be?"

"I…" My voice was gone. I could not say it, but I had made my choice—the only choice.

"Choose me," Vasily slurred, taking a couple of weaving steps towards me. "I swear I can save you both!" Then he fell to his knees.

Feeling numb, I slipped from my perch on the windowsill and retrieved the wedding-ring from the floor. "Short," I said, "did you drop something?"

He paled, and his hands flew to his shredded coat.

"Were you thinking of getting married?" I took a lurching step towards him. He caught me by the arms. His hands were shaking, but he took the ring from my hand and shoved it safely into his trousers pocket.

"Not any more," he said through white lips.

My head was spinning, my body still slack from the laudanum. Vasily was on hands and knees, remaining conscious only by a supreme effort of willpower. A little blood trickled from his mouth—the beating must have left him with internal injuries.

And yet—Short loved me, and I was in no condition to resist. I have never been a heroine, and I was at that moment in a state of complete physical and emotional collapse. I could not choose death, for in the end, Short was the man who loved me, and Vasily was only the monster who had drained me.

"Save me, Short," I said faintly.

He swept me up in his arms.

"No!" Vasily gasped. "Don't leave me to the Kabale! Forgive me, Miss Sharp—I should never have taken your blood!"

I was unable to feel anything, not even pity. "Do you remember the lightning you said would never strike you? This is it."

"Don't," he gasped one more time. "You—*promised.*"

With those words, he sank senseless to the parquetry. Then Short summoned his revenants to follow and bore me away.

Chapter XIII.

Of the journey that followed I have only the vaguest of recollections. I remember a tunnel leading from the castle's upper courtyard to a level space between the two walls, where Short lifted me into the carriage and propped me in a corner. I remember asking him, two or three times, if it was really true that he wanted to marry me. He refused to answer. Within a quarter of an hour we were in Coburg at a small house where, having dismissed the revenants, Short helped me upstairs to a large attic room and deposited me on an iron bedstead that smelled rather pleasantly of himself.

"Do you really love me?" I asked dreamily, for the third or fourth time, as he poured some water into the ewer and brought it over to me.

"Leave it till morning, Miss Sharp. You're not yourself tonight," he said firmly, dabbing at my face with a damp cloth.

"But do you, though? Because here I have been telling myself all along that a stuffed short like you would never go for a face like mine. I mean, a shirt. What are you doing?"

"Your face is all over soot, and there's a cut on your chin."

"Really? How did that happen?"

"I threw a bomb at you, if you recall."

"Oh! Ha! So you did!"

"I don't think these will need stitches," he mused, tilting my face up with both hands.

I sighed, melting into his hold. "Shall I tell you a secret, Short? I'm pretty mad about you myself."

That startled him into letting go of me. I fell back across the coverlet. The ceiling above me consisted of pale plaster and dark beams. I stared at them fondly and said, "You're my favourite. Shall I tell you why? You're the only fellow I know who hasn't tried to kill me."

"That seems rather a low bar," he muttered, dabbing the damp cloth over my neck and décolletage. I hissed as it touched another cut—a little of the flashbang's casing must have blown off and nicked me.

"Well, it's not just that," I conceded. "I like tall, sad men. Also you helped me hide Eddy's body. That was a great relief. And you came to find me in Eger. But the most important thing is, you started off thinking I was a very bad girl, but you still treated me like a lady. And now you don't anymore. Think of me that way, I mean."

He began to sponge my arms. I couldn't see him from my position flat across the bed, but his voice sounded stiff, even unhappy. "You should rest, Miss Sharp. We can discuss it when you're in full possession of your wits."

"Who's Miss Sharp? I don't know her. You should call me Liz; and I will call you Alexander. That's your Christian name, isn't it? I think you and I will be very happy together, Alexander."

"I beg your pardon!"

"Well, why not? You aren't just going to turn up with a wedding ring in your pocket and leave it at that, are you… Alexander?"

He sighed and pulled me up to face him again, his long mouth as long and thin as I'd ever seen it. "Is that why you chose to go with me tonight, Miss Sharp? Because you thought I was in love with you?"

I didn't quite understand. It all seemed so obvious now. "Well, *aren't* you?"

It was his turn to look up at the ceiling. "Good God," he muttered. I wondered if I had upset him, for he looked nearly sick. Aloud he said: "There can never be anything between us, Miss Sharp. Look at this. Look how I've hurt you."

"Hurt me?" I paused, thinking about it, but I didn't *feel* any pain. He'd dabbed my cuts with something that stung a little, but now they were numb again. "You did hurt me a little, at the beginning," I decided at last, "when you kept thinking that one monster bite would turn a girl into a dainty. But you know better now." I looked at his mouth again, at the sharp lines etched from nose to lips. "Don't look so sad, Shor—I mean Alexander. Why don't you kiss me?"

"*What?*" he whispered.

"Told you I'd give you a kiss," I mumbled, "in Eger."

His arms around me trembled; and then suddenly he pulled me close. I sighed with anticipation, but he had only tucked me within the circle of his right arm so that he could pull back the bedcovers with his left and roll me within.

"We'll talk about it in the morning," he said more firmly, pulling off my shoes, and whisking the covers over me.

"Don't leave," I objected, realising suddenly that a *very* tightly-laced corset and a good amount of jet-beaded lace were respectively squeezing and prickling me. "Aren't you going to help me off with my dress?"

"Certainly not!" Short yelped. A moment later he blew out

the candle and fled.

This was my last memory until I awoke several hours later with an aching head and a dry throat. In corset and brocade gown, beneath a fluffy eiderdown, I had overheated. Worst of all was the suspicion that I had been babbling a great deal—had perhaps said some very silly things. Oh lor'—had I begged Short to *kiss* me?

I climbed from the bed, pressing my hands to my cheeks in an effort to cool them. A floorboard creaked beneath my foot, giving rise to a sudden hush; whereupon I realised that there must have been a murmur of voices going on downstairs.

Short and—whom?

I did not particularly wish to see Short again just now—really, I must have been babbling terribly. I debated whether it might be better to depart silently by the window, but after a moment's hesitation, my curiosity got the better of me. I wanted to know to whom Short was speaking—and after the evening's events, I thought we needed to clear the air a little before I departed.

What could I have been thinking, to babble out all my most private emotions to him? How was one to maintain one's mysterious feminine allure under such circumstances, to say nothing of one's self-respect? Really, it was too bad! His confession was such an all-consuming shock; hearing it had knocked me into a ferment of blithe hope, and for the moment that was all I had been able to think about.

It's a trap, Vasily had said, but in fact Short had refused to use—whatever he felt—to get the better of me. He had not been intentionally manipulative, as I feared when he took the lockpicks from my hair. All the same, I went hot with shame to think how neatly I had fallen into his hands.

All along I had been on the alert against Vasily, the enemy who longed to drink my blood. But now Short, the one I loved, the man who made me feel safe and trustful, had turned on me; and I felt unmoored, vulnerable, and weak.

Worse: for Short I had broken my promise to protect Vasily. I had abandoned him to the Kabale. It was not guilt over breaking Vasily's trust that I felt—I had been cured of such feelings in the dungeon of Castle Sarkozy—but rather doubt of my own will. For the first time I wondered whether I was really able to fulfil the task I had set myself.

Perhaps, if I had been wise, I would have gone out the window. Perhaps it was more of the same weakness, now, that sent me downstairs instead. After some groping, I discovered the trap-door leading down into the lower level of the house, and made my unsteady way down the stairs. A moment later I came face-to-face with Short—and a red-eyed, sharp-fanged Missy of Roumania.

I am nearly certain my heart stopped altogether.

"*You!*" I squeaked, thrusting my hand into my pocket. To my horror, I found it empty. No laudanum—no saltwater—not even the silver-loaded revolver I kept for werewolves. I was defenceless.

The room's furnishings were spartan at best, but Missy lounged in a wooden chair at the head of the table, clad in diamonds and heavy lustrous satin which reflected the dim candlelight, lighting the room like a lamp. Short stood beside her, reaching for the candlestick on the table as though he had just this moment risen to venture upstairs. When he saw me, his lips moved in soundless surprise.

Missy laughed in her attractive way, wrinkling her nose. "Don't be so surprised, Miss Sharp! Didn't you hear me tell the Kabale I meant to capture you shortly?"

"You *knew* I was there?"

"How else do you think Short knew where to find you?" Missy laughed.—I felt sick. Short had betrayed me to *Missy?*—She went on: "A ladies' room in a café is too public a place to discuss your plans, my dear."

She must have been eavesdropping while May and I spoke. I gulped, trying to remember what else we might have given away.

I should flee; at once. Instead I merely looked to Short.

"You lied to me," I said dully. "You sold me to *her.* You never meant to take me to Australia."

Short looked blank. "But I *am* taking you to Australia—"

Missy laughed, rising from her chair and cutting him off with a flat gesture of her hand. "Oh, no. That was only a little fib to secure his help. Believe me, I don't mean to let you off *that* easily."

That was my last possible cue to leave—if I could. Since my path to the front door was cut off, I must take my chances with the window upstairs. Gathering up my skirts of heavy red brocade, I turned to bolt up the narrow stair, but I was too late. Missy's hands fastened in the tight fabric across my shoulders and yanked me back.

She must have crossed the room in one swift bound. Now she turned me to face her. Her eyes were flaming with bloody murder. "You will die, Miss Sharp," she whispered, "and slowly."

"One moment, your highness." Short thrust an arm between us, as though there was anything he could do to protect me but distract her long enough to be drained himself. "You promised me you meant her no harm. Do you mean to say you lied?"

Missy laughed. "Do *you* mean to hold me to my word? Just how will you do that?"

Short thrust his spare hand into his pocket, but before he could withdraw his laudanum spray, Missy pressed one palm against his forehead. Short groaned, his eyes flashing red as they rolled upwards in the sockets.

"The girl is mine," Missy whispered; and Short replied, "The girl is yours."

"We will take her upstairs and cuff her so that she does not escape."

"We will take her upstairs and cuff her so that she does not escape."

"You will not question these orders."

"I will not question these orders."

Missy turned to me with a sharp grin. "What a shame the night is so old! It's too late to play tonight, but we shall have some fun tomorrow; and maybe we'll have dear Alexander to watch. Would you like that?"

"Let him go," I whispered, struggling uselessly against her iron grasp. "He never injured you."

"But of course!—Your wish is my command." She took her hand from Short's head, and he reeled back a step as the red glow faded from his eyes.

"Do let's hurry, Short; I haven't all night," Missy added, turning me about and pushing me towards the stairs.

"Oh—I beg your pardon, ma'am." Shaking his head with a faintly confused air, Short retrieved the candlestick from the table and led the way upstairs. Missy propelled me towards the heavy iron bedstead; and Short took his cuffs from his pocket.

"No!" I twisted in Missy's grip and tried to throw her, but she was too strong for me. We staggered to the bed, and Missy stretched out my wrists towards one of the corner posts.

"Short," I screamed, "she means to kill me!"

"Don't be afraid," he said quite calmly, cuffing my wrists around the post. "It's for your own good, Miss Sharp."

Did he really not recall her saying she meant to kill me? I yanked once against the post and then lay still, panting. Vampires had strange abilities to charm the mind—had I not experienced Vasily's glamour on several occasions?—but this was beyond Vasily's power; it was nearly as bad as siren manipulation.

"I must go," Missy said, running careless fingers through Short's hair, as though he was a favourite lap-dog. "Mind she stays put, at least until tomorrow night."

She went downstairs again, and I heard the bolt shoot downstairs as she let herself out of the house. As her carriage-wheels echoed through the narrow street, Short seemed to recollect his scattered wits and turned to me.

"Is there anything you need, Miss Sharp?"

His voice was calmly solicitous, as though he hadn't just kidnapped me and shackled me to a bed to await the sport of a vengeful vampire princess.

"Come here and speak to me," I said, with an attempt to swallow my panic.

He hesitated, but then crossed the room and sat beside me. "Yes?"

I hardly knew where to start. Some of it was clear enough. Evidently, when Short had gone to the Kabale and begged them to spare my life long enough to let him deal with me in his own way, Missy had scented opportunity. Like Short, but for quite different reasons, she did not want the Kabale getting hold of me. All she needed to do was offer Short the information that I would be attending the Kabale tonight, and the thing was done.

Her motivations were quite clear, but what about Short? How much of the man I knew was real? Could I trust *anything* he had said to me in the last few hours? Had he been operating under her compulsion all night, or even longer?

"Downstairs just now," I began, "Missy put her hand on your face. Do you remember that? Do you remember her saying she meant to kill me slowly?"

His head tilted, half in surprise, half in offence. "What do you mean? She quite solemnly promised I could take you to Australia."

"Then do it," I whispered desperately. "If that's what you want, unlock me now and we'll get on the first train out of Coburg and never look back."

"Not yet."

"Why?"

"Her highness still requires your presence in Coburg."

"Look at me, Short. Why does she want me in Coburg?"

A slight frown appeared between his brows. "She didn't confide in me."

"Whose word do you trust?—Hers or mine?"

"Please don't fret, Miss Sharp. In *my* experience Princess Marie has always been quite trustworthy, and she has promised to send us on our way tomorrow."

I yanked at the cuffs with a whine of terror. "Short, we're both in danger. We must leave *now*. Listen: I have another house, near the marketplace, so much larger and more comfortable than this one! There are—things I need there. Let's go and collect them."

"Ah, you must work harder than this to pull the wool over my eyes."

"I'll kick you in the head in another minute," I almost screamed. "Go and talk to George! Ask him why he addressed the Kabale tonight—he'll tell you he was trying to save me *from Missy!*"

"My dear! You are panicking."

All the anger went out of me, and I felt as though I was freezing into a block of ice. "Don't call me your dear."

He must not have caught the deadly cold in my voice, for one of his lightning-swift smiles flashed across his face. "Not three hours since, you promised to call me Alexander."

"I was out of my mind, and you knew it."

"Yes; I got that impression around the time you asked me to marry you. Don't worry—I won't hold you to it."

Good Lord—I really *had* let my hair down. I took a deep breath, trying to stifle a sob. "I ought to have stayed with Vasily."

"You would have died," he said sharply.

"I am going to die anyway. That way would have been quicker and easier." Another sob crawled up my throat, and I dispelled it with a deep breath. "We had an agreement. He was depending on me...I broke my promise."

"I think Vasily will find a way to survive."

"If he does, he'll never forgive me."

"Indeed." An edge entered Short's voice. "I'm counting on that."

"You think of everything." Perhaps I could not blame him for handing me over to Missy, since he was convinced she meant not to harm us. Yet now that my head was clear, I saw the full truth of what he had done. It was entirely his own choice to join with the Kabale and the ghastly revenants, to hunt me down like a dog.

"I made myself a liar for you, Short," I said at last, thickly. The tears were getting harder to swallow. "What have you become? You used to abominate the revenants, and now you make use of them. You preach order to me, then lose your head and torture Vasily for the sake of a selfish vengeance.—And no, don't tell me you did it for me. You did it to make *yourself* feel better. So tell me: if you take your orders from the monsters, and give orders to other monsters, and stand by in silence while the monsters beat and drain their enemies, then how are you any better than a monster yourself?"

Short closed his eyes. "I am better," he said in a strained voice, "because I can and will choose my hill to die upon."

For so long I had told myself that a policeman and a scarred dainty could have no future together. I had been right, but not for the reason I thought. The truth was, I could never submit to the monsters that had ruined me; and Short somehow still thought the beastliness was worthwhile for the sake of order.

Not all of this was due to Missy's control, but the truth was that she would never allow him to take a stand against her. Short had already lost all ability to choose right from wrong, and he didn't even know it.

"Did you know they have found a way to make living people into revenants?" I asked. "The Kabale discussed it at their meeting tonight. Of course they are eager to turn us all into monsters: the army, the police force, every unfortunate soul at Saint Botolph's or the *Akbar*. And then you really will be their mindless slave."

"Never," Short said huskily. "I'll never consent to make such a change. If the time should come—"

"If the time should come," I said with a sigh, "you may not be given the choice, any more than Vasily gave me a choice in Castle Sarkozy."

His mouth drew tight and long.

"Please, Short. I know you don't want to be my enemy. I don't know if I'll ever give you my trust freely again; but I swear to you that if you let me go now I'll grant you the opportunity to earn it."

There was a long silence. Outside, the light of dawn was gradually beginning to grow, but in that half-light there was no seeing his face.

"I don't know if I deserve the opportunity to earn it," Short said at last, gently. He got up off the bed. "I've made my choice, and there's no going back now. Tell me if you need anything. I must go to the palace at eight."

"Short," I croaked. "Wait."

His eyes, his mouth, were drooping. "It's no good, Miss Sharp. I know what I have lost. I won't give up what little I have gained."

Chapter XIV.

If only I could have stopped *thinking* about him!

All that endless day, lack of sleep and burning worry sent my thoughts chasing each other in endless circles. I recalled the first days of our friendship, investigating Sal's death in London; the way we had worked together on the Orient Express; those halcyon days wandering through Europe, trying to find our way back to Coburg. The way his swift smile transformed his face when he saw me; the way he would tease me or compliment my dress; the way he liked to offer his arm when we walked down the street, or open the door when I approached.

Had I been wilfully blind, not to fathom his interest in me?—Perhaps. Perhaps I was afraid of rejection, sure that no man of Short's standing or profession would risk loving me.

Perhaps I had been wise to overlook it.

I recalled the way we had always found *something* on which to disagree—and I don't mean in the arguments I picked if I was bored or wrapped up in troubles. Short and I had never seen eye-to-eye on the subject of monsters, and it was that more than anything else that had convinced me his admiration and teasing were meaningless.

As I watched the sunlight creep across the attic walls, I

grieved not only the love that might have been between us, but the friendship which never would be again.

I was not completely idle. Soon after Short left the house, I swivelled off the bed and tried to break the iron bedstead, or the cuffs, or anything. All I got for my pains was a pair of badly bruised wrists, which Short noticed when he came back to see me at midday.

"Let me put some arnica on those," he said.

"Unless you mean to release me, it's a waste of good arnica," I said tiredly, but I let him do it. After he went downstairs, I tried if the cuffs would let my hands escape now that they were slippery with the salve. They did not.

The downstairs door closed behind Short. Half the day was whiled away, and I could find no a way to get free. What else could I do? I might try breaking the bones in my hands, but that would leave me crippled, perhaps for the rest of my life if a good doctor could not be found to re-set the bones before they healed.—Granted, if I failed to escape, the rest of my life was not likely to last long.

And if I did escape? I wondered what might have happened to Vasily because of my weakness. Had the Kabale already carried out their sentence?—Living or dead, he must be cursing my name, or vowing his revenge.

Once more I looked at the patch of sunlight falling through the window and promised myself that if no help came by mid-afternoon, I would break my hands. I took a deep breath, trying not to anticipate the pain. There was still time. Some friends yet remained to me: May would not forsake me. I could not imagine her coming to my rescue, but I would not despair quite yet.

It was at this doubtful moment, with Short barely gone

five minutes, that a door opened downstairs, and footsteps sounded on the stairs to my attic. I quaked in terror, imagining that Missy had given up my location to a pair of her cousins. Instead, Anton burst into the attic—followed instantly by Vasily himself!

"There she is!" Anton crossed the room to inspect my bonds. "You are well, Liz?—you are unhurt?"

"You came for me," I almost sobbed. "How did you know—?"

"May will explain," Anton said, lifting my right hand so that the short chain of Short's handcuffs was exposed. "Hold this, bloodsucker, and give me the axe."

Vasily must have been drinking blood, for since the previous night's beating, his urbane good looks were completely restored. Now, he hefted a substantial-looking axe and said, "Let me do it, peasant. I'll strike harder."

"Not on your worthless life," Anton growled. "You've never chopped wood a day in your life. You're more likely to take off her hand than her cuffs."

"It might teach her a salutary lesson," Vasily muttered, too low for Anton's ears. He darted me a look of terrifying amusement, but he handed over the axe.

Anton hefted it with a grim smile.

"Now hold her wrists steady. Move your hand up a bit to cover hers. Yes, if I *do* go astray, I'd rather hit you, bloodsucker. Here goes."

Vasily winced—Anton swung—and with a dull clank, my manacled hands were free. Not even my worry over Vasily could overwhelm my sense of relief. For the first time in many hours, I seemed able to breathe freely. "Did you say something about May?" I murmured, as Anton helped me to my feet. "Is she safe?"

"Ask her yourself," Anton said with a swift grin. Pausing only to collect my lock-picks, revolver, umbrella, and other weapons from the dilapidated dressing-table in the corner of the room, he and Vasily helped me out onto the street, where a brougham waited directly in front of the door. May leaned out with outstretched arms, and in another instant I was kneeling at her feet, sobbing into her lap.

"My poor Sharp!" May cried softly as the carriage got underway. "What happened to you?"

"Short," I sobbed. "Short loves me."

"Oh, good God!—did he insult you? I'll see the colour of his insides if he has!"

"Dear me! no," I gulped, mastering myself a little. "Only I was *so confused.* And I betrayed Vasily for him."

She made me get up and sit next to her; and I told her what had happened at the castle, and afterwards at the house.

"The beast! Fraternising with revenants—the *idea!*" May exclaimed, when I was finished. "And that dreadful Missy! What are you going to do about it?"

"I don't know," I murmured. "So much has changed." I put a hand to my bosom, feeling the crackle of paper hidden within my corset, where Short had never dreamed to look. "I have what I went to find—the identities of the Kabale. But what can I do about them? I won't kill them—I'm not my mother, no matter what anyone says—and besides, I'm wanted for murder. Even my friends—" I pulled myself up short. "I half expected Vasily to tear my head off after what happened last night."

"But it was he who warned us you had been taken, Sharp."

"Really?" She had handed me her handkerchief, and now I wiped my face, wishing with all my heart for a bath, a change of clothing, and a file to remove the severed cuffs from my wrists. "And how did you know where to find me?"

"Vasily returned to your lodgings this morning and told Anton how Short had taken you. Anton told me; I asked George and Short; and they didn't *lie* to me, but they wouldn't tell me the truth either. So then I had Anton follow Short to the house where we found you."

I blinked at her. "*You* masterminded my escape?"

She gave a shaky laugh. "What else was I meant to do? Remember, if they catch you, that implicates me."

"You are too kind," I said, with great feeling. "But truly you ought to be distancing yourself from me, for your own safety."

May shook her head. "I don't think I can, Sharp. Missy already knows it was my blood that defanged Ernest and Ducky. I'm sure it's only a matter of time before she turns her attention to me—and if George couldn't protect you from the Kabale, he certainly won't be able to protect me."

"But, hang it," I began.

"Let me finish," she added. "I don't want you to think that I am only helping you because it's in my own interests to do so. I understand now why the Kabale must be dealt with. They are too powerful, and they are using that power to do dreadful things. It must not be allowed to continue. Sharp dear, I have always believed I was put in this world to be of real use. I presumed—fat-headed as it may have been—that it was my mind and ambition I was meant to use, not merely my blood. But if that's the only way I can help you, I should be honoured to do so."

"Your blood," I croaked, hardly believing my ears. This would change everything. "Really and truly, May?"

She nodded bravely. "Really and truly. I only regret I didn't give it you in time to save Chlodwig. But I don't see any other way. You must fight this battle, and if I can make it possible for you to do so without bloodshed, I must."

"I beg your pardon," I stammered. "I can hardly believe it."

"Well, I…as a matter of fact, I had that little talk you suggested, with Anton." May coughed. "He made some very persuasive points."

I stared out the window without seeing. This changed everything. Armed with May's blood, I need not fear to stay in Coburg. The next Kabale meeting was tomorrow night, shortly after the wedding. All the members were assembled in one place—how long would it be before I had another such chance? Strike now, and I might cripple them at one blow. Strike now, and I might not only defang Missy, but have my revenge upon the werewolf that gave me my scars. And I still had my allies. Anton was faithful. Vasily, it seemed, had chosen to forgive me. Short—

My spirits fell. "Short is in Missy's power," I murmured.

"Will she harm him, do you think?"

"No; not so long as he's useful to her. And he *will* be useful. You're George's fiancée, and he's George's bodyguard; he has a constant eye on you. And then…" I took a deep breath. "I don't know, May. I can't stop thinking about him. I'm afraid he could vanquish me again just as easily as he did last night, and I don't know how to prevent it."

May hummed softly, thoughtfully. "Do you think it was the truth, when he said he loved you?"

That was the very question that had tormented me all day. "I think so," I said softly. "Missy had to make him believe she meant me no harm."

"Good," May said fiercely. "That means he's vulnerable to

you in the same way you are vulnerable to him."

My lips parted as the possibilities flashed upon me. "You mean—I should turn his own feelings upon him?"

"Why not?" May said, coldly practical. "All's fair in love and war, and this is both.—Unless you find yourself incapable of such action, of course. But you are generally very sensitive to what other people think and feel, Sharp. Perhaps it's time you used that as a weapon."

And heavens, I needed a weapon. I had badly underestimated Short, thinking that since he was neither a monster nor an anarchist, he must be mostly harmless. Instead, he had proven a cunning and ruthless foe, well prepared for every eventuality. His feelings for me—whether he would admit to them or not—constituted his only real weakness.

"What an appalling thought," I said meditatively. "Still…"

I had meant what I said to Short in the cold hours before dawn. If he took orders from monsters, and commanded monsters, then I had no choice but to treat him like a monster himself. But here, at least, I was on familiar ground. I had dealt with monsters before, and with Short I had one advantage that I lacked when it came to either Anton or Vasily: I believed that in his own way, Short truly loved me.

A staggering possibility struck me. Perhaps Short knew he was vulnerable to me! Perhaps that was why he opposed me so vehemently!

"I'll do it," I declared. "It might just work."

May smiled and offered me my own hat, with the veil pinned to it. "Put this on; I think we'll need it."

"Why, where are we going?" I inquired, perching the hat on my unkempt hair, and swathing my face in the thick black veil.

"To the palace, to collect some of my things. Didn't Anton tell you? I'm to be kidnapped."

This announcement was a trifle startling; but as May pointed out, it was important that she should be able plausibly to deny that she had assisted us in gaining her blood. I didn't choose to argue. It was heartening to see that in my absence, she had taken up the cudgels with a vengeance.

Having arrived at the palace, we crept through the corridors in a nervous procession, but met no one. It was about lunchtime, if lunch was taken fashionably late, and the palace seemed well-nigh deserted. At last we made it to the door of the Tecks' suite, whereupon May let out a little sigh of relief and led us inside.

We interrupted Mary Adelaide in the midst of pouring tea.

"Oh, May! You're back. Prince George just looked in to take you for a picnic."

Whereupon, to our collective dismay, the gentleman so described arose from the depths of an armchair that stood with its back towards us.

"Lovely afternoon for it, what!" he began—but then he caught sight of me, and his mouth dropped open. "Sharp! Demme!"

I was scarcely less horrified myself. George certainly meant me well—last night before the Kabale he had shown a great deal of courage on my behalf—but when it came down to it, he was still in league with my enemies. I looked about anxiously, half expecting Short to burst in to arrest me.

But May said, as though it was the most ordinary thing in the world, "Language, George! Sharp is only here to collect some belongings."

"But—demmit—I mean, hang it—I thought—"

Vasily glided between me and the prince. "No need for you to worry, your Grace," he said smoothly. "Everything is well in hand."

"Oh," George said, reassured. *"Well,* then—in *that* case..." and he turned to May with a wave of his natty straw boater. "What about it, then, May? Picnic?"

I raised a confused eyebrow at Anton, but he seemed quite unbothered by George's abrupt change of tune.

Mary Adelaide popped out of her armchair and retrieved a frilly white object from the umbrella-stand in the corner. "Of course she will! Don't forget your parasol, May; the sun is quite strong today!"

May took the sunshade, but refused the hint. "Oh, George, I'd love to, but I'm afraid I have a prior engagement."

Mary Adelaide gestured frantically, urging May to cancel the engagement.

George frowned.

"What kind of prior engagement?"

May hesitated, and I thought we were certainly done for; but then she chuckled fondly. "Oh, George! Ducky and Ernest are getting married tomorrow afternoon, and you ask what kind of prior engagement I might have?"

Mary Adelaide threw up defeated hands and subsided into her armchair.

"Ah." George seemed both enlightened and confused. "Don't know how you ladies do it, by Jove. Looking so fresh and pretty all the time. Must be a devil—must be a jolly lot of work. Will I see you tonight?"

"Of course," she lied unblushingly.

"Counting the minutes, by Jove." George kissed her on the cheek. Then he reddened and recoiled. "I say! Beg pardon!"

"For what?" May replied, equally startled.

"Er—thought we had an audience, you know! Must pretend to be engaged and all that! Forgot everyone here knows about it."

"Oh," May said, turning faintly pink herself. "Do—do they? I didn't notice."

"Can't tell you how sorry I am! Know you don't care to be kissed in private. Won't happen again."

"Oh, no. You mustn't blame yourself—"

"Ought to be whipped through Piccadilly—"

"George, I am happy for *any* of my gentleman cousins to salute me on the cheek."

"Oh." George deflated. "Forgot I was your cousin—that is, yes! Just a cousin, like any other.—Goodbye."

He retreated in great disarray, leaving May with her fingers splayed against her cheek where George had kissed her.

Beside me, Vasily cleared his throat.

"I'm tempted to give them the name of an excellent psychologist I know in Vienna," he murmured in my ear. "Those two need help. I've never seen such a tragic love affair."

His eyes were half-closed and laughing, and I shivered a little. He was at his most dangerous in such a mood, and I was horribly conscious of how I had last seen him, begging for help as the Kabale closed in.

Why had they not killed him? Why was he here, helping me, when the Vasily I knew ought to be plotting his revenge?

May heard his words, for her cheeks went pink. "George and I are not in *love,* Vasily."

At that, Mary Adelaide erupted from her chair. "Not in love! Victoria Mary Augusta Louise Olga Pauline Claudine Agnes of Teck! It's time you were honest with yourself! Why else would George agree to such a harebrained scheme as this pretended engagement unless he *was* in love with you?"

"Hush, mamma—I know he *thinks* he loves me; but the truth is—"

"The truth," Mary Adelaide trumpeted, "is that that poor young man only agreed to the engagement because he cared for your safety, and hoped that spending time with you might help him strangle his hopeless passion—but now he's worse off than ever, and lives in dread of the day you break it off!"

"Mamma!" May's voice was a high-pitched squeak; then she swallowed and added in her normal voice of chill calm, "If he confided in you, I must say I think it a very shabby trick to betray his trust."

"No shabbier than to treat him like a mat to wipe your feet on," Mary Adelaide said with energy.

"I have told him all along that I cannot marry a werewolf! How am I to be any clearer than that?"

"Hear! hear!" Anton said approvingly, throwing himself down in the vacated armchair. "No fraternising with monsters."

"Thank you, Lupei."

"Any time. How about a cup of tea? I'm parched."

"Oh! to be sure." May picked up the tea-pot. "Milk, as usual, but no sugar?"

I gaped. "May! You never made tea for *me!*"

"You never asked." Oh, she *was* feeling contrary today.

"We can't train him to be respectful." Mary Adelaide sighed. "Believe me, we've tried. Seed-cake, Lupei?"

As this singular tea-party got under way, I gathered up my courage in both hands and turned to Vasily. "What was all that about just now? George was about to call every policeman in

Coburg, and then you told him you had me in hand."

"Oh, that!" Vasily gave a slight shrug. "After you left me last night, I struck a deal with the Kabale. I had no choice."

An alarming confession! I chose my words carefully.

"I owe you an apology, Vasily. I promised you my help, only to desert you."

Vasily shook his head. "Both of us acted in the heat of the moment, Miss Sharp. You were at a great disadvantage, and could not have helped me by remaining to die. I have no hard feelings."

He could not, I thought, possibly be sincere. All the same, it was better to appear to trust him. I took his hand, although his chill scent of pine and corruption still made my skin crawl.

"Is this where we part ways, then?"

His lips curved in a smile that didn't touch his eyes. "Not necessarily."

"But—your agreement with the Kabale—"

"Oh, that! Cousin Nicky offered me clemency in exchange for you. Naturally, I accepted." A slight shrug. "Or so *they* think. It is easy for them to overlook how they scapegoated me for my Emperor's sins. For me, it is a little more difficult. I do not forget my debts so easily."

I was just meditating upon how ominous *that* sounded, when his grip became steely, and he pulled me close to whisper in my ear.

"Occasionally I forgive, Miss Sharp, but I *never* forget. And neither should you."

It took all my self-command not to break away from him with violence. "Believe me, I don't."

He released me, then, and I retreated, trying not to let him see me shiver.

"So George thought me your prisoner?" That was bad news. Either he had accepted the fate the Kabale had in store for me—or worse, he might even now be sending Short to rescue me from their clutches. My heart quailed at the thought, for despite the plans I had laid with May in the carriage, I found I was still nervous about facing Short again. "In that case, we mustn't stay here. We must leave at once."

Vasily and I had conducted our conversation in an undertone, but when I turned, I found Mary Adelaide watching us with thoughtfully pursed lips. "What are you planning *now*, Sharp?"

I hesitated, hardly knowing what to say. The plan was to stage a kidnapping, of course; but was Mary Adelaide to be in on the secret? Did May expect us to start brandishing weapons and twirling moustaches? and if so, how on earth would we achieve that, since not even Anton had a moustache?

May solved the problem in her own way, sipping her tea and replacing the cup primly on its saucer. "Oh! Sharp is about to kidnap me, mamma.—*With* my consent, of course; but you mustn't tell George that."

Chapter XV.

"Where's the bloodsucker?" Anton asked when he, May, and I had gathered once more in safety at the little house near the Marktplatz.

"He said he must report to Nicky," said I. "The Kabale is keeping a close eye on him, and I thought it might be as well to keep an eye on them in return."

Anton grunted suspiciously. "I don't like it."

"Nor do I, but I think we can afford to risk it. He is much angrier with the Kabale than he is with me."

Anton narrowed his eyes suspiciously. "No matter how trustworthy, he'll always be the parasite who killed my cousin and half drained you."

"Not if May's blood does what we think it does."

"Oh yes." Anton snorted. "He's been hounding us day and night for the cure, that's for certain. At least, without the bloodsucker, we have the chance to lay our plans in private." He waved a file at me. "And to get those manacles off properly."

After bidding Mary Adelaide farewell, we had split up in an effort to make our way back to headquarters on foot and in secrecy. As it happened, the Duchess of Teck had *not* been prepared to countenance her daughter's going off with a wanted criminal, an impertinent anarchist, and a disreputable vampire, especially not when she might have been picnicking with the heir to the British Empire. Still, May was eventually able to carry her point by dwelling on the untenable nature of her own position.

"I do think it's terribly dangerous," Mary Adelaide had said at last, reluctantly. "But I suppose you must do as you judge best. You've always been the sensible one of the family—except in this matter of poor George, of course. Well, I shall do as you ask, and wild horses won't drag the secret from me. Only let me tell Papa that you will be safe."

To this May gave her fond assent, and with a promise to bring her back in two days at the very latest, we had muffled up our faces and ventured stealthily forth.

Now we gathered in the downstairs kitchen of the house as I boiled the needles with which I meant to draw off May's blood. "Ah, plans," I said meditatively. "Vasily says he agreed with the Kabale to hand me over by the time they meet again the night after the wedding."

Anton nodded. "That only leaves us tonight and tomorrow to defang the lot of them. It isn't much time."

"As a matter of fact, I thought I might allow Vasily to hand me over."

Anton swore explosively, but I lifted a hand.

"I noticed the Kabale drinking freely at last night's meeting. Wine mixed with blood, unless my nose was mistaken. I thought that if May's blood could be mixed with the appropriate vintage, we might defang all or most of them at a single stroke."

"Oh, Sharp! That sounds terribly dangerous," May said faintly.

"I hate to admit it, but the aristo is right. It's too risky."

"I do wish you wouldn't call me that, Lupei. It makes me feel as though you're about to hang me from a lamp-post."

"All right, May." He spoke casually, and I opened my eyes to see this strange new rapport that had sprung to life between them. Anton went on: "I don't like handing you over to the Kabale, Liz. I certainly don't like entrusting you to the bloodsucker a second time. And I don't like pinning all our hopes on May's blood without some firmer indication that it's really going to work."

"It's a fair point," I conceded, "but as luck would have it, we have thirty-some hours to perfect the plan and test the blood. I vote we begin by defanging someone. I don't suppose you have been able to discover who gave me *these,* May?"

I touched my scars, and she shook her head.

"I am so sorry! I did try to ask, but I don't think my Württemberg cousins like me very much these days."

I gnawed my lip. If the monster himself wouldn't confess, then how was I ever to identify him? Between the shapeshifting and the way the monsters closed their ranks to protect each other, it was next to impossible ever to know for certain.

"Forget him, Liz." Anton seemed to have divined the thoughts passing through my mind. "We may never know for certain, and in any case it's no use obsessing over one of the monsters when the whole system is rotten."

He was right, no doubt; but it was still a wrench. "In that case, I suppose the most likely candidate is Missy."

"Not if you want to knock her out of the fight altogether," Anton said. "I'm thinking that would only make her angrier and more desperate, not less. Leave her until you're ready to flee the continent. Is there anyone more strategic? I vote the bloodsucker."

"But if Vasily's to make a good show of handing me over to the Kabale after dark tomorrow evening, he'll need all his teeth."

Anton growled. "Oh, this is all very convenient for him! Hasn't it occurred to you that we have only *his* word for it that he is on our side?—What else do we know? Only that he promised the Kabale to hand you over. And you'd put yourself right back into his hands?"

The benefit of my plan was that, treacherous or not, I would far rather deal with Vasily than Short, for I was vulnerable to Short in a way that I never had been to the vampire.

"If Vasily wanted me dead, he might easily have left me in Short's custody."

"Not if he wanted the credit for your capture.—You ought to have let me kill him days ago."

"I'm not in the habit of killing people indiscriminately; for which you ought perhaps to be more grateful, Anton Lupei."

My words hit home, for Anton subsided, reddening.

"What about Nicky?" May said brightly into the silence that followed. We gave her blank looks, and she rushed to explain: "The poor boy! he wants *terribly* to marry Cousin Alicky, but she won't have him because he's a monster. If we tried my blood on him and it worked, Alicky would consent to marry him on the spot."

And who knew? with Nicky defanged and no longer a Kabale member, that might be a very good thing for Vasily. "How would you describe Nicky's personality? Vengeful?"

"Sheepish."

"You think he'd be grateful?"

"N-not precisely; but he's less likely to be *angry*."

"All right," I said, fitting one of the sterilised hypodermic needles into a syringe, "let's try it."

Evening shadows had fallen by the time Anton and I perfected our plan, and dusk found us loitering suspiciously on a street corner in the south of the town, inspecting the large and extremely charming house where the heir to Imperial Russia had been lodged during the wedding. The ground floor of the house was built of red brick, but the rest of it was cream plaster, red lath, and red tiled roofs; there were oriel windows, little gables, and even a turret. I sighed wistfully, for while I had lodged in palaces and castles, garrets and hospitals, this looked like a *home,* and I had never had one of those.

"What a hole," Anton grumbled beside me."

"What do you mean? I think it's charming!"

"The windows are tiny. It must be terribly dark and *cold.* Houses should be built in a more rational manner."

"Well, speak for yourself. I want an *irrational* house someday," I said. Checking in my pocket to be sure that the hypodermic containing May's blood was safe and easily to hand—Anton had filed off Short's handcuffs over the course of several hours this afternoon, to my great relief—I eased open the wooden gate and slipped through into the garden beyond. This was a small area filled with green bushes, and Anton and I were soon lost in the shadows. Together we hurried towards the low semicircular windows in the red brick at the house's base, that looked into the dark basement.

"All right, Anton," I said, having satisfied myself with an ear pressed to the glass that the room beyond was empty. Anton broke one of the square glass-panes with a quick jab of his elbow. The muffled crack resulted in no disturbance, and after a moment, Anton reached gingerly through to trip the latch on the window. This was a ticklish job, and he had just worked his arm through to the elbow when someone lit the gas within, and George's *doppelgänger* entered by the stairs, wearing a red silk blouse and loose trousers. To my surprise, the room was fitted up as a gymnasium, complete with bench and dumb-bells and all the other paraphernalia of *Sandow's Physical Training*.

Anton withdrew his arm as quickly as he could. Nicky did not notice the intruder, for he was speaking to someone behind him. "It won't do, sir," he said pleadingly. His voice was perfectly audible through the broken glass. This side of sunset, he spoke without any lisp. "She doesn't want to marry me, and that's all."

"Nonsense, my boy! Of course she wants to marry you. It is only this foolish scruple of hers that stops her."

The voice was loud and blustering. Its speaker quickly came into view, and I drew in a startled breath, for the gentleman who appeared was familiar to me from any number of newspaper portraits and satirical cartoons. A querulous-looking man of middle age in a uniform dripping with medals and braid, wearing a set of upturned moustaches nearly as preposterous as those of the Crown Prince of Greece, he carried his left arm tucked behind his back almost as though he was ashamed of it. This, then, was the German Emperor of whom my royal betters so often spoke as though he were some untamed beast who must be petted and stroked lest he lose his temper and break out into some dreadful catastrophe.

"I confess I do not understand Alicky's scruples," Nicky said dubiously, "but of course I cannot press her to violate them."

The Kaiser's moustaches quivered. "Why the devil not?"

Peeling off his shirt, Nicky spluttered with indignation. "I *beg* your pardon!"

He tossed the blouse onto the bench and picked up a formidable pair of dumb-bells. I blush to say that I could not repress a sound of surprise at the sight of the young tsarevitch's physique, which resembled nothing so much as a finely-chiselled marble Adonis.

When I first met Nicky he was bleating pitifully at Alicky while dressed as Attila the Hun. A dashed unconvincing performance—and yet: "Who knew *Nicky* had such a figure!" I murmured.

Hearing me, Anton clicked a disapproving tongue. "For shame, Liz! Those are the abdominals of a *monster!*"

Thankfully, the German emperor's booming voice drowned out our commentary. "But think what an excellent thing the alliance would be for both our Empires!"

"I would prefer to consider whether it would be an excellent thing for Alicky. She, at any rate, thinks not."

"Oh, women get these tomfool notions into their heads all the time, God bless 'em! Look at my sister Sophie, wanting to become a siren in order to marry Constantine of Greece. A siren!—when she might have been a proper German wolf!"

"But she got her way in the end, didn't she?"

The Kaiser chomped furiously on his moustache. "Sophie doesn't signify! I can't think why you wanted to drag her into it! The important thing is, Alicky will say yes. I've instructed all her sisters, her cousins, and her aunts to convince her she must do it, for the good of Imperial Prussia!"

"I beg your pardon! I must insist that this question is left between Alicky and myself!"

"Nonsense, boy, don't you know how the world is run? When all the royalties are one big happy family, all the empires in the world get along! Diplomacy," Kaiser Wilhelm added immodestly, "is my forte."

"That may be true, but I must insist you stop hounding Alicky," Nicky said with anxious determination. "I won't have her browbeaten into marrying me or anyone."

"Browbeaten! I resent that comment! We are not browbeating her; and anyway, naturally it's up to you to administer the *coup de grâce*—"

"The *mercy kill?* Really, I cannot think that is appropriate language—"

"Stop interrupting! It's a *metaphor,* for heaven's sake. Here's what I would do, Nicholas, and I strongly advise you to follow suit. Put on your most impressive uniform—come to think of it, what about that honorary admiralty I gave you last year? I can recommend that uniform, for just last week I added another three feet of gold braid—"

("On the other hand," I murmured, "he might just try taking off his shirt." Anton gave a snort of disgust.)

"Put on your uniform, I say, wear a proper sword, and go ask Alicky to marry you. If she says no, just pick her up and kiss her until she says yes."

"I couldn't—I couldn't possibly intrude on her like that." Nicky looked dizzy. "Really, if everyone's been at her like that, it might be better if I don't try to see her at all!"

"Such poltroonery!" boomed the diplomatic prodigy. "Is that the spirit of 1812? Your ancestors would be ashamed of you! Well, my boy, that settles it, since you are so easily cowed. I refuse to set a foot out that door until you do as I ask!"

"Cousin William, I am in the middle of physical cultivation!"

The Kaiser glared at Nicky's dumb-bells. "Bah! You are

holding them all wrong. Let me show you."

"Please—"

"Using *my* method, I can lift twice this. I have the best physique in all my regiments. Watch—!"

"All *right*," Nicky said in defeat, surrendering the dumb-bells. "If I go to see Alicky, and she turns me down again, will it satisfy you?"

"H'm! what? Yes! Yes, excellent. And she won't turn you down, not if you do it properly. Now, pay attention: you plant your feet beneath your hips, like this—"

"But," Nicky added with a spark of defiance, "I won't do it in any German uniform. It's me she's taking, not a German admiral." Snatching the blouse from its resting-place, he went upstairs pulling it over head and shoulders.

"Nicholas, wait!" the Kaiser bellowed, dropping the weight on the bench with a crash, and hastening upstairs on the tsarevitch's trail. "Is your good-for-nothing cousin Vasily about?—I want a word."

With that, silence and darkness fell once more upon the basement. Anton said, "Ah, damnation! We should have taken the opportunity to deal with both of them!"

"Not the Kaiser," I said hastily. "That really *would* touch off a war—you should hear Vasily's stories about how much bowing and scraping the Kabale must do to keep him in check. Strictly Nicky—and the best of it is, we can catch him going a-courting. Quick, get the laudanum ready, and let's be out on the street when he comes."

Anton saw the sense in that, and we withdrew, taking a short-cut over the brick-and-picket fence. After a wait of ten minutes, the front door opened, admitting our quarry. Three men followed him down the path towards the gate. I met

Anton's eyes: he gave me a curt nod.

The picket-gate opened and our man emerged, muffled up in a great-coat, for despite the sunny April days the weather was frosty at night. Anton sprang upon him, forcing the vial of laudanum between lips slack with surprise. I slammed the gate in the faces of his startled bodyguard. A chill pierced through me as I saw the pale glow in the eyes of the two foremost.

"Revenants," I gasped, tightening my grip on my umbrella. "Quickly, Anton!"

Behind me, someone swore roundly in German. There came the sound of a blow, and Anton recoiled from our target with a grunt of pain.—I turned in horror, and found myself facing the German emperor!

I must insist that until this precise moment, all had gone quite according to plan. Our ambush, together with our stratagem for delaying the police escort, had gone perfectly smoothly. Beneath that overcoat and muffler, how were we to tell the difference between Nicky and his bellicose cousin? Neither were very tall men, after all.

Well—it was no use repining, and the time was ripe for a decision. The two revenants flung themselves at the gate, clawing and barely more than an arm's length from my face. They were too frantic to think of opening the gate, which was sturdily constructed of cast-iron. Anton was still reeling beneath the wild impact of the Kaiser's fist, and as for the Kaiser himself—well, as a werewolf, he was no more vulnerable to a few drops of laudanum than you or I. I hesitated, considering the uncomfortable likelihood that I had just struck the match that would plunge Europe into war. What now? I had my silver-loaded revolver in my pocket, but

I did not wish to repeat the tragedy of two nights ago.

All this went through my mind in a flash between one heartbeat and the next; and then I caught the fist the Kaiser swung at me. Responding in the way I had been taught, I rotated his extended arm behind him, driving him to his knees on the ground. For a moment he was helpless, and the syringe was ready to hand. I jabbed the hypodermic into his wrist and depressed the plug. The Kaiser howled in mingled outrage and pain. Then someone shouted at the revenants to stand aside and flung open the gate—the third man—Nicky, his red eyes enormous with shock.

"Here, thtop that at onthe," he protested.

He grabbed for my wrist as I withdrew the syringe, but never caught me. Instead, a stream of saltwater struck him in the face. Nicky screamed, recoiling into the path of the revenants, which had just now managed to get out the gate.

"Quickly." Throwing aside his empty canteen, Anton caught me by the hand and set off down the narrow street at a run, hotly pursued by the revenants. The last thing I saw as we fled was the Kaiser, half collapsed upon the ground in front of the gate, clasping his right arm to his bosom.

Chapter XVI.

"You assaulted *the Kaiser?*" May covered her face with her hands. For a moment I was not sure whether she was about to burst out into laughter or a stern lecture. "Oh, *Sharp!*"

"What else could we do?" I said mournfully. It was difficult not to wonder what Short must think of me *now*—now that I had added to my crimes by kidnapping a princess and assaulting an Emperor. "It seemed as though Nicky would be the first to leave—idiots that we were, we never even *thought—*"

May shook her head. "It isn't my place to criticise you when I was sitting at home all night in comfort. The main thing is that you got away safely, and Cousin William lived to tell the tale."

Anton and I had been forced to lead the Kaiser's revenants a merry chase before reaching the house near the Marktplatz sometime in the small hours. We had run far and fast—and been obliged to borrow some horses from a farmhouse on the southern outskirts of the town—before satisfying ourselves that we had evaded the creatures.

Now I stifled a yawn and accepted the bowl of porridge May set on the table before me.

"I made it myself," she said proudly. "Though I'm afraid it's a bit burnt."

"Toasted," I corrected her. "Burnt porridge is a dreadful prospect in the morning, but toasted porridge sounds quite nice, all things considered. Pass the salt?"

She did as requested and sat down to watch me eat my breakfast. "What about my blood? I suppose it must have worked?"

That was the question I had hoped she might not ask. "If it had been Nicky we attacked, we might have seen the effects at once. But the Kaiser—werewolves don't transform until moonrise, and when we met him he was in human shape. As an experiment to prove our theory, it was a wash, I'm afraid."

"That must be why Anton went out.—He said he meant to buy a newspaper." May frowned at her saucepan, in which a little left-over porridge was flecked with toasted flakes. "I think I'll make him another batch of porridge. This one isn't very good."

I raised an eyebrow at her. "You and Anton seem matey all of a sudden."

"I must admit, I rather enjoy his company. He was terribly rude all the time, at first…and of course he's still terribly rude, asking for cups of tea, and calling me what he likes, without so much as a by-your-leave…but things changed when you went missing at the Kabale."

"Oh?" I said, taking a leaf out of May's own book.

She let out a wistful sigh. "Life as a royalty…there are so *many* rules of precedence—who goes before whom, and all that. And when you're morganatic you're nobody; or if you're thought of at all, you're put the very last of all. But when I'm talking to Anton, none of that matters in the least, and it's no use keeping one's distance to maintain one's dignity, for he won't hear of it. I'm astonished to say that I find him refreshing."

"What about George?" I asked, purely out of curiosity.

Her face went through a peculiar contortion—a little careless smile, and then a swift withdrawal behind her customary reserve. "Oh! George is different. Of course *he* must play by the rules of precedence, but whenever he has the choice, he treats me as though I were as wellborn as he." And she gave a wistful sigh. "You will think me terribly fickle, Sharp, but I can't help thinking about…that is to say, I think you were right when you said that he would suit me terribly well if only he wasn't a monster."

"Well," I said gently, "now we know he needn't be. He intended to make *you* a monster; but why shouldn't it go the other way? *You* might render him harmless."

May's gaze fell to her bowl of scarcely-touched porridge. "That had occurred to me."

"Have you spoken to him about it? Do you think he'd agree?"

May gulped. "Oh! I couldn't. If he even knew I was here, helping you—why, I don't know what he'd do!"

I remembered the objections she had made at the beginning of our eventful stay in Coburg, at the gaol. "You told me once that you needed to respect George as your king," I pointed out. "Of course we can't jeopardise our present work but surely you might tell George something of the truth, about your feelings. I can understand deceiving someone because you know they would use the truth for evil; but if there's one thing I've learned at great personal cost, May, it's never to hide the truth from anyone I truly respect."

May did not look me in the eye, but a faint blush burned on her cheekbones, making her look more than ever like a flaxen-haired china doll.

The front door opened, and Anton called a greeting from the hallway.

"What news, Anton?" I rejoined.

Having bolted the front door behind him, he tramped into the kitchen pulling his cloth cap from his head with a shrug. "Not a thing. I didn't even bother getting a newspaper."

"Nothing?" I frowned. "No gossip? Not even about an attack?"

"Oh, there was gossip all right," Anton pulled back a chair with a dreadful scrape and dropped into it. "Did you know that the Kaiser was set upon by a band of at least a dozen anarchists last night, and escaped with his life after a running battle up and down the Marienstrasse?"

"That sounds terribly exciting."

"It was. He covered himself in slathers of glory and single-handedly saved the tsarevitch's life. But no one has heard anything about an injury, let alone a defanging."

I passed a hand across my forehead. Several nights with little sleep were catching up with me again. Why must everything in my life fall to pieces precisely at the full moon each month? "Does this mean May's blood didn't work?"

"Not necessarily," May said from the stove, where she was furiously stirring porridge over scorching heat. This, as anyone will tell you, is exactly the wrong way to make porridge. If we outlived the night, I decided, I really must give her some cooking lessons.

"What makes you say that?" Anton demanded. "Surely if the Kaiser had been defanged his revenants would be crawling all over Coburg looking for revenge."

May sighed. "How to explain... Did you notice his left arm?"

"No?"

"Wait," I put in. "He kept his left arm tucked behind his back all the time. Even when he was demonstrating weight-lifting to Nicky."

May nodded. "It's shrunken. Some sort of birth defect, I believe. I'm *told* it's about six inches shorter than his right, but nobody really knows because he keeps it out of the way as much as he can. I saw him at Cowes several years ago, you know, and he moved in the queerest manner, right shoulder foremost, almost like a crab. The point is, if Cousin William *had* been defanged, I think he would go to almost any lengths to conceal it."

"Good heavens, I hadn't thought of that."

"I wouldn't put it past him to go the rest of his life pretending he's still a werewolf." Having scraped the porridge into a bowl, May looked in a resigned way at the brown crust once again covering the saucepan's base. Then she set the bowl before Anton.

"Aren't you forgetting something?" she asked him sweetly.

"Forgetting…Oh. Thanks for making breakfast."

May raised an eyebrow. "I meant the villainous slouch."

I nearly choked on my laughter. Anton had, of course, spent the last four weeks in May's company sprawled impertinently across every available surface. This morning, he occupied his chair like an ordinary person—he hadn't even put his feet up on the table.

To my great surprise, he reddened. "You're all right, May," he said gruffly, shovelling a spoonful of porridge into his mouth. "Your old mother's not bad either, once you get to know her."

"Why, *thank* you," she said with a curtsey.

"Does this mean you're exempting the Tecks from the revolution?" I teased.

Anton took a mouthful of coffee and slanted a sidelong glance at May. "As I see it, the Tecks *are* the revolution."

"Oh, dear!" May said faintly.

"Take it as a compliment, May. You should have heard the wild denunciations he made about you on the Orient Express. Very bitter."

Anton jabbed his spoon towards me. "I see your strategem, Liz Sharp, and I'm not falling for it. I'm still demanding you hand the bloodsucker to me when this is over."

"Vasily, you mean?" I could scarce repress a shudder as I recalled his low whisper—*occasionally I forgive, but I* never *forget.* "Not for my sake, I hope. Vasily and I are even. He stole my blood; I abandoned him to the Kabale. Now that we've each done horrible things to the other, I'm ready to move on."

"Which will give him all the opportunity he needs to stab you in the back again," Anton grumbled, giving voice to my own unspoken doubts. "Speaking of the bloodsucker, did he ever come in last night?"

May shook her head.

At that moment the front door rattled to a loud knock, saving me from the embarrassment of trying to answer. "That's probably him now," I said brightly.

Anton rolled his eyes, but he must have at least partly agreed, for he took a swallow of tea, and went down the passage to open the front door.

From the kitchen, I heard the door open quite clearly. There was a moment's silence. I heard a scuffle; and an all-too-familiar voice said, "Anton Lupei, you are hereby under arrest."

Beside me, May stiffened in shock.

"The dickens!" I bolted to my feet, knocking over my chair. Down the narrow passageway that led from the kitchen to the front door, I saw Anton blocking the way with his hands lifted in protest. Beyond him I caught a glimpse of Short.

Short! I was overwhelmed with conflicting emotion. I wanted to flee from my own weakness. I wanted to belt him over the head with a sauce-pan, just to see if it would knock some sense into him.

I wanted to walk into his arms and melt that grim mouth with kisses.

Anton's shout recalled me to my senses.

"It's the bootheels! Run! Get her to safety!"

With the sound of a blow, Anton staggered and fell. Why, it was George—George, flattening him with a single right hook.

Stifling my shriek, I slammed the kitchen door and looked wildly about for some means of fastening it. There was neither lock nor bar, but a heavy oak dresser stood against the wall nearby. With a groan of effort I drew it across the doorway.

I was only just in time. The kitchen door rattled against the makeshift barricade as our assailants reached it. I turned to find May sitting motionless at the table with one hand raised to her lips, her blue eyes wide in shock.

"George—" she murmured, "that was George—he hit Anton."

"And Short was with him," I said mechanically. We stared at each other a moment, and then I managed to unearth my sense of humour. "May dear, I always knew we were cursed with beauty beyond compare, but I never expected to be besieged by admirers in my own kitchen! Certainly not by *George and Short.*"

"May!" George called frantically between hammering blows at the kitchen door. "May, are you there? I've come to save you!"

The light of battle kindled in May's eyes. "If they mean to drag us about like the spoils of war, they're quite mistaken! Are we Helen of Troy, Sharp?"

"Not on your life! I have been Athene and Nemesis, but at present I am going to mimic Odysseus, and beat a cunning retreat. Come along." So saying, I gathered her up and swept her towards the door at the rear of the kitchen. This gave onto a narrow area leading between two other, larger houses to the street behind. As I threw open the door, however, a whiff of corruption drifted to my nostrils. A pair of bowler-hatted figures loitered in the shade of a oak tree growing in the cul-de-sac. Both turned horrible, eyeless faces upon us.

"Revenants," I gasped, bundling May back into the kitchen and slamming the door. Being an external entrance, this was fitted with a bolt; but would it hold against the efforts of two or three determined revenants?

Apart from the door I had barricaded with the dresser and one or two small windows opening onto the area, there was no other mode of egress. We were trapped.

"We're trapped!" May whispered.

"Well spotted, ma'am; you're really getting the hang of this." May permitted herself a small, pleased smile. I glanced about the kitchen. What were we to do? Surrendering to Short was as bad as surrendering to Missy; for me, at least. Yet here we were trapped in the kitchen with enemies at both doors, and Anton a prisoner in the hands of revenants! I beat an impotent fist against my bosom. How desperately I had attempted to save him from just such a fate—and now at last he had met it through his loyalty to me!

Was I to lose all my friends, one by one?

"Miss Sharp." Short's voice echoed hollowly from behind the barricade. "You are surrounded. We know you have Princess May with you. Release her at once, unharmed, and we will do our best to ensure you are treated with clemency."

"Never!" May murmured. "Death before surrender!"

"No, May: think. They have Anton a prisoner—and we're hardly any better off. Our one advantage is what they don't know—that you're here by your own free will. They still think I've kidnapped you. Please, let me exchange you for Anton."

"But you need my blood for tonight!"

"We still have two syringes full. It will have to do. *Please.* You won't be in any danger, for you'll still have George's protection. But if I don't get Anton back, who knows what they will do to him? They might even hand him over to the Kabale for execution."

From the way May's lips pursed, I could tell that her blood was up, and the thought of surrender was bitter to her. She let out a beleaguered sigh. "If Anton's in danger, then of course I'll do it, Sharp. But don't fail us tonight, or we shall all be for it together."

"Stout feller." Taking a deep breath, I went towards the door. I must attack Short's vulnerability—but how? It wasn't easy with a door between us.

"Hullo, Alexander."

An echoing silence ensued before his reply drifted through to me in a stiff, emotionless voice. "Miss Sharp? Your answer?"

"Well, I hardly know what to say," I said, affecting a girlish modesty. "Naturally I am sensible of the compliment—the very great compliment you have paid me—and I hesitate to cause you pain, for I think of you very highly—but—"

"I *beg* your pardon?"

"Don't interrupt, old man; I'm trying to let you down gently. As I was saying, as highly as I think of you, dear Alexander, I find myself wholly unable to accept your offer. In time, I hope the wound may heal."

"I'm asking you to surrender, Miss Sharp, not to marry me!" Short said in exasperation. "I haven't complimented you at all."

(May sniffed. "Never a truer word."—I pretended not to hear her interjection.)

"Oh! surrender, marriage, a trifling difference! I don't hold it against you. Charity shall cover the multitude of sins," I said magnanimously. "In either case, much though it pains me to do so, I cannot accept."

"By Jove, is she refusing to let May go?" George asked, unseen.

"I warned you she might," Short responded, *sotto voce.*

"Au contraire, I'm not refusing at all," I put in. "I only said that I cannot accept Short's terms."

"Now look here, Miss Sharp—"

"Wait, Short, let me!" There was a scuffle at the door, and George added in stentorian tones: "I warn you, Sharp, I mean to have May back unhurt! Might as well give in! Have you surrounded, demmit!"

"I'm sure we can work something out," I said equably. "The fact is, I have someone *you* want, and you have someone *I* want. I would be quite prepared to hand May over in return for Anton, *if* you'll give up Short as a hostage for our safe departure."

"Sir, I really *don't* think...," Short hissed from the other side of the door.

"I warn you, I'm not as silly as I look," I called. "Once you have May, I need *some* guarantee that I'll be allowed to leave the house safely! I want Short, and if all goes well I shall release him when Anton and I are both in the clear."

There was another brief interval of agitated whispering. "And if we refuse?" Short asked at length.

It was all horribly awkward. I must put on a show of desperation, without making them too frightened to let me go free. The trouble was, Anton had followed me into a great deal of trouble, and I *must* rescue him.

"Then if you want May, you'll have to fight your way into this room," I bluffed, withdrawing my little revolver from my pocket, and spinning the cylinder so that they could hear I was armed. "Believe me, I much prefer a quick death on my own terms, to a long, slow one at the hands of the monsters. Do we have an agreement?"

More whispering from behind the dresser. May stood by my side, her grasp upon my arm slowly tightening as we waited. What if they called my bluff? Did they really believe I was reckless enough to expose May to the dangers of a gunfight? And if they did, was there any coming back—would anyone after this believe I was not every whit the bloodthirsty anarchist I seemed to be?

May sent me an anxious look. "You needn't do this," she whispered. "I could *tell* them I came of my own free will."

I shook my head. "No, don't."

There was no time to explain why.

"We accept your terms," George announced. "By Jove! Expected better of you, Sharp."

"As did I of you, your grace," I said. "Bring Short and Anton around to the back door, and send your pet corpses away. We shan't want them."

I turned from the door and took a deep, slow breath. My stratagem had worked!

May looked troubled—that is, she gazed into the distance with a faint furrow between her brows. "Oh, Sharp. They really think you've gone cracked."

"It can't be helped," said I. "I can't leave Anton in their clutches, and I can't face the Kabale with you in danger, as you will be if anything harms this alliance you have with George. Now, in case I don't see you again—"

"Don't say that!"

"It's a possibility," I said gently. "I want you to know that I think you're an absolute brick. May dear, it's been an honour, and I'll never forget everything you've done for me—starting with that Whitechapel werewolf business."

"Oh, Sharp," she said, much affected. "I only wish there was something more I could do, now that those two blockheads have ruined everything!"

"Not everything." I patted the pocket where the two remaining hypodermics, with their precious contents, rested within their cases. "Tonight, please God, we shall defang the Kabale and end all these dreadful cover-ups. After that, I suppose I shall take myself off to another hemisphere—Australia, or South America, or something. But I'll always remember you fondly, May."

"As will I, Sharp," she said, grasping my hand warmly, "always, always."

Perhaps two minutes elapsed before George and Short could be seen approaching via the cul-de-sac with their prisoner. I was relieved to see that Anton seemed undamaged. The two revenants who had been loitering at the rear of the house turned away and departed. Once the coast was thus cleared, there was no putting things off.

Drawing a deep breath, I opened the back door.

"Here's May," I said, drawing her onto the step beside me. "Now will you let Anton go?"

Short looked rather more pale and interesting than usual this morning. His burning eyes never moved from my face as he thrust Anton forward as though disposing of a soiled garment. I released May, and a tense silence prevailed as the princess and the anarchist approached each other in the space between Short and myself.

The two of them paused as they met. May put out her hand; Anton took it. His head bowed imperceptibly. "Ma'am," he said in a voice almost too low to hear, even for me.—Then they parted.

As May reached George, he uttered a cry and swept her into his arms. "May! Safe! By Jove—I thought—I feared—are you hurt?"

"I am perfectly well, George. This has all been blown quite out of proportion, you know." From the chill in her voice, it must have been like embracing a marble column.

"Overblown?" George nearly squawked with indignation. "'Pon my word I don't know what you mean! Kidnapped by your own bodyguards! I mean to say!"

May sent a look of mute appeal towards Anton and myself. I shook my head imperceptibly before turning to Short.

"Now, Alexander, will you join us?"

His mouth thinned stubbornly, and I felt a terrible sinking at the pit of my stomach. For a moment, I wondered if he meant to honour our bargain at all. A word of refusal, now that May was secure, and he might take Anton and myself as prisoners and scotch all our plans. It was what Vasily would have done in his place—but of course, despite all my fears, Short was not Vasily.

"I'll hand myself over in exchange for the blood," he said at last.

The dickens! He might not be Vasily, but he was not playing quite fair, either. I forced an insouciant smile.

"The blood? I beg your pardon? What blood?"

"The morganatic blood, of course," he said. He always *had* been indecently perceptive. "Why else would you go to all the risk and trouble of kidnapping a princess, without any sort of ransom demand? We know what you're planning, and we can't allow it to proceed. Give it up, and I'll gladly hand myself over."

"That wasn't our agreement," I objected.

"It is now, I'm afraid."

He had us at a disadvantage, and it was all very well for May to send frantic, silent signals, but there was no choice but to comply.

"Never marked *you* for such a slippery blighter," I muttered, forgetting for a moment that I meant to sweeten him up.

Short smiled bleakly. "I'm matching wits with *you* now, Miss Sharp. Desperate times, desperate measures."

Reluctantly I reached into my left pocket; but May, goaded beyond bearing, interrupted with four imperious words.

"Sharp! Don't you *dare!*"

From the way George stared at her, she might have turned and bitten him.

"May, no!" I cried, recognising the blazing look she turned

upon Short.

"Look here, Mr Short! I'll thank you to remember that it's *my* blood you are talking about, and *I* will give it away if I see fit!"

"I beg your pardon!" George stuttered. But Short made a violent gesture and cried:

"I *knew* it!"

"May, no," I murmured again, but it was much too late. May had the bit between her teeth, and all I could do was ride out the storm.

"Have you any idea of the *trouble* I've had because of this interference? Compelled to flee my family—compelled to slander my best friends as violent kidnappers—and now kidnapped in return by a pair of blockheads who ought to know better!"

"May!" George protested. She turned upon him with heaving bosom, looking far more like a Valkyrie in that moment than her mother ever had. The effect was not lost upon George, who, after some effort, retrieved his tongue from the back of his throat, where it seemed to have gotten tangled up among his tonsils. "May! Don't mean to say—you came here—on *purpose!*"

"And why not?"

"Why not?!—Give your blood?—Destroy your own family?"

"Destroy them? What nonsense! I'm no more an anarchist than Sharp is!"

"That's quite anarchic enough as it is," Short muttered; and I must admit he had a point.

May softened as quickly as she had exploded. "Oh, come, George, do you not understand? I have done this not to destroy but to *preserve* our family. After Eddy—and poor

Toria—don't you see why I must act?"

George paled, and all the indignation drained out of him. "Oh, Lor'!" he groaned. "Oh, damn and blast! If you put it like that…If this had only happened in time to save all those poor girls Eddy killed…Still! Hang it, May, this ruins everything! It won't do, having an anarchist queen!"

"Allow me to remind you that I never consented to be your queen!"

"No, hang it, I didn't mean…that is to say…I can't do this anymore, dear girl! One thing to pretend an engagement for your safety—quite another to give cover to anarchist activities! Ought to have spoken to me plainly, by Jove!"

"You are correct, of course." May drew herself up to her full height. "My one regret is that I was not quite candid with you from the beginning. Naturally this pretense must be abandoned."

George shuddered as though stabbed to the heart. "Naturally," he managed, and I don't know how he said it without bursting into tears.

"May," I repeated feebly, but of course it was no use. I could feel my hair turning grey with each moment. This was exactly what I was afraid of. May *mustn't* break her engagement with George—it was the only thing standing between her and the Kabale's wrath.

"The blood, Miss Sharp," Short now cut in, advancing towards me with an outstretched hand.

I could have gnashed my teeth—*everything* hung on my being able to use May's blood tonight—but there was no help for it. Without a hostage, there was no getting safely away from the house that had so recently become a trap. I dug into my pocket and surrendered a syringe.

"The other two as well," Short said inexorably. "Three were taken from the hospital, I believe."

Oh! he *was* on the ball. Wordlessly, I withdrew the remaining two syringes—one empty, the other full—and added them to his collection; whereupon he offered them to George, who accepted them with a bleak sigh and extended his arm to May.

"Shall we, ma'am?"

"Thank you, your grace," May replied icily, "but I can find my own way back to the palace."

With that she turned on her heel and set off, George following like a beaten dog.

In the echoing silence, Short turned to face Anton and myself, looking from one to the other of us with something like despair in his drooping eyes.

"There," he said, "it is done. Now I give you my word of honour not to escape."

Chapter XVII.

The words, the look, were too much for my wounded heart, and I turned away from Short's despairing gaze.—The next moment I could have kicked myself. My strategem was to let Short *see* my feelings, not to conceal them.

For so long I had been branded a danger, a temptress. For so long I had worked to prove myself anything but. Now that I fancied a man, I could not even show him what I felt, though it might be the world's best hope for peace.

I resolved never again to laugh at May and George. Compared to me, they were a miracle of eloquence.

"Are you all right, Anton?" I asked. "Did they hurt you?"

"They must hit a great deal harder to hurt *me*," Anton said. Despite the bruise forming where George had struck him, I could well believe it. Stocky and tough, Anton looked as though he might almost have been hewn from oak.

"You didn't need to give up May for me," he added. "I don't mind being monster bait, so long as I know the Kabale will fall."

"It's no use, Anton. Neither of us could bear the thought of leaving you in the hands of the monsters, and you're more help to us alive and free."

Anton looked so moved by my words, and I felt such longing

for an affectionate touch, that I threw my arms around his neck. At this, Short turned abruptly and stalked past both of us into the kitchen with his hands thrust deep into the pockets of his greatcoat and his shoulders hunched like a wet bird of prey.

"Smells like burnt porridge in here," he muttered.

It wasn't like Short to grumble, and I was conscious of a feeling of guilty triumph. He felt *something,* at any rate.

"Toasted porridge," I amended, following him within. "Best we pack our things and go, but first, Alexander, may I ask a question?"

His lips thinned. I could tell that he hated my using his given name, but dared not object. "You may always ask me anything, Miss Sharp; only I will not promise to reply."

"Oh, it's nothing personal," I murmured, brushing a bit of imaginary lint from his collar. "How did you and George know where to find us?"

Two bright spots lit up on his cheekbones; and he tried to step back, but the table was in the way. "I can't answer that," he said.

I curled my fingers around his cravat, pulling his head down until it was on a level with my own. "Only four people knew the location of this hideaway, my love."

He might have tried to push me away from him. Instead, he closed his eyes and turned away a face drawn with pain and anger. "Please, don't do this."

The appeal cut me unexpectedly to the heart. Perhaps this would require greater resolve and a harder heart than I possessed. If I was unable to hold my purpose, how could I be the friend Short truly needed? Just as I had stood up to Anton and my parents at Castle Sarkozy, I must stand up to

Short now.

And yet, what was this? For all my good intentions, I had already recoiled from the lines of agony etched in his face—I had done as he asked, and the moment was gone.

I cleared my throat to cover my confusion. "The four people who knew of this place were myself, Anton, May and Vasily. Which of us gave it away?"

Behind me, Anton snorted. "Need you ask?"

"Or was it none of us?" I suggested. Perhaps I might bait Short to correct me. "Were Anton and I followed last night?"

"You might as well save your breath," Anton growled. "The bootheel will never tell us the truth."

"All right," Short said. "If you want to know who betrayed you, it was the tsarevitch, Prince Nicholas."

"I *knew* it," Anton shouted. "Liz, you have to face the truth."

"You're confusing me, Anton," I said plaintively. "Am I supposed to believe this man, or not?"

Anton scowled. "You know it's the truth! You know the bloodsucker's in Nicky's pocket!"

"Of course I know it." The Kaiser had mentioned Vasily last night, as though he expected to find the vampire infesting Nicky's drawing-room. Given that the only other options were May, Anton, or myself, Vasily was the obvious culprit.

Yet it troubled me to find that I was reluctant to disbelieve in Vasily. I had betrayed him to the Kabale, and my conscience prompted me to give him the benefit of the doubt now. He had rescued me from Missy, after all—I ignored the inner voice that suggested he might have done so merely to gain my trust.

"Even if it was Vasily, it all comes to the same thing, which is that we must find ourselves a new hiding-place, and that quickly." I looked meditatively at Short. "I think I know the place."

Anton followed my gaze. "I hope you don't mean to bring *him* along."

"We shall *have* to bring him if we go to the place I mean—unless you like the idea of going about Coburg interviewing landladies with a pack of revenants baying for your blood. Here, give us a hand with this."

I seized the heavy dresser barricading the kitchen door and, with Anton's help, succeeded in heaving it aside. This done, I threw open the door and came face-to-face with Vasily, who had just entered by the front door of the house.

"Speak of the devil," I said in an undertone to Anton. He, for his part, expressed himself in more forceful language. Seeing there was no help for it, and hoping that Short had still a little laudanum spray about him, I beckoned Vasily to enter the kitchen.

"Explain yourself, young man! Where have *you* been?"

Vasily spread his hands in a shrug. "Now I am back in the Kabale's favour, I am expected to spend my time with my own kind.—Where is Princess May?"

"Gone back to the palace." I scarcely paid attention to the question. If Vasily had indeed betrayed us, how best to surprise a confession out of him?

Anton took the choice entirely out of my hands. "Short here was just telling us how you betrayed our hideaway to the Kabale."

"Short?" Vasily breathed. "The bootheel is here?"

He brushed past me like an icy breath of air on a winter's day and moments later had seized Short's lapels in his fists. He grinned savagely into the taller man's face and said, "When you've finished with him, I want this one to eat."

"That's out of the question!"

Vasily looked murderous. "I have forgiven you for leaving me to the Kabale, but I will not forgive him."

"Don't pretend you didn't deserve it," Short put in. And he accused me of a deficient sense of self-preservation!

"The bloodsucker has a point," Anton said unexpectedly. "Come, Liz, wouldn't it work nicely? The vampire can kill the policeman, and then I can kill the vampire, and the world will be a better place for it."

"Thank you, Anton, but no.—Vasily, if you damage my policeman, I will stake you myself. No killing."

I spoke mildly, but I drew my saltwater-bottle from my pocket as I did so. Hearing the slosh of the water, Vasily turned to me with a snarl.

"You told the peasant he could have me when our agreement was over. Fair is fair. I want the bootheel."

I hoped that by the time our agreement was over, Anton would have learned to see past his lust for vengeance—but I could hardly say that in front of him.

"First the Kabale must be dealt with," I told them. "If we are to be conspirators, I expect you to honour my wishes. Afterwards—well, I don't approve of feuding, but I don't suppose I can prevent you if you all decide to slaughter each other."

And if they were rotten enough to do it, then Anton was right, and the world *would* be a better place with them gone, I thought. But I could hardly say that, either.

A reluctant grin stole across Vasily's face. "Miss Sharp," he said, releasing Short, "you are not like any lady I know."

"And *you* are evading the question. Did you betray us to

Nicky?"

"I did not," he said, this time without a moment's hesitation. "Not that you'll believe me, of course; but it's the truth."

Of course it was difficult to believe him. He had only made an alliance with me because he wanted my help; and now he was, as he had said, once more in the Kabale's favour. What reason had he to tell the truth now?

Yet there was something in his face that had not been there yesterday, in Mary Adelaide's drawing-room. Something else had happened—or was about to happen. Something dreadful.

"Why do you say I won't believe you?"

He nodded towards the area door. "Look outside."

I nodded to Anton, who moved to the window giving onto the cul-de-sac outside. Almost at once, he recoiled from the light.

"Revenants!" he cried. "Dozens of them!"

My heart crawled up my throat. Whisking the sturdy wooden pin from the hair coiled atop my head, I set it against Vasily's heart. "Monster! Is this *your* doing?"

"I am only the messenger, Miss Sharp." His smile was mocking, as though he dared me to contradict him. "Do not, I beg you, do anything foolish. The house is surrounded by revenants in the Kaiser's employ."

"The *Kaiser?*" Short choked. "What on earth—"

"Good heavens," I said with a ray of sudden illumination. "Don't tell me we succeeded in defanging him?"

"Suffice it to say that he now has a very personal stake in your capture."

"You defanged the Kaiser?" Short whispered, horrified. "This will mean war for certain."

Defeat was thick in my throat. I could have kicked myself.

Vasily must have been delaying us all this time, holding us in argument while his revenant cohorts surrounded us. "I certainly chose the wrong moment to start trusting *you,* Vasily."

"I knew you wouldn't believe me."

"Very well: satisfy my curiosity, and explain to me exactly why I should."

Short made a noise of protest, but Anton growled. "Go on, bloodsucker. This ought to be entertaining."

"I don't ask you to trust me," Vasily said, ignoring their interruptions, "but here is the truth of it: after you shook off the revenants, the Kaiser sent werewolves to track you—and since you failed to cover your tracks with saltwater, you led them directly to this house. He informed Cousin Nicholas, and Cousin Nicholas, when he heard of Princess May's disappearance, informed Prince George. That is all. I had nothing to do with it."

I had half feared such a thing—dash it, I had suggested it myself when questioning Short just now. Yet, in Vasily's mouth, the explanation seemed hollow.

"A likely story!" Short muttered.

"Oh, so I take it you knew nothing of all this, Alexander? You merely happened to come here and retrieve May, just before the Kaiser's revenants arrived?"

Short flushed. "Prince Nicholas didn't inform us of the Kaiser's involvement, and that's the truth. We had no intention of betraying you to the Kabale."

With that, we seemed at an impasse. I scarcely knew what to do. Was Vasily telling the truth? Was Short? How the dickens were we to extricate ourselves from this trap?

"Don't worry, Liz," Anton told me. "We'll find a way out of

this. Wait here; I'll be back in a minute. Don't let either of them go, and don't trust them one inch."

He went into the hallway, doubtless meaning to reconnoitre the front of the house. A moment later his footsteps echoed on the stairs. Outside in the area, the revenants began to beat against the door with their closed fists, summoning us to open up in the name of Imperial Prussia.

It was a warning, nothing more. When once the revenants received their orders to attack, nothing short of a miracle would help us.

In the silence, Short took a step towards me. "It's no good, Miss Sharp. Surrender to me, and I'll see that you come to no harm."

"You won't keep that promise," I told him bleakly, and he nearly flinched. My own tears rose dangerously close to the surface. Short was my friend—Short was my ally—Short had put himself willingly into the power of the monsters and was little more than their tool. He might not be a revenant, but he had surrendered his will and conscience to Missy; and much as I wished to depend upon him now, I should be a fool to risk it.

I turned back to Vasily. "Why are you here, then? Have you come to gloat?"

"Hardly. I've been sent to offer terms."

"You have terms?" Until a moment ago I had not been aware I would have a choice.

"Such as they are: here is what the Kabale is willing to offer," Vasily said. "Turn yourselves in now, and Miss Sharp will be converted to an unliving revenant. Anton Lupei will be hanged like the mad dog he is, and May of Teck will be confined in a lunatic asylum."

"A revenant?" I said faintly.

Short made a wordless sound of protest. "How can they expect her to consent to that?"

"They will leave her with her life," Vasily said with a shrug. "To them, that is a great concession."

My life!—and what kind of life would I have, when every conviction, every principle was blurred out, and I was pressed into the mould of obedience?

Short was pale to the lips. "They must offer something better than that."

"Don't be naïve," said Vasily. "You will be a revenant yourself one day, and soon. Your masters have already set things in train to convert the English police. Doubtless you will be given the chance to resign first, although I would counsel you to do it quickly, before they fill your head with glamours, and convince you it is your dearest wish to be relieved of your own mind."

Short sunk into a chair, burying his face in his hands. I ran the tip of my tongue across my lips, which had become dry, and turned to Vasily.

"And if I refuse these terms—what then?"

"Then the revenants break down the door and beat you to death, and you become one of them in any case."

He said it with brutal indifference, and I could not help shuddering. "I meant about May."

I thought I could bear anything that happened to Anton and myself, so long as May could be saved.

"Oh, she will be locked away regardless."

Horrible fate!—to be shut up in one of *those* places—neglected at best, tormented at worst, and eventually to be driven mad in truth!—May, May! What had I brought upon her?

Another blow came at the door, and one of the panels splintered. If this went on much longer, the door would be gone. I glanced towards Short, but his face was still hidden. A pang of unexpected sympathy went through me. With what burdens had he laded his conscience in the hope of saving my life, only to see me brought to this pass?

But Vasily was waiting for his answer.—"Kill me," I said softly. "If Anton is to be consigned to a literal, and May to a figurative, grave, then I had rather a thousand times not be alive to know of it."

Vasily watched me with something odd in his eyes—a softness that hinted at sorrow, or perhaps only respect. "I expected no less from you, Miss Sharp. But I would offer you a different choice."

"What do you mean?" I found that my voice was scarcely a whisper.

"Accept the Kabale's terms and surrender yourself.—No, hear me out. There will be a few hours, at least, during which I might be able to help you escape."

He could not possibly be sincere. I shivered, remembering the evening several weeks ago when Vasily had betrayed me for the first time, in a cell beneath Castle Sarkozy. I knew him to be treacherous and merciless, but if I refused him it would surely signal the onset of the revenants. That was why I did not turn him down at once.

"What about Anton?"

"Him too, if I can manage it."

"Why?" I demanded huskily. I kept the stake pressed against Vasily's heart—for all the good it might do. It being daytime, he had no fangs with which to bite me; but he was still strong enough to break my neck if he really wished it. "Why do you offer me this?—you, who fear neither the judgement of God nor the vengeance of man—you, who no longer need my help against the Kabale, since they have accepted you once more into their bosom."

"Do I not?" His voice was soft, wellnigh overwhelmed by the sound of the revenants as they clawed the walls and shook the door. "Yet I have found something to fear, Liz Sharp. Until now I never knew what it was like to be marked out as the Kabale's enemy. It seems that there are consequences to creating a juggernaut of ruthless power with which to crush one's enemies. Believe me, that machine crushes its own as easily as anyone else."

"And Miss Sharp is to turn herself over to them on your word alone?" Short broke in, lifting his face from his hands. He looked downright haggard.

Vasily didn't acknowledge Short, but he must have seen from the look on my face that I agreed with him. "You don't believe me," he said in some resignation. "I suppose it is poetic justice, that I shall never be free of the Kabale because of what I did in the dungeon beneath Castle Sarkozy."

His words were like a knife twisting in my heart. If he had not asked such a thing of me—surrender to the Kabale!—I might have been tempted to trust him. Instead—

Instead, something entirely different happened.

For some minutes now I had heard Anton's feet going to and fro above us. Now came the sound of a window opening above. Something heavy fell into the area, where the revenants swarmed the rear of the house.

Instinct told me what to expect, and I turned to Short with a shriek of warning. At the same instant he rose from his chair, folded me in his arms, and threw us both to the ground with his body shielding my own. There was barely time to close my eyes and clasp my hands over my ears before there came a roar of sound and a wave of billowing heat reeking with the sweet scent of dynamite. Shattered glass from the kitchen windows rained down on us, mixed with flakes of soot and burning embers.

When all was still, Short groaned and slid aside. I got up, shaking and coughing. My ears rang painfully, but I had saved my eyesight and could look about me. The first thing I saw was Short curled up in agony on the floor. There was a nasty shard of glass embedded in his back beneath the right shoulder-blade, and the scent of blood was thick on the air.

I drew in a sharp breath and seized my hairpin-stake, ready to defend him from the vampire. But Vasily was not, for the moment, interested in blood. He still leaned against the wall where the force of the explosion had blown him, staring dazedly out the splintered kitchen door.

I followed his gaze and found the area beyond full of burning, wriggling pieces of revenant.—Anton, I thought in shock, had saved us all. I had never thought to be grateful for an anarchist's bomb. But I must take Short and flee at once, for more of the undead were sure to be on their way in a moment.—I staggered to my feet and snatched the great packet of salt from beneath the table.

"No, wait!" Vasily cried, seeing what I was about to do.

With one flick of my arm I emptied the sack in a great arc that cut the kitchen in two, dividing the vampire from myself and Short. He threw himself against the invisible barrier and beat desperately against it.

"I can help you," he insisted—upstairs, Anton's footsteps

descended the stair at a run.—"Take me with you."

What he asked was reasonable—yet all his words had been calculated perfectly to wring my heart. How could I trust him when all he had were plausible words, and no deeds? Within the past five minutes he had wellnigh induced me to hand myself over to the Kabale, and now who was to say he meant not to follow me to my new hiding-place for a new betrayal?

"I can't risk it," I told him, backing away and putting my arms around the bleeding Short. "I bear you no ill will, Vasily."

Anton swept through the door into the kitchen, cleared the line of salt in a bound, and paused just long enough that I was able to recognise Veronika's double sword-stick in his hand. There was a click and a hiss as he unsheathed the blades. "Come, Liz. Stay behind me."

With that he charged out the back door and into the burning area. I was aching, bruised, singed, and terrified for May; but I was made strong by wolf bite and vampire bite and utter desperation. I lifted Short to his feet and followed Anton at a stumbling run.

I could feel Vasily's eyes desperate and angry on the back of my neck, but this time I did not look back.

Chapter XVIII.

The house in which Short and Missy had imprisoned me was happily not far, but finding our way there without attracting attention was difficult, given that all three of us were somewhat the worse for wear. Short had a great bleeding gash in his back, and after Anton had employed his double swords to dismember the last of the revenants in the area, he didn't look a great deal better.

I addressed part of this problem by stealing a handcart and tarpaulin from a house behind ours in the cul-de-sac. I helped Short into the cart, but before covering him with the canvas, I laid a gentle hand against his cheek.

"You're a chump," I whispered as Anton sprinkled us with saltwater to confuse the scent. "A splendid, gallant chump; but I'm grateful to you, all the same."

After that we set off in a hurry and arrived at the scene of my captivity and rescue within ten minutes.

"Where on earth did you get that sword-stick?" I asked Anton with some curiosity as we went. "I thought I gave it to May."

"She passed it on to me. She said that she would be bound do to herself an injury if she tried to use it herself, and that since I was her protector, I should have it."

There was something self-conscious in his look as he said this—a faint blush that mantled his weathered cheeks. Naturally I could not allow *this* to pass without comment. "Why, Anton! She's given you her favour, like a lady of old to her knight—and I do believe you *like* it!"

"Humph!" he said. But then, after a moment, he added: "As I recall it, being a knight wasn't always about snobbery with violence. Sometimes it was about defending the defenceless, and that is something every anarchist should do."

"Defending the defenceless?—Is that what you were doing when you bombed the Café Terminus?"

Anton's flush deepened. At first I thought he would not reply, but then at length, he said: "I did wrong, Liz. I thought everyone in that café was a monster or a bootlicker, and deserved death in consequence. But I was wrong about your friends, so who else might I have been wrong about?—Don't say *I told you so.*"

"*Would* I say such a thing?"

"Between one heartbeat and the next, and well you know it.—But in those days I was in despair. I saw no way to break the monsters except with bombs and stakes." He sent me a brief smile. Then, as we approached our new hiding-place, his eyebrows rose in surprise. "*This* is the place?"

"It will have to do, for now." Short having already surrendered his key, I let us into his house. Painful memories assailed me. Here was the chair where Missy had sat in her finery of white and silver; there was the staircase by which she had meddled with Short's mind; up in the shadows was the bedstead to which I had been shackled.

Pulling back the tarpaulin, I found Short with a hand wrapped about his ribs, a little blood still trickling between his fingers.

"Are you badly hurt?" I asked.

"I've been impaled," he said testily.

"The answer is *no*, I take it." His breath was a little quick, but not laboured, as one would expect had the lung been punctured. Anton and I helped him off the cart and inside.

Anton scanned our surroundings with a scowl. "And how long are we planning to stay in this hole? You realise the Kaiser won't rest until we're dead."

"No," I admitted, "but do look on the bright side. We have proof now that our experiment worked.—May's blood does what we hoped!"

"That's nice, but we don't have any left."

"Perhaps not, but the day is young." I peered into the quiet street—there was no sign that we had been followed—and shot the bolt. "It can't yet be noon, and the wedding this afternoon will keep the monsters busy until the Kabale meets tonight. Once we've seen to Short, we can consider ways to retrieve May, or at any rate her blood."

Alarmed, Short shook off Anton's half-restraining, half-supporting grasp. "Miss Sharp! You promised to release me once you were safe!"

"And I will release you, Alexander, but you're in no shape to leave at present. Let us patch you up first; and afterwards we can have a chat."

His jaw clenched. "I gave you my parole, not my allegiance. I will tell you nothing."

"Help him upstairs," I told Anton, remembering my resolve to give Short a taste of his own medicine. "As I recall, there's a nice sturdy bed up there where we can cuff him."

Short muttered something I was sure he would not ordinarily say in the presence of a lady.

"Criminy?" Anton muttered. "Who taught *this* one how to swear?" He shot me a wink and turned, dragging Short along with him. "Wait down here, Liz. I want a word with the bootheel myself."

"All right, but don't damage him," I warned.

The two men vanished upstairs together. I sank onto a chair—Missy's chair—and dropped an aching head into my hands. The back of my neck was hot and red, scorched from Anton's explosion, and I pressed my cool fingers against it with a sigh as the morning's strain ebbed away. I had put up a brave front before Anton and Short, but the truth was that we had never been in a worse fix. Vasily could no longer be trusted, and even if we were able to retrieve May's blood, how would we smuggle it into the Kabale's wine? Worst of all—worse even than the thought of being made into a revenant—May was no longer under George's protection, and the Kabale wanted her consigned to the living death of an insane asylum.

I could see no way around it, and it made me feel pretty sick. Even if I did manage to defang the Kabale, without George's protection May would be marked for the rest of her life as a traitor to family—to class—to Empire.

I was her friend, I was meant to be her protector, and I had brought her to this! Oh, that foolish nobility of hers—a nobility not of blood but of heart, that made her confront George with the truth to save me from slander!

Anton's voice rose and fell steadily upstairs, not punctuated by any response from Short. At length, with one final comment, he tromped downstairs and slammed the trapdoor behind him.

"What did you say to him?" I demanded.

"Oh, nothing much," Anton replied. "I thought he would feel better if I made some blood-curdling threats while he was refusing to answer my questions."

"Anton, you'll spoil everything. I'm trying to sweeten him up, not frighten him."

"Oh, I know! It's a trick the police use—at least, they do in Hungary," Anton said, sitting down and rolling himself a cigarette. "One of them will threaten you and knock you about a bit, and then the other will come in to play the ministering angel, and you weep all your secrets into their bosom. Two-faced insects. Well, off you go and play the angel."

"If you've knocked him about at all, I'll have your guts for garters."

Anton watched me, his eyes knowing but thoughtful. "No," he said deliberately, licking the paper and rolling it shut. "I know you're sweet on him, Liz."

I remembered the day I first met Anton in the Gare Saint-Lazare. Then he had greeted me with a passionate kiss, thinking me Vera Livius, the girl he had once loved—the girl who had followed him into anarchism and agreed to become his wife. Once I *had* been Vera Livius; but since the Kabale had stolen my memories, I had become someone else. Someone not of the Kabale's making; but not of Anton's making, either.

In Hungary I had tried to explain this to him. He told me he meant to hope, to teach me to love him again.

Now, I cleared my throat. "Does it bother you if I am?"

He lit the cigarette and leaned back, watching me through the smoke. His eyes were soft and affectionate, if sorrowful. "Somewhat," he confessed. "I know now that you were right.

My Vera is gone. She is never coming back to me. I can yield with dignity, because I see all the ways in which Liz Sharp is a better woman…" He gestured broadly. "But why a woman like you should moon about over bootheels and bloodsuckers is more than I can understand."

"I once told Vasily that the whole human race suffers from a desire for things that are bad for them. That doesn't mean we're fool enough to take them."

"Not you," he acknowledged with a faint smile. Then it faded. "You have a level head on your shoulders, Liz. But the bootheel upstairs is your weak point, and don't you forget it."

"Believe me, I spent the better part of a day chained up on that very bedstead with little else to think about. Still, we have no choice. We must draw the Kabale's fangs before they destroy us." I checked my reflection in the mirror set within my pocket-watch. My hair had fallen down when I removed my hairpin to attack Vasily, and now I dragged my fingers through its glossy black length to tame it. "To do that, we need May's blood—and after George himself, Short is the only man in Coburg who might be able to help us."

Anton nodded. He didn't warn me again, but I could see the worry in his eyes as I turned away and went up the stairs.

Tethered to the bedframe by his right hand, Short sat on the floor with his knees drawn up and his free arm folded protectively across his bloodstained ribs. When I entered, his lips drew into a hard, determined line.

Was he angry? Did he think I meant Anton to threaten him?—Almost, I quailed and ran away.

"Short," I began.

"You promised to free me," he interrupted. "Do you mean to break your word?"

I must set my face as flint, or lose him altogether. Rather than flee, I went to the dresser for the washbasin and cloth. "Turn and turn about, Short. I am altering our agreement just as you did, not an hour since. Have you a first-aid kit?"

He looked mutinous, but then nodded towards the dresser that stood by his bed. "Bottom drawer."

I located the kit and kneeled before him. "I must apologise. I ought not to have allowed Anton to bring you up here alone. Whatever he said to you, I don't countenance it."

Short gave no acknowledgement of my words. "You won't get away with this, Miss Sharp. Prince George will wonder where I am."

"And the first place he'll search will be your own home?" I asked with gentle incredulity, reaching out to undo his jacket.

Short's eyes narrowed—how could I once have thought those eyes sad and sleepy?—and he reached out to seize my wrist with slippery, bloody fingers.

"That trick won't work a second time," I told him. "I left the key with Anton."

"What have you done, Miss Sharp?" His eyes burned with every kind of pain. "The Kaiser is the most volatile man in Europe, and you have paid him an insult he'll never forgive. It's the end…the end of the world."

"Or the beginning of a new one," I said. His grasp on my wrist trembled, and I gently pulled myself free. "I'm afraid I can't call a doctor, but you might let me tend your wound. They taught us this sort of thing at Saint Botolph's."

He didn't answer, but neither did he resist when I unbuttoned his jacket. Beneath, his shirt was soaked in blood. I unbuttoned that too, careful not to look in his eyes, for I felt that doing so would be another breach of his privacy. This done, I saw that the wound, which was not deep, had already ceased to bleed freely. Having satisfied myself of this, I peeled his collar back from his neck.

Short drew back. "What are you doing?"

I looked up and saw something like panic in his eyes. Hardening my heart, I leaned forward, breathing in his scent until my nose, my lips, nearly touched his skin.

"Stop it," he said in a husky whisper.

I looked up again. It was just like this morning in the kitchen at the old house, but this time his emotions were all played out on his face, as though the pain of his wound had dragged them all to the surface. Anguish, yearning, desire—he was too exhausted to keep them under wraps now.

I sat back, feeling a little breathless myself. "You've spent a great deal of time in Missy's company lately. I was afraid she might have bitten you."

"She wouldn't bite me."

"Would she not?" Not that I thought it would help at all, but I added: "Don't you realise she has you under some kind of glamour? It's just as Vasily said. They'll tinker with your mind until you have none left."

Short made no reply. I worked in silence for a while, cleaning the wound, stitching it and adding a dressing. There was nothing I could do to numb the pain of the stitches, and his breath caught with each stab of the needle. When I was finished, he leaned back against the bed with his eyes closed and his face very white. He looked pale and soft and vulnerable, half shelled out of his clothes like that; and I told myself it was high time I got on with my interrogation.

"Does that feel better?" I asked, sitting back to wash my hands.

He opened his eyes and managed a tight smile. "Yes, although I hope never again to have stitches without anaesthetic."

For a moment I caught a glimpse of the Short I had once known, the man who had been my friend. He looked into my eyes, and I found that I could not look away. For a long moment, neither of us spoke or moved. He took a long, steady breath; then he reached up and traced the three livid scars that seamed the left side of my face.

"And these?" he asked gently. "Did they put stitches in your face, when it happened?"

"Yes; I remember them coming out." His touch was so gentle—I closed my eyes, suddenly certain I was about to weep. I had to say something, anything, to bolster me up. But all that came out was the truth: "I know I'd be prettier without them."

"Without them," he said gently, "you wouldn't be the Liz Sharp we know and…"

The sound of what he didn't say left me almost breathless.

"If you care about me, you'll let me go," he added.

His words pulled at my heart. Surely he was right—none of this awfulness between us could be repaired so long as I kept him captive like this. But then something in his hopeful stillness warned me. I caught his gaze as it shifted, only for a moment, to the bright window, where the sun was reaching the day's zenith—a look as furtive and full of meaning as though he had pulled his watch from his waistcoat pocket. My heart stuttered, then began beating again, a little faster than before.

Oh, how wise he was, how cunning. Warmth rose in my cheeks as I realised how close he had come to using my heart against him a second time—and this time, by design.

"N—o," I said, pulling back a little as though I was thinking it over. "No, I don't think I will let you go; at least not if you mean to thwart me."

His face fell. "But I must. Can't you see that I am only trying to spare you any more disastrous mistakes than the ones you have already made?"

This was far worse than facing my parents in an airship bomb-bay. I knew Short and loved him. Everything within me wanted to please him, even as I warned myself I could not. He had aligned himself with the monsters and their undead henchmen, knowing full well how vile they were. There could be no peace between us until he could see the horror of what he had done, and so I hardened my heart to adamant.

I meant to win this game: not merely for myself, but for him.

"What mistakes?" I asked, putting a steely edge into the words. "—Trusting you?"

"Will you force me to enumerate them? You have killed one royalty and injured two more. You kidnapped May, a reckless thing to do whether she went willingly or not. You assaulted the most dangerous man in Europe, and all of it in blind disregard for the peace and safety of yourself or anyone else."

"I might have had the means by which to fight the Kabale in safety, if you remember. But you would not share your sedatives, and you insisted on my giving up May's blood."

"You can't go around defanging royalties!"

"No?" I let out a little hard laugh, but I was beginning to feel hopeful. Short angry and flustered was much better for my purposes than Short calm and calculating. "Oh, I see. They murder our neighbours, and you expect us to write strongly-worded letters to the editor, or perhaps submit a petition. If anyone paid any attention to that sort of thing, do you think men like Anton would exist in the world? People don't wake up one morning and feel the urge to throw bombs. They are driven to it only by long despair."

There was an echoing silence. I leaned a little closer to him.

"You said you would fight within the system. How have you fought? What have you achieved in the way of justice? The system is monstrous, built on blood and murder—so naturally, to remain a part of it, you were compelled to make a monster of yourself. Now they will complete the change and make you a revenant indeed; and there will be nothing you can do to stop them."

He looked away from me, brushing a hand through his hair, as though by unruffling his head he might unruffle his spirit. "It isn't true," he said in a low voice. "Vasily was lying—trying to get under my skin. They cannot make such a change by fiat. It would need to be passed through Parliament, and a democratic Parliament will never countenance such a thing."

"Won't they? The Republic of France did it without a qualm." There was a great deal of strain etched into the lines around his mouth and eyes, and my heart told me to take pity on him. I touched his hand. "Don't think me ungrateful for what you did this morning."

He looked at me sadly. "Thank me by letting me go."

"Oh, why so anxious to leave me?" I leaned a fraction nearer. "You asked me for a kiss in Eger. Perhaps I'll kiss you in thanks, and we might trade something else for your freedom."

There was something like panic in his eyes—but then his gaze dropped to my mouth. Only for a moment. Then he tried to get his free arm up between us as a barrier. "You're mocking me, Miss Sharp."

"Am I? Try me." I caught his hand—brushed my lips against the knuckles. "Answer me one thing, and I'll let you go."

His eyes, a moment ago wide and confused, now narrowed in exasperated certainty. "You want something?—Of course you do."

"Both of us want something, Alexander. Why shouldn't we come to an agreement?"

"Stop calling me that," he said angrily, but there was a ragged edge to his voice. "We cannot make an agreement."

"Why not?" I returned, in a voice as raw as his own. "We trusted each other once, didn't we? Don't you *want* me to trust you again? God knows I wish you trusted me."

"We cannot," he repeated.

I studied his face. "It isn't because you don't want to. So which is it, Short? Is it that you are afraid of becoming like me? Or because you think you don't deserve me?" I traced my fingers along the faint shadow of stubble at the corner of his jaw, as I'd so often longed to do. "Please, Short. Look at me."

He turned his face away and fixed his gaze on the window, as he had done before. But it wasn't out of calculation this time. It was out of fear.

Fear, not of me, but of himself.

I knew then that I could break him—break him, and heal him.

"Short," I whispered, leaning close, until my lips brushed his ear, "you told me you had forfeited any right to my heart; but it's too late for such noble gestures. Didn't you hear what I said two nights ago in this very room? You've had my heart for a very long time, and it isn't yours to be sent from you, like an old shirt to the laundry.—Since I love you I must fight for you. Grant me that right, at least."

His tongue traced his lips. "That may be, but I still cannot help you."

"But you can't look me in the eye and say you don't *want* to."

He forced his head around to meet my gaze. "I can and will."

"But it wouldn't be the truth, because you have already given yourself away, you see. It wasn't just the ring in your pocket. It was your resolve to give me up, once you realised how it had affected me. *There can never be anything between us,* you said. I would have loved you for that, if nothing else."

He closed his eyes. "Stop."

"Why? Why ask me to stop, when you love me so?"

"You are wrong—I never said it."

"Then say it now." I twined my arms around his neck, and he shivered from head to toe. "What are you afraid of? Why won't you kiss me? You were the one who began this game."

"Please." Only a whisper. So close, I could hear his heart going; his chest suddenly expanded in a shaking breath. "Not…not like this. I couldn't bear it."

"Why not? Are you afraid I might use your own heart as a weapon against you, as you did to me?"

"No—I am afraid I might hurt you again, as I did then."

"I never suffered a sweeter wound, since it proved your love for me."

I was starved for love; yet even now he could not say the words. Who knows? perhaps he was right. Perhaps a love confessed in chains is no love at all. At any rate, he shook his head, tight-lipped like a man on the edge of endurance.

"Please. Whatever information you want, I'll give it to you. Just ask what you must, and go."

So it came to this: that he would give me what I asked, even the means to destroy the Kabale, before he would admit to loving me. I drew a deep breath.

"I believe the Kabale can change—without a war, even. But not if things go on the way they always have. They must be stripped of their power, and May's blood is the key."

"You want my help getting her back?"

I shook my head. "Not May. Her blood."

Chapter XIX.

Bells shook the air in blithe, triumphant peals. In half an hour, Ernest of Hesse and Victoria Melita would be married. Never mind the affliction that had befallen the bride and groom, or the disasters that had stalked the guests; never mind the fear that made the populace bar their doors at night or hurry through the streets by day in fear of monsters and revenants—the wedding must and would go on.

With every dignitary in Coburg flocking to the cathedral, Anton and I had the perfect chance to slip into the palace to retrieve May's blood. As we took the road leading from the Marktplatz to the rear of the palace, the sound of the cathedral bells rang like a warning. We had left Short securely handcuffed to his own bed—I was hopeful of him, but not trustful, and besides, he needed the rest—but what of May herself?

Anton's mind must have been running in the same direction, for he nodded towards the church towers and said, "Suppose May is in there?"

"I suppose she is." May would no doubt walk dutifully through all the social obligations of her class until the very moment they locked the asylum door behind her. "I'll wager she knows nothing of what the Kabale has planned for her.

If things go badly tonight…" Glancing at my watch, I found that it was now two o'clock in the afternoon. Time was yet with us, but I dared not trust my warning to a letter, which May might not even receive until it was already too late. The festivities would run late into the evening; it was unlikely that she would return to her apartments before—whatever was to happen tonight. "Perhaps we should warn her."

As usual I wore my black veil to conceal my scars—a far from uncommon sight in a town holding so many dignitaries. Anton, however, had only a cap pulled low over his eyes to conceal his face. "Why don't you step into that pub," I suggested, "and I'll be back before the service begins."

He agreed, evidently worried about May, and I turned towards the church. The possibilities were grim—I might be stopped, recognised, and arrested. But at least I would get my warning to May, and I felt that any triumph over the Kabale would be hollow and meaningless if it doomed May in return.

Still, even if we succeeded, what sort of life awaited her? Without George's protection, she must flee Coburg at once. I could not imagine what she might do then. Perhaps the two of us might go to Australia, after all, and live a comfortable, obscure life together as eccentric old maids.

There were a great many plain-clothes and revenant police-men watching the church, but I slipped into place behind a family with three children and trotted purposefully after them as though I was some sort of governess. This got me quite easily into the church, a large and beautiful Gothic building which inside was painted white and filled with a great crowd of people. Two galleries on each side of the nave held yet more observers; a windowed royal box hung on the first level directly opposite the high pulpit on the right.

Within the door I hesitated, struck with momentary dread. The whole place was quite packed with people; how would I find May?

A shiny, freshly brushed-and-combed young usher stood at my side, plucking my elbow. "Your name, ma'am?"

I summed him up at a glance—no doubt the son of a local dignitary. Not one of the monsters themselves, and thus unlikely to suspect a veiled woman connected with the Tecks. "I'm Princess May of Teck's lady's maid," I told him. "I've brought her some necessities."

He pointed. "There, behind the fifth pillar."

I caught a glimpse of May's pale, crisp hair—her mother's maid must have dressed it, for the style was not the most becoming—wedged beside her parents in the shadows of one of the great square piers holding up the galleries. I slipped through the crowd and laid a hand on her shoulder. May paled when she saw me but did not speak. Whispering an excuse to her parents, she joined me in the shadows of the church's rearmost corner.

"Is something wrong?" she murmured, glancing nervously behind her at the church full of royalties. "I mean—I am so happy to see you free and well, but you ought not to be here! It is so dangerous!"

"First tell me what has happened since I saw you last," I replied. "I suppose it's all definitely off with George?"

"Yes, but…" She turned, glancing across the church. Some distance away, in the royal box near Queen Victoria's elevated seat, a young man with a neatly-trimmed beard was staring our way from behind a pair of opera-glasses.

May turned back to me with a sigh. "I told George I never

wanted to see him again, but he was very kind; he said he didn't mean to *tell* anyone it was off."

I shook my head. "I am sorry to break the news, but I think they already know."

May's face didn't change, but she fidgeted nervously with the brooch at her throat. "I think they might. We—we've had policemen watching us all day. Not Scotland Yard men: revenants." I forebore to mention that at this point, the distinction was pretty academic. "And then we were seated down here, at the back, behind a pillar. It isn't the sort of place they ought to put a future queen. But I can't imagine that George would have given me away."

I sighed. "It might have been Missy, but I'm afraid it was most likely Vasily."

"Vasily?—Oh, *Sharp.*"

"I blame myself. He swore he was on my side—but then, he swore the same thing to the Kabale two nights ago, and now I don't know *what* to believe."

"You mustn't blame yourself," she said fiercely. "We couldn't have kept the secret forever. I must simply brazen it out, if that's what it comes to."

"You, May—brazen! I should like to see *that.*" I lowered my voice. "Anton and I still mean to go ahead tonight, but I must warn you that the Kabale means to have you locked away in an asylum—and now that you're no longer engaged to George, I'm afraid that even if we succeed—"

"May!" A breathless voice interrupted us. May and I sprang apart as the newcomer descended upon us. It was Alicky of Hesse, the pretty, brown-haired girl who had helped May free me at the ball, and whom the Kaiser's sisters and cousins and aunts had been besieging with urgent pleas to marry Nicky.

This morning she wore a gown of pale, icy blue that made her look impossibly fragile and pretty.

"May," she repeated in a whisper, threading her arm through that of my friend—"I say, have you seen Nicky anywhere?"

Sending me a look of apology, May said, "Why, no, Alicky, I can't say I have."

Alicky bit down on her lower lip. "May I sit with you, then? Nowhere else is safe—I mean, I know that if I take a seat elsewhere someone is sure to get up and then the next thing I know Nicky will be sitting next to me and I—I don't want to see him!"

"He didn't happen to call on you this morning?" There was a mischievous twitch at the corner of May's mouth. I had, of course, told her everything I had overheard between the Kaiser and Nicky on the subject of Alicky's marriage last night.

"No, he didn't. Why do you ask?"

"Oh, it was only a hunch. But why run from him? Are you so afraid of him?"

Alicky's face crumpled. "What a coward you must think me! I'm afraid that if he asks me again, I shall consent. Oh, May, I am *so* unhappy; it is *so* unbearable to think that when this is over, I must go home to Hesse. I shall never stop loving Nicky—never, never, never—and he will marry someone else and forget *me*. And I shall be the maiden aunt in the corner watching Ernest and Ducky having their children and living their lives. I shall feel like an intruder all my life; and Ducky is sure to resent me!"

May stiffened a little. "Who has been putting such thoughts in your head? I'm sure Ernest and Ducky would be very kind to you." But there was doubt in her voice, and I remembered that she had always feared just such a fate for herself.

"No one has been saying such things, only I cannot help thinking it." Alicky trailed off with a sigh. "Dona, you know, has been telling me it is my duty to marry Nicky, that I ought to think of it as an alliance between two great powers, and a way to help Nicky in his very terrible task of ruling an Empire."

May glanced at me, and I read in her eyes all the same considerations with which I knew she had tormented herself. "You might," she said slowly. "You might be a very great help to him."

"You don't think it would be a sin to love a monster?"

"It isn't a sin to *love* a monster," May said thoughtfully. "I think it might be a sin not to *oppose* a monster, though—to turn a blind eye to his depredations, or to let him make you into another monster."

Alicky's eyes widened. "But if I loved Nicky, how could I oppose him?"

"If *I* truly loved a man," May said—and her voice was soft and sad—"if I *truly* loved a man who was truly doing something wrong, how better to show my love, except in opposition?"

Only I knew what bitter personal experience underlay her words, and my heart wrung. I glanced up at the royal box, but George was no longer in sight. I wished he might have overheard her—I wished I might have asked him if he could have any doubt that May loved him, since she was willing to stand up to him.

But then I caught sight of him. He had descended the stair behind the gallery, and was making his purposeful way through the crowded cathedral towards May and myself.

The dickens! Wistful thoughts vanished.—He must not be allowed to capture us. I seized May's hand, and tilted my head towards the approaching prince.

May paled. "Alicky, I—there is something I must go and fetch from my rooms in the palace. You might sit with mamma and papa if you wish. *They* will not abandon you."

"And don't weep for Nicky," I put in, thinking to shock her a little with the realities of his condition. "He got a face full of saltwater last night, and it burned him horribly. If he's late, it is only because he must be half draining the blood from some poor creature to restore his looks."

For the first time in our conversation, Alicky turned to me with a look of horror. "Nicky is hurt?"

She had evidently gleaned entirely the wrong significance from my words. "Well, only a little—"

She put a hand over her mouth, and I realised, to my astonishment, that she was about to burst into tears. For a moment she struggled. Then she whispered, "Oh dear," and fled towards the church door.

I looked at May helplessly. "I didn't think she would—"

May, however, was far more alarmed by George's approach. "We really must go, Sharp.—The nerve of that man! I *told* him I would not see him again."

We left the cathedral hurriedly—nearly all the guests had arrived by this time, and the crowd at the doors was thinning. There was a wide, open square before the church, but I beckoned May and we cut up a small side-street before George could sight us from the great door. Ten minutes later, we had collected Anton and entered the palace by a small side door for which the anarchist, during his time as May's bodyguard, had obtained the key.

"Do either of you know the way to George's rooms?" I asked as we hurried through the palace's long corridors.

"I will show you," May said primly. "Do you mean to search for the syringes? I have more blood, you know."

"Yes, but we have already taken a deal of it, and I don't mean to drain you!—If Short was telling the truth, we ought to find the syringes easily enough. He said they would likely be in George's safe."

"Oh, brava, Sharp." Then the full meaning of my words sank in. "*Short* told you? What did you do to make him tell?"

"Exactly what you suggested, more or less. To be perfectly honest, I threatened to kiss him."

"Oh, Sharp, how bold!—You must tell me all about it; I want to know everything."

"And if we end up fleeing the Continent together, I'm sure we'll have all the time in the world."

With all the great dignitaries attending the wedding, the palace was almost deserted, and the servants left behind were too busy preparing the festivities, to concern themselves with Princess May and her entourage.—Not for the first time that week, I felt grateful for the Kabale's predilection for secrecy, which worked in our favour as well as theirs. We experienced no difficulty until we reached George's suite and entered to find his valet sitting on the sofa with his feet propped up on an occasional-table, drinking lemonade and reading a newspaper.

"Hullo, Mr Brock. You seem to have made yourself very comfortable," I said breezily.

"The anarchist!" Brock cried, attempting to rise; but Anton moved quickly and struck a stunning blow to his jaw. The valet crumpled, and Anton dragged him into the dressing-room, whence we heard the sound of cravats being torn up for restraints.

"Short said we would find the safe in the cupboard beside the fireplace." Following his directions, I flung wide the cupboard door. The safe confronted me, its dark surface engraved with graceful gilded lines, but otherwise featureless save for the dial and knob. I took a deep breath, wriggling my fingers.

May peered over my shoulder. "Why, Sharp! Do you know the combination?"

"I'm afraid not. But a safe must be like any lock: if you listen closely enough, you must be able to hear the tumblers fall. I have a knack for locks, and with my hearing I think I *might* be able to do it."

"Or I could try," May offered. "When I was here two mornings ago, George opened the safe before we went to the café for breakfast. Come to think of it, he must have been retrieving that diamond. Allow me."

Frowning a little, she twisted the dial to and fro with quick, assured fingers. "I *think* that was the combination," she said at length. "Try it!"

The knob turned at once, and I swung the door open, blessing May's eidetic memory.

The safe held only one item: a forlorn little jewel-box, containing the aforementioned diamond.

"No, no," I breathed, running my hands over the interior, as though touch might reveal what sight could not. "They aren't here!"

"I shall just have to give more blood, Sharp." May picked up the ring-box and opened it, letting out a wistful sigh at the sight of the splendid jewel within. "I had to give it back to him, of course. Poor George! He told me to keep it to remember him by, but it wouldn't have been proper."

That was beside the point, surely. "We shall have trouble drawing off your blood without the needles," I pointed out.

"Search the rooms first," Anton suggested, returning from the dressing-room, where he had evidently overheard our debate. "It could be the syringes are still lying about somewhere."

"Hush," I cautioned them, lifting a hand in warning. "I believe I hear something."

May and Anton hushed, and I stood for a moment listening. All of us heard slow footsteps in the passage outside, venturing nearer. Expecting them to pass by, I lifted a finger to my lips. But suddenly May seized my arm.

"It's George!"

"It can't be!" I hissed in reply; but then the footsteps slowed as they approached the door. In another moment he would be with us. "The bedroom," I whispered; and the three of us fled silently into the adjoining room as George opened the door.

He seemed to be alone. As he entered he let out a gusty sigh, which cut off partway through as he caught sight of the open safe.

"Brock!" he shouted, but there was no answer.

His footsteps trod towards us, and Anton tensed, slipping a hand into the pocket where he carried his revolver. Seeing what he intended, May sent the anarchist a terrible frown and stepped into the doorway to confront her former betrothed.

"Good day, George," she greeted him coolly.

"May!" he gasped, and it sounded as though he recoiled a step. "I say—you—by Jove!—what—"

"You seem surprised," she observed; but she had her hands behind her back, and now signalled emphatically in the direction of the windows. I understood her meaning, of course. Of the three of us, she was the most likely to be able to distract George; and while he was still trying to overcome his shock, Anton and I might make some sort of escape. I patted my skirts thoughtfully, feeling the light, strong coil of rope I was currently using to pad my bustle. I had not come unprepared, but I certainly didn't like the thought of leaving May in the power of one who apparently had neither the ability nor inclination to protect her.

As these thoughts flitted through my mind, May advanced into the sitting-room, swinging the bedroom door almost, but not quite, shut behind her. "Please believe me when I say I would not have come if I had imagined you would be returning so soon. I do not wish to intrude upon your privacy, but—"

"Intrude—hang it! Always happy to see you, May, and you know it!"

"But, your grace, I really *must* insist on having my blood returned to me."

"Your blood!" That reduced him to stammers once again. "I—ah—depends on what you mean to do with it, by Jove!"

What May intended to say next, if anything, remains lost to history. There was an imperious rap at the door leading into the corridor, and then it popped open and the Prince of Wales said, "Family meeting in five—*May!*"

"*Who?*" an elderly female voice inquired from the hallway; and I risked a peek into the sitting-room as footsteps flowed in. Leaning on a walking-stick, the Queen limped through the door and planted herself, with a faint groan, in the largest of the armchairs. Behind her, the Prince of Wales said something chaffing about boys being boys. George's beautiful siren mother followed, looking confused and startled; and then Mary Adelaide sailed in with a shriek of motherly horror; and the next moment the whole apartment was overrun with royalties, most of them speaking at the top of their voices. An unexpected and most unfortunate development, for they were all supposed to be at a wedding for the next hour at least.

What the dickens was going on?

Wringing her hands, Mary Adelaide descended upon May in a swarm of one. "Oh, May! What *are* you doing here? Is it not enough that Ducky should bring down our grey hairs in sorrow—but that *you* of all people should be sneaking into gentlemen's rooms is really the last straw!"

"What can you mean, mamma?—what has Ducky done?"

"Eloped!" Mary Adelaide screeched, "run off with a horrible Russian duke, and left her intended at the altar!"

Really, it was too bad! What a performance I must have missed, running away from the church like that!—and what had we gained? The blood was missing, and George and his whole family had caught us anyway. I might as well have stayed in the church to observe the drama.

A loud sound echoed through the room, restoring some silence to the apartment—in fact it was the Queen, stamping her walking-stick against the floor.

"Will someone *kindly* explain what is going on here?" Queen Victoria demanded, in her most imperial tones. "George?"

"I..." George began, before coming to an awkward halt. A moment's silence passed, and then he said rather defiantly, "I was having a private interview with Princess May, ma'am. Don't see that it particularly requires the presence of the whole family!"

"Oh, don't be histrionic. Barely a fraction of the family is present!"

Indeed, when I surveyed the assembled royalties, I was forced to admit that she was right. I counted only the Prince of Wales and his family; the Duke of Saxe-Coburg and Gotha and *his* family; Mary Adelaide, but not her husband; and—oh, *dear*—Missy herself—Ducky's vengeful sister, and my own bad angel, her eyes alight with wicked glee. Glancing at Anton, I saw the agreement in his eyes. We could not leave the apartment while May was surrounded by those who might prove to be her enemies.

As George visibly wilted before the family's collective gaze, the Queen continued in a voice that was quiet but not soft. "As the head of this family, it is my duty to govern it well, little as it becomes a woman to do so. I have made a terrible misjudgement, no doubt, in arranging this match between Ernest and Ducky. I dare not make any similar mistakes with *you*, George, who will one day be King." Her gaze moved to May. "It has come to my attention that there has been—*agitation*—within the family. This must not be allowed to continue."

May had gone a little pale at the Queen's words, but she had enough self-command to make a deep curtsey. "Ma'am, if I may speak?"

"You may! I should very much like to hear what you have to say for yourself."

It was not a particularly inviting tone of voice, but May had once made a deeply favourable impression on the old Queen—due, no doubt, to the very self-command and decorum with which she now spoke: "I believe I may be partly at fault in Ernest and Ducky's misfortunes, ma'am. It was my blood—morganatic blood—which they tasted by accident at the ball, and which seems to have rendered them toothless."

"So I have already been informed."

"I assure you I had not the least wish in the world to harm anyone," she added earnestly. "But it now seems certain that morganatic blood has wonderful properties. I—George will tell you that I have steadfastly refused to marry him. The truth is, I do not wish to—to make the change, nor can I bear the thought of marrying one who already has."

George started. "By Jove! Is that the *only* reason?"

May's eyes remained fixed upon the Queen. Her throat worked, and I could see what an effort it took her to say such things, to such an audience. "Ask poor Alicky of Hesse—she feels the same way about Nicky." She turned to George, her voice softening. "The very same."

All the world knew how desperately Alicky and Nicky loved each other, for all their inability to admit it. I saw the wheels turning within George's mind as he followed the implications of May's words—I saw the moment at which he grasped her unsaid meaning, and knew at last that she loved him.

He did not reply. Instead, he turned abruptly to the window behind him, so that only Anton and I, from our hiding-place, could see his look of revelation—wellnigh of rapture.

"At any rate," May went on, still addressing the Queen, "I know that in England it is all the most dreadful secret; but if in public we claim not to be monsters, then why should it not be the *truth* that—"

The Queen broke in sharply. "To think I should live to hear such language in my own family! We are not *monsters;* we are seasonal eccentrics!"

"We are *killers,*" May cried, clasping her hands. Her words fell into that room like one of Anton's bombs. "If it is not monstrous to murder people at a masquerade ball with champagne and music, what is? With my blood this could all end—and I would give it freely to any of you."

She turned to George with an imploring look, but he remained fixed where he was at the window, his back turned to the room.

"I see what has happened," Queen Victoria said, in a soothing voice quite different to the indignation I expected. "This is most unfortunate, May! You really *don't* seem quite healthy in your mind."

Oh, the dickens.

At that, George turned from the window. "I say, don't let's jump to conclusions! May is quite right in the head, I assure you! Think she has a point, myself. Magna Carta, I mean to say—"

"Thank you, George; I am sufficiently well-versed in the intricacies of the British Constitution. Now, May, I am afraid your fate is not quite up to *me.* The Kabale is aware of you now, and a committee has been delegated to handle the situation. I am informed that they met last night, after your blood was used in an attack upon William—the Kaiser, that is. Excellent doctors have been consulted, but they are all in unanimous agreement that nothing will restore his prerogatives. You are thus in a very serious position, my dear—very serious indeed, and even I may be unable to save you; so I beg you to answer me quite honestly. Were you aware your blood would be used for such purposes?"

May swallowed before replying. "Yes, ma'am."

"And yet you gave it willingly?"

"Yes, ma'am."

"And you have nothing more to say for yourself?"

"Only this: that I have always known I was meant to achieve something in this world. I am more sorry than I can say that it had to be this."

Queen Victoria gave a heavy sigh. "Then I am afraid it seems as though the Kabale's decision is quite correct and necessary."

Mary Adelaide gave a gasp of horror. May turned quite pale, but George drew her suddenly close and tucked her arm into the crook of his own. "Here," he protested. "Can't chuck May into a loony-bin! She's quite as sane as I am!"

"If she *is* in her right mind, then they'll have to hang her," a new voice put in. Missy of Roumania sounded as though she relished the thought. "Isn't that right, Uncle Wales?"

"Well—as a matter of fact—no," the Prince of Wales said rather ponderously. "Most of the time we make it look like a suicide, or an anarchist attack. The Crown Prince of Austria, for example—"

George's mouth fell open. "Prince Rudolf!—that was *your* doing?"

"Dear me, no! it was the Kabale acting as a body," his father replied uncomfortably. "Boy wanted to give up the throne and run away with his mistress. Got as far as Peru, in fact, before we brought them back. Made it look like a double suicide."

George was speechless. I felt rather dazed as well. Not content with terrorising those beneath them, the Kabale made attacks upon its own class? It scarcely occurred to me to doubt it. Perhaps I had done Vasily an injustice! Perhaps he was sincere when he claimed to wish the Kabale's destruction!

Within the sitting-room, Mary Adelaide grasped her daughter by the shoulders. "May, tell them you are sorry! Tell them you'll never use your blood again! Think of the dreadful scandal it will be! Don't let them do this to you, my darling!"

"Thank you, mamma," May murmured, "but I think my fate is no longer in my own hands."

It was really high time I was preparing our escape. Signalling Anton to avert his eyes, I hitched up my skirts and rummaged beneath them, looking for the rope that hung there.

"Hang it, there must be another way," George said pleadingly. "What if May was to marry me? She'd be no danger to any of us then, surely?"

"Out of the question! I'm afraid May has shown an independence of mind that makes her quite unsuitable, even if she did make the change."

"Alix, please," Mary Adelaide burst out, turning in desperation to George's siren mother. "Can't you do something to her mind? Make her herself again?"

"Mamma, no!" May gasped, goaded into horror at this suggestion. "Imprison me—subject me to anything, rather than that!"

Let the reader not judge the Duchess too harshly: she did not know of May's experiences with siren compulsion, and of course had no acquaintance with it herself.

"Of course, May cannot be sent to an asylum in full possession of her memories," the Queen put in, dashing our hopes at once. "In fact it might be best if it was done at once. Alix, if you will—"

"Oh," May murmured in a stifled voice, "I cannot bear it."

Beside me, Anton swore under his breath and unholstered

his revolver. But I had my eyes fixed on the room beyond; and I seized his wrist to hold him back.

At May's stifled cry, George stepped in front of her. "Keep back, Motherdear!" he cried. "Don't lay a hand on her!"

"I don't need to lay a hand on her, poppet," Princess Alix murmured dreamily, but Queen Victoria spoke in a voice as hard as a diamond-saw:

"What is the meaning of this, George?"

"What I ought to have done long ago." On the deck of a ship, his voice might have been heard from Ushant to Scilly. In the small apartment, it was quite overpowering. "No one shall meddle with May. No one shall drain her, or explode her, or send her to an asylum. Never heard such a lot of tosh in my life!"

"What *are* we to do with her, pray?"

"Nothing at all, and if the Kabale wants to bother her, they will have me to reckon with, demmit!"

"George, as your sovereign, I order you—"

"I abdicate," he boomed. "Louise can be Queen after Papa."

"George!" his sister screamed, "you *beast,* how could you say such a thing?" and after that the room dissolved into pandemonium.

Dashing a proud tear from my eye, I released Anton.

Reader, I wish you had been there. Anton threw open the door through which we had been peering, and sauntered into the midst of all those clucking and fretting royalties. May stood behind George, clutching his arm, and looking rather dazed as he traded shouts with his family. Then she saw Anton, and her face lit up.

He bowed to her—actually bowed—and the room hushed as one by one, the family realised there was a stranger in their midst.

"Care to retire?" Anton said to May.

"Oh, *yes,* please," May said.

Anton unlatched the window-casement and threw it open. I slung the rope quickly around the central mullion at its middle—thank goodness for neo-Gothic, say I.

The Queen was the first of the monsters to regain her wits after our sudden appearance. "Mary Adelaide," she cried, turning to May's mother. "Have you nothing to say? Will you stand by as your child defies you?"

The Duchess of Teck looked conflicted—but after a moment, maternal instincts won the day. "As far as I can tell, ma'am, it's you she means to defy; not me."

"Ingrate! Do you mean after all these years in which I have supported your spendthrift habits—"

"—That I still mean to keep a mind of my own? Indeed, ma'am. You have put me under an obligation to do my duty by the Crown, but I'm hanged if you'll make an unnatural mother of me."

"I shall cut off your allowance!"

Mary Adelaide made a large and dismissive gesture. "I shall go begging in the streets, and tell the world you put me there."

"Oh, mamma!" May breathed, her eyes a little starry with pleasure. There was no time to say more, for Anton and I had completed our arrangements. He put an arm around May's waist, whisked her through the window, and rappelled away.

"Wait!" George cried, turning to the casement as though he meant to throw himself out after her. That seemed my cue to intervene. Stepping onto the windowsill, still holding the trailing end of the rope, I reached out a beckoning hand to him.

"Coming with us?"

"Ra-*ther*," he said, stepping up beside me.

Missy of Roumania pointed at me. "Stop her! That's Elizabeth Sharp!"

"Who the devil did you think it was, Missy?" George said rather severely. "The Great Cham of Tartary?" and on that note, we too departed.

Chapter XX.

George and I reached *terra firma* within moments of Anton and May. The instant our feet touched the cobblestones of the street, George released me and seized May by both her hands.

"May!" he said in a voice of half-choked passion, "did you mean it?—Is it true?"

"Of course it is, George; every last word."

In this way, without a single plain word spoken, they came to understand each other!

"I didn't know—ah, May!" Overcome, George raised both her hands to his lips and kissed them. "Your blood—give me your blood to drink."

At that, Anton cast me a look of mingled confusion and horror. "You'll need to explain what the blazes is going on, Liz. I am baffled."

I was practically hugging myself in glee. "Why, don't you see? She told them she felt the same way for George as Alicky does for Nicky—Alicky is out of her mind in love, but she won't marry Nicky because he's a monster. Weren't you paying attention, last night?—So now, of course George will defang himself, and May will be quite safe again." I danced up to the lovers, and narrowly restrained myself from throwing my arms around them both; they had had enough shocks over the last half hour, and I did not want to entirely unseat their reason. "May—George—let me be the first to congratulate you. I'm sure you'll both be very happy together. Shall we adjourn to a more private setting?"

May glanced up. There were faces peering down at us from the windows above. "George!" the Prince of Wales bellowed. "I shall cut you off with a shilling—see if I don't!"—"Papa, you *beast!*" Princess Louise shrieked. "I won't be Queen! I won't!"

A slight shudder ran through George's slight, dapper frame. "'Pon my word, yes," he murmured, "let us move on!"

The moment the royalties upstairs rallied sufficiently to call upon their henchmen, we should have the police on our trail. Anton and I took the lead, almost at a run; George and May followed with clasped hands, and in this manner we cut down the Herrngasse and emerged into the Marktplatz. This had been transformed into a fairground, with free food, drink, and music for the celebrations of the townspeople. I am sorry to say that the festive spirit seemed sorely lacking: whether because of the dread that had hung over the town all week, or because of the sudden levanting of the bride, the celebrations seemed as much a wash as the marriage itself. Anton, May, George and myself hurried across the empty square towards the small house where Short lay awaiting us; and at the foot of Prince Albert's monument we came quite suddenly upon Alicky and Nicky.

They had their arms around each other, for we had startled them in the midst of kissing. It was me and Anton they saw first, and both of them paled.

"Miss Sharp!" Nicky yelped; and suddenly we were surrounded by his revenant policemen, who now appeared from within the otherwise empty pavilions.

Anton unsheathed the swordstick, but George, with a tutting sound, put himself between the anarchist and his cousin.

"Nicky! I say! Are we to congratulate each other?"

Nicky looked astonished, and a little breathless, although that might have been the effect of Alicky. "You too? George, old man! I thought it was all off with you—not that I'm not frightfully pleased!" He waved his grey top-hat in May's direction. "Allow me to congratulate you, ma'am! You won't regret it."

"It is a great deal better than spending the remainder of my life in a lunatic asylum, to be sure." May spoke in a very composed voice, but Anton, beside me, whistled; and Nicky looked as though he had been struck between the eyes.

"Er—naturally!" he said. "Please believe that I strongly opposed that verdict, ma'am."

May relented. "I would never have dreamed otherwise."

"Thing is, none of them ever listen to me," Nicky put in in an undertone, turning back to George. "A seat on the Kabale isn't all it's cracked up to be! You shall see when you are on it yourself! But what are you doing in the company of—er…
" he sent an anxious glance in my direction and whispered, "Isn't Miss Sharp an anarchist, then, after all?"

"Er—If you can't beat them, join them, what!" George guffawed in a manner that was just a little too hearty, then changed the subject. "Anyway, what about you, Nicky? Going to defang yourself? I'm sure May will fix you up with the needful!"

"Oh, dear me, no!" Nicky said at once with every evidence of shock. "What could have put that thought in your head?

Alicky has consented to convert."

May's swift stillness told me with what shock and displeasure she greeted this announcement; but Alicky had her arms wound around her betrothed, and was looking up at him adoringly. Even George seemed struck with astonishment. After a moment, Nicky looked at me and went on:

"I suppose it's my duty to have you arrested, Miss Sharp, but really, I ought to thank you for bringing us together!"

"But how?" I protested faintly.

"Well, er—*when pain and anguish rack the brow, a ministering angel thou,* as one of your British poets would have it! Seems there's a bright side to being doused with saltwater." He waved a dismissive hand at the revenants, and they moved back into the shadows of their hiding-places. "For having done me this service, I shall this once look the other way. Don't make me regret it, Miss Sharp!"

"Why don't you chuck me a tenner for good measure?" I said to cover my confusion. He was letting me go, but at what cost? At the cost of Alicky's conscience? The thought was as bitter as gall.

"Is the wedding over already?" Alicky put in anxiously. "Or are you late for it, like us?"

"No, it's quite over," George said.

"And we've missed everything! Come along anyhow, and let's tell Grandmamma," Alicky added to Nicky, and hand-in-hand the pair of them ran off—for all the world like happy schoolchildren, save for the rotting undead shuffling in their wake.

May and George watched them depart in silence. "Oh, Sharp," May murmured. "That poor girl—in that den of vampires!"

"It's all my fault," I said, stricken. "I never should have told her he had been hurt."

"Nonsense," said Anton, with brutal cynicism. "She would have heard it from someone else, if not from you, and she would have responded in the same way. If you ask me, she was looking for an excuse."

"I thought Alicky understood," May said numbly. "I thought I could depend on her…"

"You can depend on *me*," George said, tucking her arm within his.

May smiled at him. All the same, as I led our small party in the direction of Short's lodgings, I could tell that Alicky's choice weighed as heavily on her as it did on me. To both of us, Alicky had represented hope. Hope that the younger generation of royalties, perhaps even Nicky himself, could be brought to give up their dreadful power of their own free will; hope that not just their bodies, but their hearts might be changed.—No! I could not allow myself to fall into such despair. No one was beyond hope. Alicky might yet be saved, and Nicky rendered harmless, if tonight's mission went as planned.

Although I write these memoirs with the benefit of hindsight, I swear to you, dear reader, that a premonitory shadow had fallen across my soul in the Coburg square, at the foot of the Albert monument. I recall quite clearly wondering what horrors might yet befall Imperial Russia, and poor Alicky herself, because Nicky would not of his own free will give up the bloodthirsty traditions of his forefathers.—Naturally I could not have imagined the terrible reality; but all that was then twenty years distant. Hurrying home through the golden April afternoon of Europe, we let ourselves into the downstairs room of the house where Short lodged.

"It is a little cramped, I know," I told George, "but I'm afraid we had to leave our former lodgings in rather a hurry."

He reddened with embarrassment. "Beastly conduct, Miss Sharp! Thought you'd kidnapped her. Ought to have known better. When I think of it—"

"Then pray don't think of it," I said, relenting. "But you know I mean to deal with the Kabale tonight, don't you? Do you mind very much?"

"You mean to defang them, using May's blood?"

"Yes; and having seen how Ernest and Ducky were treated after *they* were defanged, I am sure the Kabale will lose all its influence if we succeed."

He grasped my hand. "I am with you, Sharp. I am quite happy at home in England; I don't wish to run to Peru and then be assassinated anyway, not even by my own family. I say, is Short still with you?"

"Yes—he's been upstairs resting. Let me run up and see if he is awake." So saying, I left Anton to explain the morning's developments and went upstairs.

I lifted the trapdoor. "Short?" Then I caught a whiff of scent, and my heart stood still, for I knew something must have gone terribly wrong. Swiftly I climbed through the trapdoor and closed it behind me.

A man lounged on the bed, smoking a meditative cigarette. When I entered, he turned to me with a smirk. It was not, of course, Short.

It was Vasily.

It was Vasily; and he must have taken Short away, for the policeman's familiar scent of pipe-smoke and gunpowder had faded, in a way that suggested he must have been gone an hour at least.

"Good afternoon, Miss Sharp," Vasily said. "I must warn you to remain silent, if you wish to see the good inspector again."

My first impulse was to call for assistance and then, perhaps, to fly at Vasily and do him an injury. I indulged myself so far as to withdraw the hairpin from my coiffure.

"Where is he?"

Vasily stood in one graceful, fluid movement and offered me a letter with a mocking bow. I opened and read it in moments. Unsigned save for the mark of a wolf's head, it informed me that the man Alexander Short would be converted to a revenant that evening at sunset; that is, unless I turned myself over to the bearer of the letter to take his place.

I remember that my fingers felt cold and numb as I read. How did the Kabale guess to what lengths I would go to save Short?—Vasily must have told them.—Or no doubt Missy knew of my weakness, given how Short had succeeded in capturing me at first. No, this was bound to happen—the marvel was that it had not happened sooner. That left the question of how Vasily had known to come *here*. Possibly he had followed Anton and myself from the house beyond the Marktplatz this morning; or perhaps Missy had deduced the most likely place for Anton and myself to take refuge.

Whatever the truth, it hardly mattered. The game was over.

Vasily spoke. "You ought to have accepted my offer this morning when there was still a—"

I blinked my gaze away from the letter. "Take me to him."

That surprised him. "What, without a fight? This is unlike you, Miss Sharp." He prowled towards me, his feet barely making any sound on the wooden floorboards. "Go on! Call for help. Fly at me with that stake. Leave Coburg and never return."

I threw the stake at his feet, following it with my battered umbrella. That halted him in his tracks. Then I reached through the slit of my skirt and tugged the band that fastened the two roomy pockets to my waist. They fell to the floor with a rattle, carrying with them saltwater, revolver, laudanum, and wolfsbane. Without them, I felt light and defenceless, but I would rather leave them here than turn them over to the Kabale when I surrendered. Perhaps Anton might find them useful.

"There. *Now* will you take me to Short?"

Vasily's eyes narrowed in suspicion. "Whatever plan you may be revolving in that teeming brain of yours won't help you now."

"I have no plan," I said. Not only my fingers, but my lips felt numb, but I was mercifully conscious of a vast inner calm. Of course it was the calm of sheer terror; but there was something restful in it, too, for I had ceased to struggle. So long as I turned myself in, the Kabale could have no reason to harm Short. They must be unaware he had ever been anything but my hostage.

Presuming that Vasily meant to cuff me, I held out my hands.

Vasily was not reassured. If anything, his suspicion had progressed to disquiet, and he hesitated before fastening the gyves about my wrists.

"This will achieve nothing, Miss Sharp. The Kabale is on its guard now. Whatever game you are playing—"

"You think I mean to play games with Short's life?"

"Ah," he said with a curl of his lip. "I still can hardly believe you have such a weakness for the bootheel." With that he threw open a window that led onto the sloping roof, whence, I saw, he meant us to clamber along the tiles and in at the window of the house adjoining this one.

"Why, I believe you're jealous of him," I needled, when this journey was over, and he was ushering me down the stairs.

It was dark in the house, and the sun was westering in a golden glow. Vasily's eyes glinted with a suggestion of red. "Perhaps I *am* jealous. No hunter likes to see another capture his prey."

He threw open the door at the rear of the house. Beyond, a sturdy brougham was waiting, together with an escort of half a dozen revenants. Their eyes glittered hungrily in their grey, decomposing faces as Vasily escorted me towards the carriage and put me inside.

He took his own seat opposite. As we got underway, I watched him in quiet thought.

It hardly mattered, for I was about to die in any case; but it struck me as odd that he should have spoken as he did, with such bravado. Odd, and not entirely consistent with some of the things I had seen him do, or heard him say.—He might be conveying me to the Kabale, but he had given me ample opportunity to escape, and had indeed begged me to do so—whether sincerely or not, I could not tell.

"Prey?" I asked softly. "Is that all I have ever been to you?"

"You told me so yourself. Don't you remember? *An untempted Aphrodite,* you said."

"There have been times, of late, when I have wondered if I was wrong."

"You have chosen a convenient moment to appeal to my humanity." He leaned forward, and I wondered if his teeth were becoming more pointed as the sun slid lower in the sky.

"Why is that? Do you desire me now that I am about to kill you?"

I knew I was balanced on the grave's brink. Outside the shadows were lengthening in a glare of gold and rose from the west; the whole world, and the creature opposite me, was limned in liquid light and flowing dark shadow. Even now it was strangely exhilarating to stand on the edge of death with my murderer, if that was what he meant to be, and bare our souls to one another.

I knew that heady sensation now for terror, not desire; and much as it thrilled me, it was a temptation to which I had never been fool enough to succumb. Sometimes I think we women are wiser than we are given credit for.

"Neither more nor less than I have always desired you," I said, "and as constantly as I have always known you would one day kill me."

"You seem determined never to forget that I drank your blood when you refused it."

"And I never will forget it; although I may, in time, forgive." I let the mocking repetition of his own words hang between us like a noose before I added, "But tonight I choose to remember something else; and that is how for a night and a day, at least, you respected my choice."

"I was weak and in pain," he snarled. "I respected your fighting spirit, not your choice."

"No, I don't think that was all," I said. "Don't you remember?"

And I put out my hand, and stroked my fingers through his hair, in the way that only his nurse and I had ever touched him: not as a dainty, not as a mistress, but as a friend.

He jerked away from my hand as though it burned him.

"That trick will not help you now. I am in my right mind tonight."

"As you were not, that night. Do you remember? I stroked your hair, and you told me about Ioanna. I think she is why you didn't kill me; isn't that true?"

The words must have touched him in a sore spot, for swiftly he reached out and fastened his hand on my throat. "Do not try me, Elizabeth Sharp. Remember who you are dealing with."

"I do," I said, through the numb layer of cold that surrounded my every movement. I was almost too terrified to blink, for I felt as though I might at any moment wake and find myself back in the cell beneath Castle Sarkozy, where I had been locked into the cell of a very hungry and not entirely sane Vasily.

"Something is different about you tonight," Vasily observed with a frown. "You are different when you are really frightened. You fight."

"That was for myself," I said. He was not holding me very tightly, but I knew he could feel the hammer of my pulse beneath his fingers. Why could he not understand how frightened I was? "Tonight I am here for Short. I told you I mean to come quietly."

"Then perhaps I'll kill Short myself, and take you away with me."

"Guarantee his safety, and see what I do then."

He scowled. "You would still fight me."

"I suppose I would. Why? What does it matter?"

For an instant, his hand tightened on my throat. Then he released me, but there was a murderous glare in his eyes. "Because he is your *enemy.*"

"And you are not?"

"I have *said* I am not!" He struck an open palm on his knee. "Twice now you have abandoned me to my enemies, and twice I have attempted to help you regardless. *Bozhe moi!* I am still ready to help you, even now, even though it is as much as my life is worth. You refuse to trust me, but you will throw yourself into my power to save *Short?*" His voice was an anguished cry: "Why? *Why?* Why does he have your forgiveness and not me?"

I stared at him in surprise. Was this the root of it, then?

Did Vasily, in fact, feel something more for me than simple, predatory appetite?

I touched my tongue to my dry lips. "My forgiveness is not yours by right."

"No," he said bitterly, "and there is the problem with your plans for the Kabale, Miss Sharp. No one would forgive us for what we have done. Strip us of our power, and you leave us helpless before our enemies to be devoured in our turn. None of us will admit it, but it is the truth all the same. For all that I would help you still, if you asked it. Speak now, before we enter the castle gate—while there is still time to save you."

Outside the park rolled by; we were rising up the long winding road through the park, up towards the castle. The sun was about to kiss the western horizon. I sighed.

"And if I refuse?"

"Then I have no choice but to obey the Kabale. They are stronger than I, and if *you* will not help me, I have nowhere else to turn."

"I cannot ask for your help," I said at length.

"Because of *him?*—Or because I am a monster?" He sent me a ferocious smile.

"Yes, but I suppose one can afford to be generous on the brink of the grave." And I reached out and slid my hands through the hair on his forehead.

He startled, his eyes widening; and for a moment he and I sat facing each other in the garden of the estate I had never visited in Moldavia, where he had killed Ioanna.—Only for an instant; and then he got control of himself, and the glamour winked out in the dark blaze of sunset.

"I forgive you, Vasily," I told him.

"I don't want your forgiveness," he snarled. "Not like this."

But he was not in control of his own glamour. The sunset slipped away and once again we faced each other in the grotto. The sound of the carriage-wheels was swallowed up in the sound of running water. The light was soft and diffuse rather than bright and harsh. I brushed his hair away from his eyes—he was a younger Vasily now, the boy who had known Ioanna; and I thought the shape of my arm had changed, and that if there had been a mirror before me I would not have looked into my own face.

"I forgive you for taking my blood," I said softly, in Ioanna's voice. "I want no revenge on you, Vasily; only to save you. If you do not believe me, then listen to the beat of my heart. You know I am telling the truth."

He looked at me with haunted eyes. When I lifted my hand from his face, the glamour faded.

Vasily did not speak again. He fell back on the seat opposite, and spent the brief remainder of the journey staring into the bleeding sky.

Chapter XXI.

Vasily led me into one of the great stone bowers of the castle, but he did not conduct me directly to the hall where the Kabale would meet later that evening. Instead, he ushered me into an empty antechamber.

"Am I not to see Short?" I asked, looking about the echoing room.

He hesitated a moment. "You don't wish to see Short."

"For pity's sake, Vasily! You terrify me. Take me to him at once!"

"Very well; but don't say I didn't warn you." Towing me by my bound wrists, he led me upstairs to a more private part of the castle. Having knocked at the door of a receiving-room, he opened the door and stood aside.

The sun must have set as we walked, for his eyes were now certainly red, and his teeth were long and sharp. He was a terrible sight. I hesitated with all my senses crying out in reflexive fear—but then I heard a faint groan from within. Abandoning restraint, I crossed the threshold in a single bound.—Ah! the sight that met my eyes!

The apartment was a large one, lit in the last dim bloody light of sunset. It had been done up as a sitting-room with Persian carpets, large sofas, and the painted red and gold panels that decorated the rest of the castle. In that red room filled with red light, Short half sat, half reclined on one of the sofas. It was his groan I had heard. A girl in a dress of pale, rose-coloured tissue had her arms around him. As I entered, she lifted red eyes and a face smeared with blood.

Missy, still in her finery from the abandoned wedding—Missy, her eyes blazing in triumph—Missy, covered in Short's blood! I felt beside myself in a chilly, detached sort of way, as though I watched all this through binoculars from a distance.

Missy tightened her embrace and licked her glistening lips. "Ah, Miss Sharp," she said softly. "I am *so* pleased you could join us."

"Don't touch him," I said through numb lips. I turned to Vasily, who had closed the door and now leaned against it with folded arm. "You said he would be safe if I turned myself in. The Kabale promised—"

"As you promised me?" he murmured.

"He has lost too much blood," I cried. "Vasily! Will you punish him for *my* faults?"

At another faint groan from Short, I turned to see that Missy had bent once again to her frightful repast. Meanwhile, Vasily watched me with a stony face.

"You said you did not hold these things against me," I said wildly. "Do you retract your forgiveness, now that I have offered mine?"

His mouth was set into a cold line, and his blood-red eyes were like points of angry fire in the gathering dusk. Still, after a moment they left me and moved to Missy and her victim.

"Leave him, ma'am," Vasily said, striding over to the pair and laying a hand on Missy's arm. "The Kabale promised he would be unharmed if Miss Sharp surrendered herself."

Missy struck Vasily's hand away. "Impertinent!" she hissed—but all the same she unwound her arms and got up from the sofa.

"Don't be afraid, Miss Sharp," she said with a hungry smile, trailing a cold finger from my temple to my jaw, and down to the pulse in my throat. "I haven't drained him; only left him a little something to remember me by. Fair is fair. You ruined my sister; I have ruined your pet."

As she departed, I rushed to Short's side and pressed my fingers against the flow of blood from his neck, trying to stanch the flow with my handkerchief.

"Miss Sharp?" he murmured.

"I'm here, Alexander." I turned on Vasily in desperation. "Why are you standing there? Won't you send for a doctor? He needs help!"

Vasily shrugged. "The Kabale meets in less than an hour. Only royalties and their servants will be admitted to the castle tonight. Don't be alarmed, though. Princess Marie knows exactly how much she can take, none better."

He spoke dispassionately, and I was overwhelmed with loathing. His conscience, it seemed, was awake only when it came to myself. "If you won't help him, then you might at least leave me alone with him."

Vasily lifted an eyebrow and glanced around the room, his eyes lingering on the windows.

"I don't mean to escape, if that's what you think," I added, for I had already considered the possibility myself. I had no rope, and without one I could hardly climb that sheer wall myself, much less with shackled hands and a half-dead man on my back. "Apart from anything else, I don't mean to abandon

Short."

"No," Short murmured.

"I'll set guards," Vasily warned. "Don't try anything foolish." With that, he followed Missy from the room. Once the door closed behind him, I heard him giving instructions to the revenant guards that had followed us from the courtyard.

Not that it mattered to me anymore.

"Try to stay awake," I told Short, steadying his drooping head between my hands. His heartbeat was a rapid, labouring sound. His eyes focused on me dizzily. "Missy's bite will change you. You'll clot quickly and heal fast."

Short's throat worked, and his tongue ran over his lips. His voice was only a faint croak. "I…"

"You need water?" I looked about me and quickly saw a decanter of brandy and a soda-siphon on a sideboard to one side of the room. The liquor would be deadly to him, but the soda-water might help. "Here," I said, taking Short's hand, and pressing it against the sodden cambric wisp I had clamped to his wound. "Hold this."

His weakened grasp tightened on my fingers. "Miss Sharp," he rasped—but I slid my shackled hands from his and went to the small bar. A moment later I returned with a tumbler half full of liquid and held it to Short's lips. He drank all of it gratefully. Beneath my hand, his heart slowed a little—a good sign. I sighed in relief; but as I set the cup aside, Short's hand covered mine, and I found him looking up at me with a frown between his eyebrows.

"Miss Sharp," he murmured, "you came."

"Could you doubt it?"

The frown deepened, and his bloodless lips thinned. "You shouldn't be here. They'll kill you."

"Don't look at me like that," I protested. "What did you expect? that I would leave you to die?"

"If I *was* dead, would you save yourself?"—He gestured towards the handkerchief at his neck. The blood was already clotting, but for a moment I thought he was about to tear the wound open. An anguished sound escaped my lips, and I arrested his arm.

"Don't ask me to save myself at your expense!"

"No fear," he murmured. "You're too late to save me now… You were right about Princess Marie. She came to the house and—and I don't know what happened after that. I came here. Why should I have come here? I gave you my word not to escape."

"She must have been playing with your mind again." I could almost taste the bitterness on my tongue. How Missy must have loved it, getting Short to follow her willingly to his own destruction!

"You should go." He touched my cheek with chilly fingers. "I don't matter. Find May. Finish what you started. Only stop them doing this to anyone else."

Was I being a fool again? Once already I had ignored greater responsibilities for Short's sake, yet surely this was different. Then I had wronged Vasily; but now, if I left, it felt as though I might wrong Short.

"There is no escape," I said, taking his hand. I could not make myself sound sorry. "Vasily has told the policemen outside the door to shoot me if I try to escape, and I cannot scale the wall with my hands tied. For the moment, I'm afraid you're saddled with me."

"*Liz.*" He wove his fingers into my loose hair as though he could hold me against the whole world. "Liz, they'll kill you."

Ah, how long I had longed to hear my name on his lips! There was something intoxicating in the way he said it, breathing it out like a lament; and I was ready to discard my life as a child discards an unwanted toy.

"So long as it saves your life, it doesn't matter to me."

He took a deep, shaking breath. "It matters to me. This is all my fault. I ought to have believed you—about the revenants, Missy, everything…A part of me knew you were right; only I didn't want to see you lose your life in trying to fight them. When I thought of enduring the rest of my life without you, it hardly seemed worthwhile…and now, of course…"

I forced a smile. "With any luck, you won't have to. You understand they will likely take your memories and send you to the *Akbar,* or worse still make a revenant of you. You will forget me either way."

"Better than to endure a living death remembering you."

"Don't," I whispered. "How can I make up my mind to die when you tell me such things?"

His eyes lit with purpose, and his fingers curled in my hair. My mouth was suddenly dry as I realised what he meant to do.

"No," I whispered, "oh, no, you don't."

"You promised," he said, and I was quite beyond any ability to resist. He drew me down and kissed me very gently, as though he thought I was made of glass and might shatter. My heart beat with suffocating force. I broke away from him after a moment to catch my breath, but he drew me closer, and I felt his lips move against the scars that crossed my cheek.

"I have one to match yours now," he murmured through his kisses.

"I am so sorry," I whispered, restraining my tears with

difficulty. "I came the moment I heard—if I had not been late—"

"Don't apologise," he told me, releasing his hold just enough to let me look him in the eye. "I consider it an honour; do you hear?"

Overcome with emotion, I hid my face against his uninjured shoulder.

"Liz! What's this—did I say something to hurt you?"

"No, you duffer! Only I never thought I would hear you say such a thing."

"I beg your pardon," he said with a sigh. "What a beast I was!—I ought to have gone home myself, and you would not be in this fix now."

"Or they might have taken Anton instead, and I should have been here in the same fix with him."

Short made a thoughtful sound. "I'm a generous man, but I'm not sure I'm sufficiently generous for *that*."

"It does seem as though we're stuck with each other for the term of our natural lives."

"Till death do us part," he added, with a twinkle.

"If by some miracle I live to see the morrow, you'll regret saying that."

"No," Short said firmly, "I won't."

"Aha! so the ring really was for me!"

"I never denied *that*." His lips brushed mine again. "It's yours. Only promise me not to let them kill you without a fight."

And how the dickens could I argue with that?

Chapter XXII.

The last glow of sunset had long faded, and it was dark in the receiving-room when Vasily came to collect us both. Weak as he was, Short had to be half carried by a pair of revenants. Meanwhile, Vasily linked his arm through mine and drew me a few paces ahead of the others.

"They mean to offer you a settlement," he murmured in my ear. "Take it and come away with me."

"A settlement!" I wished I could see the look on his face, but the passages of the castle were too dark to see him properly. "Why ever should they do that?"

"You still have friends in high places, Miss Sharp."

Did he mean himself?—Or George and May? I had no opportunity to ask, for we had descended the stairs into the vestibule; and now the double doors swung open, admitting us to the room where the Kabale sat at its long table. There my question seemed answered, for as the Kabale turned to look at me, I found George sitting at the table beside his father.

Alas, George! Having defied his family for May's sake, had he now been coerced or cajoled to return?—My spirits fell. It would have been something to know that George and May, at least, were free.

This evening the upper galleries were empty. Only the

Kabale itself sat watching as I was led to stand before them. Catching my gaze, Missy of Roumania ran the tip of her tongue across her gloating lips, as though to remind me of what she had done to Short—as though I *could* forget, with his drying blood on my hands, and smudged across the front of my dress!

George glanced at me with an unsmiling face, but then returned his gaze to the table before him. As for the others, they watched in suppressed triumph.

In a far corner of the room, a kind of steel frame awaited beside a table which contained a number of sharp and glistening tools. The frame, tilted at an angle, was fitted with leathern restraints of a type with which I was all too familiar, and my breath caught in my lungs at the irresistible recollection of the laboratory in Castle Sarkozy. No doubt this was the apparatus of revenant-making!

The chairman—Willie, the Kaiser's heir, if I recalled correctly—dismissed the revenants that had escorted Short. They left him leaning against a wall for support, and bowed themselves out. After that, Willie picked up a piece of paper from the table before him, perusing it in dignified silence for a full minute.

It was really rather funny. There they all sat champing at the bit to drain my blood, but they stretched the moment out purely to show me that I had not, in fact, consumed all their attention for the past five days. I must be put in my place, after all.

At length Willie cleared his throat. "Elizabeth Sharp?"

"Hullo, Jim!" I said. I was sure that if I spoke with anything less than hilarity, my voice would have quaked in fear.

The Prussian crown prince overlooked my familiarity.

"Your crimes are as follows: bombing a royal train; escaping custody; impersonation of a royal personage; seven counts of reckless endangerment of a royal personage; resisting arrest; theft from a hospital; the murder of Prince Chlodwig of Lippe; spying upon the meetings of this body; conspiracy against this body; possession of proscribed substances;"—that must be May's blood—"three counts of aggravated assault against royal personages resulting in permanent impairment of same; three counts of kidnapping."

"How busy I've been!" I murmured, more to keep my spirits up than anything else.

"Many of these are capital crimes; and yet, *astonishingly*," Willie announced in a disapproving tone, "it seems that a member of this body has spoken on your behalf."

This must be the agreement of which Vasily had warned me. I glanced at George, presuming that I must have him to thank for this way out; but he only looked up in surprise as his cousin Nicky, resplendent in a fine uniform, rose from his seat.

"Mith Sharp," he began, "in conthideration of thervitheth rethently—ahem." He cleared his throat and began again. "Following a thertain happy event thith afternoon, I should like to render my thankth. The Kabale hath offered the following termth: if for the future you remain thilent on the thubject of thith body, and abide by itth ruleth, we will exthempt you from conversion to revenant, and withdraw our recommendation that Printheth May be committed to an athylum." Nicky cleared his throat. "Altho we would be prepared to extherthithe our influenthe—that ith, you will be given the name of your attacker from two yearth ago, as you requethted at firtht."

I am not too proud to admit that I gaped.—The Kabale's last offer had been so parsimonious, I had not for a moment imagined they might actually offer me something I truly wanted. Immunity for May—freedom for myself—and the name of the beast who scarred me! Let it not be forgotten that for two years I had dreamed of nothing else; that I had taken service with May in order to learn that name; that I had followed her to Europe in a ferment of eagerness to learn it. Three nights previously I had come face to face with the monster at last—only to lose him again in the aftermath of Prince Chlodwig's death.

At last, I might face my attacker and find some sort of reparation!

"Say yes," Vasily whispered behind me, his words little more than the motion of his lips by my ear.

But I hesitated.—I had once before been swayed by the prospect of something I very much wanted, and I could not quite bring myself to accept this promise now. I must think coolly.—What was to prevent the Kabale giving me the wrong name?—Prince Chlodwig's, for instance, dead and beyond my reach; or some other scapegoat, chosen to preserve the reputation and safety of the wolf who had scarred me. And say that they did give me the right name: would that bring back the memories I had lost? Would it prevent the victimisation of more unfortunates?

There was more at stake here than my own pain—there was more wrong with the world than one or two bad royalties, like Missy or the wolf that had scarred me. They could not even solemnise a marriage without bloodshed. If I needed more proof, there was the fact that the Kabale was willing to name my attacker at all, in exchange for their own immunity.

It was exactly how the royalties always behaved. They would scapegoat the weak, and count the cost cheap if it protected the more powerful.

I glanced to where Short waited leaning against the wall near the door. His face was in shadow, so that I could not read it.—Alas, Short! I had promised to fight for my life; but I could not sell my soul for him or anyone.

"I'm afraid you seem to be labouring under a misunderstanding," said I. "It isn't revenge I want; it's justice. I want you to stop killing people altogether."

I thought Short gave a tiny grunt, as though in pain. At the Kabale's table, Nicky blinked.

"You refuse?"

"I have no choice," I said dully. "I cannot make the promises you require."

"What did I tell you? Bad blood will out," Missy murmured.

—And who knew? Perhaps she was right. There was a great deal of Vera Livius in me after all—the trouble-maker, the rebel, the anarchist—or as near as made no difference.

I would never submit to this.

Nicky's mouth hung open in surprise. "But—you don't underthtand," he said very earnestly. "We shall have no choithe but to make a revenant of you."

George was silent, staring at the untouched wineglass on the table before him.

"You *do* have a choice," I told the tsarevitch. "You might do as I ask, and stop this reign of blood."

He threw up his hands. "I am thorrier than I can thay, Mith Sharp." Pushing back his chair, he bowed to Willie. "Gentlemen, I mutht go. My fianthée awaitth."

George moved then, jumping to his feet with a cry of

entreaty. "Nicky—!"

Everyone around the table stared curiously at the young prince. Beneath their scrutiny, George reddened and sank into his chair again.

"Never mind. I'll speak to you later," he said gruffly. Nicky nodded to him and departed.

I wondered mightily what George was playing at, but my thoughts were interrupted by the sharp rap of Willie's gavel.

"Elizabeth Sharp, you are hereby condemned to revenant conversion, the sentence to be carried out at once, without prior execution. Gentlemen—and Princess Marie—you asked to witness the procedure yourselves. I think you'll find it a simple enough affair." He raised his voice. "Professor Schmidt!"

All this time Vasily had been standing behind me. Now his cold hands fastened upon my shoulders, holding me in place. I did not struggle, but a chill struck at my heart. Until now I had remained calm, partly by dint of telling myself that surely, surely there would be some eleventh-hour reprieve, some form of rescue. George was here! May could not have forgotten me! Anton, surely, would do something!

In the event, it was Short who acted. Pale, covered in blood, his clothing and hair disarranged, he pushed away from the wall and staggered towards the table.

"Short," George yelped, noticing him for the first time. "What the blazes has happened to you, man?"

"Begging your pardon in advance, sir," Short gasped, withdrawing something from his pocket. It was a small canister of a type I had seen on a previous occasion, not two nights before. Falling against the table before any of the assembled royalties recovered their wits enough to move, he lit the fuse at a candle-flame and then sent the sputtering flashbang rolling down the table, scattering papers and knocking over wineglasses.

The Kabale recoiled with shouts of alarm, calling for guards or diving beneath the table. Only one of them kept her wits. Missy captured the device and, with a yank of her delicate fingers, removed the fuse. She threw it underfoot, ground out the flame against the parquetry, and raised an eyebrow at Short.

"What's this, Inspector? Have *you* turned anarchist, also?"

Short could not answer: he sank to his knees, gasping for breath in the aftermath of his exertion. The doors burst open. In another moment we were surrounded by revenants.

"It's only a flashbang," I declared hotly, since Short could not answer. "It wouldn't have done any of you a bit of harm."—Only it might have allowed both of us to escape; and now the effort was useless.

"York!" Chairman Willie arose from the floor, poked his nose above the tabletop and sent a censorious look at George. "Is this *your* bodyguard?"

"I...er...I suppose it must be," George said lamely. His forehead was covered with a sheen of sweat. He said nothing else, even when the Prince of Wales managed to untangle himself from the remnants of his chair, which had shattered beneath his efforts to get away from the table, and rose wheezing to his feet.

"Short, I am affronted!" George's father swung about to face the two gentlemen who had entered the room unobtrusively and wheeled the frame and the table forward while all this disturbance had gone on. "Professor Schmidt, is there any reason both these insurgents cannot be safely turned tonight?"

"No, sir; none whatsoever."

"Excellent. Deal with both of them," said the Prince with a wave of his hand, sinking into a new seat offered thoughtfully by Missy herself. "And don't forget to explain the process as you go along; we are quite interested in your methods."

So Short and I were both to make the change!—I had known the same fate awaited us both, of course; but I had comforted myself that perhaps Short would not be condemned at once—that he might yet contrive an escape. Now it was over: all the sands had run through the glass.

"Vasily," I cried, as Short and I were seized by the revenants, "for pity's sake—!"

He relinquished me without a word. As we were dragged towards that ominous frame, I was nearly ready to weep with vexation.

"Why can't you let me die in peace, Short?" I demanded. "You chump!"

"But a gallant chump, at least?" Although still breathless, he seemed indecently cheerful. "Don't wish me away, my dear. I had rather share in your fate, than watch it from afar and know I did nothing to stop it."

The professor and his assistant affixed their frame to stand upright. Short and I were each placed against it, back to back, and strapped in at arms, wrists, and waists. The professor, I noted, was rather a young man, very blonde and blue-eyed and icy, with a jaw and cheekbones sharp enough to butter bread with. His assistant looked nearly alike enough to be his brother, but had the vacant, glimmering stare of a living revenant. I shuddered, partly at the thought of soon becoming like him, and partly at the thought of a brotherhood so unnatural. What dreadful falling-out, what unholy rivalry had led to *this?*

The professor went to his table and uncorked a bottle of some white, cloudy tincture—I smelled the strong, flowery scent of laudanum. "Sirs, ma'am—you will be aware, of course, of the method by which a corpse is revivified. It was long presumed that living persons could not be so transformed, because the alternate consciousness required an empty shell to inhabit: the patient's native personality would not allow the incursion of an alien. My modest contribution to the field of revenant studies is simply this." He flicked a forefinger against the bottle in his hand. "Laudanum, the simple tincture known to you all. Once the native personality is unconscious, the procedure is more simple than revivifying a corpse, and requires less specialised equipment.—First, I administer a dose of the tincture to each patient."

The professor and his dead-eyed assistant converged upon us. "So long, Alexander," I muttered. "I'm sorry I brought you to this."

"I'm sorry I wasted so much time trying to defend the indefensible," he replied, with equal composure. We had said our more heartfelt good-byes half an hour before in the receiving-room.

The revenant assistant seized my chin, squeezing mercilessly until he forced my mouth to open. In went the spoon, and for the second time in a week I found myself gagging on the overwhelming taste of far too much laudanum. Once I had been forced to swallow, the Schmidts moved to Short, whose more determined efforts to resist were crowned with no better success.

I watched George. There was a wineglass in his hand. His fingers tapped against the stem, and his gaze bored through me as though he was looking at something a thousand miles away. I wished I could have told him that whatever he had done, I would forgive it, so long as he remained true to May.

Schmidt stepped in front of me again, seizing the collar of my dress and pulling open the row of small buttons to lay bare my décolletage.

"I *beg* your pardon!" I spoke frostily enough to make May herself proud of me—but of course, a woman's honour is only sacred above a certain social level.

"As you know," Schmidt announced, turning to the table to pick up a scalpel, "the most important part of the procedure is the carving of the Dunwich Signature. Once the patients are fully inert beneath the effect of the laudanum, this completes the conversion. Your living revenants await.—Alphonse, your scalpel!"

The professor handed his assistant the instrument and came at me, brandishing his own. I shrank back, hearing Short's heartbeat racing as Alphonse approached. Our restraints rattled, but they had been built for monsters, and Short and I were still common mortals.

Schmidt thrust a hand against my shoulder to hold me in place. The tip of his tongue protruded in concentration as he took his scalpel and drew it over my heart in a circular motion (not once did he look me in the eye; I might have been an animal or a mannequin). I caught a painful breath as my flesh parted beneath the razor-sharp blade, but Schmidt was practiced at his work: the steel cut just deep enough to draw blood, but no deeper.

I was grateful for the laudanum, then, for it dulled the pain a little. But as I had already discovered, it was not enough to deprive me of my senses. I could not stop thinking of what might come next for Short and myself, and cold sweat formed on my brow.

A chair scraped in the silent room. George rose to his feet, his hand playing with his pocket-watch as though he was about to make a speech. His face was pale as he cleared his throat.

"A toast," he announced in a voice loud enough to rattle the chandelier. "All your glasses charged?—Allow me to refill that, Tino. Now, ma'am, gentlemen: to the future!"

Glasses clinked. Voices repeated the toast at a murmur. George must be up to something, but for the moment I could not think what. The scalpel cut deeper now. I risked a glance down and caught a glimpse of an emblem or sigil carved across my heart in blood, the symbols that surrounded it strange and evil-looking. What was the meaning of this—this Dunwich Signature, as Schmidt had called it? There was nothing of science in this: we were in an older and darker world now. Terrible as were the things Vera Livius and her father had done, they were not of this order.

I felt my mind slipping; I felt my surroundings melting away. I sensed a void full of malice and darkness, and a hundred souls crying out in desperation and agony and guilt, and it seemed to me that I was fated to be among them, as a will stronger than my own crept into my body and seized control of my limbs.

I was saved by a sound: at the table, a glass smashed to the floor, and Missy screamed.

"Poison!" she shrieked. "Treachery!"

I came back to myself with a jolt. There was no darkness: I stood in the bright, civilised hall at the Coburg castle, and the wailing I heard was from the princess, who stood with both hands pressed to her cheeks and a look of horror on her face.

Consternation reigned at the Kabale's table. Just as he was about to cut the final mark, Schmidt hesitated, turning to glance behind him.

"Finish it!" Missy screeched, throwing up a finger to point at me. "Finish the procedure!"

But Schmidt never had the chance. Vasily moved too fast to see. There was a flash of white teeth, an awful gurgling sound, and the overwhelming stench of blood. Then Schmidt fell to the floor with his throat torn out, and Vasily spat shreds of flesh, the entire lower half of his face covered in the professor's blood.

Behind me, Short was the only locus of silence and stillness in the room: his only movement was the beat of his heart, the ebb and flow of his lungs. I could not see Alphonse Schmidt, nor gauge whether his Signature was complete.

"Short!" I cried, "wake up! Don't yield to it!"—As Vasily seized my wrist, meaning to unbuckle my restraints, I shook my head and rattled the frame. "Leave me! Save Short!"

He hissed at me through his bloody teeth, but he turned away from me to obey.

Missy stood behind him, a wooden stake clenched in her white, shaking fist.

"You *snake*," she declared.

My heart leaped into my throat as she struck home, driving the spike deep into his body and tearing it out again for another blow. Vasily caught her wrist and hurled her from him. Missy struck the floor with some force and burst into tears.

In the sudden quiet, Vasily hunched over his wound, breathing hard. The stake had missed his heart, but it must have hit an artery, for there was a great deal of blood trickling between his fingers.

At the table, the sensation had died down enough for the Prince of Wales to stand up and point an accusing finger at his erring son. "George! What is the meaning of this?"

George paid no attention at first: his body hunched, and he bent over the table with a groan of pain. For a moment I wondered, horrified, if he too had been wounded. But then a sulphurous glow kindled in his eyes as he fought free of his jacket—as the shirt across his shoulders ripped—as he began to grow in size.

The moon must have risen, and now there was a new commotion, as the German royalties discovered that they remained unchanged.

"Gentlemen of the Kabale," George panted in the throes of his transformation, "you have just tasted the blood of a morganatic princess. You are no longer monsters."

"George," I muttered, "you *marvel*." Vasily had undone my right hand. Now I tried to release the restraints on my left wrist, but my head was swimming, and my fingers seemed about twice their ordinary size.—I must try to rid myself of some of this laudanum. With my left wrist free, I fell to my knees and performed an indelicate operation involving two fingers and a natural bodily reflex. Once the spasms had passed, my head felt clearer. I found I was able to address my ankle restraints with more exactitude.

Meanwhile, the Kabale still struggled with their discovery. They had not yet considered anything beyond their own catastrophe: their revenants stood motionless at the borders of the room.

"George! You *ingrate!*—After all this family has done for you!—And *you*, Vasily!"

"Traitor!" cried Chairman Willie, leaping to his feet, and throwing the dregs of his tainted blood at the transforming George. "I *will* have satisfaction for this! You *shall* fight me, sir!"

"Demmed if I do." George gave a whine of pain as his limbs thickened and grew. "I have no quarrel with you!"

"Guards!" Willie howled—a thing I had believed only happened in productions of Shakespeare. He pointed at George, then Vasily, who was still on his knees, bleeding. "Arrest these traitors!—And the anarchist!"

With a sob, I got my feet clear of the frame at last and staggered to my feet.—But when I turned to see what had happened to Short, my blood ran cold.

Alphonse, the living revenant, was just unshackling his last restraints. Short stepped away from the frame and both of them turned to me.

The cold, unholy corpse-light flickered in Short's eyes. His jacket and shirt hung open, revealing the bloody sigil carved across his heart. The final symbol—an eye—stared at me from the centre of the circle.

The Dunwich Signature was complete. Short was a revenant.

The two revenants advanced upon me, moving as one. Speechless with horror, I caught up the first weapon I saw—Schmidt's fallen scalpel—and backed away from them. Short!—To come to this, after all we had been through together! I reached Vasily and helped him rise unsteadily to his feet, one hand clamped to the wound in his chest.

Revenants converged upon us from all directions. I raised my scalpel in a shaking hand, knowing it for a hopeless gesture. The blade was too small to do any kind of good against the revenants—and, revenant or not, I could not stomach the thought of doing Short an injury.

"Sharp!" George barked. Now fully transformed to his lupine form, he leaped the table in a single bound and landed beside me. "Time to go, what!"

"Where to?" I cried.

With one brawny arm, George threw the bleeding vampire across his shoulder. "After me!" He charged towards the door—towards the thickest line of revenants.

It struck me, then, that he must not know of the revenants' berserker rage.

"No, wait!" I shrieked, but I was already too late. George struck one revenant aside and then another; but then the whole hive of them went mad, throwing themselves upon him with fists and truncheons. In a moment, he and Vasily disappeared beneath their swarming mass.

I was not to be overlooked: the Short-revenant seized me by the arm.

"Miss Sharp, you are under arrest. Do not resist." That dear voice was flat and toneless. A pang went through me at the sound worse by far than the bleeding, incomplete sigil carved on my breast. Ah, to have lost him now, when we had begun to understand each other!

—No, I would not believe that. I had been able, just for a moment, to resist the transformation. Short, like me, was a living creature, with a will and a mind. I turned, gripping his arm in turn, gazing into his weirdly-shining eyes.

"Alexander," I pleaded. "If you can hear me, fight, fight, fight for us. Don't you know that I love you?"

I pulled down his head to mine, imprinting a burning kiss upon his cold, motionless lips. Did I imagine it, or did a muscle twitch beneath my thumb where it rested upon his cheek?—But then a punishing blow struck me in the ribs, throwing me to the floor. I gasped for air as the Short-revenant advanced upon me with knotted fists.

"No more mistakes," Chairman Willie announced. "Kill the anarchist, Short—throttle her, if you must!"

I threw a despairing glance towards the scrum where George and Vasily still struggled beneath the weight of the other revenants. There was no help for me there, and Short—Short was about to kill me, and all I had was a scalpel for a weapon.

With that, an idea occurred to me—a wild and foolish notion, one that might only seal our doom.

Yet it was the only course that still remained open to me.

Gritting my teeth, I lifted the scalpel to my own heart. With a few swift, searing strokes, I completed the Dunwich Signature.

At once my surroundings faded to dim shadows. Another mind beat upon my own: an entity of rapacious appetite and terrifying willpower. There was a struggle. My mind was alert and would not give up its place without a fight. But I succeeded in the end—gave up my body and allowed my unseated mind to drift.

Some slight tether still connected the two: far away in the Kabale's chamber, I was aware of my body rising to its feet and standing motionless before Short as he, too, came to a halt.

We were all puppets on the same string. I could feel them now, the hundreds—perhaps thousands—of revenants in the world, all of them controlled by the same dark mind.

I followed that string, an unseen passenger along dark,

twisting tendrils of power. I found myself looking through other eyes. I saw glimpses of the streets of Coburg as the revenants there stood guard or patrolled on their beat. I stood at the gate of the palace, saluting as a carriage rolled by. I was in the police station, dragging a boy into a cell, and striking him viciously when he resisted. I was in the courtyard of this very castle, glaring with dull suspicion at a carriage waiting in the shadows; atop it was a hunched coachman, playing with the lacquered walking-stick he held across his knees.

I was in a hundred places within the council-chamber of the Kabale, surrounding a groaning George and Vasily, determined to cut off their escape, to beat the defiance out of them.

I was looking at my own mask-like face through Short's eyes.

"Alexander," I whispered to the darkness where the lost souls lurked. "Where are you, my love?"

The answer came at once.

"Liz!—Here?…Then all is indeed lost!"

"All is lost," a thousand voices echoed in the dark.

"Don't say it," I told them fiercely. "They're *our* bodies, aren't they? It has no right to them. It can't hold us—not if we all rise together."

"We can't, can we? Is it possible? Could we get out of here?"

"We're signed over to it," said Short dubiously. "It's the *rules.*"

"Hang the rules! Whose rules are they, anyway—*his*? There *must* be a higher law than this. There *must* be justice, in this world or out of it."

"It's too strong. It will never let us go."

"We don't need to be stronger," I said. The certainty cut

through my doubt like a ray of light through clouds. For days I had felt adrift, scarcely knowing what to believe. Now I knew for certain that I *did* believe—that I *must* believe. The world was full of evil things so much stronger than myself, and I could never fight them alone.

"We needn't be stronger," I repeated. "We only need to be *right.* Give us back our bodies, you thief! They were given to *us,* not to you!"

That other consciousness seemed suddenly aware of me—of the uprising of lost souls. Throughout Europe, every one of the revenants turned from its business and lifted its head to stare in the direction of Coburg—of the castle—of Short and me where we stood facing each other silently in the council-chamber.

The *thing* reacted with a flood of vengeful malice. Within the council-chamber, my nerveless hand reached out, still clutching the bloody scalpel: I knew that whatever this dark power was, it meant to cut Short's throat and with it, whatever faint thread still connected him to life.

A miscalculation. That dreadful sight gave me the last strength I needed to fight.

That will of iron faltered beneath our concerted assault as it found its hold not so strong as it thought. My own mind was clear, scarcely impaired by the drug. As that alien grasp slipped, I flew back to my body like a bird—and my first sight, as I took command of my limbs, was Short's eyes clearing of that terrible revenant fire.

My hand was already extended: it was but the work of a moment to slash the scalpel across Short's breast, adding one more bloody line to the sigil and ruining it forever. Somewhere in the back of my mind, I heard something like a shriek of hatred and despair. Swiftly I turned the scalpel a second time upon my own flesh, scoring a defacing line through the centre of the sigil. The shriek cut off abruptly. Then I pocketed the blade and flew to Short's arms.

I opened my eyes after a moment, for silence had fallen over the room. Alphonse was on his knees. With one hand he had wrenched open his shirt; his own scalpel, freshly blooded, lay in his other hand; and his eyes were human again, and filled with tears as they gazed upon his brother's body.

Elsewhere in the room, the corpse-light faded from the eyes of the undead revenants as they paused from their attack. A change came over their rotting faces: a momentary look of peace, or even happiness, before they laid themselves down for their final sleep.

The Kabale were dumbstruck. In the silence, George got shakily to his feet, dragging Vasily with him and looking much the worse for wear.

"Miss Sharp! Not sure how you managed *that*," he panted. "Not a moment too soon! Shall we?"

The four of us limped to the door in silence. There were more dead revenants in the antechamber, and still more in the courtyard. A carriage waited in the shadows not far away. Anton sat on the box. When he saw us, he sheathed his swordstick with a gesture of relief and picked up the whip to urge the horses into motion. George bounded to the carriage door and slung the injured Vasily within. I helped Short in after them; and in another moment May folded me in her arms, and the carriage was rattling hastily through the gatehouse and across the moat to safety.

Chapter XXIII.

George had taken a seat on the box beside Anton. Afterwards I was not sure whether the breakneck pace at which we dashed into Coburg was a result of Anton's whip or the scent of wolf, but the horses certainly managed it in record time. Short and I supported Vasily the whole way, listening to his ragged, labouring breath.

"What is wrong with Vasily?" May breathed. "And you and Short—you're covered in blood!"

"We're all right, but Vasily…Missy staked him through the chest."

"Is he going to die?"

"I don't know." I steadied him as we went over a jolt. "He *said* he was throwing in with the Kabale, but then he tried to help me again. I don't understand…and you! and George!"

"Oh yes—I should explain. After we found you and Short missing from the attic, it was clear that *something* was wrong. Then I found one of Vasily's cigarettes on the floor next to the bed—I remembered seeing him smoke them in London; they're an English brand—so we knew he had been there, and after that it was not too difficult to track him down."

"You ought to have been a detective, ma'am," Short said admiringly.

A glimmer of laughter silvered her voice. "Perhaps I'll need to become one, if George's family cuts him off with the threatened shilling."

"But Vasily," I prompted. "What's this you say, about finding him?"

"Oh, yes! While Anton was collecting my blood from where George had hidden it—Sharp dear, can you believe it? that man had left the syringes in *the pocket of his coat*—George and I came up to the castle to spy out the land, and we found Vasily wandering the corridors like a guilty spirit, quite willing to help us. It was his idea that George should pretend a reconciliation with his father, and propose a toast once the procedure was underway."

I felt a little dizzy with surprise. "But then—everything Vasily said was true. He was on our side all along."

"Of course," May added, "we were not entirely certain we could trust him, but at that point there didn't seem to be much other choice. Then it was only a matter of lacing the wine, and sending George to beg the Family's pardon and ask very nicely to be allowed to witness the procedure. Oh! And I brought your old journals over from the palace. They're in the attic of Short's house, along with a passport in case anyone bothers you on your way out of Germany. I'm afraid it's a fake, but it should serve."

"May," said I with feeling, "I don't know how to thank you."

"Then don't," she said promptly. "But I *do* insist on being godmother to your eldest daughter. May Short will make a lovely name, I think."

I gaped at her. May blushed. "Oh dear! Have I said something terribly wrong? Is the wedding not going ahead?"

"The wedding?" I protested feebly.

"Why, yes! Don't the two of you have an understanding by now?"

I glanced in Short's direction, but the carriage was mercifully dark. "Oh, dear! is it *that* obvious?"

"My *dear...!*"

"There is an understanding," Short put in—and even in the dark I could hear that he was smiling. "Of very recent date, although I admit that I *did* make an impulsive purchase in Eger..."

But at that moment the carriage jerked to a halt, and I looked out to behold Short's lodgings. It was a risk, I supposed, for Missy knew we were using the house as our headquarters; but we had left Missy and the rest of the Kabale with a great many other things to think about. Two minutes later the Georgewolf, May, Short, Anton, and myself were gathered in the downstairs room looking at Vasily. I had laid him across the tabletop, where he sprawled pale and still, staring into the shadows with unseeing eyes. His breath was an ugly-sounding rasp.

"That sounds like a punctured lung," Short observed.

"Are you quite sure?" My hands fluttered over Vasily's breast and the terrible stain there, uncertain what to do. "We must do *something.*"

"Must we?" Anton laid a hand on the stake at his belt.

"Anton! what are you doing?"

"You promised me I could kill him when the Kabale was dealt with," Anton growled. "He killed my cousin Ioanna, Liz. He drained your blood at Castle Sarkozy, and he betrayed us to the Kabale this morning."

"*And* he saved my life tonight," I protested.

Anton ground his teeth. I looked down at Vasily, remembering what had happened when he drank my blood at Castle Sarkozy. All the same: "I can save him," I said.

"Let him rot!" Anton cried. "You may forgive him for what he has done to *you,* but I will never forgive him for what he did to Ioanna!"

I kept my temper with an effort. "Very well, Anton. Do you really think your cousin would want this man dead, if she could speak to us now?"

"If she could speak to us now, she wouldn't be dead."

"Look me in the eye and tell me in all honesty that she wouldn't forgive him," I insisted.

Anton met my gaze angrily.

"In all honesty," I pressed him.

Anton's lips worked; his face reddened; and after a moment he turned away angrily. "Ioanna was a fool for him."

"Better to be a merciful than a vindictive fool," I said, dipping into my pocket for the scalpel. So it came to this, that I would break my one first rule, and for such a one as Vasily! All the same, I owed him my life, and had freely given him my forgiveness. I did not trust him, or even particularly like him: but this I could do—I could bleed for him.

I made a neat cut in the vein of my wrist. George whined softly at the scent of blood, and May gave a little gasp; but Short met my eyes and nodded.

Sliding my right hand beneath Vasily's head, I held my bleeding arm to his wrist, and let the blood trickle between his lips. For an instant there was no change. Then his mouth moved slightly against my wrist, and he took a convulsive swallow. A moment later he clutched my arm and began drinking in great strong gulps. Even as we watched, the wound in his breast knit together, and his laboured breathing calmed. I waited until the last wheezing sound faded away and his heart was beating no faster than anyone else's in the room before I twisted my arm from his lips and stanched the flow with a tea-towel.

When I turned back to the table Vasily was sitting up on it, watching me with something between awe and astonishment on his face. He touched his fingers to his bloody lips.

"You gave me your blood," he whispered. "You saved my life."

"I told you I forgave you," I said through my dizziness.

Overcome, he buried his face in his hands for a moment. Then he slid off the table, onto his feet. "I could kiss you," he declared.

"Try it, and it'll take more than my blood to save your life."

At this Anton stepped between us brandishing something that glinted red in the candlelight—the third and last hypodermic full of May's blood.

"It's true that Ioanna would have forgiven you," Anton announced. "But if you are truly sorry, you will give up the power you gained when you took her life."

"Miss Sharp!" Vasily appealed to me with an ingratiating smile.

"Oh, no," I said, falling into the chair Short had silently produced for me. "I promised not to interfere. I've saved your life, and now you must dispose of it as you see fit."

"If you are *not* truly sorry for killing my cousin," Anton added in a conversational tone, brandishing his stake, "then I will have no choice but to finish you. To spare other lives, you understand."

Vasily's eyes narrowed. "You will let me live if I defang myself?"

Anton hesitated a moment. A glance—not towards me, but towards May. "Yes," he said at last. "I swear it."

Short's hand found mine and squeezed. Perhaps he had seen the look of happiness on my face, for I felt the taste of victory. It was difficult enough to defuse a bomb, but I had succeeded in defusing the bomb-maker—an infinitely more ticklish and uncertain operation. As for the vampire—well, I had never really hoped to show Vasily the error of his ways; and yet…

Vasily held out his arm, wincing as Anton jabbed a vein none too gently with the needle, depressed the plunger halfway and drew it out again. Vasily grimaced and ran his tongue over his suddenly very human teeth.

"I feel fragile," he said mournfully. "Weak."

"No, you don't," Anton said with his customary brusqueness. "You feel the same way the rest of us do now; only you've lost your unfair advantage." He turned to May, and offered the hypodermic with a flourish. "Princess."

"Thanks, Anton," she said, leaning over and kissing his cheek. He turned as red as fire, and retired in disarray.

Short stepped forward, offering Vasily his hand. The ex-vampire regarded it with a raised eyebrow and a quizzical expression.

"What's this?"

"My apology," Short said stiffly.

"Very well, then; say your piece, and let us bury the quarrel."

"I won't say you didn't deserve to be beaten by revenants within an inch of your life, but it was wrong of me. I forgot my duty, and acted on my worst impulses."

"Did you, though?"—I had something to settle with Short, myself. "—Forget your duty, I mean. It seems to me that both you and the revenants did exactly what you were created to do, which was to stamp out dissent with violence and impunity."

Short winced. "Miss Sharp—"

"Liz," I put in, relenting a little. It was difficult to remain exasperated with such a well-intentioned sort of face.

"Liz," he amended with a smile, but he did not go on at once. Only he went on looking at me, half touched, half wistful.

"Well?" I prompted, feeling my cheeks become warm.

"It doesn't matter," he said with a sigh. "You are quite right. I had not merely the opportunity, but the right to commit violence with impunity. I never took the Livius Serum; I was a revenant for scarcely two minutes; but I have been a monster all the same. Say no more. I telegraph my resignation to London in the morning."

"Resign?" the George-wolf yelped, from his position crouched at May's feet. "Hang it, Short! Supposed to protect me! What's the meaning of this?"

"Only this, sir: that Miss Sharp is making an honest man of me."

"We shall find a new bodyguard, no doubt." Raising the half-full syringe, May looked down into the adoring eyes of the George-wolf. "And you, George? Shall I make an honest man of you?"

He uttered a soft whine. "Dem shame! Keep you safe like this, what!"

She kissed him between the eyes. "George dear, you're a prince of the greatest empire in the world. That will never change; certainly not now that Uncle Wales is defanged as well. If you can't keep me safe as a prince, you'll hardly have any better luck as a wolf."

George considered this a moment. "Need to set right what

I did wrong," he admitted at length. "Lupei's right. Can't give back the life I took. Least I can do is give up the power I gained." He stretched out a great hairy arm to receive the dose. "Nice not to tie myself up each month, what!"

Unfortunately, the young lovers had forgotten that when George was transformed once more into a man, he would find himself without a stitch to his back. A certain amount of embarrassment ensued, scarcely resolved when Anton tossed George a second tea-towel from the kitchen dresser.—Thankfully, Short's valise upstairs was quickly raided, an operation that soothed May's embarrassment—though it did little for George's peace of mind, since the outfit thus procured was unfashionable as well as ill-fitting.

It was late, and despite the cramped quarters, none of us felt much like venturing out into the streets upon this, the last night of the full moon. Therefore it was decided that the gentlemen should make themselves as comfortable as possible downstairs, while May and I shared the bed in Short's attic. Vasily and George, being able-bodied, climbed across the roof to scout the empty house next-door for anything they could find in the way of spare bedding; May disappeared upstairs to offer moral support for the journey; and Short and I were left sitting wearily at the kitchen table. Short had not released my hand for some time. It felt rather nice to sit there hand in hand like that. I could imagine we had grown old together and had a full and busy life behind us.

Of course, given the eventfulness of the past few months, we arguably *did* have a full and busy life behind us.

At length Short sighed and withdrew from his pocket the gold wedding-ring that had so complicated things on that memorable evening at the castle. Very pretty it was, with a floral scroll etched around the band—and very pretty it is to this day.

"This was meant to be a surprise," he began mournfully.

"Oh, believe me, it *was*."

"A pleasant surprise, I mean.—And I warn you," he added severely, as I opened my mouth again, "that if you keep arguing, I shall just put it back in my pocket."

"I like that! I was only going to ask if this was what you meant before, by an impulsive purchase in Eger."

"I find it best to be well prepared. Well? What about it, my dear Elizabeth?—Shall we elope in the morning?"

"My dear Alexander," I said fervently, "I don't care where or how we get married, so long as it is not in Coburg."

* * *

What else is there to tell? George and May returned to the palace the next morning and were received with voluble remonstrances; but there was nothing anyone could do. The heir to nearly every throne in Europe had been rendered toothless at a stroke; the Kabale was in complete dissolution; and when it came down to it, even if Uncle Wales had had the slightest intention of stepping aside to surrender the Crown to a properly monstrous sibling (which he most certainly did not), how could the change possibly have been explained to the Nation? As far as the English were aware, theirs was the only royal house in Europe that loudly boasted of *not* being monsters. Pretty silly Uncle Wales would have looked, admitting otherwise.

I'm fairly certain that there was an effort on the part of the Kaiser to have something unpleasant done to George, but nothing came of it. Certainly, after the Kabale was dealt with, the royalties of Europe were a great deal more distrustful of each other than they once had been, and the diplomacy that had once been carried out by princely cousins and dowager aunts passed quickly into the hands of ministers of state and ambassadors, so that a new Kabale soon became unthinkable.

George and May were married the following year. I was not present, but I received a handsome photograph of the happy couple in return for the set of hand-sewn baby clothes I had sent. May and I still write to each other, and I believe she and George are very happy together, in their own very steady and reserved way. We don't hear from George as often, but after the War they put up a statue of him in King's Domain. I always give it a wave and a kind word when I happen to pass, although Short tells me that I ought not to greet His Majesty, even in effigy, with "Oi, Georgie!"

I don't, of course, presume on our friendship to the point of publishing these memoirs during their lifetime. Can you imagine!—No, I shall seal them up and pass them on to the least harebrained of my daughters with instructions not to open them for a century at least.

Of course there was a war eventually, as all the world knows. By that time the anarchist ranks had thinned a good deal, for the defanged royalties of Europe had in many cases chosen to listen to the anarchists' grievances and do something towards a remedy. The diplomatic Kaiser lost his throne, but poor Nicky and Alicky lost their lives, for Nicky—ever the dutiful son, and bound by tradition—never did agree to defang himself. I liked him a great deal, but he believed himself obliged as a matter of filial piety to rule with bared fang and iron fist. Luckily for us, George and May proved more amenable to the changing times; and I flatter myself I can take some of the credit for that.

Alexander and I were married in Switzerland a few days after the memorable wedding at Coburg. Reaching England after a hurried journey, we stayed in London only long enough to collect our personal belongings and book our passage on the next ship to Australia. We settled quite happily (if not particularly quietly) in Melbourne and went into business together as private investigators. Our eldest daughter is named May, as instructed; but she takes after me more than after her godmother.

I am afraid that the secret of revenant-making was not lost, even after the death of the terrifying Professor Schmidt. On the contrary, it was merely refined, until the Americans perfected a means of turning their policemen into living revenants that look and behave almost exactly like real people.

After the defanging of the Kabale, Vasily disappeared not only from the Russian court but also from European high society. May and George's discreet inquiries uncovered only the fact that his property had been confiscated by the emperor. Twelve months passed with no word; and then Vasily sent me, as a wedding gift, a rather remarkable diamond necklace. I was fairly certain I had seen the diamonds on a previous occasion about the neck of Missy of Roumania; and I had quite recently read in the papers about a jewel robbery, the culprits of which had never been caught. Be that as it may, I have never heard from Vasily since—which makes me think that the rascal must still be alive and well somewhere or other.

As for Anton: if you'll believe it, he married Hannah Bunker, the Old Botolphian who once tried to explode May, and followed Alexander and myself to Australia, where he went into politics. We see each other often, and I sometimes suspect his eldest son of fancying my May.

There is nothing else to tell. The night grows late, and for the last couple of hours Alexander has been asking me to stop chuckling over past exploits and come to bed. Since I have already thrown both my slippers at him, I suppose I had better do as he asks.

NOT TO BE OPENED UNTIL THE 31ST OF AUGUST, 2020.

S.D.G.

Grand Duke Vasily Nikolaevitch Romanov will return.

Unhistorical Note

It is peculiarly exhilarating to write a work of historical fiction as devoid of historical fidelity as this book. Nevertheless, the reader may be interested to know that while practically all the events in this book have been exaggerated, fabricated out of whole cloth, or at best turned inside-out and rifled for spare ideas, a certain amount of inspiration was certainly found in the history. There was a grand royal wedding in Coburg in the spring of 1894, though the bride—Victoria Melita ("Ducky")—did not run away with a Russian Grand Duke for another decade. It was at the Coburg wedding that the tormented amours of Nicholas II and Alix ("Alicky") of Hesse were brought to a decision through—or perhaps despite—the strenuous efforts of Kaiser Wilhelm II.

In reality, George and May were already married at this point, and had settled into a rather dull life at Sandringham, where George dedicated himself to collecting stamps and shooting a really astonishing number of birds. I am quite sure I have painted a much nicer portrait of the two of them than they merited in real life; just as I have, without the slightest provocation, turned the melodramatic Marie ("Missy") of Roumania into a villainess. That said, there is a grain of truth behind this story: it seems clear that George and May, and the British monarchy, survived the upheavals of World War I at least partly because of their adaptability to changing times.

I'm grateful to books such as John Merriman's *The Dynamite Club*, Miranda Carter's *The Three Emperors: Three Cousins, Three Empires, and the Road to World War I*, and Deborah Cadbury's *Queen Victoria's Matchmaking* for informing my picture of Europe during the eventful 1890s.

As always, I must thank my wonderful beta readers for their help: Christina Baehr, Schuyler McConkey, and W.R. Gingell, who did sterling work in convincing me that there's only so much backstabbing a book of this sort needs.

Suzannah Rowntree
  April, 2021.

About the Author

Suzannah Rowntree lives in a big house in rural Australia with her awesome parents and siblings, drinking fancy tea and writing historical fantasy fiction that blends real-world history with legend, adventure, and a dash of romance.

You can connect with me on:

🌐 https://suzannahrowntree.site

Subscribe to my newsletter:

✉ https://www.subscribepage.com/srauthor

Also by Suzannah Rowntree

The Miss Sharp's Monsters Series
The Werewolf of Whitechapel
Anarchist on the Orient Express
A Vampire in Bavaria

The Watchers of Outremer Series
A Wind from the Wilderness
The Lady of Kingdoms
Children of the Desolate
A Day of Darkness

The Pendragon's Heir Trilogy
The Door to Camelot
The Quest for Carbonek
The Heir of Logres

The Fairy Tale Retold Series
The Rakshasa's Bride
The Prince of Fishes
The Bells of Paradise
Death Be Not Proud
Ten Thousand Thorns
The City Beyond the Glass

www.ingramcontent.com/pod-product-compliance
Lightning Source LLC
Chambersburg PA
CBHW021809110726
47902CB00006B/1706